RARE EARTH

About the author

Michael Asher has been hailed as one of Britain's two most distinguished desert explorers and has received awards from the Royal Geographical Society and the Royal Scottish Geographical Society for his expeditions. A fluent Arabic speaker, he has travelled over 16,000 miles by camel and lived for three years with a traditional Bedouin tribe. In 1987, he and his wife Mariantonietta Peru became the first people ever to cross the Sahara desert from west to east on foot and with camels – a distance of 4500 miles.

He is the author of twelve books, including two previous novels, and in 1996 was elected a Fellow of the Royal Society of Literature. He has also presented television documentaries on TE Lawrence and Sir Richard Burton for Channel 4.

A former soldier with the Parachute Regiment and SAS, he has a degree in English from the University of Leeds. He has lived in the Sudan, Kenya and Bali, but currently lives near Rabat, Morocco, with his wife and two children.

RARE EARTH

MICHAEL ASHER

HarperCollins*Publishers*

HarperCollins*Publishers*
77–85 Fulham Palace Road,
Hammersmith, London W6 8JB

www.**fireandwater**.com

Published by HarperCollins*Publishers* 2002
1 3 5 7 9 8 6 4 2

A catalogue record for this book
is available from the British Library

Hardback ISBN 0 00 713645 5
Trade paperback ISBN 0 00 713023 6

Set in Times New Roman by
Rowland Phototypesetting Ltd,
Bury St Edmunds, Suffolk

Printed and bound in Great Britain by
Clays Ltd, St Ives plc

'It is a maternal mystery, this primordial darkness. That is why the sun's birth in the morning strikes the native as so overwhelmingly meaningful. The *moment* at which light comes is God. That moment brings redemption, peace.'

CG JUNG Memories, Dreams, Reflections

'It was taught by the Buddha, oh monks, that the past, the future, physical space ... and individuals are nothing but names, forms of thought, word of common usage, merely superficial realities.'

MADHYAMIKA KARIKA VRTTI

'Our normal waking consciousness, rational consciousness as we call it, is but one special type of consciousness, whilst all about it, parted from it by the filmiest of screens, there lie potential forms of consciousness entirely different.'

WILLIAM JAMES The Varieties of Religious Experience

'Laws of nature are human inventions, like ghosts. The whole blessed thing is a human invention, including the idea that it isn't a human invention. The world has no existence whatsoever outside the human imagination. It's all a ghost, the whole blessed world we live in.'

ROBERT M PERSIG Zen and the Art of Motorcycle Maintenance

'No man can live this life and emerge from it unchanged. He will carry, however faint, the imprint of the desert, the brand which marks the nomad; and he will have within him the yearning to return, weak or insistent according to his nature. For this cruel land can cast a spell no temperate climate can match.'

WILFRED THESIGER Arabian Sands

ACKNOWLEDGEMENTS

I would like to thank Donald Young for the kernel of the idea, though the result is radically different from the original concept. Similarly I am grateful for the suggestions of Susan Watt at HarperCollins, who helped me create the 'second concept'. My neighbour in Nairobi, Patrick Towers-Picton, told me about columbite-tantalite, literally over the hedge one evening, and later suggested palladium complex as a mineral of suitable value. The title 'Rare Earth' also came out of our conversations, as well as the 'sampo' and the basic scenario of the strike. Much of the mining background came from Patrick's colleague (Jean François Damon) whom I also thank wholeheartedly. Any inaccuracies in the text are my own, not theirs. Peter Speke, a former geologist with Rio Tinto, gave me the idea for 'One-Eyed' Ben Harris, though there is of course no connection between Rio Tinto and the Rand Corporation. I am deeply grateful to my agent, Anthony Goff of David Higham Associates for his continuing support. Finally, this book would not have been possible without the help of Mariantonietta and Burton. I thank them both.

To Mariantonietta
Burton and Jude

RARE EARTH

1

A GUNSHOT CRACKED OUT LIKE A lightning bolt, and Truman sat up sharply, blinking, groping in limbo to retrieve his personality, letting his dream diaper into fragments like a shattered mirror. There were two more shots in quick succession, then another and another. He grabbed his hat and rushed out into the blinding desert light, past the dining marquee, the water-bowser, the gaggle of ducks, the dog's leg of labourers' tents. The puff of blue smoke that hung over the huddle of shadows on the sands told him he had not dreamed the five gunshots. It was his system that every find was saluted by a salvo of bullets – the number depended on its importance, and five meant a discovery of the first quality – perhaps a Ptolemaic burial, perhaps even the *big one* – the tomb of the Oracle, the Hidden One herself.

He held on to his hat and dashed across the dunes, leaving little explosions of dust like cotton wool where his desert boots touched the surface. In the distance Miflah Barud, the foreman, was running towards him, a curious little hunchback figure with his pistol still in his hand.

'What is it?' Truman yelled at him.

'A corpse, *ya duktoor*!'

'Is it Ptolemaic?'

Miflah snorted, shaking his bearish head. 'Not Ptolemaic, *duktoor*,' he said. 'This one been dead 'bout three weeks.'

Truman stared at him. 'What are you talking about?' he demanded.

The hunchback beckoned, and Truman followed his shambling figure on to the dunes, brushing past the labourers who were huddled up together, shouting frenziedly and pointing at something on the ground. In their midst he found Mike Eliot, his American graduate-student, crouching and scooping handfuls of sand away from the raddled body of a big man, lying profile down like some large recumbent animal. The man was clearly *homo modernis* – unless the blue Levis he wore were the ancient Greek version – but his skin was the yellow-brown of dried parchment, so tight on the bones it seemed almost to have been pasted on. The cadaver was untouched by insects or scavengers – not even vultures ventured into the emptiness this far from the Nile. Truman had found predynastic corpses buried on the edge of the Nile Valley no more decomposed than this man – and some of them had lain there for eight thousand years.

The cadaver had a wild mop of dark hair and an equally shaggy beard, and its enormous frame was pinned under the weight of a tubular-steel back-pack that looked far too heavy for any human to carry. Eliot brought a Swiss Army knife out of his pocket, bent over awkwardly on his stiff leg and slit the carry-straps of the pack with the largest blade. He shifted it, gasping at its weight.

'Holy shit!' he said. 'Feels like lead!'

Truman sank to his knees and examined the dead man's face. The skin was wattled taut like an old leather draw-bag, the mouth an obscene purple gash, and the one eye Truman could see was tight shut. The other – the right – was covered with a sinister-looking black patch. The labourers fidgeted and gasped when they saw the eye-patch, and some began making the sign for protection against the evil eye.

'Hell's Bells!' Truman said. 'We've been digging here for three months. How come we didn't find him before?'

'He must have been here when we started on this phase two weeks ago,' Eliot said. 'But he was completely covered. That storm last night must have uncovered bits of him. The boys said they saw a hand sticking out of the sand.'

Miflah the Hunchback hunkered down next to Truman.

'*Al-'atsh*' he said. 'This man died of thirst. See the way his face is screwed up like an old water-skin? I've seen faces like that a dozen times on men lost in the desert.'

'Yeah,' Truman said. 'Poor bastard. I mean, if he'd pushed on another few kilometres he would have reached Siwa.'

He turned the corpse over gingerly. The body was light and stiff as a post. The coagulates in muscle fibre that made the human frame rigid after death had kicked in, and the moisture had simply evaporated like a vapour.

'I don't know where he came from,' Truman said, scanning the ceaselessly boiling flow of the erg. 'But this guy must have had rocks the size of Gibraltar to cross the Sand Sea on foot. There's nothing out there for hundreds of miles – not a tree, not a blade of grass, not even a bloody fly.'

'A *Jinn*,' one of the men growled. 'Don't you know the Sand Sea is the land of *Shaitan*?'

Truman and Eliot exchanged stifled grins.

'So what do we do now, anyway, Doc?' Eliot asked. 'Take him with us?'

'Not a chance,' Truman said. 'If we take him to Siwa, the police will only bury him there. It's a waste of time. We'll just shove him right back in the sand, mark the spot, and report the death to the police-post in Siwa. If they want to investigate they can come and dig him up, but you can bet your last cent they won't bother. What we can do is return his belongings to the next of kin – if we can find out who they are.'

'There're no documents on him,' Eliot said. 'I've checked.'

Truman eyed the huge back-pack curiously. The obvious thing to do was to open it, but somehow he felt reluctant. Miflah probed the pack with his callused fingers and tested its weight.

'Allah!' he muttered. 'What's in there? Solid gold?'

The workmen were staring at the pack in half-terrified fascination now, and Truman took Eliot's penknife from him, slit the

3

top straps and lifted the flap. Inside was a scuffed and torn map, a small GPS unit, and a veteran leather pouch. The rest of the space was filled with packets of dust in plastic sample-bags, each one sealed with a metal clip and labelled with a number. Truman couldn't help snickering.

'So much for your gold!' he said, lifting one of the packets out and holding it up for display. 'There must be fifty of these things in here. This guy died carrying a sackful of dirt.'

Miflah touched his bent nose with a stubby finger.

'Sometimes even dirt is valuable,' he said.

Truman put the packet back thoughtfully. He took out the leather wallet, opened it and found inside a British passport with an Egyptian entry stamp dated two months before. The passport showed a wild-looking man with a cheerful face and a tangled beard: it belonged to a Benjamin John Harris born Johannesburg, South Africa, 1950. It also contained an international driving permit in the same name, a wad of around $1000 and the business card of an Augustus Maynard, CEO of Kortex Mining Co. Ltd, with an address in Hanover Square, London.

'Well now we know who he is,' Truman said. 'And what he was doing out there.'

'I should have guessed it,' Eliot said. 'The guy was prospecting for minerals, and those bags are mining samples.'

'Right,' Truman said. 'But I never heard of anyone prospecting in the Great Sand Sea.'

'Those guys don't go on foot. Where's his wheels?'

'Probably be found in fifty years' time,' Truman said, 'nose down in a dune.'

'Yeah, but what if there's more of them out there, Doc? I mean, prospectors work in teams, and somebody could be alive.'

Truman scratched his broken nose. 'Not likely, Mike. Not if this one's been here three weeks already. And why would he lug this damn great pack out with him if there were others sitting on the vehicle? Anyway, there's not much we can do. We've got no four-wheel drive jeeps with us. All we can do is report it to the police right away. It's their baby now.' Truman put the documents away and tucked the wallet, map and GPS unit under his arm.

'These go to the address on the card,' he said. 'We can bury the samples with him. He won't be needing them any more.'

Eliot looked troubled. 'Seems a pity, Doc,' he said. 'I mean the guy humped them out of the desert. He could have ditched them any time, but he kept on humping them till he dropped dead. Like Miflah said, they had to be pretty valuable to him. Cost him his sorry ass.'

Truman frowned. 'Jesus, Mike,' he said. 'That pack must weigh a hundred kilos and we're pushed for space. We're going to end up dumping some of our own kit, and I'm not checking in at Cairo International with a hundred kilos of dirt in my suitcase – not at eight dollars a kilo for excess baggage. I'm strapped enough as it is.'

Eliot shrugged. 'You won't have to, Doc', he said. 'We've got a whole container going back to the UK. You can just slap the stuff in there.'

Truman weighed it up for a moment. 'I don't want to get involved in any red tape,' he said. 'I've got enough on my hands with Whealan closing us down and the committee hauling me over the coals. I had a colleague die on me on a dig once, and you wouldn't believe the hassle involved. It's going to cost us all tomorrow just reporting this to the police, for a start.'

'I'll have the samples put in the container,' Eliot said. 'I'll even do the paperwork with the cops. Seems like the least we can do for the poor bastard.'

Truman sighed. 'OK, I'll leave it to you, Mike.'

He turned to the hunchback. 'Miflah,' he said. 'Have the pack put in my tent. After that you can bury the body, and stick some kind of mark up.'

Miflah gave him a mock salute. It was fitting, Truman thought, that Harris's corpse would lie here forever, as a monument to the end of his archaeological career.

Truman and Eliot hung around until the labourers had reburied

5

the corpse, then watched them shuffling back to camp with their shovels over their shoulders, humming a solemn melody like refugees from a *Snow White* remake. Truman listened to the drum of the wind, bass profundo harmonics so similar to the men's voices that it seemed as if the earth itself was alive and chanting a hypnotic mantra. You could hear it in the endless riddling of the sands, the wave-motion of light and shade, the rhythm of savage colours pulsing across the spectrum – out here in the desert the planet's song was virgin, but in the city it was drowned under a cacophony of noise and traffic fumes. He saw the sun painting curried rills of gold across seams of dust-cloud and swallowed hard. Beautiful wasn't the word for it, he thought. Out here you could feel the earth was part of yourself.

'I feel famished,' Eliot said. 'What's for dinner?'

'For something completely novel,' Truman chortled, 'roast duck. There are half a dozen left, but they've been mighty quiet these past few nights.'

Eliot guffawed. This season they'd imported a couple of hundred ducks from Siwa as fresh meat, shutting them up in an old tent at night. At first the birds had made an appalling racket, but the cook had solved the problem by choosing two or three of the noisiest ones every day to be killed and served for dinner. Either the ducks had cottoned on to what was happening or the cook had simply eliminated the vociferous ones, because for the past few weeks the duck tent had been curiously silent.

'Come on,' Truman said. 'We can put the last of the whisky to bed afterwards.'

The sun had turned red ochre and was taking its leave in firework bursts of colour slashing like searchlights through the glowering sky. The quartz-flats below them had become a shimmering molten gore. As they walked across the skirts of the dunes towards the camp, Miflah came shuffling towards them, a parcel of dark on the smouldering blood-colours of the desert. He was now dressed in a full-length army trench-coat and a woollen scarf arranged into an elaborate head-dress.

6

'Excuse me, *duktoor*,' he said urgently, 'I must talk with you.'

He looked serious, and Truman hoped desperately he wasn't going to come out with some nostalgic farewell speech. He nodded at Eliot. 'I'll catch you up.'

Miflah looked unusually flustered as he waited for Eliot to move out of earshot.

'What is it?' Truman asked. 'You look like you've seen a ghost.'

The little man was panting as if he'd been running. He brought out a piece of dirty cotton from under his coat and unfolded it. Inside was a folded piece of paper.

'It was in the dead person's pocket, *duktoor*,' Miflah said.

The paper showed a sketch done in pencil of what appeared to be a rock aiguille – almost like an ancient Egyptian obelisk, but created by erosion rather than man-made. The rock was covered in scratchings and carvings and the artist had gone to great pains to copy them. Prominent among them was the head of a ram – a domesticated ram with whorled horns, bearing the ancient Egyptian sun-disk, the oldest and most sacred of symbols. For a moment Truman stared at the sketch spellbound, feeling as if a new ratchet had just tumbled into place somewhere with an audible 'snick'.

Then Miflah touched his arm gently.

'I heard of that sign,' the hunchback growled. 'It is the camel-brand of a tribe called the Saghrana, who live far away from everyone in the deepest stretches of the *Mufarida*. A place they call the Funeral Plains.' He shivered. 'The old folk tell stories about them. That they are blood-suckers who can leave their bodies and fly away like bats.' Truman was looking at the little man with his head to one side, only half taking in the words. Miflah scowled.

'What is it, *duktoor*?' he said. 'You think this is all, how you say . . . *mumbo-jumbo* – eh?'

'No, no, it's not that,' Truman said distractedly, 'It's just that this symbol – the ram's head and the sun-disk – well it might be the brand of a nomad tribe, Miflah, but it also represents the Oracle of Ammon – the so-called "Hidden One". I know, because five years ago at Aghurmi I found an identical image in a cartouche on the Santariya column.'

2

TRUMAN ALIGHTED FROM THE TAXI IN Regent Street and was engulfed by crowds of Christmas shoppers. A flurry of Union Jacks snapped in a vicious cold breeze above the mock-Tudor facade of Liberty and outside Hamleys toyshop there stood a giant teddy-bear in Beefeater uniform with frost on its nose. Last night's snowfall was a memory – a scum of grey slush along the gutters – and cars and double-deckers were moving cautiously, their tyres crackling on salt-grit. Truman dodged between vehicles and hurried down Hanover Street. He lingered for a moment under a Queen Anne facade by the revolving door of the Jones, Laing, La Salle building, mingling with a wedge of clean-cut young associates in navy blue Crombies heading out to the pub for a cheery Christmas pint. The holiday was three days away, and everyone seemed to be high on the usual festive camaraderie. It only nauseated Truman and made him feel more of an outsider. Since he'd got back from Siwa two weeks ago he found he'd developed an aversion to crowds. *How did we end up like this*? he wondered. *How, after 3 million years of evolution, have we come to a point where we lock ourselves up at close quarters with millions of people we don't know and don't feel we belong to?*

The Hanover Square address was a courtesy title, he discovered. Actually, the Kortex office lay down St George's Street nearby, next to a wine shop – a Regency porch of bevelled blocks, an oak door with its statutory Christmas wreath, a bell-pull, and a big brass plate engraved with the title Kortex Mining Company Ltd. Truman halted there for a moment, smoothing wisps of wayward black hair out of his eyes. He glanced down the street, glimpsing the neo-classical exterior of St George's Church with its array of pillars, pedestrians trudging along wet footpaths in anoraks and greatcoats. He loosened the upturned collar of his faded ankle-length overcoat, sighed and leaned heavily on the side of the portico, wondering whether to go in after all.

A week after arriving back in Oxford, Truman had found himself sitting in front of the entire Ashmoleum committee, in an austere hall in the museum. He'd looked along the row of expectant faces and detected not a mote of sympathy there – they reminded him of jackals closing in for the kill. The Chairman, Sir John Oldfield, prided himself on being a bluff Yorkshireman who had walked with nobs without losing the common touch. His manner had been deceptively blythe.

'You are here, Dr Truman,' he said 'to answer certain allegations of the mismanagement of funds disbursed to you by this committee for the Oracle of Ammon Project at Siwa. We've had our accountants go over your books, and they find at least twenty thousand pounds unaccounted for.'

He peered at Truman over his half-moon glasses. 'Would you care to say what happened to the money? Have you perhaps been playing the horses, Dr Truman?'

There were restrained titters from the stuffed-shirts. 'Or did you take the opportunity to pay off the mortgage on your house?'

'That's preposterous,' Truman said. 'There may be anomalies in the accounts, but all that money has been spent on the dig in one way or another. You know as well as I do that there are invisible overheads – incentives paid to local big-wigs, bonuses for the labourers – items that aren't specifically allowed for in the budget, but have to be paid. Normally they're covered up under other headings, but I've been too busy. I never had any interest in accounting. That's my mistake, I suppose.'

A surge of anger swept through him as he stared at the truculent, vulturine faces of the committee. 'But that's not what this is really about, is it?'

'What on earth do you mean?' Oldfield asked blandly.

'There are at least three members of this committee who've written papers on the tomb of the Oracle,' Truman said, 'all of them agreeing that her body was removed from Siwa before the Muslim invaders arrived. The Santariya Column suggested to me that she was buried secretly in the Sand Sea. That's what this is about, Sir John, and you know it.' He was standing up now, shouting. 'It's about your damn reputations! You know perfectly well I never siphoned off a cent in my life. You just couldn't stand the idea that I might actually find the tomb of the Hidden One and prove the lot of you were barking up the wrong tree!'

For a moment there was an embarrassed silence. Then Oldfield said quietly, 'You had three years looking for the tomb of the Oracle, Dr Truman. 'You had your innings and you came up with nothing. You were wasting your sponsor's money. Unless you can reimburse the missing funds, no one's going to take you on again – not even as a field assistant. If you behave yourself you might just manage to get a job teaching English to foreign students.'

And that had been that. Truman had walked out of the meeting, knowing there was no point in arguing. One part of him felt relief. In the desert he'd grown accustomed to the slow rhythms of a more primitive existence, and now the world he had come from seemed a frightening, frenetic and unpredictable place.

He'd been wondering what to do next, when out of the blue there had come a phone call from Gus Maynard. Maynard had been low-key, polite, and very persuasive, asking if he could possibly call at the Kortex office in London some time in the next two days.

'I would very much like to talk to you about Harris,' he had said. 'I want to thank you personally for getting Harris's personal effects and the samples back, and perhaps discuss a matter of mutual benefit. Were you aware that I offered a reward for the discovery of Harris's body?'

Truman said he wasn't, and explained rather brusquely that he'd brought the samples back only because he'd had a space in a container that happened to be going back to the UK the following day. Maynard paused, obviously noticing Truman's surliness, but repeated that he would be most obliged if Truman would call in at the office in the next two days. At first Truman had declined firmly. That evening, though, he had phoned Maynard back, saying he'd reconsidered. He had added that he was curious to know what Harris had been up to in the Sand Sea. Maynard had agreed to tell him the full story, and they had made an appointment. Now, loitering in the cold outside Maynard's door his nerve almost failed him. He blew a smear of condensation over the brass plate, then rubbed it off with his bare hand as if he might rub the name Kortex Mining Company off the face of the earth. It was still there when he took his hand away, so he pushed the door open and went in.

A giant Rastafarian with dreadlocks was sitting behind a desk in the reception hall amid gilt-framed mirrors, frayed kilims and a smell of floor polish. The desk looked far too small for the man, who must have weighed twenty-two stone and had a build somewhere between an armoured car and a rhino. The big fellow's presence was immediately threatening, and it was that more than anything that drew Truman on. Truman was hardly the macho type, but he had an uncontrollable urge to challenge those he felt threatened him, just as he had challenged the Ashmoleum committee when he should have kept his mouth shut.

The Rasta stood up and took a neat dance step out from behind the desk, raising himself to full height like a grizzly. A plastic badge pinned to his barrel chest bore the name *Cliff*, in big cursive letters.

Truman drew himself up straight.

'I have an appointment with Mr Maynard,' he said. 'Dr Truman?'

'It's cool,' Cliff said truculently. 'But I gotta frisk you, see if you're carryin'.'

'Carrying what, exactly?' Truman enquired.

Cliff glared at him. 'Whaddya think, man?' he said. 'A piece.'

'A piece of what?'

'A gun, man. A gun.'

Truman shrugged. 'Are you kidding?' he said. 'In Hanover Square? Kortex must get some creeps for clients.'

'You wouldn't believe it.'

Truman allowed himself to be frisked. Cliff worked on him with cold detachment, laying a massive hand between his legs and patting his trousers all the way down to the parquet.

'Is Mr Maynard in?' Truman said drily. 'Or not?'

Cliff grunted. 'The boss is upstairs,' he growled. 'He's expectin' you.'

3

MAYNARD WAS WAITING FOR HIM ON the second floor in a room that looked more like a down-at-heel gentleman's club than an office. A coal fire blazed in an antique fireplace decorated with Dutch tiles, and there were threadbare Kirghiz rugs and shapeless leather armchairs. A ball-and-claw footed desk was the only hint that anything commercial might be undertaken here, and that impression was countered immediately by its adornment of photos of teenage children, and of the strikingly handsome Scandinavian-looking woman Truman assumed was Maynard's wife. Half of the wall space was taken up with fitted bookshelves and over the mantelpiece hung a portrait of some forgotten Scottish nobleman, with a gilt frame six inches wide. Maynard stood up to greet him. He was anything between sixty and seventy-five, a small man with a prosperous waistline, a silver goatee, and the remains of his hair brushed back sharply from a forehead that was an atlas of liver spots and wrinkles. His face had red patches from some allergy and his eyes, red veined and watery, stood out in a puff of tissue, half disguised by severe school-ma'am glasses. He was wearing a comfortable kashmir cardigan, and exuded the clubby air of a college president rather than a Mining Company CEO.

'Dr *Truman*,' he said in the same prim Scots patrician Truman had noticed on the phone, '*Such* a pleasure. Sorry about the patting down – a bit gruff, Cliff, but believe me there's a heart of gold under the beef.'

Truman accepted Maynard's handshake, looking into an inscrutable mandarin grin that seemed to show everything but give away nothing. Maynard might be grinning like that when he stuck a knife in your back, Truman felt.

'Mr Maynard,' he said. 'I really don't know what this is about. I returned the things I found. You sent me a cheque to cover my expenses and I considered the matter closed. As I told you, if I'd had my way I'd have buried the samples with the cadaver.'

Maynard assumed a pained expression and moved over to a carved blackwood chest that doubled as a drinks cabinet.

'Scotch?' he asked, as if whisky was the panacea for all social awkwardness.

Truman shook his head. 'A bit early for me,' he said.

'Poppycock,' Maynard said pleasantly, topping his own drink up with a generous shot from a bottle of twelve year old single malt. 'It's never too early for a dram, and anyway, it's Christmas – at least, almost.'

He lifted the cut glass in salute. 'Cheers,' he said. 'Merry Christmas to you, Dr Truman. Please sit down.'

Truman shrugged and plumped down in one of the leather armchairs next to the fire, warming his knuckles. Maynard sat opposite.

'Now, whatever the case,' he said, 'I owe you a huge debt of gratitude for bringing those samples home. Thank God you didn't bury them.'

'Look,' Truman said, 'you thanked me in your letter.'

Maynard flapped the air with a pudgy hand.

'Now just hear me out a minute, Dr Truman,' he said. 'I'm talking more about what we could do for each other.'

Truman gave a hollow chuckle. 'I'm an archaeologist, Mr Maynard,' he said. 'I don't do mineral samples. OK, so trowel-jockeys work in the good earth like miners do, but with a different object. I think you've got your professions muddled up.'

Maynard put down his glass and placed his hands together as

if in prayer as he considered the undulating flames in the fire-place. When he glanced up he looked like a vicar about to perform a funeral service.

'I don't need a prospector,' he said solemnly. 'Tell me, did you examine the map, the sketch and the GPS unit?'

Truman thought about it for a moment.

'Yes, I did,' he said. 'The map showed the whole Western Desert of Egypt and the Sudan, but there was a circle round a place called the Bint Hammou Plateau – a desolate mountain massif straddling the Sudanese border. The GPS had recorded landmarks in the same area. The sketch I don't know about – it's of what they call an aiguille, a rock obelisk fashioned by erosion. It's covered in graffiti – mostly tribal camel-brands. At first I thought the samples must have come from Bint Hammou, but the plateau is about five hundred miles south of Siwa across the Sand Sea, so Harris couldn't possibly have walked from there carrying that bloody back-pack with no water. He could have got the samples from Bognor beach, for all I know. He had a visa for Egypt in his passport but none for the Sudan.'

Maynard's eyes were opaque under the deep glasses. 'So you thought about the matter quite carefully,' he said.

Truman glanced at him feeling a twinge of guilt. 'OK,' he said. 'I was curious, and reconstructing things is my job.'

'Weren't you also curious about the samples?'

'I suppose so,' Truman said non-committally. 'But I was more interested in how Harris turned up a stiff in my camp on the edge of the Great Sand Sea. He wasn't collecting samples in the erg, I'm sure of that, and if he was prospecting in the Sudan it wasn't on the up-and-up because he had no papers, not even a visa.'

Maynard smiled almost gloatingly.

'You've got it,' he said. 'Harris was geologizing illegally in the Sudan. He couldn't afford to take chances. There's a civil war on there. The Bint Hammou Plateau is inhabited by unadmin-stered nomads, and if the nomads had found official papers on him they'd probably have rubbed him out. He started off with a Land Cruiser, but it must have conked on him somewhere. My guess is he started walking and just dropped dead from thirst.'

'So *you* sent him to the plateau?' Truman said.

Maynard blinked.

'Yes,' he said. 'And he was overdue back. When he didn't show I offered a reward for the body.'

'You were so certain he'd kicked the bucket? Didn't you consider he might have done a runner?'

Maynard looked annoyed.

'Not Harris,' he said. 'He was one of the most loyal men who ever worked for me. Been with me twenty years. Did you notice the eye-patch? He lost the eye in a cave-in while he was working for the Rand Corporation. Ever heard of it?'

Truman shook his head. 'Miners and archaeologists are oil and water,' he said.

'Rand's is a big mining cartel based in Johannesburg,' Maynard went on. 'Harris served his apprenticeship with them – his father and grandfather had worked for them too, so it was the family tradition you might say. He was a mining engineer and a damn good one – one of those guys who can read the ground like a story. Eye like a snapshot when it came to strata. Rand's shoved him on the fast-track, but the cave-in put the kibosh on that. Actually he'd already warned them that the shaft was unsafe, but no one took a blind bit of notice. Six people ended up strawberry jam, and Harris got off with a rock splinter through the retina. He was lying in hospital recovering when some slick young company lawyer breezed in and told him Rand's wouldn't employ him any longer because of his partial sight, and that he could forget the compensation. If they'd admitted culpability they'd have had to pay through the nose for the six stiffs, you see, and the stiffs were all blacks. Sordid business. Harris tried to bring a civil action, but Rand's boss – guy called Marcus Rand – sent his heavies round to threaten him. Ben was so pissed off he decided to get the boss back personally. He was a dab hand with explosives, was Harris, and he rigged up a booby trap with a timing device on Rand's car. He always said he never meant to hurt anyone – they all knew Rand left his car in the exec parking lot every day from nine to twelve, regular as clockwork. The idea was to rubbish the car and do collateral damage to a few others. What he didn't know was that the day he'd chosen for his little op was the birthday of Rand's eight year old daughter, Jenny, and Rand was taking her out to McDonald's or somewhere as a treat. At 11 a.m. when the car went up, Rand and his girl were on their way downtown. The girl got vaporized and Rand waved bye-bye to his legs – or most of them.'

Truman thought automatically of Jonathan, who'd also been killed on his eighth birthday.

'Jesus!' he said. 'What a bastard!'

Maynard gulped like a salamander.

'Not really,' he said. 'Harris never forgave himself. Wore a hair shirt for the rest of his life. Never got hitched – just devoted himself to work, swearing one day he'd prove Rand was wrong to sack him. A few weeks ago in the Bint Hammou Plateau he finally got the chance. He found the *sampo*.'

Truman peered at Maynard curiously.

'The *sampo*?' he repeated. 'What the hell is that?'

'The *sampo*, Dr Truman,' Maynard said, 'is a term out of Norse mythology meaning the "golden dream" of the gods in Valhalla. It's used whimsically by prospectors to denote the legendary strike of a lifetime – the crock of gold at the rainbow's end. When he pegged out, Harris had just made the best strike of his life.' Maynard's holy expression was replaced by an almost palpable look of cupidity. He didn't quite rub his red-backed hands together, Truman noticed – but almost.

'I had the samples analysed last week,' he said in a reverent whisper. 'They contained high deposits of palladium complex. That, my dear Dr Truman, is the *sampo* – a matrix of palladium, platinum and iridium, the most valuable minerals on earth.'

18

$$\boxed{4}$$

MAYNARD PICKED UP A SILVER-CHASED humidor and flipped open the lid, displaying a selection of exquisitely expensive cigars.

'Have one,' he said. 'No, take two. To celebrate the strike of the century.'

Truman picked a cigar out, sniffed it and looked at the label. It was a genuine Davidoff. He replaced it in the box.

'This isn't some kind of publicity stunt, is it?' he inquired doubtfully. 'Last I heard, palladium was only found in Russia.'

Maynard took a Davidoff from the cigar box and brought a silver cutter from his pocket. 'My doctor says I shouldn't,' he commented. 'Says it doesn't do my heart any good, but I say what the hell?'

Truman watched his small, deft fingers as they fed the cigar butt into the cutter for execution. There was a crisp snap as the blade descended and a tiny wedge of cigar dropped on to the carpet. Maynard examined the excision with interest, then poised in the act of lighting it.

'It's not a publicity stunt,' he said. 'True, the Russians have seventy percent of the palladium market, but there are smaller deposits in South Africa, where it's mined by Harris's old chums, the Rand Corporation. This new find in the Sudan is going to upset the whole applecart – the samples reveal a yield of about a kilo of palladium per cubic metre.'

19

Truman whistled. 'That's a lot of palladium.'

Maynard examined the end of his cigar again and licked it with the tip of his tongue. 'Palladium is what we call a rare earth. It's vital to the computer industry, but it's also a precious metal in its own right. The current market price is $550 an ounce, which makes it about twice the value of gold, at $260 an ounce. Platinum trails a bit behind palladium at only $520 an ounce, but I'm sure you'll agree that's better than a poke in the eye with a burnt stick. I don't know how good your maths is, Dr Truman, but mine isn't bad and I calculate that at $550 an ounce, palladium sells for about $20,000 a kilo. There's a whole mountain of it in the Bint Hammou Plateau. With a kilo per square metre, you don't have to have a degree in calculus to work out the profits.'

Truman shook his head. 'OK, I see why you're so grateful I brought the samples back. The strike is worth a king's ransom, and Ben Harris got there before Rand's. But I fail to see what all this has to do with me – I'm an archaeologist.'

Maynard showed a set of predatory teeth. 'Correction, Dr Truman,' he said. 'You *were* an archaeologist, but they kicked you out on your ear for mismanagement of funds. You're currently unemployed.'

The verbal blow was delivered so unexpectedly and with such force that for a moment Truman felt genuinely shocked. He reeled back stunned as if Maynard had punched him. 'How the hell do you know that? It's none of your damn business!' He stood up abruptly and reached for his coat, but Maynard flapped a yeasty hand at him.

'Hey, now hold your horses, old boy,' he said. 'Don't let's get in a tizz. I know all about you. I've made it my business to know. You came here out of curiosity and I like a man who's curious. Now you can satisfy that curiosity, or you can walk out in a huff.'

Truman wavered for a moment, as if wondering what twilight-zone of insanity he'd just let himself into.

'All right,' he said, sitting down again. 'I give you ten minutes then I walk.'

'Ah,' Maynard said, his eyes glistening. 'I thought a little straight talking would appeal to a man of your calibre. I know the mismanagement business was trumped up. You're a very straight man, Dr Truman. Straight, honest, direct. You have never kissed an ass in your life. You could call yourself Sir Daniel Truman-Keynes, Bt., but instead you prefer a title you earned on merit – plain Dr Dan Truman. Your father was a City barrister who died in a climbing accident in the Alps when you were four. The family money had gone walkies even before he was born, and all he left you was the title. You and your mother were dirt poor – genteel poor's the worst kind, because you have to keep up appearances. An uncle paid for you to go to a public school – Sherborne wasn't it?'

Truman sighed. He'd left the title in abeyance where it belonged almost twenty years ago. 'Mr Maynard, this is all ancient history. Are you under the misapprehension that you can blackmail me somehow?'

Maynard peered at him reproachfully through his glasses.

'Not a bit of it,' he said. 'I don't think I've ever met a less blackmailable man. I know you're a brilliant archaeologist. You studied law at St John's, Oxford, got the best first class honours they'd had in years, then spent two years travelling. When you got back you switched to archaeology and took your PhD at Magdalen. You got work as a graduate student with the expeditions led by Freiburg and Churl studying the Greek, Roman and early Islamic periods in the Nile Valley. You gained a reputation for man-management as well as remarkable insight and insatiable curiosity. Only trouble was, you got on better with the gyppo labourers than with your bosses. They reckoned you were anti-social, arrogant and rebellious. You have a very marked streak of personal ambition and you've always challenged authority.'

'Yes, and I've mostly turned out to be right.'

'So I see the assessment was correct. Now what else is there? I know you married a girl called Natalie – the daughter of a bread-delivery man from Brighton. She was a graduate of Essex

21

University and went into publishing, worked her way up to commissioning editor with one of the big London houses. You had one son – Jonathan – he was killed in an accident.'

'The guy was drunk,' Truman said, trying to keep the tremor out of his voice.

'I'm sorry, Dr Truman. I have a son. It must have been terrible for you. Anyway, you and your wife split up after that. You suffered depression and started hitting the bottle yourself a bit, but pulled out of it when you found a thing called the Santariya Column at Siwa. That gave you a clue that the Oracle of Ammon was buried there, and you dropped everything to search for it. Problem was you never came up with anything. Then, a few weeks ago your sponsor – a redneck US real-estate tycoon called Dennis Whealan – pulled the plug on it. Tough luck, but trowel-jockeying's like mining, I suppose – sometimes you come up with the goods, sometimes you luck out. Anyway, Dr Truman, the fact is you're out of a job, and they're after you for twenty grand. That more or less the size of it?'

'More or less. Where the hell did you dig up this stuff, and in only two weeks?'

Maynard tapped his nose. 'A little bit here, a little bit there, I have good sources.'

Truman swept the wayward strands of hair out of his eyes. 'Mr Maynard, tell me, are you proposing to help me reopen the Siwa dig?'

Maynard sipped whisky, chortling. 'Sorry, Dr Truman. I'm not. This, alas, is a tale of filthy lucre, not academic research. Still, if you could help me out here, you could pay off your debt to Whealan and run any dig you want anywhere in the world without worrying about wee timorous beasties like him.'

'Oh?' Truman said, glancing at him doubtfully. 'How?'

Maynard rubbed his hands together and studied Truman with gangrenous eyes. 'Have you ever wanted to be rich?' he asked, 'I mean *rich* rich.'

Truman smiled securely. 'Mr Maynard, I have degrees from the best-known university in the world. I could have chosen

22

almost any job I wanted – barrister, stock broker, merchant banker – you name it. If I'd wanted to be rich, do you think I'd have chosen archaeology? In my experience, the only people who are *rich* rich, as you put it, got there through some kind of crime. Wasn't it Balzac or somebody who said that? My ancestors came over with William the Conqueror and got rich by turfing a lot of Saxons off their land and butchering them when they resisted. The English gentry – my family included – are just descendants of a bunch of medieval delinquents.'

Maynard's eyes twinkled, not altogether pleasantly. 'Good,' he said. 'That's just what I'd have expected you to say. But you do want to reopen your dig, don't you? Pay off the twenty thousand? Find the Oracle?'

'Yes, I do.'

'Well then.' Maynard's face assumed its former solemnity. He picked up his discarded cigar and played with it for a moment, then fixed his gaze on Truman. *Now we're getting to it*, Truman thought.

'The Bint Hammoud Plateau belongs to a group of nomads called the Saghrana,' Maynard said. 'They are real tough fighters who hate outsiders, and who are even shunned by the other peoples of the region. Seems they have their own religion or something, and the area is a kind of holy site. Has the only water-source for hundreds of miles, and the natives call it ''The Sacred land''.'

Truman thought of the sketch found in Harris's pocket – Miflah had told him that the ram-and-sun-disk motif was the brand of a nomad tribe called the Saghrana.

'How do you know all this?' he asked.

Maynard grinned. 'The Blythe-Devereld papers. They're what put us on to the plateau in the first place. Blythe and Devereld were two subalterns in the Long Range Desert Group during World War II, who tracked a German Brandenburg platoon into the Sudan. They'd both been explorers before the war and they kept copious notes on what they found. It seems they spent some time in the Bint Hammou Plateau, where they took preliminary samples that suggested the place might yield platinum.

Anyway, Blythe and Devereld ended up dead – only one of their drivers got out. He brought one of the jeeps back but was stark-staring bonkers by the time he got home. The journals he salvaged confirmed the Saghrana as owners of the land. A recent report from the CIA says that the tribe is led by a chief called Ossama Hadab, who sounds a real charismatic leader, but even that report was based on hearsay not first hand data. If Ossama exists, we need his moniker on a contract.'

He straightened up and his rheumy eyes went cold and hard. 'I need a man to go out and negotiate with this Ossama. It has to be somebody who speaks Arabic like a native and knows the country and local ways. It has to be someone straight, like you, because I've had dealings with Bedouin in the Middle East before, and those guys might be illiterate, but they cut through bullshit like a knife through butter. That's why I can't send some whizz-kid, cocky lawyer from the City. I need you, Dr Truman. You're the man for the job.'

Truman gasped. He'd been expecting something bizarre, but this took the biscuit. He felt a laugh rumbling up like distant thunder from somewhere deep inside and he let it come out in a raucous guffaw into Maynard's face. 'You must be kidding,' he said, still rumbling. 'I'm a trowel-jockey, not a negotiator. No thank you very much. There's a civil war on in the Sudan, and you want me to go and broker an illegal deal with a bunch of xenophobic nomads nobody knows anything about. You must reckon I'm the biggest sucker in Christendom. And you think the Sudanese government is going to sit by twiddling its thumbs while you sign a deal worth billions of dollars with a totally unadministered tribe? It's a perfect recipe for a hole in the head.'

Maynard scratched at a raw patch on his face, and Truman saw a brief smudge of exasperation in his eyes. 'The Saghrana own the land. It's theirs to sell.'

Truman chortled. 'So what?' he said. 'You can't just go turfing up any place you please, even with the consent of the site-owner.

There are things like permits and mining rights to be obtained, and they're only provided by governments. The agreement will be toilet paper as soon as the government wins the war and has time to concentrate on backwoods regions – which they'll be guaranteed to do if they hear there's a fortune to be had there. And how much does a mining operation like that cost? Ten million dollars? Fifteen? No bank's going to lend that kind of money on a project in a war-torn country against the signature of some illiterate troglodyte war-chief with a bone through his nose.'

Maynard hiccoughed at the joke, and winked slyly at Truman. 'You leave the finance to me, old boy. That's my department. The investment capital's there. All we need is the contract. As for permits, the *Mufarida* is huge – one of the most arid places on earth, and it's a no-go area to the government. Only the nomads can survive there. Now, I've had it from a blue chip source that the CIA thinks the civil war will go on for another thirty years. Ample time for Kortex to get in and out and fiddle about. It's our business to make sure the government never do take over the area. Money's not much good to the Bedouin, so we'll pay them in arms – M16s, rocket-launchers, machine-guns, L2 grenades, mortars – any damn kit they like. They've got the terrain on their side and with regular infusions of modern clobber they'll be more than a match for government troops any day. It'll be just like buying our own security.'

Truman stopped laughing and looked at him incredulously. He understood the scheme clearly now. It was a dirty deal with him earmarked for Puss-in-Boots while the fat-cat Marquis of Calabas here sat at home and smoked his Davidoffs. He watched as Maynard finally lit his cigar, took a deep toke and blew out the smoke with a sigh of satisfaction.

'Maynard,' Truman said. 'It stinks.'

Maynard poised the cigar between thumb and forefinger and grinned playfully. 'Ah,' he said. 'Certainly it doesn't smell like roses, but then – as you rightly said – making money never does.'

He put the cigar down carefully in the ashtray and leaned forward, till his knees touched Truman's. His fishlike eyes, raw with determination now, fixed on Truman's face. *Here it comes*, Truman thought. *The punch-line. The final gambit.*

'I need you in on this, Dr Truman,' Maynard said. 'and to show you how much I need you, I'm not offering you a flat rate. I'm offering you a cut. Ten percent of profits over the next ten years. Think about it. The palladium alone is worth billions. The platinum too. This'll be the first and last job you'll ever have to do outside your own field. After this you can reopen your dig at Siwa or any damn place you like and live there forever as happy as a pig in sewage.'

'You mean if I still have my *cojones?*'

Maynard blew a smoke ring. 'I didn't say there's no risk. But fortune favours the bold.'

'Like hell!' Truman said. 'My maths might not be as good as yours, but even I can calculate that ten percent of bugger-all's still nothing. Get someone else, Mr. Maynard. Get one of your City lawyers. You might think I'm some kind of Oxford pointy-head who was born yesterday, but I'm not.'

Maynard stayed bent forward, his eyes never leaving Truman's face. 'There's no one else for the job,' he said placidly. 'I need you. You're not some shitty third-rate solicitor. You're a straight guy and you know your onions when it comes to the Arabs.'

'I know nothing about the nomads. I've never been into the *Mufarida* beyond Siwa, and I've never met any Saghrana. In fact I never even heard of them until a couple of weeks ago.'

'That doesn't matter. You know the lingo and the culture, and you *like* the Arabs, that's what counts.'

'Forget it.'

'You're the only one who can do it. That's why I need you.'

'No way.'

Maynard sat back and folded his hands across his mouth in contemplation.

'You're a hard bargainer, Dr. Truman,' he said at last. 'And

 26

that's just what I need. All right, twelve and a half percent. But believe me, I can't go any higher.'

Truman glanced at Maynard's poisonous eyes in disbelief. *This guy actually thinks I'm stalling to up the ante*, he thought. But he couldn't help doing the calculations anyway. He didn't know how much palladium they could expect to extract in a day, but 2.5 kilos didn't sound too much, and that amounted to nearly 1.5 million dollars a month, 18 million dollars a year. At twelve and a half percent that would give him about 2.25 million dollars a year, 25 million in ten years. And that was only the palladium. The platinum might double that, and Maynard hadn't even mentioned what the iridium was worth.

Truman couldn't imagine what such wealth meant, and he told himself he didn't really want to know. But there was a fascination in it – that he had to admit. He stared at the fire, then out of the window at the grey English morning. To strangers, the world out there seemed eminently civilized, a world of ivy-bound Saxon churches, pubs and village greens, of honest, industrious, upright folk who tended their roses and loved their dogs. Truman had known since childhood that it was an illusion. Under the civilized exterior it was a cattle-market where people's lives were bought and sold. And here he was sitting by a Christmassy fire, bargaining away his life for money. And not only his own life. Maynard was proposing to sell modern firearms to illiterate nomads. Somewhere along that road, innocent people were going to get whacked.

He stood up and stared at the fire for a few moments, composing himself. 'Look, Maynard,' he said. 'I don't know if this is flattery or insult, but I can't take it whatever the case. I'm not a mining company wide-boy. I'd be useless to you.'

Maynard twitched and watched him through eyes that were pill-box slits. 'I told you I don't want a wide-boy. Believe me, it's the only way you're going to pay off Whealan and get your dig open again.'

Truman hesitated. To reopen the dig at Siwa was just about the only ambition he had in life right now, and he felt a surge of anger that Whealan had reduced him to this. The desire to get back to Siwa was so keen it was almost a physical craving. He'd found a profession he loved and was good at. He'd never expected to be rich, but had been content that he would never need to be. Now, at the age of thirty-seven, he'd simply been kicked out because he refused to play academic politics. This job had dropped from the blue, custom-built for him, and suddenly it seemed ungrateful to providence to turn it down out of hand. Maynard had asked him to do something dangerous, probably immoral, but right now, however you looked at it, this was his only path back to Siwa.

'Can I think about it?' he asked.

Maynard smiled with satisfaction, seeing that Truman was tottering on the brink, and came in with the double-whammy. 'Sorry, old boy,' he said. This is a once in a lifetime offer. You say yes now or you forget it. If you walk out that door now, I won't take any calls, and if you ever come back here, Cliff won't let you past his desk. The strike is highly confidential, so you tell me now whether you're in or out.'

Truman scratched his broken nose with a forefinger. 'And if I'm out?' he inquired.

Maynard's gaze was as intense as a cobra's. 'You should be all right as long as you keep your mouth shut.'

Truman flared with anger. 'Are you threatening me?' he demanded.

For an instant Maynard's eyes flickered on him, surprised at the outburst. 'Threatening you?' he said. 'I'm offering to make you a very rich man. What's it to be?'

Truman turned it over in his mind for a few more moments. If he took the job he reckoned he had only an even chance of getting back alive. But if he ended up feeding the vultures, so what? Natalie had left him: Jonathan was dead. All he had to live for was Siwa, and if that was closed to him anyway, what was the point in going on? He'd already come to a decision, and his mouth went dry in anticipation of the risk he would be taking. 'When do I start?'

Maynard beamed. 'Bravo, old boy,' he said, picking up his cigar, 'I knew the extra two and a half percent would tip the balance!'

Truman smiled back wanly, knowing he didn't give a tinker's cuss about the extra two and a half percent.

'I'll have that whisky now,' he said.

5

WHEN TRUMAN LEFT THE KORTEX OFFICE, Sergei Rybakov was standing pressed in a doorway across the street, holding a cigarette in one leather-gloved hand, while the other was thrust deep into the false pocket of his navy-blue Kashmir coat, teasing the butt of his Makarov pistol beneath. He recognized Truman at once from the snap Maynard had shown him – a lean-looking guy about thirty-five or so, in a threadbare black overcoat, with narrow features, fine as an antelope's, unkempt dark hair that kept blowing in his eyes, and a trim goatee beard. He didn't have that apple-pie pinkness of the British, Rybakov thought – he could have been Italian or Portuguese, but on the surface anyhow, he looked a wimp – definitely the arty-farty type. Only the double-stepped broken nose stood out as an anomaly on the sensitive face.

Truman gazed around him speculatively and for a moment Rybakov froze, wondering if the guy had spotted him. There was something penetrating in Truman's gaze that smacked of street-awareness – as out of place on the aesthetic features as the broken nose. Maybe he was more switched on than he looked.

Rybakov flicked his cigarette away half smoked and it sizzled in the slush. He watched Truman curiously as he disappeared round the corner by St George's, then glanced briefly at his gold wristwatch, wondering how much longer he'd have to wait. The watch matched his two gold teeth, the gold Dunhill lighter in his pocket, the gold cufflinks, the gold tie-pin and the gold earring in his left ear. They were like the emblems of his trade, and he had the parvenu's fascination with such baubles – his life was an unashamed imitation of the advertisements in glossy magazines. Despite the ugly jobs he had done in his time – the stabbings, the garottings, the slashings and maimings – Rybakov didn't think of himself as a gangster, but only as a survivor, an entrepreneur looking after his own in a world where poverty meant starvation. In this day and age you had to do some desperate things to survive, he thought, and he knew he was walking a tight-rope on this one. He hadn't slept well for weeks, wondering when the walls of the affluent little bubble he'd created were going to cave in. In his more confident moods, though, he fancied himself as some latter-day Russian count in his designer suits and handmade pinstripe shirts. He had long, stately limbs, a long-boned face with just a touch of Chechen around the eyes, gypsy-dark hair cropped short as iron filings, and black eyes that were still and keen as a hunting-dog's.

It was only five minutes before Maynard emerged. Behind him and looking about twice his height, came Cliff, a fearsome dark wizard in his dreadlocks, floor-length black oilskin trenchcoat, and broad-brimmed black hat. Maynard saw Rybakov and marched across the road to him, his leather-soled shoes scrunching on the salt.

'You don't want to walk on the ice with those shoes,' Rybakov told him when he came near. 'I know, I'm Russian. You'll slip over and break your leg.'

Maynard smelt of good whisky and good cigar smoke. 'These are Lobbs' shoes,' he said primly. 'They are guaranteed. You ought to get some, Sergei. Anyway, if I slip I've always got Cliff to pick me up.'

Rybakov sent a resentful glance in Cliff's direction, 'We have a saying in Russia. The bigger they are the harder they go down.'

Cliff eyed the Russian back with raw hostility, 'Oh yeah? You wanna try me, Ivan?'

Rybakov squared up to him, though the Rastafarian had a good two feet to his advantage. 'It's *Mister* Ivan to you,' he said.

Maynard wafted the air with his fat hands. 'Now! Let's not fall out. You know, Sergei, Cliff has been with me for seventeen years. He is the most loyal man I have ever employed – him and One Eyed Harris.'

'Yeah, look what happened to Harris,' Rybakov sneered. 'He was another one thought he was tough.'

'Come on, Sergei,' Maynard said soothingly. 'Forget it. Let's decide what we're going to eat. Chinese or Italian?'

They'd eaten at *Il-Pensiero* before, and Rybakov knew Maynard was at home there because he could sit in his own little private nook at the back – a querencia where he could pontificate without anyone overhearing. A big, soft Indian girl with hair like black velvet brought the menu, and Maynard let Rybakov choose for all of them, knowing how much he liked to show off his recently-acquired culinary sophistication. He ordered *antipasto misto, lasagna al forno, spigola arrosto* and a bottle of Chianti. He tasted the wine, swilling it around the glass and sampling the bouquet as if it was a very big deal, before allowing the waitress to pour. When the glasses were filled he raised his to Maynard, then, grudgingly, to Cliff who was sitting at a separate table facing the door – not because Maynard was too high and mighty to eat with a Rastafarian, but because Cliff was a pro and liked to hang loose. Rybakov was happy about that – he couldn't stand the way the big guy sneered at him from behind his high, mahogany-smooth cheekbones.

Maynard sipped wine. 'A very sound choice, Sergei, if I may say so. So, did you see him then?'

Rybakov savoured the Chianti. It reminded him of golden sunlight and bronze skinned girls on the Tuscan hills – not that he'd ever been to Tuscany, but he'd seen an image like that in an advertisement somewhere. 'Truman? Yeah, I saw him. Looked a wimp. He take the bait?'

'Hook, line and proverbial sinker, my dear boy.'

Rybakov's eyes narrowed suspiciously. 'You sure that creep's kosher?' he asked. 'Seems he make his mind up pretty quick for an egg-head type. How can you be sure he didn't have samples analysed himself?'

Maynard chortled. 'You're too suspicious, Sergei. Dr Truman agreed to the deal because he had no choice. He's been kicked out on his behind, accused of mismanagement of funds, and has nothing else to live for but his precious excavations.'

'Maybe, but I tell you there's something about him I don't like. I went through the file you give me on Truman. Reads pretty smooth till you see there's two years missing out of his life after graduation. What the hell was he doing?'

'A lot of young graduates take a few years off after university to see the world,' Maynard said. 'There's nothing odd about that, believe me.'

Rybakov fixed Maynard's self-satisfied face with a piercing gaze. 'I still say we send my boys in.'

Maynard snorted again. 'This is a job for the rapier, Sergei, not the bludgeon. Trust me – the English are the best in the world at this sort of thing. Comes from generations of experience.'

The waitress brought the *antipasto misto*, and Rybakov picked at the *salchiccia* with his fork, looking surly. 'It's our money. You should have let us decide.'

Maynard chewed *prosciutto di parma* and wiped his mouth with a paper napkin. 'Any of your gung-ho ex-Spetznatz types speak Arabic, Sergei?' he inquired.

'No – they're soldiers, not bloody linguists.'

'Precisely. This job requires someone sensitive. Someone with nous, who's not going to end up doing a raspberry in some Arab's face and ogling his wife. He's going to be operating among people about as different from us as Martians, and that takes knife-edged sensibilities. A sniff out of place could mean no deal, and no deal means toodeloo to your chances of hiking your greasy cash down the laundromat.'

Rybakov sipped wine and sneered. 'Sensibilities, my ass,' he said. 'I learn all about sensibilities when I was Spetznatz sergeant

33

in Afghanistan. Saw my comrades with their dicks sliced off and sharpened sticks shoved in their butts. Only way to deal with ragheads is give them a dose of forty-four magnum.' He speared an olive and held it up curiously, 'We got ourselves an army of Afghanistan veterans, and if your man don't come up with the goods, Maynard, I send them in.'

Maynard put his fork down on his plate and took another sip of wine. 'Very well. It's your money, after all.'

Rybakov looked happier now he'd asserted himself. 'Does this Truman geek know where finance is coming from?' he asked.

Maynard drew in his breath with a theatrical sucking noise. 'No way,' he said. He's got qualms enough. He doesn't need to know.'

'So when does he leave?'

'I've got him booked on a BA flight tomorrow evening, straight through to Cairo. He'll be met by Costas Giorgiu, our fixer on the ground. He'll set Truman up with a professional smuggler who runs camel-caravans across the border south of the Kharga oasis. After that he's on his own.'

'Camel-caravans! Shit, is this twenty-first century or what?'

'These caravan guys have been evading the police for generations. They know how it's done.'

The waitress came to clear away the antipasto plates. Rybakov took another sip of wine. 'What about opposition?'

Maynard waved his fork and frowned. 'Now that's the bad news. I have a stoolie in Rand's camp, who tells me Marcus Rand has got a whiff of the palladium find.'

Rybakov stopped forking lasagna and watched Maynard furiously. 'How the hell?' he demanded.

Maynard sighed. 'I've been over this in my head a dozen times. There's been no leak at my end. Truman knew nothing about the strike until a couple of hours ago, so that rules him out.'

'What if he had samples analysed himself, and he's playing us for schmucks?'

'Sergei,' Maynard said, with exaggerated patience, 'Truman

 34

just isn't the type. He's an intellectual, living in his own little dimension of academia. Straight as a die. Not a trace of graft in his record. You suggesting he had the stuff analysed then just dropped into my office to see the colour of my carpets?'

'For a billion dollars, people do funny things.'

'OK, but this isn't the first time sensitive data's gone astray. Unless Rand's got himself some kind of oracle, I'd say a better shot is Qurayshi's – the lab that analysed the samples last week.'

Rybakov took a double gulp of wine and rubbed his mouth with his napkin. 'Who was analyst on Harris samples?' he inquired.

Dr Amersadiqi – Iranian fellow. One of the best they've got. There's no way he could have known where the samples came from, but he'd know that Kortex put them in – and how much they're worth. If it does turn out to be him, I shall be most disappointed, but I do recommend you have a word in Amersadiqi's shell-like ear.'

Rybakov laughed. He loved the delicate way the British understated the most heinous threats. 'A word in his shell-like ear,' was a job that would suit him perfectly. 'Rand got ex-South African secret police as security. If they get on site first they make mince pies of that wimp Truman.'

'Meat.'

Rybakov cocked an eye at him. 'No meat, my friend,' he said. '*Spigola arrosto* is grilled sea-bass.'

Maynard bubbled with laughter and patted his lips with his napkin. 'I know that. I mean mincemeat. Not mince pies, mince-*meat*. You meant Rand's security would make mince*meat* of Truman, but I wouldn't be too sure. Truman was a karate black belt at 20 – a national youth champion in free-sparring. Might be a bit rusty now, but I'd say he could handle himself. See that broken nose he's got? He copped that in a fight-off match with a black guy called Willie Richardson for a place in the Olympic team. Truman lost by a point – and Richardson went on to win the silver medal.'

Rybakov laid his fork down and belched discreetly. 'Fucking

Bruce Lee!' he scoffed. 'Another one who died young. I never saw black belt yet could dodge a nine millimetre shell. Is the ones without broken noses that worry me.'

'Well then,' Maynard said, signalling to the waitress to take their plates. 'Perhaps you'd better stick a minder on his tail. Have you got anyone available?'

Rybakov smiled at a private joke. 'Is old man Paretsky,' he said. 'He's around in Cairo. I'll have him put on job.'

'Who's old man Paretsky when he's at home?'

'Federal Security Service deputy head of station in Cairo. USSR dinosaur who survived perestroika. He's an old bugger but he can – how you say, *wipe the floor* with most of them. Now *he* speaks Arabic – one of the die-hards who think we better going back to days of Brezhnev. Good at what he does, though.'

The waitress brought the fish and Rybakov attacked it with a vengeance. 'Man,' he said, 'this is what you call fresh fish, no?'

Maynard forked a piece of fish, peered at it through his severe spectacles, and sampled it tentatively. 'Now *there* we disagree, Sergei,' he said. 'Yesterday, I should say.'

He put the fork down. 'You could have Paretsky liaise with Costas Giorgiu,' he said. 'But I hope he knows his chickens, because I wouldn't like Truman to get whacked out before he strikes paydirt.'

Rybakov watched him resentfully, like a child scolded for not knowing its alphabet. 'Paretsky?' he said, sullenly. 'You can rely on him hundred percent to get Truman into field. What to do with him when he comes out with contract is problem. I tell you, my bosses will not be happy making him present of twelve and a half percent.' Maynard called the waitress to take his uneaten fish and drained his wine.

'Don't worry about Truman, old boy. I chose him because he's expendable. Once we've got the contract we'll take steps to ensure that Dr Truman never makes it back.'

6

Truman's house was a mausoleum of memories, despite the fact that he'd tried to exorcize every trace of Natalie and Johnny from the place. But you couldn't erase memories from your head, he thought, no matter how hard you tried. There would always be Johnny's voice there – Truman couldn't ever forget how the little boy would sing loudly to himself whenever he was left alone, even for a minute, as if to remind you he was still around. Things had never been right between him and Natalie after Jonathan had been killed. It wasn't exactly that they had blamed each other for his death, more that whenever they'd looked at each other they'd seen Jonathan there.

The room had an air of obsessive tidiness to it – as if everything was in its place. Truman lit a wood fire with white cakes of Zip and stood by it, warming his hands, drinking Nescafe from a mug. There was a frost this morning – through a silvered window he could see traffic lurching down Banbury Road towards the city centre, and gardens with threadbare May trees the colour of ice. When the flames were licking nicely around the logs, he sank on to a cushion near the fire, and flipped through the notes on the Saghrana he'd made in the Bodleian the day before. The earliest reference he'd found to a people called the 'Saqranae' had come in a folk tale from an Arabic manuscript dating from the 12th century, in which they were referred to as 'vampires whose voices twitter like bats.'

The word 'Sagrarna-Ghararna' was to be found on a map dating from 1570 – the *Africae Tabula Nova* of Ortelius – straddling what was now the Sudanese border, but neither Herodotus, writing in about 500 BC, nor Strabo four hundred years later, had mentioned them. That suggested they had arrived in the area between 100 BC and 1500 AD – a long period to work with. For the modern era there was a report of a tribe called the Saghrana raiding a village in the Dakhla oasis in Egypt in 1938, and carrying off eight or nine young virgins. Their origin was not known but they were thought to have come far across the desert. Similar raids had taken place in Kharga oasis in 1941 and at Bahriyya in 1945, and in each case the abducted girls had never been seen again.

And Miflah had been right about the ram's head symbol – all the modern sources agreed that the Saghrana camel-brand was a ram with the sacred sun-disk between its horns – the same symbol he'd found on the Santariya column. The Saghrana were a tribe that was 'lost' to history, it seemed – a people entirely cut off in the desert. He started to understand why Maynard couldn't send some fast-talking Jack-the-Lad – to these people any outsider was going to look like he'd been beamed down from the moon.

Truman put his notes down, stood up and stretched, glancing out of the window. A shadow across the street moved quickly out of view behind a privet-hedge and Truman's attention was drawn to the movement. It was funny, but when he'd left the Bodleian yesterday, he'd had the distinct feeling he was being followed, and there'd certainly been a man waiting for him outside Maynard's office – a tall, slim guy with an elegant Crombie, a gold earring, and something oriental about the eyes. He shrugged as he went upstairs to collect his things together for the trip. The best bet was that it was one of Maynard's boys keeping tabs on him, making sure he didn't gab to anyone. After all, he was now privy to a multi-million dollar secret and

Maynard couldn't afford to take chances. He wondered if the guy had tapped his phone. He looked discreetly out of the bedroom window as he packed his Ziplock bag, but the shadow behind the hedge was gone.

It was only as he approached the airport that he noticed the tail – a black car that stuck to him and now seemed to be gaining. It was a Renault or an Opel, he thought – something European, though all cars looked the same these days, anyway. He drove into the North Terminal, located the Avis compound, gave the keys to the attendant and signed his clipboard. When he emerged from the compound a tall, barrel-chested man in a fur-lined parka was waiting for him, leaning against a rail, smoking a pipe. It wasn't the one who'd been outside Maynard's place. That guy had been spindly and expensively dressed, whereas this one was solid-looking, with a creased face, a boulder-shaped head and sandy hair beginning to go thin. He looked almost thuggish at first sight, but the pipe lent him an air of sophistication, like a stage prop, and closer up there was intelligence and deep watchfulness in the bright blue eyes.

'Dr Truman, sir?' the man said, standing up straight. The voice was north country with the harsh edges filed off, and deceptively gentle, Truman thought. He was wearing thick-soled brogues, and faded blue jeans under the parka, and there was the earthy athleticism of a shot-putter about his bulk. He put out a large hand and smiled. 'Whitehaven,' he said. 'With the Foreign Office.'

'Foreign Office?' Truman repeated in surprise, shaking the hand automatically. 'Are you the one who's been following me?'

The big hand removed the pipe and jammed it into a breast pocket. 'Sorry if it worried you, sir, but I had to talk to you. Could we go somewhere quiet?'

If you were the one who tailed me from the Bodleian, you could have picked a better time,' Truman said. 'Right now I have a plane to catch, and I really don't know what the Foreign Office has to do with me.'

Whitehaven was a big man. He shifted his weight so that it

rested equally on both feet, and stuck his hands to the parka's side pockets. 'It's quite important, sir. It's about Kortex.'

His manner was outwardly deferent – almost apologetic – yet there was the slightest hint of compulsion there, Truman thought. The big man seemed to have no doubt he could force Truman to do what he wanted if necessary. He looked at his watch. 'I don't know what this is about,' he said. 'But I'll give you ten minutes, that's all.' It was the same deal he'd given Maynard, he remembered, and he suddenly regretted it – the whole direction of your life could be changed in ten minutes.

They sat in a self-service restaurant in the retail area called The Village – a place done out like a Disney version of an English pub, with a fireplace, old books and a mantlepiece with china dogs. Truman seated himself at a formica-topped table, watching passengers trailing past with their trolleys, while Whitehaven brought filter coffee in mugs. He sat and stuck his unlit pipe in his mouth, looking for a moment like a granite-faced griffon. Truman sipped his coffee experimentally. It was unexpectedly good. At the next table sat a young couple with day-glo rucksacks at their feet – a half pretty girl with a bob of blonde hair tied in a scarf, trying to baby-talk a long-haired young man in a leather jacket who glowered over a cigarette.

'So what *is* this about?' Truman asked.

Whitehaven sucked on the unlit pipe. 'Gus Maynard,' he said. 'I understand you're working for him, sir.'

The young man at the next table was pouting like a small child and the girl was caressing his face with her hands. He snapped something and shrugged her off angrily. They seemed lost in their world, entirely oblivious of anything outside their own private bubble.

Truman turned his attention to Whitehaven. 'You understand wrong! I don't know who you are, Mr Whitehaven, but my business is my own, and as far as I understand it, I'm not obliged to reveal the story of my life to somebody just because they happen to have followed me all the way from Oxford, and throw out the words ''Foreign Office'' without any identification. Last time I looked, only the police have the right of arrest in this country, so unless you're lying you can't touch me, and if you are lying, you're obliged to show me ID.'

Whitehaven regarded him with opaque eyes, set the pipe down on the table, but didn't reach for any identification. 'Touchy aren't we, sir?' he said. 'No-one said anything about police or arrest.' His voice remained controlled but Truman detected fury there, itching to get out.

'You're a free man,' he went on, 'and you can go where you damn well please and talk to who you damn well please. You can work for anyone you like, but I thought maybe I should put you in the picture before you get dragged into the shit out of your depth. You're an educated man, Dr Truman, and I had you down as a reasonable one. I thought maybe we could have a little heart-to-heart.'

Truman kept his face deadpan. 'If you know so much about me,' he said. 'You'll also know I don't take kindly to being threatened, and I call tailing a man for two days a threat.'

Whitehaven blinked at him half apologetically. 'Listen, sir,' he said in a low voice. 'We know Kortex hit the jackpot recently. We also know you brought the samples back in a container from Egypt, so you're up to your eyeballs whether you like it or not. And we know you were at Maynard's office yesterday morning.'

Truman sighed and glanced at the two disenchanted love-birds at the next table again. The boy appeared unmoved by the girl's pleadings, and had turned his face away from her, concentrating hard on his cigarette.

He raised his eyes to Whitehaven. 'Who is this Maynard, exactly?' he inquired.

Whitehaven chuckled. 'Have it your own way, sir,' he said. 'But I warn you, he's a shyster of the first order. Talks honey but the guy's got some very nasty playmates. Guys you wouldn't want to collide with down a dark alley. His chums are stictly *persona non grata* in this neck of the woods.'

Whitehaven nodded as a speck of interest lit up in Truman's eyes. He lowered his head towards Truman's. 'Russian *mafiya*,'

41

he said. 'They've got a pile of dirty cash from hawking dope, running gambling joints, rent-a-thug rackets – you name it, they've got their gungie thumbs in it. We're talking very big potatoes – megabucks, and all those dirty shekels have to be sanitized. The mineral market's the ideal business. They work through companies like Kortex, buying up raw materials, processing them in cheap Heath Robinson set-ups back home in Mother Russia, and playing them out on the international market at a mark-up. Hey presto! The money's become hygienic enough to eat your lunch off.'

Whitehaven had spoken with energy, but Truman eyed him sullenly.

'What's that got to do with me?'

The girl at the next table had given up caressing and was sobbing now. The boy was jabbing his cigarette out furiously in an ash-tray, ignoring her.

Whitehaven frowned. 'Don't you get it?' he said. 'Kortex is a front for the mafiya, and if you're mixed up with Maynard, you're mixed up with international money laundering. This recent strike's just up their street. You're a pawn in the game, Dr Truman, and one way or another you'll get scragged. These boys have been on a feeding frenzy since the wall came down, and they don't give a monkey's, believe me. In New Jersey ten years ago, they took over from the Italian mafia by hanging guys on meat-hooks and cutting their bodies in half with chain-saws. They'll promise the moon and all you'll get is a point thirty-eight Christmas present.'

Truman finished his coffee and watched the boy next door picking up his rucksack with grim determination. The girl was still crying with her head in her hands, her face obscured by the flop of blonde hair.

'This is all very interesting,' Truman said. 'Fascinating, actually. But I still fail to see what it's got to do with me.'

There was a twist of desperation in Whitehaven's face now. 'We've had tabs on Kortex's action for years. But we need proof. You could help us get that proof, Dr Truman. You could be our inside man.'

The boy in the leather jacket was standing up, tossing on his rucksack, while the girl tugged hopelessly at his arm.

Truman guffawed. 'You mean a stool-pigeon? I'm afraid you've got the wrong guy, Mr Whitehaven.'

Whitehaven surveyed him patiently, and picked up his pipe, tapping it softly on the table. 'I know a little bit about you, Dr Truman,' he said. 'You're not the bent type – a bit eccentric maybe, that's all. OK, you got kicked out on your behind over some academic wrangling, but don't let that affect your judgement. Even if they don't bump you off when they've done with you, you'll go down with them when the shit hits the fan, and it will, believe me, it will. You work for us and I'll make sure you're in the clear.'

He paused and watched Truman steadily for a few moments studying the effect of his words.

Truman coughed nervously. 'Mr Whitehaven,' he said. 'As I told you, I have an aversion to being threatened. It brings out the worst in me. So might I suggest you stop flogging a moribund horse and let me get my flight.'

The big man shrugged. 'You're in the crap up to your armpits, Dr Truman, and a little bird tells me you'll regret it. This isn't some chicken-feed deal, and the world's not going to sit by while the mafiya stuff their faces from the pork-barrel. This is the real sleazy, shitty world we're talking about here. Sooner or later people are going to get scrunched and I don't mean just the slime. I mean people who can't count past their fingers and never heard of a rare earth strike. Are you going to stand by and let that happen?'

'Oh please,' Truman said sarcastically. 'The holier-than-thou pose doesn't suit you, Mr Whitehaven.'

'Maybe not. What I do know is that you're playing with fire with the big boys, and you're going to get burnt. Don't wreck your life for a sleaze-ball like Gus Maynard.'

Truman glanced at the sobbing girl at the next table and felt suddenly sorry for her. The boy was stomping off towards the entrance without a glance over his shoulder.

'My life's already wrecked,' he said. 'But thank you for the advice. I'll bear it in mind. Just now I have to catch a plane.'

Whitehaven sighed, stood up and laid a white business card on the table. 'Think about it. If you change your mind, ring one of the numbers on here – day or night, from any place in the world – and ask for me.'

He shoved the card over to Truman who took it without looking and put it in his pocket. He pushed his chair back and stood, picking up his Ziplock bag. 'I don't think I'll be seeing you again, Mr Whitehaven.'

Whitehaven nodded gravely. 'Maybe not,' he said. 'But you might like to know that the analyst who worked on the Kortex samples – a Dr Amersadiqi – was found dead in his flat this morning with a bullet in his skull. His wife was lying in the next room – she'd been raped and her breasts slashed before they finished her off. Perhaps we will meet again, Dr Truman. Who knows?'

7

THE REINFORCED STEEL DOORS OF THE Rand building slid back and Colonel Julius Stein entered jauntily, nodding at the surveillance cameras and whispering a throaty greeting to the uniformed security men. The building was already an anomaly in downtown Jo'burg – muggings and shootings were now commonplace even in daylight hours, and most big businesses had fled to the suburbs to escape the growing insecurity. Not Rand's, though. The towering concrete and glass fortress had been built on the site of the original premises erected by Marcus Rand's grandfather in the 1920s, and Rand had inherited the laager mentality of his forbears. Here he would stay.

In the lobby an old man in an ill-fitting blue overall was pushing a cleaning trolley across Stein's path, and it grazed the Colonel's leg as it passed. The old man froze and scanned Stein's face warily with eyes that looked almost opaque from trachoma. 'I'm sorry, Sir,' he stuttered. 'I don't see so good these days.'

The Colonel watched him curiously. 'What's your name?' he demanded in a coarse whisper.

'Juma,' the old man said wearily.

'How long have you been with us, Juma?'

The old man sighed. 'Nearly thirty years,' he said. 'I'm sorry, I didn't see you coming, Sir.'

Stein stood up straight. 'That's all right, Juma,' he said affably.

45

'Accidents happen. You should get those eyes looked at, though.'

He inserted his ID card into the slot on the turnstile, and passed through to the reception desk, where a thick-set half-caste woman with a brush of dyed red hair eyed him guardedly. 'Good morning Colonel Stein,' she said.

'Morning Mrs Gillespie,' Stein croaked. 'You see that old man over there? If he's still on our staff by tomorrow morning, *you* will be scrubbing the floors for the rest of the week. Now please open the executive elevator. I wish to see Mr Rand.'

The woman blanched. 'But it's Mr Rand's dialysis time. He gave orders not to be disturbed.'

Stein smiled, showing two rows of sharp little teeth. 'Just open the elevator, Mrs Gillespie,' he whispered.

As the elevator shot up to Rand's 'command den' on the twentieth floor, Stein preened himself in the mirror. It had taken him a decade of hard graft to work his way up to the dizzy heights of the twentieth from the security section in the basement, he reflected, and no bitch of a receptionist was going to tell him he couldn't go up there now. He had travelled a long way from the slag-heaps of Russian-occupied east Germany where he'd grown up as the son of a drunken miner, but he still wasn't where he ought to be. He'd come to Rand's as security chief during a period when the country was changing over to black majority rule, and whites were fleeing the country in droves. Shareholders had been pulling money out, and Rand himself had been on the point of losing his grip. It had been Stein who had rallied his confidence, installing new state-of-the-art security systems, training a small army of all-white mercenaries recruited from the old government forces, and turning the office building into an impregnable fortress.

Stein's innovations – and his ruthless methods – had impressed Rand. So much, in fact, that he'd eventually appointed 'the Colonel' company trouble-shooter with the post of assistant deputy CEO for Exploration, and an office on the eighteenth floor. Stein was determined that he wouldn't stop there. He knew his talent had never been properly recognized. He'd always had to struggle up the ladder from the bottom, only to be robbed of his prize on the top rung. Nobody appreciated his vision – not even Marcus Rand. Given the opportunity, he believed, he could halt the Corporation's failing fortunes and turn it into the global empire it deserved to be, but over the years Rand had become increasingly distrustful of other companies, and reluctant to expand. What he wanted deep down, Stein knew, was the cosy family business the company had been in his grandfather's time, when the whites ruled the roost and the blacks were so much grist to the mill.

He smoothed his sleek dark hair back with a curiously effete gesture and studied the finely tuned features that stared back at him from the gilt-framed mirror. At school in East Germany, back in the tough years of the post-war era, they had called him a sissy because of his slim figure and almost effeminate good looks. They had jeered at him for his refusal to play 'manly' sports like football and rugby – until he'd stabbed one of his tormentors in the testicles with a pocket-knife, that was, and they'd realized the 'sissy' had reflexes as fast as a snake's. After that they'd given him a wide berth.

He grinned at the memory, and straightened his impeccable dark suit. When his father had drunk himself to death, Stein had been left a penniless fourteen year old with a mother dying of tuberculosis. They'd offered him his old man's place at the pit, but even at that age Stein had realized it was tantamount to a capital sentence. Instead he'd joined the Party, grovelled his way into the good books of the powerful by doing any shitty job they demanded, and at eighteen had been rewarded by a post in the Stasi – the secret police. Even then it had been a hard grind, forcing himself to take on the tasks nobody else wanted, forcing himself to be obsequious to his superiors year after year until he was almost exploding inside. He'd worked his way through from lieutenant to major, and then, just as his colonelcy was pending, with the chance of real power, that bastard Gorbachev had come along with his bloody perestroika, and instead of being a force to reckon with, he'd ended up a name on the wanted list.

He'd fled to the west, got himself installed as a security advisor in a firm with prospects, and everything had looked rosy again. Until some snooper had identified him, and he'd been forced to move again. He'd had to start a third time with Rand's, and he was damned if he was going to be thwarted again. He relaxed his body into an easy posture and assumed his customary expression – a permanent grimace like a ritual mask with blank holes where the eyes should have been.

The elevator door opened with a hiss, and Stein stepped languidly out into the 'command den'. Marcus Rand was sitting in his automatic wheelchair next to an IV stand, growling, and being fussed over by a smart doctor and two young black nurses in crisp white smocks. The light in the room was dim and artificial – Rand would often have the automatic shutters closed for weeks at a time, to block out the view of what he called 'The Eyesore' – the sprawling maze of central Jo'burg beneath. Ever since the bomb-blast that had taken his legs and his daughter, Rand had suffered from agoraphobia, but he felt safe in his electronic nook amongst flickering TV screens linked both to international satellites and in-house spy networks, computer terminals, video systems, satellite and terrestrial phone links. His facilities produced forecasts constantly, and Rand was obsessed with them – intelligence forecasts, political forecasts, economic forecasts. It made him feel omniscient, Stein guessed – sitting up here on top of the world, always one jump ahead.

Stein insinuated his way silently into the luxurious hospitality suite. Rand waved an imperious hand at him, and he sat down without a greeting and crossed his legs elegantly, watching the dialysis procedure with the detachment of a bug-collector examining a specimen. Rand looked like Humpty Dumpty, he thought, waiting for the doctor to insert the IV tube into his naked torso. His legs were shrivelled almost to ciphers, but his body was grossly and obscenely fat, his bald head elevated with the impertinence of a cockerel's, and something of the cockerel's bland arrogance in the set of his nose and eyes.

'Ouch!' Rand growled, glaring at the doctor who had just

pinched his skin with the IV attachment. 'Can't you be careful, Sommerville?'

Dr Sommerville was a tall, fresh-faced man with blue eyes and a placid, almost obsequious demeanour. He virtually bowed to Rand when he talked, Stein noted. 'Sorry Mr Rand,' Sommerville said. 'We're almost done now.' The doctor finished his work on the IV, and the two nurses laid sterile pads over Rand's knees. Both were pretty, with nubile figures and long bare legs, their short frizzy hair cut into fetching symmetric patterns. One was a head shorter than the other, and for a split second Stein's caustic eyes fluttered over her, caressing the curves beneath the starched medical dress.

'All done, Mr Rand,' Sommerville said, dipping his head. 'We'll see you in an hour.'

Rand grunted and cast a glance at the receding posteriors of the nurses as they entered the elevator. Stein watched them too, his eyes smouldering, until the doors swished closed.

'We lost our snout in London,' Rand announced. 'Amersadiqi was found dead in his apartment this morning. He'd been well worked over, which means somebody was on to him.'

Stein watched him through eye-slits. 'A great pity,' he commented. 'But at least he got the report out before he croaked.'

'So what?' Rand barked. 'All we know is that Kortex have struck the world's biggest deposit of palladium. We haven't any idea where it is.'

'And Harris?' Stein asked blankly. 'He made the strike?'

Rand's bloated Buddha face screwed up like a rag, and flushed red. 'That filth's croaked too,' he gasped. 'I should have had a contract put out on the bastard years ago.'

A ghost of a smile played round Stein's thin lips, and his eyes rested on the remains of Rand's legs – tapering stumps under loose trousers. All his precious forecasts hadn't predicted that some maverick mining engineer would booby-trap his car twenty years ago, Stein thought. Forecasts were all well and good, but there was always the chaos element – the random chance that defied prediction. That was where the real danger lay.

'Relax, Mr Rand,' Stein said. 'If you squeeze any harder you'll cut off the drip. How come you're so certain Harris is dead?'

Rand looked disconcerted for a moment and made a visible effort to relax. He picked up a remote and flicked a button. The largest of the video screens came to life, showing a shaded map of Egypt and the Sudan, with areas of vegetation in various shades of green, and desert in saffron-yellow. He put down the remote, picked up a laser-pointer and flashed a red spot on the screen. 'That's where Lambart's boys lost him. Last seen on October 4th heading out of Kharga, going south. Disappears into the storm and is never seen again. On 30th November Maynard offers a reward for information about his death or present where-abouts. There were no takers.'

'It could have been a ruse,' Stein said. 'Did you think of that?'

'Of course I thought of it,' Rand snapped.

He watched Stein with hooded eyes, trying to master the rage within. The 'Colonel' was insufferable, but Rand had to admit his assessment was correct, as usual. He'd sent Lambart after Harris to cut Stein down to size a bit, but the gambit had misfired. Lambart's little cadre of company investigators had screwed up big time and he knew he should have used Stein's trained mercs instead. There was no doubt that Stein was the best trouble-shooter he'd ever employed. He was so completely without qualms that at times even Rand was afraid of him, and Rand didn't scare easily – not if he was within four walls that was. There was a cut-glass intelligence to the man too, and he'd gradually insinuated himself into almost every aspect of Rand's operations. Rand liked to believe he could out-think everyone, and he was sometimes startled to find that Stein was two jumps ahead of him. No wonder he'd eluded the law for so long, Rand thought.

Stein claimed to have come to South Africa a decade ago to seek his fortune after a successful career in the French Foreign Legion Para Battalions, having made his way up from trooper to colonel on merit. Rand's discreet investigations had stuck a pin in that legend. 'Colonel' Stein was actually Major Hoth of

50

the former East German Secret Police – the Stasi – a Communist party-hound who'd done every dirty job the state had offered him with gusto. He'd spent a lot of his time carving up dissidents, or so-called dissidents, with a butcher's knife. Stein was a survivor all right, but the fact that he was on the EC's most wanted list gave Rand a certain reassurance. He'd never told Stein he knew, but there was a fat file stashed away in a place the Colonel would never find it – a file that would make diverting reading for the German police should the day ever dawn when Stein had outlived his usefulness. The way the guy was hustling in on him lately, that time might well be soon, he thought.

He put down the laser pointer and switched off the screen. 'I did some checking in Egypt,' he said, more calmly. 'It took a truckload of cash but I finally came up trumps. A Benjamin John Harris was reported found dead near Siwa Oasis at the police post there in early December.'

'Who reported it?'

'A guy called Mike Eliot – an American archaeology student with an address in New England. No other information on him, but he had Harris's passport and driving-licence. The police made no investigation. Now, it might be a con as you say, but there's a two month gap between Harris disappearing at Kharga and turning up dead near Siwa – ample time for him to have made a strike and got the samples back. I think we have to assume Harris is dead, but Maynard's still laughing through his teeth. There's another piece of shit I should have taken out years ago, before he got pally with the Russians. Can you imagine how much this strike is worth? If the palladium goes to the Ivans we'll be out of the market, and that can't happen. I need that strike, Stein. The way the government has been leaning on us lately to provide benefits for the miners and up the salaries, it's a wonder we can stay in business. I've got the board on my back and the shareholders whingeing about restructuring. If we lose this one, we could both be out.'

He stopped to catch his breath, his grotesque upper body covered in sweat.

Stein shifted position slightly. 'OK,' he said stiffly, 'but Maynard's backers are tough cookies, Mr Rand, and they have a lot of cash. Wouldn't it be better to consider a joint venture?'

Rand's cockerel eyes widened almost imperceptibly. 'With the mafiya? You've got to be joking. Those guys are crawling all over Africa like termites – have been ever since the wall came down. Next thing you know they'll be launching a take-over bid. It was better when Russia was run by the Commies.'

Stein's face creased ironically. 'The mafiya *are* the Commies. The same people who have ruled Russia ever since the revolution. Lenin and his Bolsheviks were mafiya, so were Stalin and his crew. My father was a miner all his life – he worked damn hard, but we lived on the edge of poverty just because he never would join the Party. He thought it was politics, but it wasn't, it wasn just survival. He was a fool. I myself never made that mistake. I have always tried to make sure I stayed on the winning side.'

Rand snorted. 'Then you better make sure we snaffle the palladium before Maynard gets his greasy palms on it.'

Stein stared at him hard, then turned his gaze away. 'Kharga and Siwa are both in the Western Desert of Egypt. So unless this is all some elaborate decoy, the strike was made somewhere west of the Nile. That narrows it down, but the deserts out there are huge. It's going to be like looking for the proverbial grain of sand on the beach.'

Rand coughed. 'We'll never find it on our own. We have to get a little birdie to tell us where we start looking. Maynard plays his cards close to his chest, but he's got to send somebody out there sometime soon, and that guy has to know where he's going. Kortex have done a lot of business in Egypt at one time or another. Do they have an agent in Cairo?'

Stein looked pensive. 'No one full time. But I could probably find out who they've used as a fixer in the past.'

'Good. At least that would be a start. Get on the next flight to Cairo, Stein. Find Maynard's fixer and make him squeal. Cut his rocks off if you have to, I don't care, but don't come back until you've located the strike.'

'I'll need technical backup – and I want to take some of my own boys with me.'

'I can spare you two Pumas – I'll have Ridgeway ferry them up for tomorrow night. Take ten of your best men.'

Stein nodded and stood up, pinching the creases of his trousers. 'There's a flight to Cairo at 4 p.m., Mr Rand,' he said. 'That's another four hours. I don't know what I'm going to find to interest me for all that time.'

Rand sighed and rolled his eyes. 'Perhaps you need nursing.'

Stein smiled, and Rand was reminded of a hyena he'd once shot in the veldt, just before it attacked – back in the days when Jenny was still alive and he'd still had legs.

'That little nurse who was just in here looked very comforting,' the Colonel said.

'Just so long as you don't do what you did to the last two,' Rand said. 'It cost a small fortune to pay the families off.'

Stein tilted his head to one side. 'Perhaps my tastes are getting too expensive for you?'

'No,' Rand said. 'You see, they're one of the things that gives me a handle on you, and don't you forget it. You can consider her my Christmas present.'

He pressed a button on his wheelchair and almost at once the door to the connecting office whispered open and a gray-haired woman with a rawhide face hurried in. 'Yes, Mr Rand?' she asked.

'Miss Parker,' Rand said. 'What is the name of that little nurse who was just here? Not the taller one – the shorter of the two.' Stein averted his gaze.

The lady looked flustered. 'Oh dear, Mr Rand,' she stammered. 'I can't keep track of all the . . . I think her name's Cherry.'

Rand beamed, showing grey, bloodless gums. 'How appropriate. And how old is she?'

'About eighteen I think.'

Miss Parker stared nervously at Rand's disgustingly fat torso and the clear fluid seeping through the tubes. She peeped at Stein and then looked at Rand again, her eyes filled with fear. 'Not again, Sir,' she begged. 'Please.'

'Miss Parker,' Rand said. 'Colonel Stein has a headache. Tell Nurse Cherry to present herself at his room in twenty minutes. That's an order.'

'Very well, Sir.' She turned pale, cast a horrified glance at Stein and marched out.

8

Truman awoke with the billows of the dream thrashing in his head like the torn fragments of a sail, and took in the hum of the Boeing's engine and the ping of the seat-belt warning. He closed his eyes for a moment and struggled to retrieve the image, reconstructing the fabulous crystal cave that seemed to have been produced by a holocaust, freeze-dried on the point of final meltdown.

The cave was vast and full of chambers and distorted columns, its great vaulted roofs, as high above him as those of a cathedral, pitted with the spikes of a billion small stalactites. Truman had dreamed of the cave many times and it always reminded him of the design of Cologne cathedral, except that this was a surreal version of a cathedral that had achieved its skewed and asymmetric form over millions of years of slow evolution, like some incredibly old and immensely slow-growing fungus. In the cave there was the sound of water, and the sound of fire. Water dripping into shallow pools, a fire crackling in a hearth of stones – the smell of wood-resin.

There were strange pictures on the walls, of pipe-cleaner men leading giraffes on strings, swaying in mesmerized rhythm around some animal-headed god, racing figures with the limbs of athletes done in primary colours chasing antelopes with bow and arrow, warriors with heads like goldfish bowls or simply with stalks for heads and limbs so extended they went on forever. By the fire sat a girl with a face like a brown almond and eyes like polished jade, her hair a cascade of coarse black silk down her back. She was sitting as still as a statue, looking at him with big jade eyes. *'You must teach us, Antara,'* she said.

He blinked and saw a stewardess standing over him pointing to his seat. He levered it into an upright position and stared out of the porthole into the night – at the lights of Cairo that twinkled beneath him like stars.

It was 7.55 a.m. when he came through to the Arrivals Hall and almost at once he realized the fixer wasn't there to meet him. He scanned the faces of the cluster of men and women toting placards with names on them in English and Arabic, and pushed through them to the automatic doors. Outside there was a chilling wind and the sun clambering whitely through a spider web of cloud. The taxi drivers and hustlers were wrapped up in gloves and duffel coats with scarves wrapped round their heads like turbans, and cigarettes drooping from their mouths. He ignored them and looked round again for Costas Giorgiu. When he was certain his fixer wasn't around, he marched back through the doors, bought a cup of lukewarm coffee from a machine and made a beeline for a public telephone. He stood the coffee on the pedestal and dialled the emergency number Maynard had given him.

The phone was picked up almost at once. 'This is Costas Giorgiu,' a voice said in heavily accented English. Truman guessed the guy had been waiting for him.

'This is Truman. I'm at the airport. You were supposed to meet me here.'

'Ah, Dr Truman,' the voice said greasily. *'Ahlan wa Sahlan. Mirhabban bik fi Masr.* I trust you had a pleasant flight?'

'Let's cut the welcome mat shall we?' Truman snapped. 'What's going on?'

There was an almost imperceptible pause, and when the voice came back it was brusque and businesslike. 'There has been a change of plan,' it said. 'You are to go straight to the safe-house in Heliopolis. Mr Maynard gave you the address?'

Truman reached for his coffee without looking and knocked it off the pedestal. The paper cup hit the floor and exploded on impact, spattering his Nike hiking boots and trousers with coffee. 'Shit!'.

'Excuse me?'

'Nothing. Yes, I have the safe-house address, but what's all this about?'

'I'll explain it all to you here. Take a taxi. Do not speak to anyone. You will find the door of the apartment block open. Enter and proceed up the steps, turn right along the corridor and enter the last flat on the left. You should be here in twenty minutes. Oh and one more thing, Dr Truman.'

'Yes?'

'Are are you armed?'

'Not unless you call packing a Leatherman armed.'

'I beg your pardon?'

'No, I'm not armed.'

The phone went dead before Truman could ask the relevance of the last question, but it wound itself over in his head as he kicked the empty coffee-cup out of the way, and walked back towards the automatic doors. A gnomish man in black-framed glasses stood in his way wearing a false smile and a double-breasted black blazer. He had a security card pinned to his lapel. 'Can I help you, sir?' he said in English. 'I am a marshal employed by the Ministry of Tourism to assist new arrivals. Can I get you a taxi or find you a hotel?'

'No thanks,' Truman growled, pushing past him.

The tourist marshal followed him irritatingly. 'I can get you good rates.' Truman stopped and the man grinned at him sheepishly. 'I am a genuine tourist marshal,' he insisted, pointing at the security card on his lapel. 'I am not a tout.'

The man must have been sixty, Truman thought, but he was wiry and fit-looking without an ounce of fat, his pale face – very pale for an Egyptian – shaved so smooth it might have been depilated. He wore large, thick framed glasses behind which the eyes were alert and intense. His English was excellent.

'Look, stop following me, will you?' Truman said, glaring at him. The man stopped, and Truman dashed for the first taxi in the rank, mumbling the address to the cabby so quietly that no one else could possibly hear it. He threw his bag on the back seat and settled beside it. As the taxi drove off he saw the trim tourist marshal hurrying in the direction of the carpark.

'You want nice hotel, cheap, clean?' the cabbie said, distracting his attention.

'Just shut up and drive,' Truman said.

As soon as they had passed the Tourist Police on guard at the main gates, the cabbie put his foot down on the gas pedal and shot into the early morning traffic along Al-Uruba Street, a modern boulevard cut straight as a die through leafy suburbs towards the old city. The driver wound in and out of the traffic, screeching to a halt at traffic-lights, turning right near the Meridien Hotel into Beirut Street and the heart of Heliopolis.

Truman knew the geography of Cairo pretty well – he'd visited the city dozens of times during his excavations. This place was far older than Cairo itself, he knew – Cairo was a mediaeval city, but Heliopolis had been here in ancient Egyptian times as the religious centre of On. He was surprised to find the address he'd given the cabbie lay in a derelict quarter of rotten tenements. *These buildings must be a hundred years old at least*, Truman thought, *and once they must have housed thousands of families*. The streets were shadow-strewn and silent in the grey morning light and Truman saw ghostly human shapes out of the corner of his eye, shying away from the car like wraiths. The cabbie's eyes were deep pits in the mirror, and Truman began to wonder if the man had brought him here to rob him. In this city, anything was possible. Suddenly though, the driver drew up by a steel door so pitted with rust that it looked as if had merged into the wall itself. 'Jesus!' Truman said. 'You sure this is the right address?'

The cabbie guffawed. 'I take you nice hotel, clean, cheap,' he parroted.

Truman checked the number on the door. It was correct. He slapped the money they'd agreed on down on the driver's shoulder and jumped out. The cabbie's laughter followed him all the way to the door.

9

A NDREI PARETSKY'S RENAULT SLURRIED TO A halt in the shelter of a broken down wall, not 200 metres from the door where Truman's cab had stopped. He climbed out of the car and ripped the false Tourist Marshal ID card from his jacket, shivering in the early morning chill. Moscow in winter it wasn't, but Paretsky had always suffered from the cold, which was one of the reasons he'd spent most of his life on assignments in warmer climes. He watched as Truman opened the rusted door and disappeared inside, then waited for the taxi to pull away, troubled. Something was wrong, he was certain of that.

He'd spent more than half an hour on the telephone the previous day while that third rate racketeer Rybakov had briefed him in detail – if Rybakov's psychopathic rambling constituted a briefing. Truman was supposed to have been met by Costas Giorgiu at Cairo International, and Paretsky had arranged to liaise with the fixer there twenty minutes before the flight got in. Rybakov had told Paretsky not to make contact with Truman, but to stay in the background and make sure things went smoothly.

But things hadn't gone smoothly – there'd been a change of plan, and Costas hadn't informed him. He'd made repeated calls to the safe house, only to have the phone hung up. It was his responsibility to ensure nothing happened to Truman, and though he didn't give a toss about Rybakov and his thugs, he'd been a professional KGB man all his life, and he'd always believed that if you were given an assignment, you did it well. Paretsky was the son of a diplomat and had learned English as a child at school in San Francisco. He had been recruited by the KGB while still a teenager and had had six years of studying Arabic before they'd finally accepted him, then five years in the Yemen as an agent. In those days the KGB really had been formidable. These young dolts like Rybakov had no idea. Paretsky was aware he would have been one hell of a sight better off if he'd thrown in his lot with the mafiya, but for him that would have been a betrayal of his entire life. It was a matter of pride, and though he had seen his whole world disintegrate around him in the wake of that asshole Gorbachev, he still had plenty of that. In fact, it was almost all he did have.

He locked the car, checked that his Makarov in the shoulder-holster had a round up the spout, and clambered cautiously forward over hunks of brickwork and piles of plaster. When he reached the door he paused, pressing himself against the crumbling surface and listening for the sound of footsteps and voices. It couldn't have been more than five minutes since Truman had disappeared inside, but Paretsky had a strong intuition that something bad was going down, and he knew he should have warned him at the airport. Truman himself had been something of a surprise. He'd expected a self-centred intellectual type with an exaggerated sense of his own preciousness, but despite his aesthetic features, Paretsky had acquired a different impression of him during their brief encounter. And there was something about him that was familiar – he didn't yet know what it was, but he was working on it.

There was a scuffle nearby and the Makarov snapped into his hand with the speed of a lifetime's experience. Two Egyptian boys were watching him with wide eyes – barefoot ragamuffins in cast-off European clothes and motheaten woollen hats. Their features were sapped to the bone from cold and hunger and their eyes stood out like balloons against their haggard faces. '*Imshu!*'

61

Paretsky hissed at them. 'Clear off!' The boys stood their ground, their big eyes following the Makarov with resignation rather than terror.

'You don't want to go in there,' the taller of the two boys said abruptly.

Paretsky grinned but his pistol didn't waver. 'Who are you to tell me what I want to do?' he demanded.

'There's bad people in there,' the other boy piped up. 'They killed the fat man, and they're going to do the dark-haired Afrangi who just went in as well. If you go in they'll do you too.'

Paretsky dropped the Makarov. 'Leave you on guard, did they?' he asked. The taller boy's face looked old before his time. '*Aiwa!* They gave us money to shout if anyone came.'

'OK, so why haven't you shouted?'

The tall boy shrugged. 'We didn't like them. If you give us something we'll keep quiet.'

Paretsky fumbled in his pocket with cold fingers and came out with a crumpled note – worth two dollars.

'That's all I have,' he said. 'I'm a poor man.' It was true, he told himself – his salary was worth about a sixth of what it had been worth in Brezhnev's day.

The taller boy took the money reverently, examined it, then put it away quickly in his pocket. He pointed to an opening in a half-demolished wall just across the street. 'They came in a big car,' he said. 'They left it in there.'

Paretsky surveyed the street up and down – the undulating remains of asphalt, the footpaths strewn with broken bottles, cigarette packs and supermarket bags. The place was deserted. 'Anyone on lookout?' he inquired.

'Only us,' the boy said.

Paretsky sprinted across the road silently in his rubber soled shoes and inspected the opening in the wall. Parked there amongst dustbins and debris, out of sight of the road, was a black Mercedes. He checked the bonnet, then picked up a brickbat and drove it through the window on the driver's side. There was a dull crash as the glass splintered. He put his hand through, opened the door, searched around for the bonnet-release and found it. He slipped his fingers under the rim of the bonnet, lifted it and propped it on the steel pole, then unscrewed the rotor-arm, twisted it out of shape, stamped on it, and tossed it far away into the rubbish. He closed the bonnet gently, then for good measure took out a penknife and slashed both front tyres. Finally, he ran back across the road to join the boys.

10

BRINDLES OF LIGHT SLATTED THE BROKEN stairs from the cavities and cracks in the tenement walls as Truman climbed to the second floor, carrying his Ziplock bag. The place was full of rubbish – shapeless cartons, bits of styrofoam, newspaper fragments, rags of clothing. There were nests of dried up excrement too – the place smelled like a rat-infested toilet, but worse, there was a putrefying stink as if some big animal had slunk into some unseen cranny to die. The staircase seemed to be held in place by a single rusted bracket, and it creaked and rattled perilously under his feet, forcing him to clutch at the fractured bannister.

It was an odd place to put a safe-house, he thought, but there could be no doubt that this was the address. The steel door had been open just as Costas had told him, and the fixer's instructions had been explicit. It was a relief to get off the rickety staircase, and into the narrow corridor from which the doorgaps of vacant flats yawned darkly, but the smell of putrescence was even worse up here. Truman stepped over little mounds of cracked plaster and approached the apartment warily. The flat's metal door stood slightly open, and he paused before it, listening. All was silent, so he pushed it fully open with his free hand and went in.

The room was surprisingly dark, lit only by flat beams of light that criss-crossed its length from cracks in the boarded-up windows. But the light was enough for Truman to make out a hump on the floor – the pear-shaped body of a fat man with a bulbous head fringed in dark hair. He was lying curled up foetally on a scrap of carpet in front of a ragged armchair, sightless eyes bulging from their sockets and a big, blood-smeared hand clutching at his own throat. The floor was a pool of blood, treacle-coloured in the pale light – the armchair was soggy with it, and there were even spatters of it on the walls.

Truman dropped his bag and shoved an elbow against the plasterwork to steady himself. He forced himself towards the corpse on the floor and rolled it over with his foot, taking in a pulped nose and a gaping wound in the neck. The fat man had been slashed across the throat, but the blood looked fresh and had only partly congealed. He'd been dead not more than an hour or two, Truman thought. *No*, he corrected himself, *less than an hour*, because he recognised the man from the photo Maynard had shown him as Costas Giorgiu, and it was less than an hour since he'd spoken to him on the phone.

Truman turned, picked up his bag and hurried through the door. There was a play of shadows in the corridor and he ducked instinctively, but not quite fast enough to dodge a glancing blow across his temple. His senses reeled for a second, and before he could react rough arms closed round both of his and something that could only have been the muzzle of a hand-gun was pressed into the cleavage between his jaw and his neck.

'One move out of place, Dr Truman,' a voice grated in his ear, 'and you're as dead as the fat Gyp!'

Truman dropped his bag and it was kicked out of the way. In the dim light he saw he'd been jumped by two big torpedoes – weight-lifter types with mean, close-shaved faces and close-cropped hair. They had the trim, efficient air of professional soldiers. They half-carried him across the corridor and through the open door of an adjacent apartment. The room was as dark as the first, unfurnished but for two chairs, one of them pushed right up against the boards of the sealed window. A man was sitting in the chair, erect but comfortable-looking, his head and lean torso in silhouette. Truman was dragged forward and forced down opposite him on the other chair – close, but not close enough to make out the shadowed features.

Dr Truman, I presume,' the man said. The voice was frayed at the edges and reminded Truman of a nail scraping on sandpaper.

He glanced around him. One of the big soldiers was standing over him with a 9mm Browning pistol pointed firmly in his direction. The other was standing by the door to prevent an escape. Both men had a good ten kilos on Truman, and both were taller by at least a head.

A trickle of blood dripped down his face from the blow to his brow, and Truman touched the abrasion indignantly.

'Who the hell are you?' he demanded.

'I am Colonel Julius Stein,' the silhouette said. 'Of the Rand Corporation.' Truman swallowed, thinking of the revolting scene across the corridor. 'Are you responsible for that – that carnage?' he said, his voice shaking.

There was a pause.

'Dr Truman,' the frayed voice came back, 'I am not here to answer your inquiries. I am here to talk about palladium, one of the most valuable substances in the world right now.' The accent was German or Scandinavian, Truman was certain, and the man had a pompous manner of speaking that seemed deliberately cultivated. He opened his mouth, but Stein cut in.

'No, don't make the same mistake as Mr Giorgiu, my friend,' he said. 'I know you have been sent here by Gus Maynard of the Kortex Mining Company in London, to negotiate a deal for the palladium strike Ben Harris made a few weeks back in the Sudan. Your mission has now been aborted, and that's probably as well for you, because knowing Maynard's reputation as I suspect you do not, I'd be most surprised if you managed to survive long enough to enjoy whatever prize he promised you. Maynard's people have a habit of disappearing, did you know that?'

'No,' Truman said, 'but going on what I've just seen, Rand's won't be winning any awards for altruism either.'

'Costas was scum,' Stein whispered. 'He knew what to expect.

 66

He thought he could warn you off with that "are you armed" business, right under our noses. He got what he deserved. Now, you don't look the stupid kind, Dr Truman. You are a lawyer?'

'An archaeologist, actually.'

There was a rasping chuckle from the shadowed head.

'That's what I call scraping the barrel,' Stein said. 'What did he promise you? A fortune, I imagine. Ten percent was it? Now, Dr Truman, the Rand Corporation is quite anxious to make sure it gets a major cut of any palladium found on this dark continent. I am empowered to offer you fifteen percent of the profits from any mining operation that ensues, in return for giving me the exact coordinates of the strike, and the name of the owners of the site.'

There was a pause, and Truman nodded, apparently considering this carefully. Actually he was thinking of the corpse in the next room, and Maynard's story of how Rand's had thrown One Eyed Harris out on his backside when he'd become an embarrassment to them. 'And if I refuse?'

'You will tell us one way or the other. My friends here are both veterans of the old South African secret police. They are well experienced at dividing sheep from goats. Look, I really don't have much time. Which is it to be?'

Truman shrugged. He had never considered himself a brave man, or that there was really any such thing. Bravery and cowardice were qualities of momentary actions, not definitive aspects of human beings themselves. But ever since he'd been a child at prep school he'd overreacted to anything he felt threatened him. So while other kids ran away from the class bully, Truman – who was probably even more scared than they were – had had the suicidal impulse to taunt him. He felt the same impulse with Stein.

'You know what?' he said. 'There's a hell of a lot of desert out there. Since you haven't got much time, I suggest you get a shovel and start digging.'

There was pregnant silence. Then the shadow that was Stein sighed. 'Very well. He's all yours, Pieter.'

A second later the man Pieter was leaning over him with a

mess of orange electric flex, momentarily obscuring the aim of the man with the gun. Truman knew that he had only one chance. He hunched forward and brought his knee up hard into Pieter's groin. The big man yelped and sagged, and Truman leapt up and hit him again on the side of the neck with a smashing closed-hand punch, facing the other soldier who was shifting position slightly to better his aim. Truman saw the gunman's eyes narrow momentarily as he made to squeeze the trigger.

'No!' Stein yelled, 'don't shoot!'

In that second Truman jumped high and snapped out a double flying kick, sending the gunman stumbling against the wall. Stein was already on his feet and bounding towards him, but Truman spun the chair against his legs as he rushed for the door. In a second he was through it and haring along the corridor, sensing heavy footsteps on the plaster behind him. He was about to dodge into one of the open doorgaps when a small figure stepped out of it. With a shock Truman recognized the impish little tourist marshal with the glasses who'd accosted him at the airport. The guy was now pointing a chunky pistol in his direction.

'Duck!' the man screamed at him.

Truman obeyed automatically, and as he sank to a crouch there was a deafening double explosion and a blast of gasses that seared over his head. He glanced back in time to see Stein's gunman crumple and fall with a bud of redness sprouting from the middle of his chest. There was smoke in the corridor and the smell of cordite, and Truman's ears rang from the shots. The 'tourist marshal' was rolling a green canister along the uneven floor.

'*White phos*!' he yelled at Truman. 'Go!'

There was a reverberating thud as the canister split open and erupted into billows of smoke. He loosed off two more shots at the ceiling, and grabbed Truman by the arm, pulling him towards the stairwell. When they reached the bottom, the man put an expert shot into the rusted bracket that was holding the staircase in place. By the time they made the street, the entire rotten edifice had come crashing down behind them.

11

Truman and Paretsky dashed for the Renault, and Truman held on to his seat as they accelerated out of the street, swerving round the corners, working gradually into the more modern, more populated quarters of Heliopolis. Truman felt like laughing hysterically, and recognized the surge of relief that came after a close encounter with infinity.

'Christ,' he said as they shot into the main artery of Al-Urubba. 'You tourist marshals know your shots!'

Paretsky chuckled. 'We aim to please.'

'By the way,' Truman said, 'was that really white phos?'

The Russian sniggered. 'Nah,' he said. 'It was just a smoke bomb I salvaged, about thirty years old. But you wouldn't believe how yelling 'white phos' psychs them out. Who were those guys, anyway?'

'Business competitors,' Truman said. 'They work for a company called Rand's – a South African corporation. There were three of them – two soldiers and a guy who called himself Colonel Julius Stein. Said he was a troubleshooter.'

Paretsky cocked one eye at him. 'The opposition. I guessed the South Africans would be around sooner or later.'

'And who the hell are you?' Truman asked.

Paretsky watched him out of the corner of his eye.

'I'm your official minder, as from now, Dr Truman,' he said.

'But if I'm right, there was a time when Truman wasn't your name. Remember Beirut 1983? You must have been in your early twenties.'

It was a shock. A shadow passed over Truman's face, and he had to take several deep breaths to steady himself. 'I've never been in Beirut. You must have got the wrong guy.'

'No,' Paretsky said, intense eyes gleaming behind the thick-framed glasses. 'I've got a memory for these things. As soon as I met you at the airport, I knew I'd seen you before, and now I know where. Downtown Beirut, 1983. It was winter, and a bunch of Palestinians had just jumped a Soviet agent working in the city. Me. They were knocking seven shades of shit out of me. They were going to put a hole in my head, but you came along and laid into them with karate moves. I never saw anything like it. You took on six men, and disarmed them all – at least one got a broken neck. OK, you were dressed in down-and-out clothes like a street Arab, but it was you all right. I never forget a face.'

Truman shivered and shook his head. 'In your dreams.'

'OK,' Paretsky said, gripping the wheel tautly. 'Have it your own way. But I know it was you. Always did want to thank you for saving my life.'

'You got the wrong man,' Truman said. He paused. 'Are you working for Maynard?'

Paretsky accelerated, overtaking a heavy truck. 'No. I'm strictly a patriot. Mother Russia's my only mistress. Oh shit . . .' He let the silence drag out while he overtook another truck. 'You get so used to spouting the Party Line that you forget it's the Party Line. The truth is, I don't know who I'm really working for. Nobody does any more. It's a crazy mixed up world, and I can't even tell the good guys from the bad guys. I'm Andrei Paretsky, KGB Deputy Head of Station in Cairo – only they call it the FSS now. I *used* to work for Mother Russia, but now I get my orders from some jackass who thinks he's fucking Al Capone – the same asshole who gives Maynard his orders.'

'You mean the mafiya?' Truman said. 'I heard they were

 70

behind Maynard but I didn't believe it. How'd that happen?'

Paretsky hiked his shoulders over the wheel. 'Things ain't what they used to be. Dr. Truman. The way I heard it, Kortex had heavily invested in the Coltan market – Columbite-Tantalite, that is – a heat-resistant metal used in missile exhausts. Kortex were buying it from local mining companies in Zaire when the mafiya moved in with their dirty cash and started paying twice the market price. Kortex couldn't compete, but the Moscow wide-boys knew a good front when they saw one and offered to rescue the company. Maynard's been in their pocket these last five years.'

He paused and glanced at Truman again. 'It was you in Beirut wasn't it? OK, you were younger – you didn't have the beard and long hair, but you had the same broken nose. I remember it because you looked such a *shlemiel* apart from that nose.'

Truman's face was deathly pale. 'Look, I'm grateful to you for the search and rescue bit, but I've never been in Beirut. I'm an archaeologist – or was, before I got mixed up in this shit.'

Paretsky went silent, peering sideways at Truman through slitted eyes. 'Have it your way. I'm still the opposition – is that what you think? You're on some covert op here – you infiltrated Kortex and you don't want me blowing your cover? Am I right? Let me tell you, Dr. Truman, I don't give a shit any more. I'm up for retirement soon and I've wasted my life working for a bunch of traitors, anyway. At least you saved my life once. I owe you.'

'I'm not on an op,' Truman said.' And I haven't infiltrated anybody. I'm an out of work trowel-jockey who got mixed up with Kortex, that's all. I'm grateful for your help, but spare me the third degree, OK?'

Truman went quiet for a moment as they passed the Cairo stadium and the international exhibition grounds with their array of stylized concrete palms. Near the Abbasiyya Flyover traffic slowed down as the great arteries converged on the city centre. There were buses with people hanging out of the doors, and electric trams with passengers packed like sardines. Paretsky halted at a traffic light, then swept under the flyover down Saleh Salem Street, heading for the Nile and the road to Giza.

'Look Truman,' Paretsky said suddenly. 'It doesn't matter who you're working for . . .'

'I'm working for Kortex.'

'OK but whoever it is, you're going to wind up with your head rearranged sooner or later – probably sooner. My advice is just to get the fuck out of here. The flak will die down eventually and maybe you'll be able to get back to your own life. If you don't bug out now, they'll get you.'

'Who will?'

'Kortex, the mafiya, Rand's – what the heck does it matter? You're in the shit and there's a bullet with your name on it.'

'I'm not running,' Truman said. 'Maynard gave me a job to do and right or wrong I agreed to do it. I'm not dipping out now. However hot it gets, I can handle it.'

For a moment the Russian squinted at him incredulously, then he laughed. 'You've got to be bluffing. You *are* on an op. You must be. Either you've got a secret agenda, or you think you're still in the world of the honourable English gentleman with the stiff upper lip. Honour went out the window, in case you didn't notice. You're living in the wrong time.'

Truman scoffed. 'Look who's calling the kettle black. Mister I-used to-work-for-Mother-Russia. We're not so different after all.'

'Maybe not, but I'll tell you something I've learned in my life – it's not the plans of the big enchiladas that matter. They might work for a while, then the wall comes tumbling down and it all turns to garbage. In the end what counts is the chance connections between the little guys like us – millions of free molecules whizzing around bumping into each other purely at random. What happens then is unpredictable, and that's how history really turns.'

'You mean you can never predict how things will really pan out?'

'Only within a limited range. I don't care if you're fucking

 72

Nostradamus, there's always the X-factor, the chance element, the unexpected. That you can never see. But one thing I *can* see is that if you bring the contract out, they'll deal you the ace of spades. The bastards will probably even ask me to do it, and at that stage I might find it hard to refuse.'

'I'll just have to take my chance on that,' Truman said. 'But I'm not running.' Paretsky snorted and Truman looked out of the window. The Nile was coming up, a pale wash of wintergreen in the dull light. The car slowed down to cross Al-Malik Salem Bridge.

'So what now?' Truman said softly.

Paretsky cleared his throat. 'Phase two was for Costas and me to motor you to Kharga to meet a guy called the Desert Fox,' he said. 'But looks like it's just you and me now. We can make it to Kharga in less than eight hours, even in this old jalopy.'

'You know how to contact this Desert Fox?'

Paretsky headed across the bridge towards Giza. 'All Costas told me is that he'll be waiting for us at a coffee house in Kharga town – place called Jaffa's. It's not much to go on, but now Costas is out of the picture it's all we've got.'

He slowed for another set of lights, and before they turned green Truman said 'OK, let's go for it.'

The Giza plateau was coming up and the tip of the Great Pyramid loomed out of sand-mist. As they turned off down the desert road, Paretsky shot another sideways glance at him. 'I swear it was you saved me in Beirut. I'm certain of it!'

Truman turned and surveyed the little Russian with shrewd eyes. 'The time you'd better be certain of it is the time they give you orders to deal me the ace of spades.'

12

I N London it was already dark on a bleak and windswept
Christmas Eve and the lights were burning in the Kortex office
off Hanover Square. Gus Maynard, dressed in an elegant dinner
suit ready for a cocktail party at a cabinet minister's, was sipping
hot toddy and toying with the idea of lighting up a Davidoff.
His last medical report had been unequivocal – he had a serious
heart condition that gave him no more than twelve months to
live, and every cigar he smoked brought the day of reckoning
nearer. He hiked his shoulders at an invisible audience and lit
up the Davidoff anyway.

He picked up the *Evening Telegraph* and glanced again
through the report on Amersadiqi's murder. Rybakov had over-
done it as usual, he thought. He'd asked him to put the fear of
God into the minerals analyst and the bloody guy had torn the
arse out of it, splattering the Iranian in bits all over his flat and
cutting up his wife too. With all the pressure MI6 were giving
them, they didn't need the advertisement. He sighed. The Russians would never learn. The idea was to terrify Amersadiqi into
confession, not to enter a Jack the Ripper copycat contest. If
extreme measures were needed, then there was always a concrete
coffin in the Thames. Discreet. Silent. Tasteful. This murder had
a vulgar quality that was Rybakov to a tee.

Maynard had put down the paper and was finishing his Scotch

when he heard a commotion downstairs – the sound of raised voices and a scuffle. He jumped up, bristling, and clicked on the intercom.

'Cliff?' he said. 'Cliff?'

Before there was time for a reply, the door burst open and Rybakov stood there, his half-Chechen face framed palely by oil-slicked hair and the upturned collar of his impeccable blue overcoat. He stood very still, hunting-dog eyes riveted on Maynard as if he was seeing him for the first time. 'Sergei?' Maynard said.

'Who were you expecting?' Rybakov sneered. 'Maybe Father Christmas?'

'What's going on?' Maynard demanded. 'Where's Cliff?'

'Cliff is sitting on floor down there with two broken arms. The big baboon crossed my path once too often, so me and my boys teach him who's boss.'

Maynard bit his lip, and his poisonous eyes bled fire. 'You're a bloody fool, Sergei. Why? Just because he was a big guy and made you feel inferior?'

Rybakov closed the door behind him quietly with a gloved hand, then turned and faced Maynard again. Shimmers from the flames in the fireplace played across the marbled smoothness of the face and glittered on the gold earring.

'Let's get one thing straight,' Rybakov said, taking a step towards him. 'I'm not inferior to nobody, right? The gorilla stood in my way. Thought he could muscle me out. Well, nobody stands in my way, Maynard – not you, not your third-rate bouncer.'

Maynard's breath was coming in gasps. He felt his heart flutter and sat down carefully in one of his fireside chairs. He deliberately reached out a quivering hand to pick the Davidoff from the ashtray. He looked away from Rybakov, put the lit cigar in his mouth and puffed it gently.

Rybakov eyed him, glowering, head lowered between hunched shoulders like a bull about to charge. He moved stiffly towards the fireplace and stood facing Maynard with both hands in his pockets, fingering the pistol beneath. 'I snuffed Amersadiqi last

75

night,' he said, his voice as passionless as an icepick. 'I had a word in his shell-like ear.'

'I know,' Maynard said wearily. 'It was all over the papers. You decorated the walls with bits of him, and his wife too. Was there really any need to make a spectacle, Sergei? This isn't gang warfare. Don't you know MI6 are just praying for something they can pin on you?'

'Shut up!' Rybakov said. 'You got some explaining to do.'

'Me?' Maynard said. 'What about?'

'Truman,' Rybakov said, opening his mouth and displaying his gold teeth. He held himself ramrod straight, Maynard noted, but there was a twitch to his eyes that betrayed a disquieting nervousness.

'Truman had samples analysed before we did,' said Rybakov. 'I suspect it all along. He is bloody mole, and you invite him right in through door.'

Maynard looked shocked. 'Nonsense. Truman had the samples sent straight to me. What are you talking about?'

Moving as swiftly as a hawk, Rybakov leaned foward, grabbed Maynard by the collar of his elegant dress-shirt, and dragged him to his feet.

'Steady on,' Maynard said. 'That's a handmade shirt, Sergei.'

Rybakov didn't let go. 'Amersadiqi told me the samples bin in before.'

Maynard blinked his bloated red eyes. 'It's got to be some monumental cock-up at Qurayshi's,' he said. 'One lot of samples looks much like another.'

'Is no cock-up,' Rybakov spat. 'I put the squeeze on Amersa-diqi. Beat him up good, had my boys gang-bang his old babushka in front of him. Slashed her nipples off with a razor till she's mewling like a gutted cat. He was blubbering before we even got started on the hard stuff. He admit he's bin working for Marcus Rand for years. Made assholes of us all. Bin passing them stuff on every major strike went through the lab. Said Rand told him to watch Kortex specially. The guy was the leak on Harris samples all right.'

'But that's exactly what I suggested,' Maynard stammered. 'Doesn't it rather rule Truman out?'

Rybakov gripped the collar tighter. His face was so close to Maynard's now that the Scotsman could smell his heavy breath. The two gold teeth were poised above him like vampire fangs.

'I'm not finished,' Rybakov yelled. 'I am just about to stiff him for good, when the guy tells me the same samples bin in the lab a week before Kortex sent them. Same samples, same proportions of palladium and platinum. Only they didn't come from Kortex. The name on the docs that time was Richard Whitehaven.'

Maynard tried to pull himself away and the shirt ripped.

'Don't fucking move!' Rybakov screamed.

'I've never heard of Richard Whitehaven,' said Maynard.

Rybakov shook his head truculently 'I found out who Whitehaven is through Kensington Palace Gardens. He's Africa desk at bloody MI6, that's who. Truman must have passed them the samples before he sent them to you. Truman's a mole, Maynard, and I'm wondering just how much you knew about him. You picked him. You recruited him. It all went off far too smooth for me.'

'Don't be ridiculous Sergei,' Maynard said.

Rybakov butted him in the nose and let him go. Maynard sat down heavily in the armchair and his glasses fell off. He put a raw hand up to stop the blood welling out of his nostrils.

'What was deal, eh?' Rybakov bawled. 'Stop the Moscow boys moving in on Africa? Ruin monopoly on palladium market? My syndicate saved your ass, Maynard. You forgotten the Coltan business in Zaire? Without us you'd have been up shit creek without a paddle five years ago.'

In spite of himself, Maynard scoffed. 'It was your lot who ruined us by paying double the price.

A triumphant gleam came into Rybakov's eyes. 'That's it.' he snapped. 'You always resent it, didn't you, Maynard? You sell us out to your own security service.'

'This is preposterous, Sergei,' Maynard blustered. 'Pure paranoia.'

Rybakov slipped the big Makarov into his hand and pointed it at Maynard. The Scotsman blanched and turned his face away.

'You had dealings with spooks before,' Rybakov said. 'I seen your record. You're in this up to the hilt.'

Maynard turned to look at the gun. He blinked and put his glasses back on.

'In my business there are always shady goings on,' he said mournfully. 'Of course I've had brushes with the Intelligence Services. Yes, I've even done them favours when there was something in it for me. But I have nothing to do with Truman, I swear.'

Rybakov slapped him across the face with an open hand and the glasses dropped onto the floor. 'Tell the fucking birds,' he said. 'I want to know where the guy is now.'

Maynard gasped and held a pudgy hand to his face. 'He's due in Kharga tonight. To make the RV with the Desert Fox.'

'I'm going in myself,' Rybakov said. 'That asshole is dead meat.'

'You'll never get in there till tomorrow morning,' Maynard said. 'And Truman will be long gone.'

'Then I'll have Paretsky do him. He's due to make report any time now. I'm going in, anyway, to make sure. And I'm sending my Spetnatz boys to settle those Bedouins.'

Maynard watched the Russian with blank eyes. He found his glasses, picked them up from the floor, and replaced them with all the dignity he could muster. Then he looked into Rybakov's face. There was a killer lurking there all right, a street thug hiding under the thin veneer of sophistication. But there was more too. He was suddenly, inexorably certain that Rybakov hadn't come here to kill him. He was bluffing, and suddenly Maynard was certain he knew why. He began to laugh roundly.

'What the fuck you laughing at?' Rybakov spat.

'Oh Sergei,' he said. 'Surely not you. . . .'

Before he could finish the sentence there was a shattering bolt of pain across Maynard's chest. He tried to get up, realizing that he hadn't even heard the shot, his hand flailing for grip on the chair arm. He found he couldn't move and he fought for breath, clutching desperately at his heart with both hands before the pain closed him off like a vice. The feverish whiteness of Rybakov's knuckles on his pistol-grip was the last thing he ever saw.

13

TRUMAN AND PARETSKY PULLED INTO KHARGA in the late afternoon after a non-stop drive along the desert road. It was
a relief, Truman thought, to find yourself among date palms,
tamarisks and water-gardens, after hours of staring into featureless mid-space. Out there they hadn't had a glimpse of water in
eight hours, but here it was everywhere – spraying in plumes
in fields of green barley, even playing across the road in rainbow colours. Paretsky halted at almost the first building they
came to – a flyblown shack with a fractured *Agip* sign outside,
and a troop of rusty petrol pumps with their intestines missing.
They both got out to stretch their legs, and a bent old man in a
turban and an overall the colour of mud hobbled out to greet
them.

'Do you have petrol?' Paretsky asked.

The old man had slate grey eyes that looked as if they'd
suffered a lifetime of being coarsened by sandpaper. He lit a
Cleopatra cigarette and exhaled indignantly. 'Of course we have
petrol,' he said. 'This is a petrol station.'

He gestured to a single oil drum standing in the sun and told
Paretsky to pull over to it, while he entered the shack and came
out staggering under the weight of a battered old hand-pump.
He attached it to the drum and began to pump the handle puffing
and panting, and blowing cigarette smoke. When the tank was

full and paid for, Truman asked if he knew a place called Jaffa's Coffeehouse.

The old man scratched under his turban with greasy, truncated fingers. 'I know it. It's right in the centre of the old town.'

It was late when they reached the old quarter, and blinding desert light was falling laterally across the grid of mud-brick streets like transparent gold, creating bays and islets of purplish shade around porticos and doors. The streets were inches deep in wind-blown dust. It had been market day, and the last vendors – men with work-worn faces in stained shirts and surreal skull-caps – were packing up their stalls, throwing dirty fruit peelings to marauding goats, feeding slivers of bad meat to skeletal dogs, strapping unsold live chickens in wooden cages to the backs of big white donkeys. Jaffa's Coffee House stood in a small square in the middle of the suq, a place of broken down doorways with awnings of reed matting, rusted engine blocks half-buried in sand, emaciated cats gnawing chicken-heads, and broad-bedded donkey-carts piled with sacks. A squinted telephone kiosk stood in one corner, part filled with drifting sand.

Truman and Paretsky left the car and walked in through the open door of the coffee shop. Inside it was cool and dark, with sunbeams melting the shadows through slit windows like heat-rays. The benches and stools were occupied sparsely with grizzled peasants in ragged robes, talking in cracked, emery-cloth voices, gasping on honey and apple tobacco from hookah pipes, and sipping from thimblefuls of coffee or glasses of red tea. The atmosphere was thick with tobacco smoke.

There was a drop in the growl of conversation when the two foreigners entered, their long shadows falling like dark shafts in the oblong of light from the door. *'Mirhabban bikum!'* someone said, and Truman looked round to see a pot-bellied mountain of a man in a well-tailored gallabiyya, a skullcap and dark glasses. He had a buttery complexion and a dark stringy moustache, and the wraparound glasses gave him a waspish look, despite his size. He was chewing gum and smelt of sandal-wood.

'I'm Jaffa,' he said in a whiny, eunuch's voice. 'What do you want? Coffee or tea?'

'Tea,' Paretsky said, licking dry lips. 'Strong and black.'

The fat man clicked beringed fingers at a ragged boy who was dickeying with a broken hookah in a corner.

'Gib itnayn shay, ya walad!' he ordered. 'Bring two teas, boy, and be quick, by God!'

Truman touched Jaffa's baggy sleeve and pulled him over to one side, smelling the feminine odours of sandalwood. The hum of conversation started up again, the two strangers already forgotten.

'We arranged to meet the Desert Fox,' Truman said in a low voice. 'Is he here?'

The fat man looked at him slyly. 'I know all about it,' he said, nodding to a skewed arch in the plaster wall, covered by a threadbare curtain.

'In there,' he said, turning away.

Truman had to duck to pass through the curtain. Beyond it was a small ante-room, with a single unglassed window that admitted a solid jet of golden light and a door that was half open on a small yard. There was no furniture in the room but low stools, crudely made and covered in goatskin, and on one of them sat a man in a puce-coloured gallabiyya and a thick woollen headcloth sucking at a hubble-bubble.

He turned to watch them carefully as they entered and Truman saw a face that was as grey and knobbled as raw limestone, eyes sunk deeply under sandblasted brows, a long pointed snout like a potato knife, and a mouthful of blunt teeth that might have been worked on with a file.

'Peace be on you,' Truman said.

The man stood up and Truman saw that his frame was lean and willowy beneath the colourless robe. 'And upon you be peace,' the man answered in a gravel voice, proffering a hand that was as dry and hard as old iron. 'I have been expecting you.'

'Costas Giorgiu told you we'd be coming?'

 82

The man nodded, his eyes darting from Truman to Paretsky as he gestured at the stools. 'Please, take your rest.'

He wore sandals made out of car-tyres, Truman saw, and as he sat down again he kicked them off to reveal feet that looked as dry-grained as tree bark. He picked up the mouthpiece of his hookah and took a deep toke of honey-flavoured smoke, letting it curl out through his nostrils. 'Where do you want to go?' he inquired, his eyes flickering towards the curtained door.

'The Bint Hammou Plateau,' Truman said.

The Desert Fox coughed over his pipe. 'God protect us from the stoned devil! Why do you want to go there?'

'That's my business. Didn't Costas tell you where I was going?'

The Desert Fox shook his head and glanced once more at the curtain.

'What's wrong?' Paretsky asked.

'Nothing,' the grizzled man said. 'Only I can't take you to Bint Hammou. More than my life's worth to go there. It's a Saghrana place.'

'So what?' Truman said. 'I pay good money.'

The Arab looked at him appraisingly and sucked in smoke. 'I don't mix with the Saghrana,' he said in a whisper, blowing smoke through his nose. 'The old folk tell us tales about them. Say they're vampires who steal virgins – keep them herded in caves like goats and drink their blood. They live in the Funeral Plains – the worst place God made. No water, no shelter, no nothing. Only the Saghrana can live out there, and they'll kill any stranger that wanders into their territory and live on his blood. The plateau has the only water in the entire place, but it's impossible to get into. No one who goes into that place ever comes back.'

He stopped talking as the boy brought in glasses of steaming black tea for Paretsky and Truman. Truman took his and laid it gently on the floor. He glanced at Paretsky, who was looking anxiously at his watch. 'I got to make a report to Rybakov in London,' the Russian said. 'It's overdue.'

'Wait a minute,' Truman said. 'You never mentioned anything about a report before.'

'If I don't they'll think something's up,' Paretsky said. 'Don't worry. You can trust me. Remember Beirut?'

He turned to the Fox and spoke rapidly in Arabic. 'Does that phone box outside work?' he inquired.

The old man blinked tensely. 'The Lord knows all,' he said. 'But last time I tried it did.'

'I'll phone through to London,' Paretsky told Truman. 'I'll only be five minutes.'

'What are you going to tell them?' Truman asked.

Paretsky shrugged, 'The truth. Everything going like clockwork. Safer that way. And don't forget, I've got to live with these morons after you've trogged off.'

After he'd gone, the Fox eyed Truman questioningly. 'Do you know what you're taking on, Mister Afranji? This is the season of the sandtides. Great storms blow up from the Sudan, so powerful they can knock a camel over. Have you ever been out in such a storm?'

'No,' Truman said, wondering what it would be like to be alone in the desert with the Fox. There was something about him – some nervous quality that made him feel uneasy. Once they were out there, his life would be in this man's hands. True, Costas Giorgiu had recommended him, but he doubted if the fat Greek had ever sat on a camel.

'There's nothing out there,' the Fox droned on. 'Only bitter water to drink and sour porridge to eat. Even in winter the heat can be terrible and the cold at night burns even worse. Why, it can be cold enough at this time of the year to freeze the water in the drippers.'

Truman sipped his tea and frowned. 'Am I to take it you've changed your mind?'

The Fox's eyes darted towards the open door again. 'You don't want to go to Bint Hammou,' he whispered. 'Forget it. Turn round, go back to where you came from. Get out quick, while you still can.'

He broke off suddenly to stare at Paretsky, who pushed his way through the curtain breathing heavily. Truman saw he'd turned deathly pale, and stood up alarmed. 'What is it? What's going on?'

Paretsky leaned on the door jamb panting, and beckoned to Truman. 'The situation has changed,' he whispered. 'Maynard's dead.'

'What?'

Paretsky grabbed his hand tightly. 'Don't react,' he hissed. 'Don't let the old guy know there's anything wrong. It's true. Rybakov says you're a mole, and he's ordered me to take you out.'

Truman watched him, trying to master his astonishment.

Paretsky gripped him harder. 'That's not all,' he whispered. 'I've got a feeling this is a set up. The old boy looks too nervous, and there was something I didn't like about the fat guy who showed us in here. Let's get out right now.'

There was a sudden movement in the curtain behind them. Paretsky swivelled and went for his weapon, but before he could grab it a barrel-like figure in combat camouflage wrenched the curtain away and smashed the Russian's skull with a pick-helve. Paretsky grunted and fell, his face a pulp of blood, and almost simultaneously Colonel Julius Stein stepped through the yard door on the opposite side. Next to him were three hard-boys, all of them pointing sub-machine guns Truman's way.

The man who had downed Paretsky stood up swinging the pick-helve and Truman recognized him as the big soldier he'd knocked down in the Cairo flat.

The Fox raised himself from his stool and blinked apologetically at Truman. '*Istaghfarallah*!' he said. 'God forgive me! They have my wife and children.'

Pieter advanced towards him and hit him hard in the face with the end of the pick-handle. 'You almost gave the game away,' he yelled. 'You'll pay for that.'

The rest of the soldiers worked their way into the room, covering Truman, cutting off any path of escape. Stein stepped lightly towards him and for the first time Truman was aware of deep eyes that seemed to burn like coals. 'Now Dr Truman,' he said, looking down sternly at the inert figure of Paretsky. 'Where were we before you and your little friend here decided to break up the party?'

14

As the soldiers forced Truman and the Fox down on their knees and trussed their hands behind them, a vast pot-bellied figure appeared through the curtain. Truman squinted to see the waspish dark glasses and the butterscotch complexion of Jaffa, exuding the cloying smell of sandalwood. 'God curse you!' the Fox shouted at him. '*Bogeitna*! You betrayed us.'

The fat man minced over to the kneeling caravaneer and yanked his head forward with a plump hand. He spat full into the old man's face.

'What about the time you said my camels were lost in the desert?' he inquired in his namby-pamby voice. 'I found them three weeks later on sale in Dara'a camel-market! You're a liar and a cheat and by God, this is what you deserve!' Before Stein's men bundled them out through the back door, Truman saw Stein slapping ten pound notes into the fat man's hand.

A Hilux pick-up and a Toyota Land Cruiser were waiting in the alley outside, each driven by one of Stein's boys. Paretsky, bleeding profusely, was carried out and thrown into the back of the pick-up, and Truman and the old man were made to squat down next to him. Pieter, with his pick-handle held discreetly low, sat at the tailgate watching.

The engines were gunned and the vehicles bumped out of the alley, across the square, and along a salt road that ran through tunnels of shade created by the intertwined foliage of date palms, dom palms, figs, almonds, olives and limes. They passed the occasional villager walking or riding a donkey.

'If there's one peep out of either of you,' Pieter growled, 'you wind up dead.'

His iron stare came to rest on Truman. 'And don't think I've forgotten this morning,' he spat. 'You'll be getting that back with compound interest. You and that little shithouse who shot Joe.'

The Fox's house stood alone amid palms and feeder-channels on the rim of the oasis – an ancient mudbrick castle of a place, half delapidated, and encircled by a mud curtain wall from which the occasional rain had taken massive bites. Stein's men drove straight into the yard and cut the motors. There was silence. No one came out to greet them, no dogs barked. A clutch of half-starved chickens regarded them balefully from behind the remains of a tractor that had long ago reverted to its constituent elements.

Pieter jumped out of the pick-up and two more soldiers ran over and began yanking them down. They dragged Paretsky out last, dropped his body in the sand, and tied his hands loosely behind him. The Russian looked in a bad way, Truman thought – his face was a mess of blood and flies were buzzing around the gash on his skull. But at least he was still breathing. He glanced up at the house – a mud-coloured edifice the texture of sun-dried biltong. It was bathed in shadow, its windows bearing down on them like sightless eyes.

Puffs of dust skimmed through the yard, bowling bits of grass and tumbleweed along with them. From somewhere came the sour creak of a door. There was a hush over the landscape. Above them the sky was submitting to night angrily, a firebrand mesh of cloud, smoky crimsons, blazing oranges, simmering golds – a whirlpool of volcanic dust and magma changing so quickly and violently that it looked as if the air itself had actually burst into flames.

'Get them inside,' Stein said, and the men carried Paretsky up

 88

a set of moulded mud steps to the studded front door, deliberately bumping his head against each one. They hustled Truman and the old man in after him, and Truman found himself in a shadowy, barn-like room, smelling of flour, hung with shapeless cooking-pots and leather saddle bags. The men rammed them down on their knees, while someone lit an oil lamp, and Truman watched as Stein crouched over the inert Paretsky, slapping his face viciously with an open hand. When he was certain the little man had come round, he grabbed him by the chin.

'Listen you scum,' he said. 'You put me to a lot of trouble. I almost broke my ankle shinning down that stairwell.'

Paretsky's eyes blinked at him dully, and Stein sighed. He stood and gave the Russian a swinging kick in the ear. Then he straightened his jacket and smoothed the rich hair back. He moved into a position in front of the light, and monstrous spidery shadows sprang from him over the whitewashed walls. He pointed a clawed finger at the Desert Fox. 'I don't think we need *him* anymore, Pieter,' he croaked. 'Put him out of his misery'.

The big South African drew a Browning pistol and placed its muzzle at the back of the Fox's head.

The old man thrashed about madly. 'God protect me!' he whimpered.

There was a single explosion, so loud it made Truman's eardrums hurt. The Fox jerked once and fell flat on his face. Truman's eyes started out of his head and he bit his lips until the blood came.   Stein took a knife from his pocket and flicked open a fang-shaped blade which he held up. In the wall-shadows it looked like the tooth of a giant shark.

'It's good to get rid of all the junk,' he said in his rasping accent. 'Don't you agree, Dr Truman? It was a nice try by our little friend, but I am afraid he just wasn't good enough. True, he disabled our transport, but then we had a couple of Pumas waiting at Cairo International, so you see we held all the aces. That's the luxury of working for a big organization like Rand's. We were here hours ago, talked to Jaffa, told him to be on the lookout for you. He guided us to this place and we staked it out. The so-called ''Desert Fox'' wasn't so foxy after all. He walked straight into the trap.'

'Why did you have to kill him?' Truman demanded.

Stein balanced the knife between thumb and forefinger. 'That was what you call *quid pro quo*. An extra inducement to our fat friend at the coffeehouse – you see, the Fox had cheated him on one of his caravan deals. I'm happy to have ridded the world of a cheat. As for his family – they're in the cellar underneath us – a woman, three little girls and a boy. And that gives me an idea, Truman.'

He turned to his soldiers. 'Bring the boy!'

There was the creak of a hinge from somewhere, and one of Stein's big mercenaries emerged from the shadows, dragging with him the whimpering figure of a little boy. He was about eight years old, brown-skinned, dressed in a torn shirt and baggy trousers, with a coxcomb of hair on his shaven head. The big soldier had him by the neck, but the boy cried and hit out at him with his little fists. Finally the South African smacked his face with a heavy blow, sending him flying.

The big man picked him up again and the boy swore and spat at him. '*Fayn abuya*?' he wailed. 'Where's my father?'

The big man guessed what he meant and dragged him to where the corpse of the Fox lay face-down in the dust. The boy stared at it with vast, disbelieving eyes.

Stein nodded approvingly. 'Now let us continue our dialogue, Dr Truman,' he said. 'You were telling me that if I wanted to find the palladium I ought to use a shovel, were you not? Ha! Ha! How drole. Your flippant answer has revealed a great deal about you, however. I pride myself on being a good judge of character, and I should say that you are the stubborn type – no, more than that – you're a man who reacts dramatically to threats and challenges. In the position you were in, in Cairo, most people would have either capitulated or tried to bluster. With you it was blatant defiance. That is not unique, of course, but it is quite unusual. Now, I could get the truth beaten or burned out of you.

No one can hold out forever. But in your case I feel that would be messy and time consuming.'

His body went rigid suddenly and he grabbed the sobbing boy, lifting him by the neck with one hand as if he was as light as a pillow. He brought his blade near to the boy's jugular. The boy stopped cursing and started choking.

'This is the Fox's offspring,' he whispered, 'and if you don't tell me the location of Harris's strike I'm going to slit his throat right now in front of you. If that fails there are four more downstairs.'

Truman, balancing painfully on his knees, lifted his eyes to the choking boy. He was about as old as Jonathan had been when he'd been killed by a drunk driver. The body count was mounting: Amersadiqi and his wife, Costas Giorgiu, Maynard, and now the Fox had already died for the sake of Harris's samples, and things didn't look too hot for Paretsky. Truman didn't have the right to be the cause of this little boy's death too, he told himself – not for a billion dollars, not even for the tomb of the Oracle. The chances were slim for all of them, but if he told the truth at least there was hope. Surely Stein would have to check out the coordinates he gave them, and even with a chopper at his disposal that couldn't be done till daylight. If Stein whacked him before checking his story out he might never know.

'All right,' he said. 'I'll tell you. The strike was near the Bint Hammou Plateau in the Sudan – just across the border, south east of here. The coordinates of the test pits where Harris got the samples are 22 degrees north, 28 degrees east.'

Stein dropped the boy, who shimmied away sobbing. Stein let him get a few feet, then seized him by the coxcomb, forced his head back and cut him across the throat with a fluid back and forth movement of his knife-blade. Blood gushed from the wound and the child coughed and clutched at his neck with a small hand.

'Papa!' he sobbed. 'Papa don't let them hurt me'. Then he collapsed in a pool of blood on the floor.

Stein watched, his face a mask of blackness. Truman tried to stand, roaring as if he was the one who'd been cut. 'You filthy animal!' he yelled.

One of the soldiers pushed him down hard, cracking his knees, and Stein oiled closer. He kicked Truman in the stomach and when he bent double, slapped his face hard. 'If you're lying there are another four in the cellar to do.'

Truman shook his head, speechless, wanting to vomit. The room was spinning. He felt stunned, as if the energy had been drained from his body. Stein wasn't even human, he thought. A fearsome rage began to build up inside him, burning in his guts like hot coals, pouring through his blood – a high octane mixture of fear and loathing. He let his head fall on his chest.

'By the way,' Stein said. 'Please satisfy my curiosity. What *did* happen to Ben Harris?'

'Harris is dead,' Truman mumbled, his mouth dry as parchment. 'I found his body near Siwa. The samples were with him. That's how I got into this.'

'Pity,' Stein said. 'About Harris, I mean. Mr Rand would have been so happy to know that he was still alive.'

He waved a delicate hand at one of his boys and a pad stinking of ether was clamped over Truman's mouth. He felt himself flying down a tunnel through strobing slats of light and shade, and into a cross-grained matrix of purple brightness.

Stein probed Truman's fallen body with his shoe, and put away his blade. He felt no guilt at having murdered the Arab nor his boy. They were casualties, nothing more, and he'd used them to obtain what he needed. He'd learned that children were expendable at the hands of his drunken father, who'd regularly celebrated his Saturday nights by thrashing him to a pulp. He practised the lesson assiduously on the children of dissidents he'd tortured and mutilated while working for the Stasi. Those children and their parents had been the price of his promotion. He'd become so good at torturing confessions out of them with the aid of his knife that they'd called him The Butcher of Berlin. After a while he'd even begun to enjoy it, to revel in his reputation, in the fear he saw in peoples' eyes when he passed. That had not been exactly what he'd wanted, but it had been enough.

Then everything had changed, and he'd been at the bottom of the pile again after his years of hard work. Rand's was his last chance. He was going to make it to the top this time whatever happened, even if it meant using Marcus Rand's head as a spring-board. One day, he'd be sitting in the command den on the twentieth floor, but to get there he first had to secure the biggest rare earth strike of the century. No one and nothing would stop him doing that.

'Get a Puma out at first light, Pieter,' he said. 'And take Truman and the other man with you. Tell the pilot to find the Bint Hammou Plateau and check out the coordinates Truman gave us. I want definite eyeball evidence of test pits, or else we shall have to think again. If you do find the evidence, then there's no need to bring either of your passengers back. Heave them out of the Huey at a thousand feet, the way you used to do it with the dissidents. It should be about a century before anyone finds them out there.'

15

THERE WERE CHINKS OF LUCIDITY, LIKE slits in the dark cloak that enshrouded him, but Truman only became fully conscious when he felt wind on his cheeks, smelt aviation fuel, and heard the throb of rotor blades. He opened his eyes to find himself lying on the steel floor of a helicopter with his head almost protruding from the open cabin, with slipstream and downthrust whipping at his long hair.

He blinked and instinctively struggled to get up, finding that his arms were still tied, and that Paretsky's inert body was lying across his legs. He guessed they must have given the Russian a dose of the same stuff they'd put him out with – no one could be in a coma that long.

Several thousand feet below him the desert lay like an endless leopard-coloured sheet – the hide of a dragon, rippled, mottled and coruscated in dunes, ridges and the black protrusions of jagged rocks.

'The sleeper awakes,' a mocking voice yelled over the roar of the motor, and Truman rolled slightly to see the big South African called Pieter, sitting in the rear cabin's only seat, wearing a flying helmet and headset, and cradling his Browning pistol easily in his big fist. Truman wriggled himself into a half-sitting position, and saw that there were two men in the front cabin, the pilot and another of Stein's boys, both staring intently at the landscape ahead.

Truman found Paretsky's head nestling in his lap. His wound looked raw and infected, but the flutter of his eyelashes told Truman he was still alive.

He tried to shift position, and a flash of agony like burning irons shot up his arms. The helicopter wobbled slightly as it hit an air pocket, and Paretsky's head banged against the floor. A second later the Russian opened his eyes.

He stared at Truman for a moment, then his left eyelid closed and opened in a slow and deliberate wink. Truman felt a surge of optimism – from the punishment the little guy had taken he ought to be at death's door, but the wink showed there was still fight in him. Paretsky closed his eyes again, and Truman became aware of an overwhelming sense of thirst.

'Water,' he croaked, 'Give me water.'

The words came out feeble and halting, and Pieter grinned at him. 'What do you say?' he demanded, screaming over the thud of the rotors.

'Water,' Truman repeated.

Pieter picked up a spare headset that was hanging on a hook and jammed it on Truman's head.

'Now, what did you say?' he said, his voice rasping in the headset.

'Water,' Truman said again through the mike, hearing his own voice chafing in his ears.

'Why bother?' Pieter's metallic voice came back. 'You're going to be a pile of bleached bones soon enough.'

'Aw, give the man water,' the pilot's voice cut in evenly through the headset. 'Ever heard of a last request, Pieter?'

Grudgingly, the big South African picked up a litre flask from his knapsack and unscrewed it. He unclipped his seat-harness and leaned over, catching Truman roughly by the hair and thrusting the water-bottle to his mouth.

Truman gulped down water breathlessly until the flask was taken away. He took a deep breath, then nodded at Paretsky. 'Now him.'

Pieter made an obscene gesture. 'The little shit's out of it,' he growled. 'He don't need water.'

'Hey!' the pilot's excited voice cut in suddenly, 'Look at that. You can just make out the Plateau on the horizon!'

Pieter sat the waterbottle back in his knapsack and leaned his big frame over the pilot's seat to see, arching across Paretsky's body. Truman saw Paretsky's eyes open wide, focussed with frightening intensity on the big man above him. The Russian tensed for an instant, his body deadly still. Then he brought up his right foot and lashed out, slamming it straight into Pieter's exposed testicles. It was a kick Truman himself would have been proud of.

The big man screamed and lurched, dropping his weapon, and falling heavily against the door-frame, teetering for a moment in the gap. His eyes bulged out of their sockets and his mouth worked like a fish's as he fought for purchase. Paretsky arched his body back and in a last superhuman effort hit the big man a smashing blow with both feet, in the balls. The chopper lurched fatally at the crucial moment, as if to emphasize the force of the kick, and Pieter's hands slipped off the shiny metal. His face contorted maniacally for a second as he clutched at the air, then suddenly he was gone. Paretsky was already up with his hands miraculously free of the plastic cord, grabbing the fallen Browning. The second soldier was mouthing obscenities through the mask, trying to turn on Paretsky with a gun in his hand.

Paretsky shot him twice at point blank range, mouthing something that Truman couldn't hear clearly. The rounds slapped through the man's chest and emerged in a shower of blood, plunging into the instrument panel. The pilot screamed as the helicopter listed heavily. 'Fucking shit!' he bawled through the headset. 'We're going down!'

For a moment the aircraft seemed to right itself, then there was a sickening bang as the engine backfired and it plunged into a nose-dive, dipping towards the desert surface at an acute angle. Paretsky pitched over on top of the pilot, dropping the Browning, and Truman clawed at the bulkhead with his bound hands, clinging on for life as the G-force dragged at him. Frantic images surged like a wild river through his mind. He could hear the pilot grunting to himself as he battled the terrifying power of gravity. An alarm beeped. Gradually, inch by inch, the chopper's trajectory levelled out, then without warning, the desert rushed up, and the aircraft's skis hit sand and broke off with a crack. The Puma bounced once, twice, and crashed headlong into a towering dune with bone-shattering impact.

Truman felt himself flying. For a moment he was helpless, hanging like a mote in the grip of the planet's remorseless physics, in a dimension where time did not flow, where all energy transformed into its opposite, where all events occurred in a suspended now. Then his body hit soft sand, rolled over and lay still. The last thing he saw was the Puma erupting into a ball of flame and smoke.

16

F OR A LONG TIME TRUMAN HOVERED between consciousness and oblivion, aware that he was icy cold. His eyes flickered open and he became aware of a stink of scorched flesh and petrol fumes, choking grit in his mouth and throat, and the pinch of thirst in his stomach. His eyelids were heavy and painful, and his arms, still tied behind him, were spasms of torment.

He knew he had to get out of the wind or freeze to death, but an attempt to move brought fresh pain coursing through his muscles like liquid fire. He was belly-down on the sand. He began to squirm snake-like across the surface, not knowing where he was going. After a few seconds he stopped, panting for breath. He tried again and suddenly sensed cold metal against his face. He squinted through narrowed eyes and identified a piece of the Puma's tubular ski, broken off in the landing. The ski was half buried, and the end of the tube had snapped off jaggedly, leaving a fracture as sharp as a knifeblade. With an effort that sent his heart racing, Truman forced himself to sit up.

The scene looked different from the vertical perspective – the frame of the Puma like a great swatted crane-fly, proboscis embedded in the slope of a dune, with a flurry of smoke wafting into a sky as blue and clear as azulene. Bits of wreckage from the aircraft lay scattered around on the low dunes. The landscape rolled away to the south – an undulating sea of amber, broken only by a grey smudge on the far horizon that marked the plateau. On the other side of the wrecked Huey he saw a nest of stones eroded crosswise into shelves and fins, enclosing a few square metres of shelter. From the wedge of darkness a pair of legs protruded. Truman didn't know if they belonged to Paretsky or the pilot, but he shouted Paretsky's name anyway. Then, fighting for breath again, he shuffled his body around, and began to saw his binding against the broken steel.

The first moments were such torture that he almost fainted, but he held on, letting the pain out in audible screams, knowing that he must have his hands to survive. He forced his muscles to work, sawing up-down, up-down, until there was nothing left in his world but this motion and the pain it brought. He had no idea how long it took, but one moment he was bound and the next his hands slipped apart, free. He flopped down into the sand, exhausted, gasping in the freezing air.

He heaved himself up again on hands that looked bloated to the size of boxing-gloves, and were now a stinging mass of poisonous needles as the blood began to circulate. Tearing off the rest of the rope, he nursed his swollen wrists for a moment, closing his eyes and praying for water. He rose unsteadily to his feet, wobbled for an instant, and collapsed in a heap on the sand. He lay there for a while, feeling the wind ravaging his body, then tried again. This time he tottered but stayed up, and slowly, wincing in the sour wind, dragging his feet like dumb-bells, he made his way to the nest of boulders, and fell into the sand by the prone body there. It was Paretsky. The Russian's face was grey and his breathing faint and laboured. His clothes were bloody rags, his head black from fuel-burns, and the septic wound on his temple bulged like a cyclops's eye. Truman felt for the pulse at his wrist with his balloon-sized hands and couldn't find it.

At his touch Paretsky's eyes flickered and opened feebly. 'Water!' he croaked.

Truman giggled ludicrously. 'In short supply, old friend.'

He cast his eyes back over the scattered wreckage of the helicopter, and suddenly backtracked to focus on something shiny and oval-shaped lying on a low dune about ten metres away. It was Pieter's water-bottle, and the last time he'd drunk from it – some time in the Jurassic era it seemed – it had been at least half full. Moaning silently to himself now, he swivelled his body round and began to crawl through the sand towards the water bottle. The surface felt like ice on his hands and face and every move seemed to take a lifetime. He remembered reading about the penitents in Tibet who made pilgrimages of dozens of miles on their stomachs. That seemed impossible – just getting ten metres to that water was an effort worthy of Hercules.

When he reached the bottle he found that the cap was still on and there was a heaviness to it that confirmed there was still water inside. Truman inched his body round and began the long trek back, shoving the water-bottle through the sand in front of him, hearing the intoxicating slosh of liquid from inside. Haltingly, he crawled his way back to the little redoubt of shelter. Once there, he pushed himself up, unscrewed the cap clumsily and held the bottle to Paretsky's cracked lips, pouring a few drops over them.

The Russian's eyes flicked open again, and Truman lifted his head and scooped sand under it, feeding him the water a drop at a time. Paretsky sucked at the liquid like a thirsty infant, choking and spluttering. When Truman thought he'd had enough, he drank a little himself a sip at a time. Paretsky blinked at him and tried to smile. 'It's cold,' he mumbled. 'I can't feel my legs.'

'You're OK,' Truman lied. 'You're going to be all right.' He grasped Paretsky's hand and found the flesh icy.

The little Russian closed his eyes. 'It was you,' he whispered. 'In Beirut.'

Truman sighed. 'I've never been to Beirut. I'm sorry.'

Paretsky gripped his arm feebly. 'It was you,' he repeated. 'Tell me it was you. I have to know.'

Truman lowered his head. 'I used to tell people I'd been in Beirut, but it was all a fantasy. After I came down from Oxford I suffered from mental problems for a couple of years. I woke up in a sanatorium in Switzerland and all I could remember was my name. I always wrote in my CV I'd been travelling. It's part of my life I closed off. I can hardly remember anything – but I get flashes sometimes.'

Paretsky's eyes opened and Truman saw that they were glinting fiercely in a last effort to concentrate.

'Bullshit,' the Russian said. 'It was you. I never forget a face. Lying in the Huey it all came back to me. When those assholes were going to stiff me in Beirut you downed them with karate moves. Best fighting I've ever seen. I'll never forget how you looked when you came racing down that street. Not scared in the least, but surprised. You looked like you just discovered Godzilla. I remember hearing a story that circulated afterwards – that they tortured you for weeks. You were almost a vegetable when they let you go.'

'No,' Truman said, feeling a wave of anguish surfing through him. 'It's not true. It was someone else.' To his surprise, he began to cry.

'It was fucking you,' Paretsky said. 'Tell me it was.'

Truman brushed tears away angrily. He realized Paretsky was dying and that he needed to know he hadn't given his life for nothing. *What the hell does it matter if I lie?* he told himself. *Let the poor bastard die in peace.* He gulped in the cold air. 'OK. It was me.'

Paretsky closed his eyes and a smiled a curiously satisfied smile. 'Then I've paid my debt.'

He didn't open his eyes or speak again, and when Truman listened for his breathing a few minutes later, he knew the Russian was dead.

He lay next to Paretsky's corpse for hours in a limbo between life and death, and by the time he became fully aware again the sun was gone, replaced by the cold hoop of the moon, and a smattering of stars. The night was still and freezing, but there was a sharp sting of thirst in his kidneys that told him if he didn't get more water in the next few hours he would die anyway. He closed his eyes against the awful immensity of the heavens.

Perhaps, he thought, it would be better to die like Paretsky.

101

He'd known right from the beginning that what he had set out to do was too difficult. And all the palladium in the world wouldn't compensate for the life of the Fox's little boy – nor the other people Stein had killed.

Something stirred against his cheek – a breath of wind at last in the stillness. For a moment he fancied he heard the patter of feet, the sound of small animals running fast on the sand, almost like the whisper of leaves blowing in the wind. Suddenly there were ghostly voices around him – a dialogue of gutteral consonants and contralto vowels, like bats twittering. The voices seemed to be all around him like an echo, trembling, waxing and fading into silence, then starting up again. Truman opened his eyes and saw only the desert bathed in blue moonlight. He smiled to himself. Funny what thirst could do, he thought.

Then he sensed a movement in the corner of his eye and he jerked his head round to catch a fleeting shadow. He shut his eyes again, and almost at once there was a vibration on the surface, the slightest tremor of sand. He opened them to see silver shadows streaming out of the darkness towards him, tall hooded figures in thick burnooses, whose faces were masked by veils with slits for the eyes – wolfish ovals of dark in the moonlight. There must have been twenty of them and they moved like a tactical military troop, spaced out with a point and flanks, carrying rifles at the ready and sheathed sabres across their chests, their bodies braced with intent alertness, their bare feet murmuring across the sands.

The point man moved directly towards the rocks where Truman lay and knelt down on one knee no more than a metre away. He held up a hand and the troop halted and crouched in all-round defense. Truman felt frozen to the spot, unable to move even to defend himself. He blinked at the point man's dark eye-slit submissively.

'There are two of them here,' the apparition said, his voice a sibilant whisper. 'One's dead, and the other – well, he won't last the night.' 'We can't take him with us, Hafid,' another voice came back. 'Finish him and let's be on our way.'

102

They were speaking Arabic, that Truman was certain of, and though it was a strange dialect full of words that were foreign to him, he understood well enough that '*Khallas minnu*' meant 'finish him'. He opened his eyes wide and rose up slowly on to his knees.

'*Maya*,' he said, his voice cracking. '*Addini maya*! Give me water!'

'By the Light Mother,' the point man said. 'He's still got spirit after all.'

He knocked back his hood, tugged at his face-veil and let it fall, and Truman saw a bearded, hatchet-shaped face, whose carved lines were picked out by the moonlight. The eyes were dark with a yellow glint, set close above an aquiline nose, and the ear-lobes had been carefully bisected into two.

'Khyar,' the tribesman whispered urgently. 'Bring water. We may save him yet.' 'Why waste water on an Outsider, Hafid?' the other tribesman said, drawling his words as if he found it difficult to speak. 'We've got precious little, and the men haven't eaten or drunk all day. We've got two men down who'll bleed to death if we don't get them to the Kahina by sunrise, and the Gharana hot on our tails. We must get back to the Sacred Land. Why waste effort on crashed flying machines and Outsiders?'

The man called Hafid held up a hand that looked the texture of lava in the moonlight. 'The law of the Kel is clear,' he snapped. 'A Son of Adam – even an enemy – must be given sanctuary, unless he is too far gone to survive. Only then may we send him to the Light Mother's mercy.'

The second man – the one called Khyar – detached himself from the squatting ranks and moved cautiously up beside Hafid. He loosed his veil carefully and Truman saw a smooth oval face disfigured by a fresh cut across the jaw, three or four inches long, running over a ridge of swollen red flesh. He looked little more than a youth, and his deep-set eyes were half-closed with obvious pain and fatigue. Apart from the lack of beard, he was out of the same mould as the older man – granite brow ridges, a face like interlocking blades, a hooked kedge of a nose. His burnoose was torn and stained with a dark substance that was probably blood, but his stance was steady and overtly belligerent.

He peered at Truman through his strained eyes. 'This is a weakling from the cities of the outer regions,' he said, speaking thickly out of one side of his mouth. 'Not worth a bowl of camel's piss. You led the troop here just for this, Hafid? You endanger the lives of the *gom*. The Gharana are near – I can almost smell them. By the Holy Imenan, let's squander no more sweat.'

He put down his rifle and touched the swelling on his face warily. The wound was deep, Truman realized, and no more than a day old. The man stood up straight and drew his sabre with a single sweeping motion. The curved blade glittered for a second in the starlight, and Truman watched it as it swept downward as inevitably as a guillotine. In that long instant Hafid snapped out a hand and gripped the swordsman's wrist.

'No,' he growled, fixing the younger man with a hawkish stare. 'He is entitled to asylum, Khyar. That is his right. If you kill him you dishonour both yourself and the Kel.'

Khyar arrested the sabre's sweep an inch above Truman's temple – an act that bespoke incredible control. He whipped it away and glared at Hafid with undisguised hostility. His sword-arm twitched.

'Khyar,' Hafid said. 'We are all tired and some of us are wounded. Don't let the pain cloud your mind or force you to take actions that you might regret.'

Khyar grimaced. 'You dare suggest that pain affects my reason? That is an insult, Hafid bin Slaym!'

The older man's eyes flashed. 'No insult, by the Mother of Light! You are a tried and proven warrior, Khyar. But pain may undermine even the sharpest of spirits.'

The youth with the swollen face paused indecisively.

'If you want to call me out, do it,' Hafid said gently, shaking his head in exasperation. 'But until you defeat me, I am leader of the *gom*.'

Khyar's face crumpled and he let the sabre fall wearily. His eyes blazed at Truman, but his body relaxed. He put away his weapon reluctantly and let out a forced laugh.

'It would have been more merciful to finish him,' he mumbled through his half-closed mouth. 'No Outsider can stand the life of the Kel Saghrana. He'll never be able to keep up with us on the Funeral Plains.'

Hafid shrugged. 'He can ride.'

'The *bil* are shot,' Khyar protested. 'If you give him a mount it'll founder.' 'He can have Wald al-Asmar,' Hafid said. 'That camel will keep going forever.'

He slung his rifle over his shoulder and pulled Truman up easily. 'Bring the *bil*!' he shouted. There was a new dappling of shadows, as a train of camels, carrying cross-ridged saddles and decorated saddle-bags, was led across the sands – huge reptilian forms, snake-silent in the blueness. The last two beasts carried long frames of wicker-work, like helicopter-stretchers, in which two men lay, swathed in dark robes and moaning slightly. The tribesmen gathered around them and Hafid glanced at them in concern. 'Are they still breathing?'

'The spirit is still in them,' someone said. 'But they have lost a lot of blood. The Light Mother damn all Gharana to hell!'

'Give them water,' Hafid ordered. He took hold of the bridle of the first camel and tugged on it making soothing sounds, until the beast lowered its great body gracefully, its legs telescoping joint by joint.

Hafid pulled an embroidered sheepskin cloak from a saddle-bag and draped it around Truman's shoulders. It was heavy, but deliciously warm. He dipped into the saddle bag again, brought out a beautifully-carved wooden bowl and filled it with water from a goatskin slung from the camel's flank. Truman's turgid eyes opened wide at the sound of water, and he moved instinctively for the bowl. Hafid shifted it deftly out of reach. He tore a strip from his layered dark headcloth, bunched it and dipped it in the bowl. He held it to Truman's mouth. 'Suck!' he ordered, 'Little by little. Light Mother's wrath, if you drink a whole mouthful at once it will kill you, even in this cold.'

105

Truman sucked and felt the liquid trickling down his throat and into his stomach, almost immediately easing the tightness there, seeping into his blood and bringing relief to the pain in his kidneys. He sighed deeply and held out the rag to be soaked again. Hafid ignored it, and grabbed him by the arm lifting him bodily on to the back of the camel.

Truman held on as the beast's hydraulic limbs uncoupled – first the forelegs, then the back, then the forelegs again. The rest of the troop had distributed themselves in a protective shield around the camels. Hafid looped the headrope around his shoulder. 'There are Gharana abroad,' he said. 'Let us go in the Light Mother's grace!'

$$\boxed{17}$$

IT WAS ALMOST DAWN BY THE time they reached the Bint
Hammou Plateau. The sun was still a promise – a predawn
roseate glow, and the desert was a series of pits and troughs of
alternate light and shadow. The massif that had seemed so tiny
on the horizon was huge at close range, a vaulted granite cordil-
lera formed into grotesque shapes – hammer-heads, dolmens,
steeples, organ-pipes – scoured, grooved, pitted and in places
slashed away by erosion. Iron and manganese, drawn out of the
strata by ancient weathering, gave the rock wall an ochreous
crust, and behind it there were the outlandish caps of mountains
– shaped like demon figures with spiked and saw-toothed ver-
tebrae, balancing between them sinister shadows of silver, purple,
black and blue.

Truman felt exhausted, wracked by the endless jogging of the
camel, his hands still pumpkins, but the nagging pain of thirst
had receded with the cool stillness of the night. The Saghrana
troop moved with a speed that was astonishing, their loose formation expanding and contracting but never losing its defensive
shape as the texture of the surface evolved from low dunes to
sand-flows, to blasted rock hammada and gravel serir. They
moved like a pack of predators – purposefully, never faltering
in their pace, never exchanging a needless word. Often hand-
signals passed between them, and the patrol would halt, blending

invisibly into the moonlit shadows, giving Truman, high on the camel's back, the odd sensation of being alone.

They pressed on and on, stopping only when the sun's red eye winked at them at last over the furthest hills. There was a hush as ribbles of firegold and transparent opal infiltrated the weft of the night, then the sun rose, a livid, crimson bubble, quivering like some delicate newborn organism on the lip of the world, and a shockwave of brilliant light struck into the darkness like the deep brass boom of a drum. Truman gasped at the beauty of the dawn, and the Saghrana unhooded their desert-hued burnooses, and stood silently for a moment, rifles slung, hands raised with palms open, murmuring together in communal prayer.

As the light thickened, Truman began to look about him, trying to read the syntax of the desert world. The serir – duff gravel on wind-graded sediments – stretched as far as the horizon, broken by saline flats and the fish-scale patterns of dunes, swept up from some ancient and invisible drainage-system. Wind and sand were the tools at work here – but water had been here too, in the past. The plateau walls had been milled and ground by rivers that had flowed out of them in prehistoric times, and the dunes were the ancient beds of those rivers, elevated and repositioned by the wind. The mountains Truman could see in the distance were the relics of volcanoes – hard magma plugs that had filled volcanic pipes and had been left standing when the more brittle outer shells had cracked and fallen away.

Close up, the wall of the plateau was overwhelming – a sheer mass of corroded and pickled granite that seemed to lean its weight on their smallness. Truman felt like an ant under its gigantic eaves. At some silent signal the Saghrana wheeled and began to travel parallel with it, pressing on and on as the sun rose higher, until Truman began to wonder if they really intended to enter the plateau at all. Then – without any signal this time – they swung left, rounding a spread-footed buttress towards what looked like a natural archway – a single spar of fluted sandstone wedged across a canyon, half disguised by a growth of dune grass and tamarisks.

'The Salaba,' Hafid announced. 'This is the gateway to the Sacred Land.'

The troop passed quickly through the arch into a rock defile ribbed with shadows, so tight the patrol had to shift quickly into Indian file. Truman heard a series of shrill whistles, sensed movement above him and craned his neck upwards, getting the impression that someone had actually jumped across the defile hundreds of feet over his head. All he saw, though, was a wing of kites whirling endlessly and effortlessly up there on the breeze. The opposite end of the tunnel was a crack in the rock wide enough for only one camel to pass through, and Hafid drew him into an amphitheatre of rock so vast that Truman caught his breath in surprise.

The space inside the plateau was truly enormous – large enough to have housed a major city – and from its quilted dune-bedding, there rose dozens of lone knappes, each larger than an apartment block, with features so fretted and twisted by erosion that they looked like melted ornamental candles on a vast scale. The knappes themselves, though, were dwarfed by the volcanic plugs of the mountains, ominous grey presences only half visible far-off in the hazy light.

As they moved out into the valley Truman began to see clear signs of human life – the three-stoned hearths of old campsites, stone cairns, boulders piled to mark graves, rock enclosures, well-worn camel paths converging from all directions. There were rich seams of halfa grass, tamarisks, acacia and palmetto like tiny oases all over the valley, and as his eyes adjusted, he could make out thousands of slow-moving black dots among them – the goat flocks of the Saghrana, he guessed.

Nests of segmented tents, like tails of giant dark lobsters, were pitched in fours and fives at long intervals right under the overhangs of the rock walls. As the patrol progressed Truman saw that as huge as this space was, it was no more than the atrium of the plateau – scores of other chasms and gorges opened out of it on all sides. Soon figures were racing towards them – warriors mounted on trotting camels, their hooded burnooses

109

streaming behind them. There was the crack of rifle-shots and Truman saw puffs of white smoke among the racing men, and heard bullets whizz past his ear. 'They're shooting at us.' he gasped.

Hafid chuckled. 'Don't worry, Outsider. That's our custom. It's a salute for our safe return.'

The riders were abreast of them now, reining in their camels, and one or two slipped from the saddle and rushed to greet Hafid, shaking his hand and slapping him on the shoulder. 'The Light Mother be blessed.' they chanted. 'She has delivered you from evil.'

Hafid threw back the hood of his burnoose and loosed his veil. He shook his head sadly, looking round at his men.

'Not all of us made it,' he said. 'The devils were waiting for us, and Goloi himself was with them. Hamud and Terash were badly wounded. There's hardly a man among us without a sabre cut. And we failed. We didn't get our camels back.'

Other riders had converged on them and all around him hooded, veiled men were jumping out of the saddle. Several of them couched the camels carrying the wounded men and Truman saw them lifting the shrouded bodies, transferring them to fresh camels.

'We must carry them to the Kahina at once,' Hafid said. 'Only she can save them now.'

Two or three men loosed their veils and stared up at Truman. 'And who's this?' someone asked.

Hafid shrugged. 'Just an Outsider.'

The men watched him silently, astonished, as Hafid led the troop on across the valley, turning up one of the side chasms – a cul-de-sac, where as many as thirty black tents were pitched in family clusters. At once there were whistles and shrieks from the shadows and people came running out from all sides – men, women and children, shouting and ululating as they gathered excitedly around Truman's camel. They were mostly tow-headed children with half-naked peach-coloured bodies, pretty girls in woad-blue robes to their knees, with tattooed faces, stained lips and plaited hair, but there were also warriors dressed in burnooses or flowing shirts, who watched guardedly from the sidelines. The children pawed at Truman's legs as he rode and a skeletal saluqi barked at him. The patrol didn't break formation, though, until Hafid halted the camels by a large black tent and called, 'Thank the Light Mother, we are home safely.'

The troop slung their rifles and helped couch and unload the camels. Hafid himself barracked Truman's camel, so suddenly that Truman tumbled off the animal's back into the sand. There was tumultuous laughter from the crowd, and Truman got up awkwardly to find himself staring into the eyes of an old man with a vulturine face. The old man was not laughing. He might have been a thousand years old, Truman thought, and his features might have been chiselled out of the plateau itself, blasted by the same scathing winds.

He was wearing a mottled burnoose, with a magnificent furled headcloth of spotless white, whose ends hung around his face like tails. He stood unstooped by age, holding in his hand a black staff with a handle carved with the head of a serpent. He carried a sabre in a baldrick around his shoulder, and round his neck he wore a chain supporting what might have been a leopard's fang. The man had the unmistakable presence of authority and Truman wondered if this was Ossama Hadab, the man he had come to seek.

'Is this the way they teach Outsiders to get off a camel?' the old man demanded drily, bringing hoots of derision from the crowd.

Truman slapped sand feebly off the sheepskin coat, then slipped it off and handed it back to Hafid. 'I've never ridden a camel before,' he said in halting Arabic. There were cries and snorts of laughter from the onlookers.

The old man cocked an eyebrow at him. 'Never ridden a camel? Then you have no business in the *Mufarida*. Kel Saghrana boys can ride a camel from the time they can walk – the girls too.'

He glanced round regally at Hafid's troop. 'Who brings this weakling who cannot ride a camel? You, Hafid?'

111

Hafid stood up to the aged man unfalteringly. 'Nazir,' he said. 'This man fell out of the sky and lived. We found two others dead, and there were the remains of one or two more, burned in the wreck of the flying machine. He was alive.'

'Our sentries saw the flying machine go down,' the old man said. 'Yesterday not long after sunrise.'

'Hafid endangered the *gom*,' Khyar cut in in an angry voice, that was almost comically distorted by his swollen jaw. 'He took us to investigate the fallen flying craft when the Gharana were following our sign. He wasted our water on this Outsider when we had two men down and many injured.' He explored his jaw wound tenderly with probing fingers. 'He gave him a camel to ride while the *gom* walked and when the camels were already exhausted.'

The Nazir smiled indulgently. 'I see you too are wounded, Khyar bin Kalash. No doubt you fought bravely against the demon Gharana?'

'I killed two with my blade,' Khyar grunted proudly.

'You are a brave warrior, but you must learn that honour and courage are the same. We are not Gharana devils who slit the throats of any child lost in the Funeral Plains.' He glanced at Truman again and grunted. 'Still, Hafid could have picked a better time to bring an unwanted guest.'

He pulled Truman inside the tent, and called in Hafid and Khyar after him. The tent was huge and high-vaulted, held in place by a double pole at the centre, carpeted by rush-fibre mats and decorated by camel-trappings and leather saddle-bags sewn with cowrie-shells. A Mauser rifle with a carved and decorated butt hung from the roof on a sling, and there were sets of gourds, pouches and leather bags everywhere. At one side there was a flimsy cloth partition, and from behind it Truman heard the whisper of women's voices.

He slumped down shakily on the fibre rug and the two tribesmen sat down opposite, one on each side of the old man.

There was a pause as the Nazir considered him. 'Why have you come here, Outsider?' he asked at last.

 112

Truman paused, took a breath and rubbed his distended wrists. For a moment he was genuinely stuck for an answer. He wondered whether he should just come out and say he'd been sent here to offer these tribesmen modern weapons in return for their land. But now Maynard was dead there was no longer any real reason for him to be here. 'I came to find Ossama Hadab. Are you Ossama?'

The old man's face went blank. 'How can an Outsider know of Ossama Hadab?' he said warily. 'No, I am not Ossama. I am Tissi bin Tamghar, Nazir of the Kel Saghrana.'

He paused. 'You are the second Outsider to have come here this winter. The other was a man with one eye, who arrived in a white car – a man who was digging for something. The warriors said he was evil and wanted to kill him, but I said anyone who digs in the sand must be crazy. Let him alone, I said, let him have his grit and dust. Perhaps the one-eyed man sent you?'

'No,' Truman said. 'He didn't send me. I came of my own free will. I wanted . . . wanted to find Ossama . . .'

His voice trailed off lamely and with a jolt he remembered Maynard's voice saying, *These Bedouin cut through bullshit like a knife through butter.*

The old man snuffled and squeezed his aquiline nose with thumb and forefinger. 'You will not find Ossama,' he said. 'Ossama is like a sand-tide moving across the Funeral Plains – here and everywhere.'

'You mean he doesn't exist?' Truman asked.

The Nazir ignored the question and stared at Truman suspiciously. 'Perhaps you are crazy like the one-eyed man, or perhaps you became crazy when you fell from the flying machine. Whatever the case, you will never find Ossama. The real question is what to do with you. You cannot ride a camel, walk or live in the *Mufarida*. A Saghrani knows how to shoot, ride, hunt, and track. He is accustomed to thirst, hunger, heat, cold and fatigue from being a child. We make no allowance for Outsiders. We can't take you home, and the code of hospitality forbids harming you, yet you can be of no possible use to us.'

'I can learn,' Truman protested.

The Nazir muttered to himself and stood up, moving with the sprightliness and grace of a much younger man, and pulled Truman outside, where the crowd of boys and girls greeted him with curious stares and laughter. The Nazir hunted round for a moment, then pointed to a track in the sand, so scuffed that Truman couldn't tell if it belonged to an animal or a human being. 'Describe the animal that left that sign,' the old man said. 'Tell me where it has come from, where it is going and why.'

Truman shook his head. 'That's impossible.'

The old man sniffed and called out an almost naked boy of about eleven or twelve years with an oddly lopsided, peanut brown face and hair shaved down except for a coxcomb in the centre. 'Yani,' the old man said, 'describe the creature that left that sign.'

The boy seemed only to glance at the tracks for a few seconds. 'The sign was made by a she-camel that has just had her second teeth,' he said at once. 'She was coming back from the well at Tarout with two full drippers. She got a thorn in her foot on the way and her master had to remove it. This camel belongs to the herds of the Bait Ghayda and passed here two days ago. Her master was Younis bin Ayer – I can tell because his sign is here too.'

The boy didn't seem to attach much importance to what he'd said, but Truman was astounded. The old man grinned at him. 'You see,' he said. 'What is impossible for you is nothing for a child of the Kel Saghrana.'

'I can learn,' Truman repeated obstinately.

'No,' the Nazir said, 'You are too old. What is written in childhood is written in stone, but your childhood is past. For now you can work with the womenfolk herding the goats, that is all I can offer you.'

At that moment there was a commotion and both Truman and the old man looked up to see a rider galloping towards them on a pure white camel. Truman had never seen a camel gallop before and it was a magnificent, graceful sight – the great neck extended like the neck of a giant swan, the long legs working with sweeping, elastic strides, and the rider, his full desert-coloured burnoose and veiled white headcloth blowing back in the wind, rolling steadily with the animal's gait as if rider and beast were one.

He reined in the camel abruptly a few metres away and dropped effortlessly from its back. All Truman could see of his face was the eyes under the face-veil, shadowed by the hood of his burnoose. 'Nazir,' the rider shouted. 'Another flying machine has come. It has landed far away, where the other one went down.'

'Send the *gom* on watch to investigate,' the old man ordered. 'Tell them to leave at once.'

18

COLONEL STEIN WAS LEANING OVER PARETSKY'S stiff body in the shelter of the rocks, examining the tracks around it with interest. He picked up the empty water-bottle and shook it.

'Not killed on impact,' he told the watching pilot. 'Died later. By the look of him he got clear just before the aircraft went up, but was caught in the explosion. He hung on for a while before he expired.'

The pilot, a stumpy man in flying overalls, scratched the two day stubble on his chin. 'They're still not accounted for, Colonel. There's old Pieter flat as a pancake in the sand, and maybe the remains of two inside the Huey. Now this one. That's four. There's one missing.'

Stein smirked and drew a hand through his rich hair. The wind had dropped and the morning was still and silent, the sun a white eye riding on a methylene-blue screen.

'Congratulations,' he sneered. 'Yes, there's one missing and I'll stake my life it's Truman. He was in the back of the Puma and the two dead are in the front. They were probably slowed down by their seat-belts and couldn't get out when she blew. Looks as though Pieter fell out or was pushed before the helicopter crashed, and Truman and his minder survived.'

He knelt again and examined the imprint of a body in the sand

 116

next to Paretsky's cadaver. 'This was Truman,' he said. 'He lay down for a while with his friend. The minder dies and Truman moves out.'

The pilot looked uneasily towards the horizon where the plateau was just visible. 'Yeah,' he said. 'Still, out there he'd have no chance.'

Stein stood back from the cadaver and squinted at the tracks again – the sign of barefooted humans and the ovoid pads of camels. 'People were here. People and camels. I think they took Truman with them.'

The pilot guffawed. 'You mean the Arabs? They'll probably be having him for breakfast right now.'

Stein walked around, occasionally crouching down to poke at pieces of wreckage. Suddenly he saw a mess of orange flex in the sand and picked it up. It had been severed raggedly. *Damn that smug bastard Truman*, he thought. He'd managed to get out against all odds and now he'd be a plague on Stein for as long as he was alive. He took a handful of sand and squeezed it hard in his palm, his eyes smouldering. They'd spotted Harris's markers in their sweep over the plateau earlier, so there could be no doubt that Bint Hammou was the site of the palladium strike.

But Truman's escape left the situation dangerously volatile. Maynard had sent Truman out to do a deal with the nomads, and maybe that's what he was doing right now. A contract with the site-owners would give Kortex the upper hand, and Stein knew Marcus Rand would blame him for the fiasco and feed him to the board like shark-bait to save his own skin. Rand needed this strike, and Stein needed to be able to give it to him cleanly. He'd slaved for years to get in this position. Nothing had ever been handed to him on a plate, but in sheer ability he'd outshone them all in the end. Only the final steps remained. If he handled the palladium operation here well, the sky was the limit. But if Truman managed to get out with a contract, all that would be chicken shit, and he'd be lucky to work out his time as a security-guard on the ground floor.

'Hey, boss,' the pilot said. 'Look at that dust. Something tells me we got company.'

Stein stood up, casting a glance towards the horizon. There was a cloud of blue dust there that hadn't been there a moment ago. He moved to the Puma, extracted his powerful binos, then climbed a sand ridge and scanned the skyline. 'We *have* got company,' he announced. 'About fifteen men on camels coming our way.'

The stumpy man looked up at him in alarm. 'Jesus, I'd better get the kite warmed up.'

Stein skated down from the ridge top and barred his way, with a ferocious smile on his face that would have sent anyone who knew him running for their lives. But the pilot didn't know him.

'I'll get it warmed up myself,' Stein said. 'I have a pilot's licence. You are surplus to requirements, actually – especially as you now know where the strike is.'

The pilot looked puzzled and opened his mouth to say something, but in that moment the colonel hit him, a sharp crack in the teeth with the heavy binos that sent him staggering against the rocks. The pilot felt blood welling from broken teeth and put up a hand to feel it. He looked up just in time to see Stein standing over him, holding a vicious little fang-shaped knife.

19

S TEIN'S CREW MET HIM AT KHARGA'S small airport, and whisked him back through the desert to the Fox's place in the Land Cruiser. The Colonel sat in the passenger seat deep in thought. Rand had ordered him to find the location of the palladium strike and he'd done it, but in the process he'd inadvertently delivered Maynard's negotiator just where he wanted to be. He didn't know what kind of shape Truman had been in when the nomads had picked him up, but the guy had been capable of severing his bindings, so he couldn't have been too far gone.

Stein had to assume the worst – that Truman would get the contract with the site-owners and get out with it. After all, the desert was a big place and if Truman was determined to get out, even Rand's couldn't stop him. The thought that an amateur like Truman might foil his plan infuriated him. Like that snooper Krause who had ended his chances with Sikor, he thought ruefully. The man had been a nothing – a cleaner – just another east German refugee who'd moved west and got himself a shit job. But the guy had thought himself clever, sticking his nose where it wasn't wanted, asking questions. He'd had a brother whom Stein had interrogated five years earlier, and who had emerged from the cells a nervous wreck, half blind and without the use of his right hand. Tough shit, Stein thought. But one day they'd been waiting for him outside the Sikor office, and the brother had identified him as the former Major Hoth of the Stasi, the Butcher of Berlin. Krause's big mistake had been to let Stein know that he knew. His little crusade had ended one day down a Berlin alley with Stein's knife across his throat. But Stein had known at the time he'd only bought himself a couple of days. The same night he'd packed as much as he could into a suitcase and taken a train to Madrid. From there he'd flown to Jo'burg and another life.

This was his big chance and he wasn't going to let some other nobody like Truman screw it up for him. This was a time for independent action. Rand had always been against mergers and joint operations, but there were certain members of the Corporation's board who disagreed. If Stein bypassed Rand and made a deal with Kortex, he reckoned he could count on those members to support him. They might not be the majority, but presented with a *fait accompli* they could well carry the rest with them. Rand would go ballistic, of course, but with the board against him he'd be forced to accept or resign as CEO. Stein might even get the job on the rebound. It would be a huge gamble, but then his whole life had been a gamble. He sucked in his breath, wondering what collateral he could offer Maynard and his mafiya backers, and how the hell he was going to bring this coup off in the next forty eight hours.

He looked at his watch. It was almost midday and unseasonably hot – the sky cloudless and radiating heat like stainless steel. They approached the old house through the zebra-stripes of light and shade made by the intertwined branches of the palm and olive trees. The car was just about to enter the broken down yard, when the Colonel held up a hand and snapped 'Stop.'

The driver, Simon – a squat South African with a bulldog's face – did a lurching emergency stop and the two soldiers in the back almost flew over their seats. Stein paused for a second, watching and listening. 'Where's the sentry?' he whispered. There was an almost imperceptible movement at one of the upper floor windows of the Fox's house.

'Get out!' the Colonel bawled. '*Fast*!'

As Stein threw himself out of the car there was a crackle of machine gun fire from the house, stitching a weft of steel blisters across the bonnet and doors, and crumping through the windscreen. Stein heard a yelp as Simon was hit getting out. The two hard-men who had been in the back rolled into cover and brought their MI6 rifles into action with lightning precision. They loosed off a concentrated salvo of single and double shots that peppered the frame of the upper storey window, ripping the woodwork to chips. The machine gun stopped abruptly, but almost at once there were bursts of drumfire from two windows on the ground floor.

Stein pressed his face into the sand as the rounds lashed over him. He heard the wounded Simon grunting and cursing to himself on the other side of the car, but a second later the big man's pistol began pumping shots with slow deliberation, supported by the staccato whine of the MI6's behind him. For a few moments the firefight blazed back and forth, then Stein heard a voice yelling his name over the gunfire. 'Stop shooting! We have your boys in here. Any more and they'll be getting gobfuls of lead!'

Stein raised his head and brushed the sand off his face with his hand. 'OK!' he yelled back. 'Stop shooting. Hold your fire.'

Smoke and dust had gathered in the yard in thick bolus, and when the breeze had taken it, Stein saw a lean figure at the door of the house. It was a man with oriental eyes and a slick mat of cropped hair, dressed in an elegant blue suit. He appeared to be unarmed. 'Your men stay where they are,' the figure shouted across the thirty metres that divided them. 'You come here. Any shit and your boys inside get stiffed. Understand?'

The man walked steadily out into the centre of the sand-filled yard. He had guts, anyway, Stein thought. He raised himself warily, smoothed his hair back and patted sand off his jacket. He walked towards the other man, his eyes darting across the leathery mud facade of the house, probing for weak spots and fire-points. Close up, the elegant man was more Slav than oriental – a peculiar blend of features one would only find in a Russian.

'Ah,' the Colonel said, 'our Russian comrades. I wondered when you would turn up.'

The man grinned truculently, showing gold teeth. 'I am Sergei Rybakov,' he said, his Russian accent clear at close quarters. 'I control Kortex Mining Company of London.'

'Really?' Stein said complacently. 'I thought Kortex was run by a man named Gus Maynard.'

Rybakov raised a mocking eyebrow.

'Maynard had an accident,' he said. He lit a Marlboro and exhaled the smoke into Stein's face. 'He smoke too much. Had a heart attack. Now, I want Truman. Where is he?'

Stein stared at him with a smile of contempt on his lips. 'You mean *Harry S.* Truman? I heard he died.'

Rybakov pulled a wry face. 'I know Truman was here because I got it out of your foot soldiers, like I got your name. I know you're Rand's gofer. And by the way, don't look for your London stoolie, Amersadiqi. He's doing analysis on daisies.'

Stein shrugged. 'That's outdated news. How did you find me?'

'We followed your trail,' Rybakov went on. 'Jaffa's to here, and we jumped the boys you left. We found a dead guy and a dead kid, and three more kids and a woman still alive in cellar. We liberated them. They will be on their way to police right now, so we don't have a lot of time.'

Rybakov dropped the half smoked Marlboro in the sand and crushed it out with a hand-made shoe. 'Where's Truman?' he repeated.

'Somewhere out in the blue, I should think,' Stein said. 'He and his little minder were involved in a helicopter accident. The minder went down, but Truman walked away.'

'You mean he's alive?'

The Colonel smiled, sensing weakness. 'You sound upset,' he said. 'I thought he was your pet negotiator.'

'Truman's a snitch,' Rybakov snarled. 'He work for somebody else. If I get my hands on that asshole he's one dead son-of-a-bitch.'

Stein worked hard to keep his face poker-straight to stifle the astonishment worming through him. Maynard was dead, and that changed the situation dramatically. He had been the mafiya's front runner, their legitimate face. He had known the mining business inside out, in a way thugs like this Rybakov would never do. Now, Rybakov claimed Truman was working for some-one else. That might be a gambit to get Stein to reveal his whereabouts, but if it was true it meant that Kortex – the mafiya – had played straight into his hands.

Rybakov watched him silently for a moment. 'You know where strike is, no?'

Stein gave him a superior glance. 'As it happens I do. But these things should be discussed discreetly, not in public.'

Rybakov turned and gestured to a reed-mat lean-to enclosing a square of shade on one side of the house. 'Over there,' he said.

Stein glanced at the space, weighing up distances. He knew the Russians were ruthless and right now his men were outnumbered anyway. There was only a fifty-fifty chance of surviving this encounter, but it was his big chance.

'Very well,' he said. 'But I assure you one thing, Mr Rybakov. If any harm comes to me, you and your men will never get out of here alive – not even at the cost of the ones you hold captive.'

The Russian beamed, knowing it was bluster. 'OK. My boys do nothing.'

There was a mud-brick step under the awning, where the two of them sat, close together.

'You know, my friend,' Stein said, 'this bang-bang-you're dead business is for the cowboys. It's very wasteful, don't you agree?'

'Kortex made strike,' Rybakov said. 'It's ours and we don't want competition. You tell Marcus Rand to back off.'

Stein shook his head, fingering his folded knife in his pocket, wondering if he could slash Rybakov fatally before anyone got near him. 'Mr Rand is an obstinate man. Once he scents rare earth, he doesn't bow out for anyone. You can kill me and all my men, but it won't mean nuts to Rand. I know where the strike was made and I've checked it out myself. I had the coordinates relayed to

Jo'burg last night. Rand will move in whether I come back or not, and I'm afraid there's nothing you can do about it.'

'Huh!' Rybakov sneered. 'We got an army – trained ex-Spetznatz men, just waiting for chance like this one. They'll wipe him out.'

Stein's burnhole eyes glinted. 'Mr Rand has his own army, all ex-South African police and Special Forces with state-of-the-art gear, all highly trained and raring to go.'

Rybakov didn't look impressed. 'I also know where strike is. We already got heavy gear promised by Libya – we done a favour once for Gaddaffi. We can move in overland before you even get your grunts off the ground.'

'That may be,' said Stein. 'But you're still going to get a little war in the desert with a lot of people wiped out on both sides. It'll cost a king's ransom, and there'll be nothing to show at the end but a planeload of body-bags. Now consider it for a moment, my friend. The rare earth there is going to be worth an incredible amount. Enough for everybody. Instead of slogging it out like street hooligans, why not consider a joint operation?'

Rybakov raised an eyebrow. 'Rand will never go for it,' he scoffed. 'He always say he don't work with Russians. My cartel made him offers before and he spit in our face.'

'Mr Rand is determined but reasonable,' Stein said, 'and I'm sure I can persuade him to come round. Tell me something – who are you going to get to do the mining? That's a specialized business and it requires a lot of experience. Rand's have that experience – in fact we have the best track record of any mining operation in Africa.'

Rybakov cocked his head to one side. 'Kortex is mining company. Now I run it myself, why do I need Rand?'

It was Stein's turn to scoff. 'Maynard's dead. Mr Rand knew all about him – it was a kind of hobby of his, you could say. Maynard was a sly old dog, and my bet is that he tied Kortex up so tightly with legal restraints that as far as you're concerned the company no longer exists – at least not in any form you could use. Am I right?'

Rybakov knocked a streak of sweat off his forehead with a flick of the fingers. 'Even if is true, we got cash. We can get any specialists we like.' 'Really?' Stein said doubtfully. 'Well that's your business, Mr Rybakov. But think it over, discuss it with your bosses. Rand's can give you the perfect front. I'm sure your cartel will agree it's pointless fighting over a bone that's too big for either of us. There's a lot more profit to be had in cooperation than there ever will be in whacking each other out.'

Rybakov went silent for a moment, trying to play the reluctant party. Inwardly, though, he was jubilant. He was aware that Stein believed he had the advantage, and at the same time he was confirmed in the belief that Rand's couldn't afford a war in the desert. He'd heard that Stein's small army was good, but with a bit of sharp manoeuvring now he might be able to immobilize them as a threat, and leave the field wide open. He decided to twist the knife even more firmly.

'OK,' he said. 'You got a point. Maybe we could do business. But there's other interested parties. Truman's working with British government.'

For the first time Stein looked disturbed. 'I don't believe it. Have you got proof?'

'Is true,' Rybakov insisted. 'Harris's samples were analysed before Maynard put them in. Name on docs was guy called Whitehaven who's Africa desk at MI6. Truman brought the stuff back from Egypt in container, so it's got to be him.'

Stein gazed at the ground thoughtfully. 'Then how come Truman worked his way in with Maynard?'

'I don't know. I think maybe Maynard was in on it. Maybe they make him deal he can't refuse.'

'Whatever the case,' Stein said, 'if you're right about Truman and he gets the mining rights from the site owners, it would be most inconvenient for both of us. We don't want the Brits sticking their noses in before we can get our operation off the ground. We have to make sure Truman never gets out of the desert. I suggest our first joint effort should be to eliminate that damned trowel-pusher once and for all.'

20

AFTER SUNSET, WHEN WOOD AND CAMEL-DUNG fires sprang up like a milky way across the length and breadth of the Bint Hammou Plateau, Tissi bin Tamghar, Nazir of the Kel Saghrana, arrived at the aiguille that had separated itself aeons ago from the pot-bellied massif of Termit cliff. The aiguille was a pinnacle of sandstone like a petrified tree, rising from a thick plinth to a narrow point some twenty metres above the Nazir's head. It was covered in graffiti – tribal scratchings and ancient rune-characters, picked out by the falling light, brand-marks of Saghrana clans, some of them long ago vanished, others still intact and unchanged since the time of the Imenan – the ancient law-givers.

Pride of place among them was the effigy of a ram with curled horns, bearing the ancient symbol of the sun-disk. Tissi touched the sacred symbol reverently – it had been carved here by the Imenan long ago in the mist of time, the Time of First Reckoning, when they had first settled in the Sacred Land. Below the ram's head was a much smaller symbol – the form of a hyena with open jaws, crudely drawn, carrying the crescent moon on its head. Tissi fingered the smaller etching and shivered. *The Gharana*, he thought, *they have been bolder than ever this year*. Twice they had somehow managed to get inside the plateau and had run off with dozens of goats.

Now they were raiding Saghrana camel-herds out in the *Mufar-ida*, and driving them off. Only a week ago they had lifted fifty head grazing in the lee of the rimwall from right under the noses of the watchers, slaughtering two herdsboys in the process. Those were the camels Hafid had been assigned to bring back, but the *gom* had returned empty handed, with Tarash and Hamud badly injured. And as if that wasn't enough, they'd brought back an Outsider who had asked to see Ossama Hadab.

The last light burned out in flame orange over the rimwall, and soon there was a moon, and the stars out in thousands. Tissi watched them, mumbling the names of the constellations he knew – the Scorpion, the Dragon, the Dark Intruder. There were faint scuffling noises around him in the halfa grass, and the old man saw the friendly shapes of hopping mice there. Suddenly there was a sussuration of wings as an eagle owl flipped out of the darkness, pouncing on the mice colony. As the bird rose, Tissi saw the wriggling legs and tail of something in its clutches, against the paleness of the night sky. Turning the sign over in his head he gave a low whistle.

Almost at once a slight figure, completely muffled in darker than dark robes wafted from behind the rock pedestal. The figure was silent, blending into the nooks and crannies of the night, so frail and flimsy-seeming it might have been a wraith. It halted before him.

'The peace of the Light Mother be upon you,' it said.

'Kahina,' Tissi said. 'The spirits of the Sacred Ancestors protect you.'

The figure threw off the hood that was concealing its face. The features that emerged, lit momentarily by the starlight, were those of a young girl – a girl with an almond-shaped face, thick long hair that was as black and glossy as the night itself. The girl ran a hand through her hair.

'What brings you here, Tissi bin Tamghar?' she demanded. 'Why do you disturb the meditations of the Kahina?'

Then she let out a peal of laughter, throwing her arms round the old man. 'It's good to see you, father. Come into the cave.'

127

She drew him past the aiguille to an entrance in the cliff face, and Tissi entered reluctantly. This was only his daughter's living-cave, but it was redolent with the smell of magic – bags of bones, gourds of coloured powders, devil-masks, dried animals and birds. On the walls were strange paintings of headless men. A fire flickered in a pit in the centre of the cave, and a bed made of sheepskins lay in one corner. The Kahina placed a leather cushion by the fire and the old man sat down, casting a nervous glance around him. At the back of the cave a natural archway opened into invisible dark recesses beyond.

'How long can you go on living alone like this?' Tissi said. 'You should have a husband and children. Your aunt Tamghart was a Kahina too, in her time, but she still had a family. Your cousin Khyar is always asking about you and I have to put him off. Did you know he was wounded in the face fighting the Gharana two days ago? He'll be scarred for life.'

The Kahina knelt down and poured water into a clay pot from a large gourd. She set the pot on the fire, and blew into the flames.

'Poor Khyar,' she said. 'Yes, I heard about it. They say he killed two of the enemy. The scar will no doubt suit him, and tales of his prowess will be whispered around campfires for years to come. Khyar's a brave warrior – brave enough when facing Gharana swords that is. But my magic worries him.'

Her father grinned. 'It worries me, too. But Khyar's getting a big reputation now, and he's proud of himself. He takes your silence more and more as an insult and I can't keep staving him off like this. When will you tell him yes or no?'

The Kahina tossed her wild hair out of her eyes. 'When the Light Mother says it is time.'

Tissi smiled and swallowed back a comment. 'What of Hamud and Terash?' he asked, changing the subject.

'If the Light Mother wills, they'll survive. They'd lost a lot of blood, but I was able to do something for them. I sent them back to their tents this afternoon, but I doubt they will ever fight again.'

128

The Nazir clenched his fist angrily. 'Those cursed Gharana!' he stormed. 'The Light Mother send them to the abyss! Two more good warriors down. It is the sacred duty of the Kel to seek revenge.'

The Kahina shuddered. 'Will it never end, father? This eternal war of Saghrana and Gharana? Sometimes I wonder if it isn't time for change.'

'Change?' Tissi said, startled. 'That's dangerous talk. The Imenan devised the *tafriq* to fight the evil that almost destroyed them. It's been that way since the Time of the First Reckoning – the law as it was laid down by the Holy Imenan. The *tafriq* is the pillar of our world. Without it the bad spirits would return.'

'Sometimes you can't just accept the past,' the Kahina said. 'In the oral history it is said "*Evil lies not within a man's spirit, but within his will.*" The Sons of Adam are not born evil, they choose evil.'

'The Gharana have chosen the Dark Mother's path,' Tissi said. 'Is it not written in the sacred scratchings on Termit cliff? The ram and sun-disk signifies the Saghrana, the hyena and moon the Gharana. They are like day and night, two halves of the whole. To end the *tafriq* would destroy the balance of our world, the balance that has allowed us to survive here.'

Ossama crouched and drew a rough circle in the dust, with a smaller circle in its centre.

'This is the Sacred Land,' she said, pointing to the inner circle. 'The domain of the Kel Saghrana. Beyond it,' she indicated the larger circle, 'lie the Funeral Plains where the Gharana survive, where we must venture in the wet season on the great southern migration.'

She made a series of dots on the edge of the circle with the tip of her finger. 'These are the Qurra oases where we trade with the oasis people for guns and metal – things we can't make ourselves. That's our world – Saghrana, Gharana, Oasis people.'

Tissi blinked at her, trying to understand her drift. 'Yes. That's how it's always been.'

The Kahina swept her hand around the outside of the circle.

'What lies here?' she asked.

'The Outside,' he said.

She watched him intently. 'We know little of the Outside, yet we are surrounded by it. Change will come, father and it will come from the Outside. The ancient enmity between Gharana and Saghrana will be as nothing in its path. Change is inevitable and we must either change ourselves or be changed and destroyed. It is said in the oral history a Kahina long ago prophesied that an Outsider would come among us – one who would show us new ways.'

Tissi scratched his corded neck muscles, perplexed. A waft of steam rose from the clay pot on the fire, and the Kahina lifted a burning twig to peer into it. 'What is it?' her father asked anxiously.

She laughed. 'Only water, for tea.'

She scooped boiling water out of the pot with a gourd and poured it into a blackened brass kettle, which she sat on the flames, adding a handful of tea-leaves. After a few moments she removed the kettle and poured tea into two bowls. She passed one bowl to her father and set hers down in front of her. Diapers of light from the trembling fire played across her face, leaving her eyes in shadow. 'Father, I hear that Hafid brought an Outsider to the Sacred Land.'

Tissi chuckled, relieved. 'Yes, he brought an Outsider, but the man can't stay with us – he's a weakling who could never stand the rigours of our lives. To tell the truth, I don't know what to do with him.'

The Kahina sipped tea and examined her father's face carefully. 'There's more isn't there?'

Tissi stopped chuckling and dropped his eyes. 'Yes. He asked to see Ossama.'

The Kahina took the news calmly. 'It begins.'

'Ach!' Tissi said. 'Maybe he's just crazy like all of them. Like the one-eyed man who came scratching for dust. He doesn't seem dangerous.'

'It's said that danger always comes from where it's least

expected' she said, her voice ice-cold now. 'In the Half-Death I've had visions of Outsiders, father, visions of fire and blood. There were strange machines breathing fire, noises like thunder, blinding light. I saw you in my dreams – saw you vanish in a cloud of smoke.'

Tears filled her eyes suddenly as she searched the old man's face. 'Forgive me,' she said, 'but I must tell you. In my dream there was a Black Kahin – a serpent in human guise, without a human soul – a Shadow-man whose eyes blazed like holes into hell. In the vision he was the king of the Outsiders, and he was here in the Sacred Land. He had powerful weapons, and he wanted to destroy the plateau. He showed me your head, father, severed from your body. I don't know what the vision means, but I fear the Outsiders. I fear them more than the Gharana. One day the Black Kahin will come.'

The Nazir shivered again. He put his tea glass down and screwed up his face. 'Maybe. But this Outsider is not a Black Kahin. I don't have to have the Gift to know that. I've seen Outsiders before. The men called Bliti and Teferelt and their *gom*. I was a small child then, but I remember them arriving in their wheeled contraptions. They spied on us, and tried to learn the secret of the *tafriq*. We silenced them, but one of their men got away in a car, and we thought more would come to try and take revenge on us. But years went by and nothing happened.'

The Kahina watched him silently. 'For years nothing. Then this year we suddenly have two Outsiders here – first the One-Eyed man, now this one. And I'm told a second flying machine swooped over the plateau today, perhaps looking for the one that crashed.'

Tissi stared at her pensively. 'Maybe we should send this Outsider to the Light Mother's mercy after all.'

The fire had burned low. The Kahina's face was grave now. 'It may be necessary, father. But let's not rush it. There is also the prophecy. Perhaps this Outsider is the One.'

Tissi looked at her, puzzled. 'But how can we tell?'

'Let me study him,' she said, 'and I will know.'

131

21

W HEN TRUMAN AWOKE THE SUN WAS already up across the valley, and the youth called Yani – the one who had identified the tracks he'd so dismally failed to recognize – was shaking him roughly. He was lying on a palm-fibre mat under a granite overhang, covered in some rags the Saghrana had given him the night before. Truman examined his wrists and found that the swelling had gone down, thanks to the herbal ointment Hafid had rubbed on them the previous night. His sleep had been deep and untroubled, and the pangs of thirst had disappeared. Yani threw him a bundle of clothes – a burnoose dyed the colour of sand, a cotton tunic, baggy trousers and a ragged headcloth.

'What's this for?' Truman asked.

'Have you forgotten?' the boy said. 'You're going out with the women to look after the goats. There are no passengers among the Kel. Everyone has to do his bit.'

'What's wrong with my own clothes?' Truman protested.

Yani tipped his head to one side and grinned, showing the gap in his teeth.

'Well, they're no good for the desert, and they look stupid.'

Truman groaned in the cold and held his breath while he exchanged shirts and pants. He tied his ordinary clothes in a bundle and stuffed them carefully behind a rock. Yani stared at the Nike hikers he'd left on. 'And the boots. Imagine the sign you'd leave with those clod-hoppers. You'd stand out like the moon if the Gharana were on your tracks.'

Truman surrendered them ruefully and shivered as he felt the cold sand under his feet. The boy's own feet were as callused as beaten hide, he noticed, and he wondered how long it would be before his were like that. He stood up and the boy adjusted the burnoose for him. 'It's warm in winter,' he said, 'and in summer it traps the cool air round your body. The colours allow you to melt into the desert when there's enemy about or you're on the hunt.'

He showed Truman how to knot the headcloth, then stood back, an expression of surprise on his oddly proportioned features. 'Mother of Light!' he exclaimed. 'You look like a Saghrani. Anyone would think you'd been wearing these togs all your life.'

They squatted for a moment by a smoky fire the boy had kindled in a three stone hearth. Truman brushed dust off his face. 'Where's the washing water?'

Yani snorted. 'Washing water?' he said. 'There is water only at Termit and Tarout and every drop has to be accounted for by the Water Masters.' He picked up a twig of sinewy wood and handed it to Truman. 'It's araq. It tastes bitter but it's good for cleaning the teeth.'

He busied himself poking in the ashes with a stick, and brought out the remains of two pathetic little rodent carcasses, badly charred, complete with fur, feet and tails.

'This is breakfast,' he said, sampling one of them. 'Hopping-mouse roasted in its skin.' He proffered one of them to Truman, who took the meat and ate a piece warily.

'Sheesh!' he said, spitting it out. 'Tastes like charcoal.'

Yani's eyes gleamed. 'Suit yourself,' he said, 'but that's all there is.'

The boy took a pocket-knife out of his burnoose and began to carve tiny morsels of flesh off the bones with enthusiasm. Truman stared at the implement. It was a genuine Swiss Army knife with about fifteen blades.

'Where did you get that?' he asked abruptly. 'They don't make those things in the Bint Hammou Plateau.'

Yani held up the knife proudly. 'Given to me by an Outsider. The one-eyed digger. You know him?'

'Not exactly,' Truman said. 'I . . . saw him once.'

'I met him when he was digging outside the plateau,' the boy said. 'In the Wadi Tum. The Kel said he was mad, but I used to talk to him. He spoke a bit of our tongue, not like you, of course, but I could understand him. He told me about the Outsiders' world – cars, boats, flying-machines, machines that can think for themselves, wires that allow you to hear peoples' voices from far off, huge tribes of people living all together, shut inside. Of course, I couldn't make head or tail of most of it. I wouldn't want to live there.'

Suddenly the boy looked furtive and spoke more quietly. 'I shouldn't have done it, but I sneaked him into the Sacred Land once and showed him Termit Rock. He made a picture with a thing called a pencil, copying the old markings. It was amazing how he could do that. It looked so real. Anyway, that's when he gave me this knife.'

'What happened to him in the end?' Truman asked.

The boy shrugged. 'He went off with lots of little bags of dust, in his motor-car. He was a wild man, but there was something sad about him. No wife or children – can you believe that? Maybe he was mad, like they said.'

Later, Yani led him out of the blind canyon and into the main amphitheatre of the valley, walking so fast that Truman could hardly keep up. Soon the women and goats came into view, a parade of black wedges and uprights trailing out among the towering knappes of granite that cast grotesque humped shadows across rose pink pillow-sand. The goats bleated as they stalked, their hooves making a scuffing, slithering sound on the desert surface, and the women, small, lean figures in brightly-coloured robes and dark headcloths, led them from the front. The sun was a burst of lemon-light above the rock walls, sending galleries of colours skating across the valley, tricking up spider-legged shadows.

Yani, evidently not pleased at being assigned a woman's role, walked sullenly, only breaking the silence to point out animal-tracks, droppings or plants. 'What is this plant, Outsider?' he would demand, cocking his lopsided head and chewing his sprig of araq. When Truman looked at him dumbly, the boy would guffaw and say, 'Don't you know *anything*? This is *aniti* grass – it has spiky seeds but they can be ground into flour and made into bread when there's nothing else,' or 'this is the track of a *jadi* – a baby gazelle. It passed here last night. By the Holy Imenan, it seems you know nothing at all! You can't track or hunt – you can't even ride a camel. Tell me, what *can* you do?'

'Nothing,' Truman admitted. 'What can *you* do?'

'I can tie hobbles and make ropes,' Yani said fiercely. 'I can make fire from a blade. I can herd camels and make water-skins, I can ride and shoot and hunt, find water and dig wells. I know all the names of the trees and the grasses and the hills, the birds and the animals and I can read the sign. That is what is needed for living here. If you don't know these things, you're useless. You are an Outsider. You can't live here with the Kel – when the time comes, Khyar will cut your throat.'

'I was given sanctuary,' Truman protested. 'Hafid granted it.'

Yani chuckled. 'Hafid is one of the Ten Bravest. Did you not see that his earlobes were slit in two?'

'I suppose I did. What are the Ten Bravest?'

'The ten chosen fighters of the tribe. Those who lead the others in battle. Hafid is a famous warrior, and Khyar is jealous of him. Khyar's father was a Burrower, not a warrior, and now he feels he has something to prove.'

'What's a Burrower?' Truman inquired.

Yani smiled faintly. 'What does it matter? He will cut your throat just the same.' He sighed. 'The one-eyed man told me that in your world there are people who can force others to do things. It's not like that here. Everyone is his own master, and no one – no group or family even – can compel anyone to do anything.'

'But the Nazir . . .'

'The Nazir is our war-leader,' Yani said, 'but he can only persuade people, he can't force them, even in war. He is leader because he has a reputation for courage, generosity, hospitality and good counsel, and people listen to him. If he lost the confidence of the Kel they would just stop listening, and turn to somebody else. No one can prevent Khyar from sending you to the Light Mother's mercy, even though it is against our code. All that would happen is that his reputation would suffer. Reputation is everything to the Kel, but Khyar might think it's worth the risk.'

Truman turned away from the boy and looked out at the walls of the plateau with their rind of ochreous patina like the bark of ancient trees. He studied the vast cenotaphs of rock under webbed caps of decomposing sandstone, great aiguilles that stood aloof like the buttress-trunks of giant sequoias. Beyond them, far in the distance, lurked the silver wraiths of the mountains.

Yani pointed a knobby hand at them. 'Do you know what that is?' he said, indicating a hill with a saddle between two blunt peaks. Truman looked, shading his eyes. 'It's a double volcanic plug,' he said, struggling to find the words in Arabic.

The boy guffawed again. 'No,' he said. 'That is Tahert, and,' – he pointed to a needle-like pinnace dominating the first hill, its screesides covered in ochre granite, and purple lava, 'that is Iyen, her lover. See there is a notch on his right shoulder – that's where Maded cut him with a sabre.'

'Who's Maded?'

The boy pointed to a squat, rounded massif, lurking in hazy shadows behind the others. 'That's Maded. He sneaked up on Iyen in the night and struck him with his sword, but in turn Iyen cut his legs off. By the Light Mother, that's something even a baby knows.'

'Maybe,' Truman said testily, 'but they're just lumps of rock, anyway.'

 136

Yani looked startled. 'Holy Imenan! Don't you know that even the rocks have their spirits? Every rock, every tree, every cave, every spring. All these things are alive in their own way. They are all part of the Great Mother's creation.'

They walked in silence again, and soon Truman saw that ahead of him some of the troops of goats were peeling off from the main column after their goat-girls, while others were heading for what looked like a well.

'This is Tarout well,' the boy announced. 'Its water comes from under the cliff at Termit through a qanat – a deep tunnel built by our forefathers, the Imenan, long ago in the Time of the First Reckoning. The Sacred Land is full of qanats – the Imenan even grew crops outside the rimwall, they say.' The boy sighed. 'But this is the only one still in use. You asked what Burrowers were. Well, in every generation there are two or three men who are taught to keep the qanat open – we call them Burrowers. The task is a very dangerous one, because the qanat is likely to collapse. Khyar's father was killed in a collapse when Khyar himself was a baby.'

There was a lone young woman at the well drawing water for her goats, which were pressing thirstily around a stone watering trough carved with tribal runes. Truman's goats shoved in among the girl's animals.

'I shouldn't be doing this work,' Yani said petulantly. 'This is girl's work. I am not a girl.'

The girl at the well wore a faded red dress, and was drawing water with a leather rope attached to a floppy, ribbed leather bucket. Her dark hood had fallen off with the effort of her work, and her thick, coarse hair spread almost to her waist. The hair was tangled wildly and black as coal. Truman watched as she arched her back against the weight of the bucket, pulling hand over hand. Her face was almond-shaped, but large boned rather than delicate, and slightly severe from the side view, with a snub nose, lips that were full and generous, and cheekbones so high they were almost oriental.

The girl wasn't attractive in any conventional Western style,

137

yet she was truly original, her features so unusual that Truman wanted to look at her again and again. There was a powerful aura of animal magnetism about her:

Cro-Magnon women might have looked like this, Truman thought, at the dawn of mankind. He watched in fascination as the muscles flexed, the collar-bones tensed, the slender but callused hands passed one over the other and the bucket emerged to be tipped into the watering trough.

'Who's that girl?' he asked Yani.

The boy glared at him and sniggered. 'Jamila. Just another girl.'

'Jamila,' Truman repeated to himself. The name meant 'beautiful' in Arabic. She was bringing up more water now, and Truman watched entranced, looking at the way she carried her head, the shape of her back, the slight bulge of her breasts.

He watched her for a long time until the boy nudged him. 'Hey!' he said. 'Come on. Your turn now.'

Truman opened his mouth to protest, but the boy pushed him roughly towards the narrow opening at the well-head, where Jamila had paused, catching her breath. Truman staggered forward shyly, hovering around the goats. He felt self-conscious, ridiculous in the clown's suit they'd forced on him. He looked about for a way of escape, but saw Yani's lop-sided face leering at him, enjoying his discomfort. Truman cleared his throat and for the first time Jamila seemed to notice him. She half turned and raised a dark eyebrow interrogatively.

'*Yimkin ta'tini ad-dalu?*' Truman said, stumbling over his words. 'Er . . . could you give me . . . the well bucket?'

The girl giggled and turned her head away politely.

'You great sissy!' Yani bellowed. 'That's not how we talk to women. Here, girl – give him the well bucket and be quick about it!'

Jamila turned back to face Truman, handing him the well-rope. He put his hand out to take it and their fingers touched – only for a fraction of a second, but the effect was electric. Truman looked into her eyes and saw that they were large, wide-spaced above the oriental cheekbones. They were a very particular colour – neither green nor blue but both at once. Jade-coloured. A surge of adrenalin flooded through his veins and left him quivering. *It's her*, he thought, *the girl in the dream I've been having half my life*!

His head spun and he had to fight to regain full consciousness. He stared at the girl. For a fraction of a second their eyes met again, and he thought he saw recognition there – or was it something else? A look of curiosity, evaluation? A moment later she turned away, walked past him and began marshalling her goats. Truman stared after her, thunderstruck. Yani shifted uncomfortably, aware that something inexplicable had just happened. 'Come on!' he yelled suddenly, breaking the spell. 'Come on, get on with it.'

Truman hefted the leather well-rope, his hands already shaking with cold. He gazed at Yani, wondering what to do, but the boy was watching him smugly. 'Get on with it!' he bawled again. Truman dropped the floppy bucket over the rim of the well and heard a satisfying slap as it hit the water, about three metres below him. He took a step closer and peered down into the dim interior. He waited a moment and then began to pull the well-bucket up in long slow strokes. It felt surprisingly light. He gave a final heave and the bucket sprang out of the well so abruptly that he staggered backwards, hitting him in the midriff and showering him with ice-cold water. Truman yelped with the cold and threw it back into the well, but by now his hands were so chilled that he could no longer grasp the rope. The end of the coil suddenly snaked out of his fingers and he heard another slap as bucket and rope hit the water at the same time.

There was a howl of unadulterated glee from Yani. 'Now he's done it,' the boy chortled. 'Mother of Light, I've never seen anything so funny. First time I've ever known anyone drop the well-bucket inside the well.'

There was the sound of contralto laughter from all around him, and Truman looked back to see that a host of girls had gathered to watch. Jamila was smiling, covering her mouth with her hands. His heart sank. He slumped his shoulders and let his head fall to his chest, feeling more humiliated than he'd ever felt in his life. He must have been mad to believe he could stay here with the Saghrana – he couldn't even throw a well-bucket without dropping it. He was reduced to a helpless child again and felt almost like crying. All his varied experience of life meant nothing. In this environment, he was simply an ignorant savage.

Jamila stopped smiling and moved as silently as a ghost towards a clump of wind-tortured acacia trees nearby. She picked up a long piece of deadfall – a knobbled branch about three metres long – and carried it over to the lip of the well, knelt down gracefully and began to fish for the well-rope. In a matter of minutes she had expertly picked it out on a cleft in the branch and handed it back to Truman silently, with downcast eyes. He took it, feeling utterly inadequate, but grateful all the same. For a moment he thought she would speak, then Yani's mocking voice cut in sharply.

'Wrap the end of the rope around your wrist, Outsider, and try again. We'll make a goat-girl of you yet!'

22

EVERY DAY FOR THE REST OF the week, Truman was up before dawn, ready to go out with the goat flocks. Yani, his constant companion, had even taken to spending the night next to him under a rock overhang. Neither of them slept much except in snatches as the nights were icy, and they had only threadbare rugs. At the crack of dawn, though, the boy would be squatting by a smouldering, acrid fire of camel dung, grinning in his lop-sided way, warming goats' milk in an earthenware pot.

'Get up you donkey!' he would say. 'You might see the lovely Jamila again today.'

Truman had to admit that the prospect of seeing the girl enticed him more than the task of herding and watering goats, though there was a certain attraction in the simplicity of the life that reminded him of the dig at Siwa, and he'd begun to feel fit and well again. The diet was basic – goats milk and any berries they gathered, with the occasional addition of game meat. Yani showed Truman how to use the wheel-trap – a hoop of straw with spokes converging on a hole in the centre. When buried in sand, a small animal – a hare or a fennec fox – might get its leg trapped in the hole and be unable to withdraw it. Yani some-times killed hares and jerboas by bopping them on the head with his stick and occasionally they ate lizard, tortoise and even snake.

141

No matter what creature they killed, though, the boy always treated their carcases with respect. 'The wild creatures share the earth with us,' he told Truman once. 'The Light Mother created them for us to eat, but the earth belongs to them, too. People are not better than animals. Plants, animals and people – even Outsiders – are equal parts of the Light Mother's creation.'

But there was never enough to eat, and Truman felt his flesh melting away with the lack of nourishment, the activity and the cold. Looking after the goats and sheep was tedious and exacting. The animals had to be watched all the time and protected from predators – the hyenas, wolves and jackals with lairs among the rocks. The hardest times though were watering-days, when Truman would spend hours at Tarout, drawing water – alone, for Yani refused to help, though he taught Truman how to jog the bucket so that it filled with water properly and to lift it with brisk, economical, hand-over-hand strokes. It was exhausting work, but Truman couldn't rest for even a moment without Yani jeering, 'See! By the Sacred Forefathers. Even a slip of a girl can do better than that!'

There was no privacy, and even when he slunk off to urinate the boy would watch him. 'See!' he would announce, tittering. 'The Outsider stands up to pee!'

Question and answer sessions still went on, but now Truman was learning to recognize tracks – to distinguish between a man's footprints and those of a woman, between a male and a female camel, between tracks made yesterday and those that were fresh. He began to retain the names and properties of plants – the herbs that were used for medicine, and those from which poisons and drugs could be extracted – grains, fruits and berries that provided nourishment if prepared in the correct way, and some that were deadly if not prepared correctly. He even started to be able to recognize some of the goats in his flock individually. As days passed Yani became less disposed to mock him, and seemed to shift more into the role of a master with an eccentric but promising apprentice. Occasionally, in fact, he seemed to delight in being his teacher, though sometimes his face would darken and

142

he would add, 'I can't see the point of this. Khyar's going to cut your throat, anyway'.

Within a few days Truman had begun to lose all idea of time. The sun rose and set, the lives of the nomads went on with a pulse and rhythm of their own. He marvelled at the harmonious simplicity of their lives. Here was a society where every man was an equal, where the leaders held authority only by common consent, where an individual was not judged by his possessions but by his reputation. 'What happens if someone's reputation is really bad?' he once asked Yani.

'No one cooperates with him,' the boy explained, 'not even his own family. That means he can't live with the tribe, and to live without the tribe in the *Mufarida* means certain death. But no one can be forced to leave – he must leave of his own free will.'

Truman soon discovered that the Saghrana did not distinguish years by dates, but named them after some significant happening. Their history was written without letters, in the seams and fissures of the rocks. Every inch of the valley was soaked in memories that had been handed down from generation to generation. And despite the doubt hanging over him, despite the biting cold at night, the bitter winds, the heat and the sand squalls, the hunger and constant thirst, Truman started to understand that these desert people had a deep connection with the earth – they were part of it in a way he had only glimpsed at Siwa, a way that his own society had lost.

Every day Jamila would be at the well, watering her goats, and Truman would find an excuse to go that way even if his goats didn't need to be watered. There, under the eyes of the gloating Yani, he would spy on her for as long as he could – taking in the way she tossed the hair out of her eyes, the slight huskiness of her voice as she shouted to the goats, and most of all the deep, deep call of those brilliant sea-toned eyes under the high cheek bones. She might have been a Tibetan, Truman thought, or some savage Tartar woman from the steppe. Her body under the loose dress looked perfectly proportioned yet without a gram of superfluous flesh.

Sometimes, while he was squatting with Yani waiting for her to finish watering, she would turn an inquisitive glance his way, a slightly haughty, severe, challenging glance. Truman thought there was an air of the aristocrat about the girl that counterpointed the wild, atavistic impression given from her high cheekbones and flashing Tartar eyes. The more Truman saw her, the more interesting her face became, as if it was blossoming before his eyes. The girl he'd thought hardly attractive at first glance seemed to have bloomed into a creature whose stunning beauty took his breath away.

Sometimes, when Truman returned her look, she quickly averted her gaze, but on other occasions she would meet his looks boldly and her mouth would pucker and the jade eyes soften with that curious, inexplicable expression he'd seen on the first day. Many times he summoned up the courage to speak to her when they exchanged the well rope – only to find his resolution evaporating when he looked into those eyes. The little speech he had prepared would disintegrate into a series of fractured syllables, and the girl would flick him an amused glance and stalk off with her goats. Yani would chortle with adolescent ridicule from behind.

As he and Yani brought the goats home to the tents at the end of the day, through layers of dust, Truman would quiz him about the girl – which was her tent, who were her mother and father, did she have a fiancee? The boy's answers were always evasive and non-committal. 'Don't worry your head over a pretty girl,' Yani would say. 'Jamila is already betrothed. In a few days' time you won't have a head, anyway, and the rest of you will be feeding the crows.'

One day when he arrived at the well, he found Jamila there alone. Yani had gone off on an errand of his own, and – miraculously – there were no other goat-girls in sight. As he sidled up cautiously, Jamila turned and smiled, sweeping her luxuriant raven hair out of her eyes with a deft movement of her tiny

144

hand. Truman looked into the radiant blue-green eyes and felt carried away by them – it was like the sun rising for the second time that day. She watched him inquisitively, weight on one leg, head cocked to one side like an animal listening for danger. There was both innocence and allure there, Truman thought. He longed to touch that coffee coloured skin, to caress the wild hair, to brush her neck with his lips. He opened his mouth to speak, but suddenly the girl froze and the smile was wiped abruptly off her face.

Truman turned, alarmed, to see Khyar standing silently by his camel, not ten metres away, his face unveiled and bloated hideously by the wound that had already become a livid scar amid swellings of purple and scarlet tissue. He stood rocking slightly on the balls of his bare feet, with a hand gripping the hilt of his sheathed sabre. He said nothing, but his eyes bored into Truman's like drill-bits. Truman turned his back on the Saghrani, and began to collect his goats self-consciously, driving them away from the well towards the massed screes along the plateau walls. Moments later there were footfalls behind him and he looked back to see Yani hurrying his way. 'I saw it all,' the boy said breathlessly when he caught up. 'Khyar was watching you. Light Mother's wrath, tomorrow he will cut your throat for sure!'

23

Truman sensed danger before he opened his eyes. He sat up straight in his rags to find a figure standing over him – a shadowed face peering out from the dark wreath of a hood, and the pale blade of a curved scimitar pointed at his midriff. 'Don't move,' the figure growled. 'I could split your guts open like a desert melon before you took a breath, Outsider.' Truman recognised the strangled tenor of Khyar's voice.

'So is this the way the Saghrana do it?' he said. 'Creeping up like a snake in the night?'

'Mind what you say,' Khyar choked, 'or by the Sacred Forefathers, I might be tempted to finish what I should have finished when we found you lying in the Funeral Plains.'

There was a scuffle beside them as Yani jumped up from his sleeping-place.

'Stop it, Khyar,' he piped.

'Shut up, boy,' Khyar barked. 'When you are a full-fledged warrior you can debate with me. Until then hold your breath.'

He drew the sword blade away and slid the weapon back into its scabbard, hidden in the folds of his burnoose. It was still night, and the Milky Way hung above them like a delta of crystals in the velveteen blueness. Truman's body was chilled to the marrow and his breath came in steamy coifs. He shivered and rubbed his hands, scenting far-off odours of camels and goats from the Nazir's camp half a kilometre away. Khyar crouched down near him and Truman smelt the woodsmoke and sour milk in his thick cloak. The warrior pushed the hood back and in the starlight Truman glimpsed a disfigured jaw and black holes for eyes.

'The law of hospitality forbids me from cutting your throat,' Khyar said thickly, 'but it's what you deserve. I saw you yesterday making eyes at Jamila. We picked you off the Funeral Plains like a dying sand rat and saved your life, and you repay us by flirting with our *haruum*.'

Truman chuckled. 'Flirting?' he gasped. 'I've never even spoken to her.'

Khyar leaned closer, touching his distended jaw. 'A wrong look is enough. You've been following her around like a lovesick rabbit. All the tribe knows about it. You may not ogle our *haruum*. By the Light Mother, if you weren't under our protection I'd cut you down here and now.'

'What's it got to do with you?' Truman answered back. 'It's none of your damned business anyway.'

Khyar twitched angrily. 'Jamila is my cousin and she was promised to me from childhood. She's mine by right, Outsider. She belongs to me.'

Truman scooped his legs under him and rested his bare feet on the cold earth, ready to launch himself at Khyar if necessary. Yani busied himself blowing fire from the moribund stumps of wood in the hearth.

'It seems to me,' Truman said, 'that you should let her decide who she wants to talk to.'

Khyar went very still. 'You're a fool,' he said slowly. 'Maybe your women give themselves to any comer, but ours don't. By the Light Mother, I'd call you out, but that would be to accept that a piece of outlands trash is the equal of a Saghrani, and that could never be, Outsider.'

'Let's get something straight,' Truman said. 'My name is not Outsider, it's Truman.'

Khyar sniggered from the side of his mouth. 'It means nothing to me. Among the Saghrana a name must be earned. You have no name here.'

Truman eased himself into a crouching position and faced the Saghrani, no more than a metre away. 'If you're not going to kill me then I suggest you leave us in peace.'

He stood up slowly, wrapping his sleeping rags round his shoulders and moved towards the hearth, where Yani had managed to coax to life a trembling flame. Khyar remained where he was, his elbows resting on his knees and his face now a pall of shadow under the hood.

'I cannot call you out,' he said, 'but I have a challenge for you, Outsider. At first light I am to take a salt caravan to the Qurra oasis to trade with the peasants who live there – sixteen camels, each carrying a *qontar* of salt. The man who was to come with me was bitten by a bull-camel today. I will take you instead.'

Truman wondered if he'd heard right. He looked up to see Yani's face, soft burnt sienna in the firelight, gaping incredulously at the warrior. 'But Khyar,' the boy said, 'the salt run is seventeen days across the heart of the Funeral Plains. The salt-road is a trial even for a hardened warrior, but for an Outsider almost certain death.'

'Don't tell me what I already know, boy,' Khyar drawled through his nose.

'To cross the Funeral Plains with a salt caravan takes a man. If the Outsider thinks he's man enough to flirt with Jamila, let him try it. If he shrinks from its dangers, as I expect he will, then I'll make sure Jamila knows.'

Truman shifted position warily. 'It's a trick. You think you can lure me out into the desert and leave me there.'

Khyar jumped to his feet, eyes molten in the light of the flames. 'By the name of the Imenan you dare to suggest such a thing.'

'It's no trick,' Yani cut in, staring at Truman with an expression that was eloquent and mature beyond his age. 'Did I not tell you that reputation is all among the Kel, Outsider? If he harmed you in any way on the salt-run his reputation would be gone with the wind. *Bogha* – treachery to a companion – is an unspeakable sin.'

'How would anyone know?' Truman asked, glancing at the boy sceptically. 'There wouldn't be any witnesses would there?'

'By the Holy Ancestors, I should carve your liver out right here,' Khyar spat. 'Of course there will be a witness. The Light Mother sees all, and no one can hide from her. No honourable man could live with himself having done such a thing, and I am an honourable man – a Saghrani warrior. Six men have I killed with my blade in face-to-face battle, and eleven times have I taken the salt run.'

'You must make the water-pact before you go,' Yani added. 'That means swearing in front of witnesses that you will protect each other unto death.' Truman stared into the flaring chips of wood in the fire. 'All right,' he said. 'If it's not a trick, why ask me?'

Khyar chuckled quaveringly. 'To be shot of you. The salt run means exhaustion such as you have never known, Outsider. It means thirst and hunger every step of the way, battling terrible sandstorms, heat and freezing cold. And if you survive that, there are Gharana raiders to finish you off. You will certainly die, but at least you won't die the death of a coward.'

He shook his head and the loose hood flapped. 'It was a stupid idea,' he said. 'Expecting honour of a creature who knows no more about nobility of spirit than a puff-adder.'

'Now wait a minute,' Truman said. He paused and scratched the beard that had grown wild and unkempt over the past week. Nothing in his situation had changed, he thought. Here at least, for all its harshness, life had the simplicity he had always craved. Khyar's challenge brought out all his fighting instincts. He knew the Saghrani wanted to humiliate him by displaying his utter superiority in his own environment, and to get rid of him finally without breaching the Saghrana honour-code. His best bet would be to refuse, but then Jamila and the tribe would know.

He'd never really expected to survive anyway – not from the

moment he'd stepped out of Maynard's office. He had no family but a mother who'd never given a toss for him, and no life to go back to. He thought of his dreams and longed to see Johnny again – the small legs pumping, the golden hair flying as the little boy ran happily to school. In the end Johnny had had no sort of life at all – never had a chance. But then existence was always precarious – a speck of light between wedges of eternal darkness – and the only thing to do was to enjoy the honey while you could. Jamila was the only chance of honey he had left, and if seeing her again meant enduring the salt road, then so be it. If he died in the process – well, he'd be with Johnny, and the tiger would get him one day whatever the case.

Truman took a deep breath, and glanced up at the stars, winking pulses of colour across the night sky. Then he fixed Khyar with a hard gaze. 'I don't care how tough it is,' he told him. 'I want to go.'

24

FOR ONCE THE ELECTRONIC SHUTTERS WERE open and brilliant sunlight filled the Command Den on the twentieth floor. Marcus Rand sat in his wheelchair staring out of the window at the confusion in the maze of streets below. When he turned his chair with a sudden burst of power, Stein saw uncertainty in the cockerel eyes.

'You sold the farm, Stein,' Rand said quietly. 'You sold me down the river.'

Stein realized this was no time for crowing. He'd briefed the board members privately and had found them receptive, even the ones he hadn't counted on. They were fed up with the way the corporation had been losing money over the past five years, and if there should be a power struggle over the issue it would be a close run thing.

'Think about it, Mr Rand,' Stein said. 'The Bint Hammou operation is going to cost a fortune. This company's been in the red for years. We need the palladium, but we also need Russian cash, and those boys are falling over themselves to get rid of it. If we try to go it alone, we'll have to deal with them and they've got an army of mercs trained just for this sort of job. That'll mean a turf war under the noses of US snoop-satellites and a lot of unwanted exposure, not to mention the added expense. You know as well as I do that nobody wins in a war like that.'

Rand glared at him with red-rimmed eyes. 'What happens after they've moved into the plateau?' he demanded. 'There'll be no way to dislodge them if they happen to change their minds. They could easily renege on any agreement, and the board won't back you up then, Stein, I can promise you that.'

Stein's voice was controlled and his manner conciliatory. 'I don't think that will happen. Don't forget we've got something they haven't. Our name. They need a legitimate front for their money laundering now Maynard's gone, and who could offer a better service than Rand's?'

Rand lowered his head angrily. 'Ivans,' he spat. 'I don't want any part of their dirty cash from whores and pushers.'

'But look at the logistics,' Stein went on. 'We've never done an op like this without making a deal with the local government. It's one thing to move heavy plant in to a foreign country by plane, but quite another to shift military hardware. Troops can go in as civilians disguised as tourists, all right, but what about armoured cars and helicopter gunships?'

'Jesus wept,' Rand said. 'Are they expecting World War Three? Last I heard it was a bunch of camel-shaggers we were up against.'

Stein scowled. 'There's no point in taking chances,' he said, 'and the mafiya can move their material in through Libya with no questions asked. That's perfect for us. They supply the military backup, and we bring in the mining gear. They shell out the funds, we split the profits fifty-fifty, and if anyone gets flak from the UN it's going to be them.'

Rand glared at him. He thought of the folder he'd secreted away with the details of Stein's background, and wondered if it was time to play his hand. Then he rejected the idea. Stein had worked a flanker on him, but he was right as usual. Rand's couldn't afford a mini-war. The company needed the new oper-ation to revive its flagging fortunes, and he was aware that pri-vately the board members had jumped at the chance of outside finance. His best ploy would be to go along with it. He'd let Stein have his operation and give him enough rope to hang himself. If it worked they would all be quids-in, and if Stein screwed up he alone would cop the fallout.

'You're playing with fire, Stein,' he growled. 'Think you can handle the mafiya without getting burnt?'

'No problem,' Stein said.

The telephone rang and Rand transferred the call to his receiver. 'Mr Rand,' Miss Parker's voice came through. 'There's the call you've been expecting from London – a Mr Rybakov. He's speaking from our office in London on the TV link.'

Rand licked his fat lips. 'Put him on,' he said.

He gestured for Stein to stand near his wheelchair, and a face flickered on the TV monitor – a youngish man with a gold earring, hair like iron filings, and a hint of something oriental round the eyes. Rand watched him closely. 'Mr Rybakov? I take it you're interested in Colonel Stein's offer?'

'If it has green light from you,' Rybakov said evenly. 'I'm authorized by my cartel to offer you 15 million dollars to set up a mining operation in the Bint Hammou Plateau, Mr Rand, but there is condition – we put in our ex-Spetznatz mercenaries as security. We don't need contract with the . . . occupiers. Our boys will crush anyone that sticks his neck out.'

Rand blinked at him and smiled acidly. 'I see,' he said. 'That's very generous of you Mr Rybakov. And you don't feel that the deployment of your troops would be spotted by US spy satellites and remarked on?'

Rybakov sneered. 'Sudan is full of troop movements – is a civil war – no? The Yanks support rebels – they're not going to turn a hair.'

'I'm pleased you're so sanguine,' Rand said. Rybakov was just what he'd expected, he thought – young, intelligent, articulate in a bluff, Russian sort of way, but a street gangster under the thin layer of sophistication. 'And what kind of opposition are you expecting?'

Rybakov hesitated for a fraction of a second. 'Can't be more than three, four thousand of the Bedouin,' he said. 'We got air support – an Apache gunship – light armoured cars, armed jeeps,

66 mm rocket-launchers, heavy machine-guns. We have hardware waiting in Libya and we can move in through desert. We finish them in a day, no fuss. I feel sorry for the bastards'. Rand nodded, impressed. 'That's going to be an expensive business. I trust you haven't forgotten the siege of Stalingrad? An army, however small, depends on its supply lines, and you'll be operating in empty desert. You'll need good logistics.'

'Hey, you think you can tell a Russian about Stalingrad?' Rybakov said sourly. 'We can do it. You like our offer or not?'

Rand drew a finger across his bulbous nose. 'I'll tell you something, Mr Rybakov. When Colonel Stein informed me of your little tete-a-tete I was very unhappy. I don't like playing with gangsters, or with cash that stinks like rotten fish.'

Rybakov's hunting dog eyes came into close-focus. 'Yeah,' he sniffed, 'like all Rand operations clean as baby's ass, no?'

'We don't deal in drugs or guns,' Rand said.

'OK,' Rybakov said. 'Suit yourself. I told Stein you don't like Russians. I offer to put up hundred percent of investment, plus cost of security and you insult me. You want war, we give you war. Mining set-ups are ten a kopeck.'

Rand pursed his lips, looking like an enormous, overgrown baby. 'Now wait a second, I said that was my first reaction. I'm not used to joint operations, especially with Russians. But now I've had a chance to consider it, I'm not sure we couldn't work well together. A war would only exhaust us both and probably end up in some international court. As for mining ops being easy to find, though – there I disagree. No legitimate concern will go for your unappetizing capital, Mr Rybakov, and you know it. You might be able to scrape together some one-horse show, but what kind of hash-up would they make of it?'

Rybakov sighed wearily. 'I bin through this with Stein. You in or out Mr Rand?'

Rand hesitated and Stein stared at the folds of flesh bulging from his shirt collar. 'OK,' Rand said. 'I'm in for fifty percent of the long-term profits. Take it or leave it.'

Rybakov snorted. 'That's too much.'

 154

'Come on,' Rand said. 'You stand to make billions. And all with greenbacks so minging you can't even unload them in Safeways. We can scour them clean as a Jew's toilet. That's got to be worth at least half.'

'I have to ask my bosses.' Rybakov said.

'If you can't make that kind of decision,' Rand said, 'then I want to meet the man who can, not the office boy.'

The Chechen's eyes flashed angrily. 'OK,' he said. 'We split fifty-fifty.'

'All right,' Rand said. 'And when exactly are you intending to start the operation?'

'We wait hot season, then we go in and hit the nomads with all we got. After that you come in with plant.'

'This Truman guy is the nigger in the woodpile,' Rand said. 'Are you certain he's a British agent?'

'Samples went for analysis before Maynard got them, and the name on the documents belonged to an MI6 officer. Truman must have handed them over to MI6, no?'

'If it's true, we can't afford to let him get out with a contract for the British government.'

'I'm working on it,' Rybakov said. 'My money says he's still with nomads in Bint Hammou. Could take weeks for him to do deal with them – even months. I have boys watching Egyptian airports, and if he tries to get out that way we'll bump him off. If he's still in desert when we move into plateau I send in search and destroy team to eliminate him. I attend to that personally.'

Rand chuckled drily. 'Very well. I'm sending Colonel Stein to London to hammer out the details. You've got yourself a deal, Mr Rybakov. We'll be in touch.'

He switched the screen off and sat silently for a while watching the dead monitor. 'Doing deals with the fucking Commies now,' he sighed. 'My old man would turn in his grave.'

25

A SOUR WIND WAS RUNNING IN over the rimwall as Truman helped Khyar couch sixteen camels between the double line of salt-packs. It was fool's dawn, and the stars were winking out one by one as a smear of cinnabar crept over the peaks of Iyen and Maded mountains. The camels were huge, scarred, obstreperous-looking beasts, bearing the distinctive ram-and-sun-disk brand of the Saghrana on their flanks. They protested as they flopped down, gnashing their teeth, blowing out pink mouth-bladders, blubbing from their prehensile lips, and threatening to take a chunk out of Truman whenever he came near them.

'They're mature bulls,' Khyar told him. 'That means they'd kill you for no reason.' He pointed at a monstrous animal at the head of the line. 'That's Maliq. The caravan leader. He's killed two men in his time – one of them he sat on and ground slowly to death with his chest-pad. Only yesterday he bit Jumayl and broke his arm – may the Light Mother heal him – and *he* has been working with camels all his life.'

'This is crazy,' Truman grunted. 'How the hell do you stop them?'

Khyar held up a straw muzzle with strings attached. 'This. And guess what? It's your job to muzzle Maliq.'

The huge camel fixed Truman with a baneful dark eye even before he got near, and began to snap its canines at him as soon as he was in range. Truman steeled himself and tried again and again to slip the muzzle over his snout, feeling like a *bandadillero* in a bullfight, each time only just evading the crushing jaws. Finally the animal vomited over him a mass of vile, half-digested plant matter. Truman retched and sank to the ground slapping sand over his burnoose, trying vainly to rid himself of the stink. Honking in glee, Khyar stepped in and fitted the muzzle over Maliq's head with studied ease. 'You have to do better than that, Outsider,' he commented, 'or you won't live to reach the Salaba.'

By the time all the camels had been muzzled, a host of spectators had gathered – small children, adolescents, and a smattering of older tribesmen. The Nazir's tents stood nearby, and Truman glimpsed the old man pottering about inside one of them. From somewhere came the dring-drang of a coffee-mortar and the wail of someone singing a dirge.

'Time to load,' Khyar said.

Each animal had been settled between two fat sacks of salt-cakes sewn up with strips of hide. Khyar pointed to the last camel in the train. 'You lift the sack on the right,' he said, 'and I'll take the one on the left.'

Truman sauntered up to the animal followed by a host of onlookers, and bent down to pick up the enormous sack. He crouched and strained, grunting to himself, but only managed to raise it a few inches before he dropped it. The children shrieked with laughter and the tribesmen chortled. Khyar's twisted face peered at him over the camel's back, leering out of his hooded burnoose. 'What's the matter?' he chided. 'The Outsider too feeble to lift a sack of salt?'

Truman stifled a rude comment and tried again. This time, with tremendous effort, he managed to raise the sack about six inches before dropping it heavily. There were more snorts of derison from the crowd. 'That's impossible,' he told the Saghrani. 'That thing must weigh over two hundred kilos. No one could lift it.'

The audience convulsed with amusement, and Khyar joined them, his face contorting painfully. 'Of course no one could lift it you idiot', he said. 'It's half a *qontar* – half a camel's load. If one man could lift half a *qontar* we wouldn't need camels, would we?'

He did a quick two-step around the camel with a cleft stick in his hand. 'This is how we do it,' he said. 'And you'd better get used to it, Outsider.'

He motioned Truman to lift one side of the sack while he hefted the other, balancing it against the camel's wooden saddle. Then he wedged the stick underneath. 'There,' he said. 'Let go.'

Truman let go of the sack, which remained in place on the stick. Khyar dragged him around to the other side and the two of them lifted the balancing sack. Khyar pegged the sacks together over the saddle while the camel quivered and snorted.

'That's the way it's done,' he said. 'That's why one man can't take a salt-caravan alone. It takes two to lift the sacks. Now, are you ready? There are fifteen more to do.'

Truman leaned an arm on the saddle and glanced round at the spectators. 'Why don't they help?' he demanded. 'We could get it done in no time. Why are they standing around gawking?'

'They would be glad to help,' Khyar said. 'But by our custom only the caravaneers themselves may load the camels. That way, if anything goes wrong on the first day no one else is to blame.'

When they had loaded all sixteen camels, Khyar ran quickly down the line, kicking them on the flanks to get them up. One by one, the great animals rose, keening and spitting, to their feet. The sun was out, egg-yolk yellow soaking through muslin cloud. Truman's blood had been warmed by the exertion, but once he'd stopped he could feel the chill undertones of the wind. Yani and a few smaller boys ran up to take charge of the caravan, while Khyar led him to the Nazir's tent. Inside, Tissi stood grey-swathed by the smoke of a brushwood fire, with Hafid at his side. Both the old man and the bearded warrior looked worried.

'Are you certain you want to do this, Outsider?' the Nazir asked as Truman and Khyar entered. 'It is a hard road and not all who take it return.'

Truman shrugged. 'I'm sure.'

Tissi held his gaze for a moment, then unstrung a bladder of water hanging from a roof-pole. Hafid held out a gourd, and the old man filled it up. 'The Light Mother protect you both,' he intoned. 'You must swear loyalty to each other by the sacred pact of water.' He held up the gourd. 'This is the water of the Kel. This is the life, the light and the spirit in the wilderness. Drink in the name of the Great Mother of all.'

Khyar squatted on his haunches and Truman did the same. The Nazir passed the bowl first to Truman, who held out a hand to take it.

'Both hands!' Khyar hissed. 'This is a holy sacrament.'

Truman took the gourd in both hands. 'Repeat after me,' the old man said. 'With this drink I swear by the Light Mother to remain faithful to my travelling companion, defending him unto the jaws of death, and giving my life for him if need be.'

The words sounded as final as a marriage service, and Truman could feel the untold ages of tradition behind the ritual, the gravity of the pact sealed in a drink of clear water. He repeated the words and the Nazir nodded. 'Drink!' he said. Truman drank deeply from the gourd. The liquid was cool and clear as meltwater. He handed the vessel back to the Nazir who passed, it reverently to Khyar. The warrior echoed the words hastily and gulped the liquid down, his face-muscles working visibly around the disfiguring scar. 'Now the pact is sealed,' the Nazir said. 'By the Light Mother's will, you will go as one.'

That's the last good water you will drink until we return,' Khyar said, rising. 'If you return, that is.'

'Only the Light Mother is all knowing,' the Nazir said. 'You are a brave warrior, Khyar, but remember – few things ever turn out as you expect them to.'

Hafid shook hands with both of them. 'Go now,' he said. 'And the Light Mother speed your safe return.'

They left the tent, pushed through the spectators, and ran to the caravan. At the head of the train the great Maliq roared and blubbered, blowing his mouth-bladder, lifting his head high and

159

looking down with slitted eyes. 'Come on, Outsider,' Khyar yelled. 'Take the lead.'

Truman took the headrope from Yani. 'Be careful,' the boy whispered. 'Maliq may try to butt you from behind. Be on guard all the time. Good luck, Outsider. Don't worry about what Khyar says – if the Light Mother wills, you will come back, I know.'

Truman touched the boy gratefully on the shoulder, then waved his stick at the camel. He pulled hard on the rope and slowly, ponderously, the camel train began to move.

26

D AY AFTER DAY THEY TREKKED ACROSS the strangeness of
the Funeral Plains, where the caravan that had seemed
so huge in the Nazir's camp became no more than a string
of beads against the vastness of the desert. The plains rolled
away in amber and black, boundless sand-sheets, dune-fields,
interminable regs of limestone pebbledash strung with clinkers
of metallic stone and scattered with grotesque nodes of petrified sand like knots of intestine. Truman recognized them as
fulgarites – the terrestrial incarnation of lightning bolts that had
struck the earth and fused the sand-grains together in their own
image.

Once the plateau had disappeared into the sand mist behind
them, it was as if the little party of men and animals had been
cast adrift in an ocean of terrifying dimensions, where the raw
powers of nature held sway. They never halted voluntarily during
the day, not even to drink, for the camels were carrying their
maximum capacity, and if their progress was halted for a few
minutes, they would sit down and roll over on their packs. Inevitably, though, there were enforced halts as a camel broke his
headrope or another went berserk and tried to throw his load.
The sacks came undone and littered salt-blocks into the sand, or
rubbed against an animal's flanks, causing a tumour that had to
be doused with oil. Every time it happened Truman and Khyar

had to work with lightning speed to put the problem right before the camels sat down.

Once, when a sack had to be restitched, the animals rolled, roaring, in the sand, scraping the heavy loads from their backs, snapping headropes and splintering the wooden saddles. That meant a whole morning's delay, while Khyar and Truman patiently re-roped the animals, then dragged each load clear, dismantled the assembly, repaired the saddles as best they could, stitched up the bags, resaddled each animal and – most arduous of all – reloaded each with the two huge sacks of salt. It was ceaseless work on parched throats and empty stomachs, and Truman soon began to understand why the salt-road was considered such a challenge, even by veteran desert men like Khyar.

There was no respite. On and on they walked, shivering in the eye of a whirlblast wind that cast drifting gravel in their faces, hearing only the maddening sea-sound of sand rasping on sand, like subliminal voices echoing in the bare chambers of their minds. At first Truman was stunned by the sheer hostility of the desert. Travelling like this, carrying their own small world on camels' backs, was quite different from the cosy life of the camp near Siwa oasis.

For Truman those first days were a marathon of pain – the endless physical effort, the dull ache of thirst in his kidneys, the roughness of dust in his throat, the keen edge of the wind, the alternate strobing buffets of cold and heat. He had to be constantly on his guard, for as Yani had told him, Maliq would lunge at him unexpectedly, trying to knock him down with his heavy skull. Soon, Truman learned to predict the attacks by the sudden snuffling and blubbering noises that preceded them, but often it seemed to him that every minute was an epic struggle against Titans. He was determined from the beginning to do what his companion did, but if Yani had been a hard master, Khyar was a tyrant. Nothing Truman did was right. When they halted the camels on the first night after an exhausting day's trek, and Truman moved gratefully towards the waterbag, the Saghrani barred his way.

'No water until after the camels are fed,' he ordered. 'The *bil* always come first.'

'OK, Khyar,' Truman said. 'But you realize we haven't drunk since before sunrise.'

'Stop your Outlands whining,' Khyar sneered at him. 'By the Sacred Ancestors, don't you know your life depends on the *bil*? They must be looked after whatever happens.'

Before the camels could be fed, though, there were a dozen tasks to complete. First the great salt-loads had to be carefully unloaded, then each animal had to be hobbled twice, once standing and once kneeling. Tying the foreleg hobbles was a task Truman didn't relish. It meant squatting under the beasts' bellies in full range of their powerful back legs – a single kick could have broken his neck. It seemed to take Truman forever to hobble just one camel, dodging the jerking, stamping limbs and the jets of urine the animals staled whenever they halted. Khyar had long finished hobbling his half of the caravan while Truman was still on his second or third beast.

The Saghrani would scoff at him. 'You'll never get to drink at this rate,' he would say. 'By the time you've finished, it will be sunrise and time to go.'

Then it was feeding time, and another painstaking chore of measuring out sorghum grain in a pot and doling it out equally into sixteen nose-bags. The task Truman savoured the least of all was removing the muzzle from the beasts one at a time and replacing it with the nosebag. The instant the muzzle came off, they would go berserk, spitting, vomiting bile and hustling up on their haunches. On the first night Truman tried five times to fit Maliq's nose-bag, only to have it tossed into the sand and the grain spilt. Khyar exploded with rage and rushed over. 'You afterbirth of a mangy she-camel!' he yelled. 'Every grain is priceless! Do you think we can afford to scatter it in the desert?' He made Truman scrabble in the sand and retrieve it grain by grain.

Finally, when all the camels were chomping on their sorghum, it was time for the first drink of the day. It was never rushed. Khyar would unlace a waterbag and fill a gourd with ritual

163

solemnity. He would set the gourd on the ground, retie the dripper, then pass the vessel to Truman with both hands.

'This is the water of the Kel,' he would intone. 'Drink in the name of the Light Mother.'

Truman would take the gourd, mutter the ritual words. 'The Light Mother be blest,' as Khyar had instructed him, and drink squatting on his haunches. He would drink exactly half the gourdful and then pass it back to his companion, who drank gravely after reciting the ancient formula. One gourd was all they drank and it was never enough to satisfy the terrible thirst that had built up through the day's exertions. Truman guessed his companion was as thirsty as himself, yet the Saghrani never once suggested that they should drink more. 'Water is life in the *Mufarida,*' he would mumble through parched lips. '*Bil* first, water second.'

Khyar would light a fire with a spark made by flint on steel, and cook sorghum porridge on smoky camels' dung. They ate it squatting around the pot with their hands. The porridge was so sour that Truman gagged as he ate, despite his hunger, and anyway the dryness in his mouth prevented him from making a good meal. Afterwards they would lie down on the cold sand under their pathetic rags, but it was too cold to sleep properly, and in any case the camels kept them awake. In the snatches of sleep Truman managed to grab, he would dream of Jamila, always hovering before him, watching, smiling, but just beyond his reach. He and Khyar never talked about Jamila, but once as Truman lay awake with his teeth chattering, he heard Khyar whisper the name 'Ossama' over and over in his sleep.

During waking hours, the Saghrani was reserved, aloof and silent, and Truman felt reluctant to talk to him for the Saghrani would twist everything he said to emphasize his ignorance. Occasionally though, Truman would try to establish some kind of bond between them, no matter how tentative.

'You and I are the same in a way,' he told Khyar one morning.

'Light Mother's wrath!' the Saghrani said. 'We're as different as the east and the west. How so?'

'Your father died when you were small,' Truman said. 'So did mine. He was killed climbing a mountain.'

Khyar snorted to himself. 'My father was a Burrower. One of the men who keeps the qanat in order. The warriors laugh at the Burrowers behind their backs, but without them there'd be no water at Tarout at all. They don't realize how brave you have to be – going into that old shaft day after day, knowing it's going to fall in sometime for certain. I have never heard of a single Burrower who died in his bed. I should have grown up to be one myself, but I was too young when my father died, and my elder brother . . . well he . . . no longer exists. I was adopted by a warrior family and brought up to fight, but they still made fun of me and called me ''the Mole''. Until I passed the *tafriq,* anyway.'

'What is this *tafriq?*' Truman asked.

In answer the Saghrani whipped off his robes displaying a torso so lean the muscles stood out like ropes. He turned his back on Truman and showed him the long whip-scars that traversed his body from shoulder to buttocks. 'That is the mark of the *tafriq.*'

Truman gasped. 'What the hell did they do to you? Looks like you were lashed with a whip.'

'It's a warrior's sign,' Khyar said. 'If you don't have it, you're not a man among the Kel. You will never be a man, Outsider.'

Before first light they would get up, have a drink of tainted water, and begin the marathon task of loading the sixteen camels. As Truman became hungrier and thirstier, the first task of the day loomed over him ominously all night. Often, as they strained on empty bellies to lift the huge bags, he would feel his head spinning and would stagger blindly about for a moment while Khyar fumed and showered him with abuse. At times Truman was filled with fury and longed to hit out at the Saghrani, but he stopped himself from retaliating. He knew that alone in the Funeral Plains he would be overwhelmed by their hugeness, and he also knew that for all his bluster Khyar could not

165

take the caravan on without him. The two of them were trapped in this together and both knew there was no escape. As soon as the camels were loaded, they were urged up, and the caravan would move off, into the pitiless, unending skirmish of the day.

The passage of time was marked only by the slow parabola of the sun as it rose and fell. Sometimes it seemed to Truman that this journey had no beginning and no end. As the days went by, though, the pain began to recede, and Truman started to take a perverse pleasure in the new rhythm of his existence. Often he felt that he had walked right through the pain threshold and could go on forever, mesmerized by the blinding light of the horizon, the crunch of the camels' feet, the occasional musical clink of stones, the swash of water in the drippers. There was a silence here in the deep desert that he had never experienced before, a sense that they were drifting along on an ocean of eternal tranquility. Everything else he had done in his life shrank to obscurity beside the task of getting this salt to the oasis. The palladium was meaningless to him, and he cackled with laughter when he thought of what had brought him here.

One morning – it must have been five or six days into the journey, Truman thought – the day dawned grey and still. There was a brooding silence to the desert that made his belly crawl. The sky was dark but cloudless, and Truman could almost feel the build-up of pressure against his sensitized skin. On the horizon there was a slow, almost imperceptible thickening of dust. As the moments passed the grey stripe on the skyline built up into a band of translucent redness, expanding faster and faster, its edges mottled black trails like wispy tentacles. Suddenly there was a crack of wind like a thunderclap that set Truman's teeth on edge, and made the camels roar. Khyar rushed to the head of the caravan, his face muffled, his tattered burnoose flying. Truman scanned the horizon again and saw that the redness had become a wall of dust, small from where he was, but close up perhaps hundreds of feet high, a million whirling vortices of sand spinning towards them like fire.

166

'The Greater Sandtides!' Khyar exclaimed, and there was a tremor in his voice. 'They've started. Light Mother's wrath, you think it's been hard until now, Outsider? I tell you, that was the easy part.'

27

THE SANDTIDE HIT THEM AT MID-MORNING as they tramped
through a field of giant dunes. It struck with the power of
a tsunami, so fast that the lead camels were spun around and
Truman was knocked off his feet. He had seen sandstorms before
at Siwa, but nothing like this. The storm had built up over the
southlands, whipping up everything in its path, feeding its energy
until it was racing at hundreds of miles an hour in whirling
vortices like thrashing columns of smoke. The noise was terrifying – a million famished banshees wailing and screeching in
chorus, a billion untuned bagpipes droning a funeral dirge.

For a moment Truman felt like a straw in the path of a hurri-
cane, helpless in the grip of inconceivably powerful forces. When
he groped to his feet, there was grit and dust in his eyes, and
the camels were already spreadeagling themselves in the sand,
shattering their saddles and casting their loads. Khyar raced
towards him, his distorted face a horror-mask of alarm, his ragged
robes flying. 'Hobble them,' he screamed. 'Double-hobble them,
or we'll lose them all.'

He dragged the mess of knee-hobbling loops from Maliq's
back, thrust half of them at Truman, and they both staggered
from animal to animal, grovelling in the sand, digging tunnels
under the animals' legs, fighting against the spirals of dust that
lashed around them, dodging the darting heads and chomping

168

jaws. When the beasts were secured, they dragged the fallen loads free and piled some of them up into a makeshift shelter against the wind. Anything that wasn't tied to the saddles was instantly whisked away. Visibility was down to a few metres and the sandtide was clawing at them, scourging their bodies with tentacles of dust. The earth seemed to rumble beneath them, and for a moment Truman could have sworn it was laughing. Khyar threw himself behind the pile of salt-sacks and covered himself with his blanket.

Truman hesitated for a moment, then hurled himself down beside his companion. 'What the hell do we do?' he yelled in Khyar's ear.

'Nothing,' the youth growled at him. 'We can't fight the sand-tides. Wait and pray.'

'But it might blow for days,' Truman roared.

'Everything is in the hands of the Great Mother,' Khyar yelled. 'She gives life and takes it away. You and I are nothing, no more than a breath of wind across the erg. What's the matter, Outsider? Scared?'

'Yes,' Truman said, almost to himself. 'Bloody right.'

He pulled a torn bit of rug over him and lay there smelling the sand, assaulted on all sides by the roar and growl of the wind.

How long they lay there, Truman didn't know. Time was a void filled only by the shuddering demonic voices of the storm that numbed his senses as if he were encased in cotton wool. He was starving and there was the squeeze of thirst in his belly, but he knew that to try and eat or drink in this holocaust would be unthinkable. Sometimes he laughed dementedly to himself at their impotence, and often he found himself drifting into oblivion and was brought back by an involuntarily jerking of the muscles as his conscious soul pulled itself violently from the brink of the dark abyss. There were times, though, when he lost contact with his senses, when his mind drifted in a blessedly silent limbo, when Jamila appeared to him, smiling. Once, the vision was interrupted by a swirl of flames out of nowhere, that licked at

Jamila like tongues, ravaging her until she became the dismembered bleached bones of a skeleton. Truman saw other bags of bones lying out on the silent erg – the bones of two men and a string of camels, long ago abandoned by the storm, the forlorn relics of forgotten lives, forgotten conflicts rendered meaningless by the crushing weight of infinity.

All day and all night the storm thundered, but when the dawn came once again it had passed, leaving only snakes of dust and spin-devils in its wake. The day was grey and sallow, the sky white as alabaster with the remnants of ochreous dust-clouds obscuring the sun. They dug themselves out from under hillocks of loose sand and listened to the silence. It was like the end of a war, Truman thought – the whole landscape seemed to have been rearranged, the sand turned over and washed with new colours. The camels were still there, half buried, and Truman's first thought was water. The pain of thirst was a cancer in his body and he fought it back as Khyar examined the waterbags gloomily.

When he looked up his sand-caked, swollen face was grim. 'All gone,' he said without emotion. 'The wind sucked the water away. We have nothing left. The Light Mother help us.' He eyed Truman stoically. 'We were unlucky. That was the Father of Storms – we call it "the Dragon" – when the whole earth comes alive. The Dragon is the creature of the Dark Mother, the bringer of death. We were accursed from the beginning, and as the Saghrana say "the accursed stays accursed though you hang a lamp upon him".'

Truman tried to speak, but his throat was clogged with grit and his tongue stuck to his palate. He shook his head and turned away.

'Come on,' Khyar said slowly, standing up, trying to brush sand off his tattered robes. 'Let's dig the *bil* out.'

Truman found his voice suddenly. 'You mean we're going on?' Khyar shrugged. 'What else? We may not have water, but we still have the *bil*.'

Truman scraped sand out of his hair. 'How many more days is it to the oasis?' he demanded.

'Six, maybe seven. We're a bit more than half way.'

'We can't go for six days without water. We're dying of thirst now.'

'Have faith, Outsider. The Light Mother will provide.'

He knelt in the sand by Maliq and began digging the beast out of the sand with his hands. The camel let out a piteous, half-hearted groan – the Dragon had leached the fight out of even the bad tempered caravan-leader, Truman realized. He dropped down on his knees to help the Saghrani.

It seemed an age before they got all the camels out, and when they had reached the end of the line they plumped down, shattered.

'How the hell are we going to lift those sacks?' Truman muttered, through cracked lips. Khyar said nothing, but lurched to his feet, 'Come on,' he said gruffly.

Then he froze, staring out across the desolate cream and grey paddled surface of the dunes. Truman knelt and looked too. There, not more than a few hundred metres away, mounted figures were loping towards them on fast camels, four dark-shrouded, hooded sandriders, hanging together in the blasted landscape like a patrol of flies.

'Thank God,' Truman said, jumping up, 'We're saved.'

Khyar didn't move. Truman strained his eyes towards the encroaching riders and felt a pang of fear. There was something menacing about their hooded forms that set a subliminal alarm bell ringing.

'What is it?' he demanded. 'Who are those guys?'

'Gharana,' Khyar said. 'The demons are upon us!'

28

KHYAR DASHED TO THEIR MAKESHIFT SHELTER and scrabbled frantically in the sand for his rifle and sabre. Truman stood rooted to the spot, watching the dark riders come closer. They began to fan out in open formation, and Truman heard the shuffle of the camels' feet as they trotted. There were cracks of musketry and bullets thumped into the sand around him. The old rifle was in Khyar's hands now, and the Saghrani was working the bolt. Truman saw him aim at the nearest rider, and heard the dull click as the weapon misfired. It had been his only chance, and an instant later the dark riders were on him with scimitars flashing.

To Truman he was watching an act in a play, unfolding in slow-motion. He heard Khyar's cry of frustration and saw him drop the rifle and draw his blade. There was the crisp ring of steel on steel as he locked swords with the first rider, then a second dropped effortlessly from the saddle and began to rain blows on the Saghrani from behind. Khyar swivelled and fought back with obstinate determination, parrying, thrusting and cutting, but the first rider jumped down, forcing him to fight on two sides. For a second it seemed as if Khyar would hold them both at bay, then suddenly one of the swordsmen pressed through his guard and skewered him in the thigh. For an instant Khyar let his blade fall and the other cut him twice or three times across the head and shoulder. Truman heard the Saghrani moan as

172

he fell, his head covered in blood and his leg pumping gore.

Truman jerked his gaze away to see the gaping jaws of a camel, a flutter of black robes, a black vacancy where a face should have been, and a curved sword raised almost on top of him. The blade swished past his ear, and he began to run up the slip-face of the nearest dune, finding his bare feet sinking into soft sand. He was aware of his pursuer behind him and his legs worked like pistons, drawing on energy he didn't know he still possessed. Higher and higher he climbed, panting, gasping for breath, expecting any minute to feel the slice of the sabre down his back. Gunshots snapped out and rounds hummed around him like bluebottles. He looked back to see that the rider had halted below, his camel shying from the soft sand. Another bullet whipped over his head, but an instant later he was over the knife-edged peak of the dune and flinging himself down in the shelter of the other side. For minutes he lay there, wheezing for breath, wondering if the raiders would come after him. Then he turned on his stomach, crawled to the dune-peak and peeped over.

The four dark riders were several hundred feet below him, and they had dismissed him, it seemed. They had dismounted now, and were working methodically, getting Khyar's sixteen camels to their feet one by one. The Saghrani still lay where he'd fallen in a soak of blood, and Truman couldn't tell whether he was dead or not. The raiders slung the camels together expertly, and seconds later they were mounting their own beasts. Each of them carried two big skins of water, Truman noticed – the gurgle of the liquid as the camels rose came to his ears from below, unnaturally loud. One of the riders worked his mount towards the standing caravan and leaned down to pick up Maliq's headrope. There was a growl of protest from the big caravan leader, and then the train began to lumber off shakily after the raider, with the other men working along its length to keep the animals moving.

Truman watched, frozen, aware that these Gharana had just removed his only chance of survival. He looked on, digging his scarred and callused hands deep into the abrasive sand, as the caravan dipped behind a dune and disappeared. As soon as they were gone, he slithered down the dune slope. The pathetic shelter of salt bags where they'd ridden out the storm was still there, with scraps of broken saddles and harnesses scattered about. Khyar lay nearby, his face and clothes soaked crimson and his gashed leg still spurting blood. Truman tore off his own head-cloth, ripped back the Saghrani's trousers, and pressed the cloth in a pad over the thigh slash. He held the pad tight with his right hand and examined the cuts on Khyar's head and shoulders. The blade had bitten furrows across his skull and another across his right clavicle, through the cloth of the burnoose. There were cloth fibres stuck in the shoulder wound, and Truman feared it would get infected, though neither this nor the head-wounds was deep.

Khyar's eyelids fluttered. 'Outsider,' he whispered. 'Did they take the camels?'

Truman grinned through cracked lips in relief at seeing him alive. 'They took the lot,' he rasped. 'But don't worry about that. Lie still or you'll bleed to death.'

He tied the cloth as tightly as possible around Khyar's thigh and lifted his feet on to one of the half-buried salt-sacks. The Saghrani gasped and tensed with pain.

'You'll be all right if you just lie still,' Truman said. 'Thank your Light Mother it's not a gunshot wound. It's a clean cut and all we have to do is stop the bleeding. The wounds on your head and shoulders look bad but they aren't serious. Those guys must've forgotten the sharpening stone. You're going to survive.'

'I can't walk,' Khyar said, his voice quivering with anguish. 'How am I going get the camels back?'

Truman smiled grimly. 'You're not,' he said. 'Forget it.'

'We have no water,' the Saghrani groaned. 'Without the *bil* we'll be dead by tomorrow.'

'Didn't you say the Light Mother would provide?'

'Yes, but. . .'

'Then she will provide,' Truman said.

 174

Khyar gritted his teeth, looking like some B-movie Franken-
stein with his bloody leg and head, and his sand-caked, distorted
face. 'The Great Mother gives and the Great Mother takes away.
Why did she give me a useless Outsider for a companion? You
stood there – *stood there* frozen to the spot, and let me fight
alone. What kind of louse are you?'

'A live one,' Truman said. 'Anyway, you had all the weapons.'

He ripped off a length of the bloody headcloth, and pulled
Khyar's hand down on the tightly-bound thigh-pad. 'Keep your
hand there,' he told Khyar, 'and don't let it come loose.' He
began to clean up the head and shoulder wounds with the remains
of the rag.

The chips were well and truly down, Truman thought, and
suddenly he felt suffused with a desperate new strength. He
swallowed, feeling the grit and the mucus under his tongue.
'*They* have water,' he said, nodding in the direction the raiders
had gone. 'Plenty of it.'

Khyar tried to laugh, but his larynx flapped aridly. 'They are
Gharana warriors,' he whispered. 'Four of them.'

'I know that,' Truman said. 'I can count. So what?'

'So you will never get it.'

Truman stood up and scanned the wall of dunes which had
swallowed up the enemy. He knew what he had to do.

'Yes I will.'

There was silence for a moment, and Truman knew he was
committed. He was hanging on to life by a thread, but he
wouldn't wait for it to break – he would fight back. Khyar looked
at him with mockery in his sunken eyes.

'You?' he grunted. 'You streak of camel's piss! You stood
there and let them down me, and now you're going to take water
from the Gharana?'

'It's that or the Light Mother's mercy,' Truman said.

Khyar licked his skinless lips with a dry tongue. 'I know those
demons,' he said. 'They'll go to ground somewhere close and
slaughter the weakest of the camels to eat. The fiends can't
control their appetites. If I could walk I could do it. Four against

one aren't impossible odds for a Saghrani warrior. But you –
you'll never do it.'

Truman turned away and picked up Khyar's fallen rifle. It was
a Martini-Henry ten-shot, and he reckoned it was at least a hundred years old. He opened the bolt and ejected the cartridge that
had misfired. The breech was undamaged and the firing pin was
intact, but it was clogged with sand.

'That was a faulty cartridge,' he said. 'Have you got any better
ammunition?'

Khyar nodded to a saddle-bag, where Truman found a bando-
lier of bullets. He slung it over his shoulder, then picked up
Khyar's sabre and belt. He rammed the blade into its scabbard
and slung that over the other shoulder. Khyar watched him curiously through dim, bloodshot eyes.

'I'll be back,' Truman said. 'Think you can hold out till then?
If you try to walk you'll start the bleeding off again and you'll
die quickly. Don't move a muscle.'

Khyar turned his head away. 'You're a liar,' he said.' You're
abandoning me.'

Truman eyed his companion wearily. 'Let me tell you something, Khyar. You said I have no name. Well I do have one. I'm
not a Saghrani, maybe, but I am an Englishman. I am Sir Daniel
Truman-Keynes, and my ancestors fought with Richard the
Lionheart.'

It was the first time since childhood, he realized, that he had
used his full name. Khyar watched him, blinking suspiciously.
Truman stood up straight and brushed sand from his mouth.
'Perhaps you've forgotten the water-pact,' he said. 'But I haven't.
Besides, I don't have to drink water and go through hocus-pocus
with someone to know that you don't dump your companion
when the going gets rough – not even a bad-tempered son-of-a-
bitch like you, Khyar. Like I said, *I'll be back.*' He left the
Saghrani staring up at him speechlessly, and began to cast about
for the raiders' tracks.

176

29

THE STORM HAD WASHED THE SANDS clean and stippled them into an amber quilt, and Truman found the tracks of the marauders almost at once, a swath of flat pad-marks as wide as a stream. As long as they stayed on the erg, he told himself, tracking them would be simple even for a man with his rudimentary skill. He glanced back at the camp once and saw that it was no more than a faint blemish on the desert's crust. He prayed that Khyar was right, that the raiders would halt within a few kilometres, otherwise he would just keep walking until he dropped with exhaustion, and death would overtake him like a shadow. He was near to it now, he knew – already dangerously dehydrated – and as he walked he tried to swallow, to generate some saliva, no matter how little, to ease his parched tongue and throat. The pain in his kidneys was so acute that he walked stooped over, his breath rasping from the parchment dryness of his lungs.

Now the wind had passed the day was still and hot, and he felt his body like a pincushion weeping vapour through every pore. He remembered the corpse of Harris – the discovery that had set this whole chain of events in motion – the grim death rictus, the *papier mache* skin stuck on the bones, the way the big man's corpse had felt featherlight without its moisture. No, he told himself, he wouldn't end up like Harris.

The will to survive at any cost gripped him, and the death visions were obliterated by images of water – cool cascades of meltwater gurgling down the mountainsides after the snow, frothing Niagaras plunging into ravines, lazy streams meandering through meadows, water spritzing from ornamental fountains in beams of light, water slopping from well-buckets, sloshing in fat waterskins, glugging from cups and gourds and bottles, running in icy ribbles down his face. He had to get water whatever happened, and he knew he would tear, shred, rip apart anything or anyone that stood in his way. The singularity of his focus drove all doubt from his mind. He was a being on the verge of extinction, on the very edge of darkness, and he had one purpose – to get water, to live. As he marched, driving his body onwards, he felt himself slipping further and further beyond the barrier of ordinary reality.

The sky was scabrous with white cloudflakes, and the dunes rose and fell before him like figures in a child's picturebook, congeries of interlocking akle in pastels of pink and apricot, lone terracotta crescents like fins, confectionery slices with icing-sugar dressings of peppermint cream and powder blue. Every step was an agony, yet he willed himself on with gritted teeth, following the raiders' trail as it wandered between the dunes, never ascending the slip-faces but always remaining on the flat carpet of dune-bedding beneath.

He could not tell if hours passed or only minutes. Even the sun seemed to stand still. The sky was a fragment of granite, blue-white, traversed by veins of darker blue, washed with shadow-shapes that suggested abstract images and objects. Many visions came into his head – of Jamila, of his childhood at Trad's Mill, of his schooldays, of his time at Siwa. He saw Johnny running to school, little legs pumping, blonde hair flying, over and over like a constantly repeated film-loop. There were rich scents on the air it seemed – smells of coffee, of tanned leather, of cinnamon and mint that evoked a host of memories as real to him as the sand and the sky. Once he sniffed the distinct smell of firesmoke, and dismissed it as another hallucination. Yet the smell lingered, pungent against the clean scents of brimstone and flint, and he halted, panting, and scanned the dunes around him. Not far off, beyond the skirts of an orthagonal dune, a wire of pure black smoke rose into the pale sky. This was no vision, he realised suddenly. It was *them* and *they* had water.

He put a finger to his parched lips. 'Shush now Johnny,' he whispered, 'or they'll hear you.'

He tensed and fell on one knee, bringing Khyar's old Martini-Henry into his hands. His shaky fingers fumbled with the bolt and slid a round into the breech. Then he made for the base of the dune at a stumbling monkey-run. He felt safer with his face pressed close to the abrasive surface of the dune, and for an instant he listened, sniffing the air. He heard no voices, and was gripped by fear that the raiders had already had their meal and moved on. Then he smelt the aroma of grilled meat, almost sickening in its succulence, and knew they were still there. He slung the rifle back on his shoulder and began to wriggle up the steep dune, writhing like a lizard, stopping every few moments to cock his ear. Soon he heard raucous voices raised so loudly that it was clear the men hadn't heard him. He continued up to the peak – a smudged and blunted sandridge – and peered over cautiously.

The Gharana bandits were there, much nearer than he'd expected – no more than thirty metres below – sitting on a flat shelf of sand between the horns of a perfect crescent. The four dark-clad figures sat round a smouldering camel-dung fire with their rifles near them, guzzling hanks of half-cooked meat. Not far away one of Khyar's camels knelt in a pool of congealing blood, its crane-like head lowered into the sand and its eyes shut. Its neck had been almost severed, and joints of meat had been sliced off its shanks. The rest of the Saghrana camels were couched in a tight squad and looked subdued and exhausted, while the raiders' mounts were standing, unhobbled, tussling over a mound of grain that had been poured on a leather sheet. They had been unloaded and their four saddles stood behind the men, each carrying the weight of two bulging drippers. Acid

179

burned in Truman's throat as his eyes riveted on the waterbags. He tore his gaze away and stared, almost fainting, as the four raiders passed around them a large enamel bowl full of water. Truman could nearly taste it.

When he'd first seen them the Gharana had looked faceless, but now he realized that they were wearing full face veils that hid their eyes, and they ate and drank under the veils without removing them. They were speaking the same dialect as the Saghrana, chuckling with laughter. 'Do you realize who that was?' one of them was saying. 'I recognized him at once. Same face, but a bit younger and lighter-built. If it wasn't for the scar it could almost be him.'

'Dark Mother's wrath! Wait till we tell the old man about this.'

'Maybe we should have finished him off.'

'No, Goloi wouldn't have wanted his blood on our hands. We're not demons like the Saghrana.'

'The thirst will get him anyway.'

'But what about the other one – the one that ran away?'

'I never saw a Saghrani who ran away.'

'That was no Saghrani. That was a slave or some wretch being sent to the oasis.'

'Whatever he was, he wasn't worth the trouble of killing. He won't get far.' Truman heard their words but didn't listen to them. To him the men were now no more than obstacles to be taken out. He guided the rifle carefully into his shoulder. He didn't remember having fired one since he'd been in the cadets at Sherbourne, but he seemed to know what he was doing. He felt detached, aloof from his body. He took the first pressure on the trigger, wondering what he would do if the weapon misfired again. Suddenly, one of the men belched massively and got up. He picked up his rifle and strode away from the fire directly towards Truman, a big-framed man in a hooded black cloak. About ten metres away he squatted down and began to urinate.

Truman took the man in his sights, gulped a breath, held it, and squeezed. There was a dull click as the firing-pin struck a dud round. The squatting man stiffened, stood and looked upwards questioningly. The other three stopped eating and began to raise themselves, scanning the dune tops. Truman squeezed the trigger again in desperation and there was a searing crack and a blurt of fire from the old gun's muzzle. The big man nearest him clutched at his chest as if he had been punched, dropped his rifle and scrabbled in the air with the other hand. He toppled over into the sand. The others were already up and bringing their rifles to bear, but Truman cast his gun aside and gripped Khyar's sabre – a curved razor-edged blade with a cross-piece hilt.

The instant he had the weapon in his hand he felt different – a primitive power filled his body from some unknown, untapped source. He leaped headlong down the dune, screaming blood-curdling animal sounds, towards the three men. He realized only later that he should have been a sitting duck, but the shots cracked harmlessly round his feet. In a moment he was on them with blood in his mouth, and possessed by a demon. He fought like a fury, slashing, cutting, thrusting, stabbing, chopping, smashing, severing flesh. He hardly felt resistance or sensed the clash of steel on steel. His mind was a hawk's red eye with only one purpose – to kill.

It was over in less than a minute, and two more of the raiders lay dead on the desert floor. For an instant Truman continued to hack at the lifeless corpses with his blade, howling like a dog. He only stopped when he realized the third raider was racing for his camel. Truman leapt after him, roaring, and for a second the man faced him, bringing his sword down with a crashing blow. Truman parried it with such force that the Gharani's blade shattered into shards. He cut to the warrior's face, slicing a scarlet canyon diagonally across his cheek, mouth and jaw. The man turned and leapt onto the neck of his camel, flipping on to its back as the animal roared and burst into a gallop. Truman flung his bloody sabre after him, and collapsed in a heap, struggling for breath.

Almost at once he thought of water. He pulled himself upright and staggered towards the water bags, picked up the water-bowl

181

that was now lying in the sand, and slumped down next to one of the drippers. He untied the skin with quaking hands and let the water splash into the bowl. It was brown and tainted with leather and tar, but to Truman it looked and smelt as if it had gushed from a mountain spring. He was tempted to swallow the entire bowl in one long, blissful drink. But caution stopped him. Instead, he dipped his hands in the water and splashed it on his face, washing off some of the blood caked there. Finally, he poured a very little – a few drops – on his parched lips. He closed his eyes in ecstasy, worked the trickle of moisture into his mouth, and almost instantly there was a modicum of relief.

He remembered how Hafid had done it after the Saghrana had picked him up. He tore a strip of cloth from his sleeve, doused it in the bowl and began to suck it avidly. The liquid began to revive him and he sat there in oblivion, sucking drops from the cloth, feeling strength and life return to his body. He realized he'd been cut in the shoulder and the side and was bleeding, but he felt no real pain yet, so he ignored the wounds. The corpses of the men he had killed grew almost imperceptibly stiffer, the blood began to dry, the camels shifted and growled. Truman felt no remorse for what he had done.

Suddenly he remembered Khyar – he had promised to return, and the Saghrani was lying out in the desert wounded, dying of thirst. Painfully, he stood up. His mind had become remarkably clear again, and he knew he would have to take everything – the camels, the food and water – and find his way back to the Saghrani in time to save his life. He grunted to himself, shambled over to the Gharana camels, and began to couch and load them methodically, one by one.

30

THE PLACE WAS CALLED *Chez Anton,* and the delicious smell of baking bread and pastries wafted into the Holborn street outside. Whitehaven reckoned they had a special fan designed to blow the enticing smells to the nostrils of the passers-by. The front part of the shop was a French Patisserie where aloof-looking girls in spotless white hats and overalls picked freshly-made cakes out of glass-fronted cases with tongs, or served customers with crusty baguettes. At the back, though, was an exclusive coffee-scented salon – oak tables in discreet alcoves, burgundy velvet upholstery, antique pictures, and formidable black-coated waiters who looked at Whitehaven as though he'd mistaken the place for Oxfam. Whitehaven ignored the looks and asked for Morgan. A waiter motioned with half-closed eyes and a bored expression to an alcove in a corner.

Morgan didn't rise to greet him, but looked up moodily from over a cup of tea and nodded at the chair opposite. Whitehaven doffed his parka, hung it on one of the chair's horns and sat down. Morgan examined the old coat with distaste. Whitehaven brought a buff padded envelope out of the parka pocket and laid it in front of him.

'What is it?' Morgan inquired, with a look as bored at the waiter's.

'A naughty video,' Whitehaven said, getting out his pipe and a tin of Erinmore mixture. 'Sorry Hugh, not bums and tits, but Sergei Rybakov talking to Marcus Rand over a secure satellite link. Only it wasn't secure. Our Cousins picked it up and passed it to me. Always make you feel like the poor bloody relation these days.'

Morgan drank tea, holding the handle of the china cup between thumb and forefinger with the little finger extended. Whitehaven supposed that was what they taught you at Eton. That and the necessity of remaining poe-faced in every circumstance. Morgan was handsome in a deceptively rugged, mature sort of way. He was a couple of years older than Whitehaven, but had miraculously escaped the middle-age spread. His hair, once blonde, had turned steel grey, but it was all there, and his legs were still the legs of the rugby forward he'd been when he'd been a Blue at Cambridge. His skin was smooth and his teeth all his own, and though he smiled rarely, when he did it was almost intoxicating.

'And who is Rybakov, exactly?' Morgan inquired.

'Moscow wide-boy,' Whitehaven said. 'Ex-Spetznatz sergeant trained as a hitman by the KGB, and now committed to higher things. Pad in Kensington with a lovely wife called Ilena, and wall to wall cocaine. Pound to a pinch of peanuts he did Amersadiqi.'

'Ah, poor Amersadiqi,' Morgan said. 'I suppose we have to assume that you've been compromised. It was rather remiss of you to turn the samples in to the same lab Kortex uses.'

'It wasn't my choice, Hugh. The Office has been using Qurayshi's for years.' Whitehaven paused and decided abruptly on a counter-attack. 'What puzzles me is how you got Truman to hand the samples over to you. I mean, when I collared him he wouldn't play pussy at all.'

Morgan glanced at him sharply. 'Who said I got them from Truman?' he demanded. 'I never mentioned Truman, and I never told you to collar him.' Whitehaven stiffened at the implied criticism. He levered the lid off the Erinmore furiously with a five-pence coin.

'I may look like a baby's bum,' he said, 'but I didn't drop

 184

out of the stork's arse yesterday. Our noble Sir Daniel brought home the samples, so you must have got them from him.'

Morgan leaned back and forced himself to relax. 'Truman didn't bring the stuff back, actually. It came in a container, which was routinely searched by HM Customs. Some bright young spark of an excise officer thought the samples were out of place among a load of archeological relics and had them sent to us. You only need a thimbleful of dust to get a reading, so no one would have noticed any was gone.'

Whitehaven nodded sagely, not believing a word of it. Thin, he thought. Just too convenient. Morgan was trying to cover up for reasons best known to himself, but then in this set-up you never knew what game they were playing. MI6 were quite capable of working both ends against the middle, just like they had in Oman in the seventies, when Whitehaven had been a sprog trooper in the SAS Regiment. He remembered Atair Khawi, 1972 – the sudden mortar attack laid by the communist *adoo* on his patrol's sangar. It had come with such ferocity and precision that Moss and Reaves had been shredded instantly. Poor old Smoky Reaves, Whitehaven thought. Talk about caught with your pants down. The guy had been suffering from the Mahdi's Revenge and had left the shelter of the sangar for a much needed crap, with Billy Moss as his escort. He'd just assumed squat position when all hell was let loose. It had been a regimental joke for years afterwards.

Not for Rich Whitehaven, though. The shrapnel from the first salvo that had taken Reaves and his oppo had also demolished Whitehaven's left calf, severed his left testicle, and made his kneecap pop out like a champagne cork. He'd crawled into a defensive position and fought off the assault that followed alone, with a GPMG and a pack of morphine ampoules. A whole bloody day and a night he'd kept it up, until a Firqan patrol had pulled him out. The Firqan were locals – tribesmen from the nomad people of the Jebel, who had risked their lives to get to him. Three of them had copped it in the process. While they were carrying him down the jebel to Salalah later, he'd told their leader he'd never seen the commies execute an attack so brilliantly. The sheikh had chuckled. 'They were trained by you Brits.'

Whitehaven hadn't believed it then. It was only years later, after he'd been recruited by MI6, that he'd come across documents confirming that the British had trained insurgents in Oman. Their purpose was to bring down the Sultan, who was himself protected by British-trained and officered troops. MI6 had backed both sides, and had been directly responsible for the deaths of Moss and Reaves, and the three Firqan who'd come for him. Secretly, Whitehaven had never forgiven the Office for that, nor had he forgotten the bravery of those nomad tribesmen who'd swapped their lives for his.

'Thing is,' Whitehaven said, flashing Morgan a shrewd look, 'Rybakov and Rand both think he's working for us.'

Morgan snorted. 'No skin off my nose'.

Whitehaven tapped his own nose with the stem of his pipe. 'I've heard it rumoured Truman was with us in Beirut in the early eighties. I've been through his dossier, and it so happens there's a gap of two years in his CV during that time. Some coincidence, eh? There's nothing on record, but then it could have been Q-ops.'

Morgan gave a hollow chuckle. 'That's nonsense, Rich. Q-ops is an Office myth. As far as I know, Truman's just a field-man for Kortex – that is, if the Arabs haven't filed him under ''erase'' by now.' Whitehaven filled his pipe moodily and lit it with a Swan Vesta, thinking of Zinoviev, the third rate KGB clerk with a cherub's face and glasses like the bottoms of Coca Cola bottles, who'd come out of the cold five years before. He'd supplied no more than low grade intelligence, most of which the analysts had written off, and had died shortly after the debrief of a very public heart-attack while walking down the King's Road. Whitehaven had done the first couple of days of debriefing, putting the screws on him about the extent of mafiya involvement in the KGB. After a solid five hour stint the guy had suddenly cracked and wheezed. 'You think my organization is the only one penetrated by gangsters? Don't you know your own office is run by crooks out to fill their pockets? What do you think Q-ops is? Don't you know who's giving you your orders?'

Whitehaven had played along with it, pressing for details and names, but Zinoviev had evidently regretted his outburst. All he knew, he said, was that the Q-ops group had done a dirty deal with the Russian mafiya in Beirut in the eighties, and that the boss of Q-ops had been at Cambridge. Whitehaven hadn't taken it very seriously at the time. Zinoviev had been ready to reinvent the wheel to get himself accepted, and in any case, Whitehaven had been taken off the debrief the following day, and had hardly thought of him again. Until today.

For a moment his solid form was enveloped in whorls of smoke, and Morgan flapped it away with a hand. 'They should make this a smoke-free zone,' he said. 'Is it necessary, Rich?'

Whitehaven considered it carefully, but kept on smoking. Morgan was his boss and the type who'd been used to giving out orders since he'd been a kid, and having people jump to it. Whitehaven believed in according respect where it was due, and considered very little due to Morgan. Actually, he didn't know how the guy had survived as head of the Africa Desk. Everyone, even the old school tie, said he was a complete space-cadet, yet somehow he'd come unscathed through all the departmental shake-ups. There were rumours of friends in the highest quarters.

'Sorry, Hugh,' he said, not looking sorry in the least. 'Helps me introspect. You have to do something to ease the pressure.'

He puffed more smoke and Morgan coughed. *Let him bloody cough*, Whitehaven thought. *It's the nearest to danger he'll ever get.*

Morgan slid a white cup and saucer over to him. 'Care for a cup?' Whitehaven put a thumb over the end of his Falcon and slotted it back into the pocket of his corduroy waistcoat. He poured himself tea and gestured at Morgan's empty cup with the pot. Morgan made an open hand sign of refusal and Whitehaven tasted the tea and grimaced. 'Cold,' he said.

Morgan's mouth creased slightly at the ends. 'Well, you *were* ten minutes late. Shall I have Bertram bring some more?'

'It's OK,' Whitehaven said. 'Wets the whistle.'

Morgan lowered his eyes and tapped his fingers smartly on the buff packet in front of him. 'I take it they've come to an arrangement?'

Whitehaven's cup clinked in the saucer. 'Yeah,' he said. 'They're going in with guns blazing. Rybakov's committed his whole private army, and Rand's bringing in the plant. The op begins in the hot season.'

Morgan regarded him questioningly. 'This puts us in a bit of a quandary,' he said. 'If we don't do something, the mafiya are going to get their foot in the door and we can't have that. Not now the Sudan's an oil producer. If the Sudan goes down, then Egypt will follow, and Saudi Arabia might be next.'

Whitehaven watched him through narrowed eyes, wondering what the big deal was. 'Best to just tip off Khartoum, isn't it?'

Morgan swallowed and for a moment his eyes were furtive. 'We need to do that, and more than that if we're going to make sure some of the new oil money comes back our way. In the old days we'd have made a deal with them and sent in an SAS sabre squadron, but the old piggy-bank's empty as far as direct intervention goes. We're not fighting wars of decolonialization now, more's the pity.' He gazed at Whitehaven curiously for a moment. 'I might be able to arrange a planeload of modern kit though. Arm the nomads like we did in Oman in the seventies. We could heavy-drop it to them in a C130.'

Whitehaven snorted. 'A plane-load of goodies is damn all use without someone to show the natives where to stick them. What about one man? One measly Arabic-speaking SAS trooper?'

Morgan's eyes lit up suddenly and Whitehaven wondered what he'd said. 'You used to be SAS, Rich. How's your parachuting?'

Whitehaven blanched. 'Are you pulling my percy? I was as fit as a fiddle then. Old codger now – almost on a zimmer frame. Anyhow I haven't jumped in years.'

Morgan's eyes dimmed momentarily. 'As you so often say,

Rich, experience increases as your reflexes get slower. You got the MM in Oman didn't you? And you speak Arabic.'

Whitehaven pulled out his pipe and stuck it in his mouth. He squeezed his eyes and raised his chin aggressively, but when he spoke there was an ill-concealed warble of excitement in his voice. 'I'm not up on weapons,' he said. 'I'd need a refresher from the Small Arms School, Ordnance, and para retraining.'

Morgan smiled his engaging smile suddenly, and it was as if the room had lit up. The smile worried Whitehaven. Made him wonder what it was concealing.

'You reckon the Russians won't make their move till the hot season starts,' Morgan said. 'That gives you four months to get your act together. What more do you need? I'd have thought this was right up your street.'

Whitehaven scratched his thinning blonde hair and fought hard to retain his composure. Morgan was right, this *was* up his street. Ever since he'd been invalided out of Oman in the seventies he'd pined for the action, the danger, the adrenaline buzz of life on the edge. The shrapnel wound he'd copped in '72 had made him unfit to return to a sabre squadron, and instead he'd been retrained for 14 Int – the Intelligence Corps unit attached to the SAS. From there he'd been sideswiped into MI6, but though the work had been interesting, it had never lived up to his expectations. In reality it was a glorified office-job. For years he'd waited for the chance to get back into the field, and now it had come. Morgan was offering him the opportunity to do something positive, and he wasn't going to squander it. Whatever else happened, he was going to make damn sure that this time the nomads got a fair deal.

He watched Morgan poker-faced, eyes made deliberately blank. He realized he didn't want to give his boss any satisfaction. Maybe it was just because he was a *yar* and a Rupert, or maybe it was something else.

'We don't know anything about this tribe,' he said. 'Except that Truman may be with them, unless he's already dead. We don't even know for sure where they are. I can't just jump into the blue with a pile of arms and wait for them to turn up.'

Morgan waved a lazy finger at the waiter and made a writing motion on the palm of his hand. He sighed. 'That's your lookout, I'm afraid, Rich.'

'And if I do go in and there's an almighty cock-up, then it's written off as a private enterprise job and I'm expendable, right?'

The waiter brought the bill on a miniature basket and Morgan fished a ten pound note from his wallet. 'Eminently, Rich,' he said. 'Eminently. Look, I don't want to push you on this. It's your call. But either you jump, or you leave the poor buggers to fight it out themselves.'

He stood up and brushed down the front of his Savile Row navy mohair. 'And if you do decide to start running round in the blue, the first thing you can do is use that sodding pipe for firewood.'

THE SIX SANDRIDERS RODE IN SINGLE file, their camels jogging at a brisk walk along the corridors of quilted sand between the dunes. Their rifles were slung under-arm ready to be brought into action at a moment's notice, and their eyes under the anonymous black veils were alert, shifting constantly from the surface to the horizon and back again. The leader of the troop was riding a magnificent white camel, hung with woven saddle-bags whose tassels swung rhythmically in time to the animal's pace. His mottled burnoose fluttered like a flag behind him in the morning breeze. Suddenly he gestured to the left with his camel-stick and turned his mount sharply up the gentle windward slope of a dune. The other riders followed him silently, until he halted at the dune-crest and lowered his veil to scan the landscape.

As far as the eye could see there were ranges of pillow-dunes in spreading asymmetrical patterns, layered in successive shades of orange, ochre brown and rose pink, their knife-edge crests steaming with a mist of sand-spray. Between the dunes were long squares of patinated limestone reg as black as asphalt. The leader shaded his eyes against the tilting sun and sought the vanishing-point on the skyline. There, where earth blended imperceptibly with the heavens, he spied a long roil of smoke undulating like a giant worm across the whole breadth of the horizon.

'Light Mother's wrath,' he growled as the others pressed close to him on their camels. 'That's the Dragon brewing down there!'

'It's the second one in a week, Hafid,' the nearest of the masked men replied.

'If we turn back now we can ride it out as far as Ra'ul's Rock.'

Hafid Bin Slaym wiped dust from cracked lips with the back of his hand. He sent the other a reproachful glance, and turned back to the landscape, smelling the fire-ash on the air. 'If we go back now, Isham,' he said, 'then they're truly lost.'

'The Light Mother protect them,' the other said, 'but you know as well as I do that to push on through the storm would be futile. Our water is low and the *bil* are tired. We'd achieve nothing by losing ourselves.'

Isham was a black cameo – gleaming eyes under the hood behind the tight-furled veil. His camel snorted impatiently and shifted its feet and he dragged on the headrope, pulling up its head. 'It's twelve days since they left,' he said solemnly. 'The Light Mother is all-knowing, but the odds are they're already dead. These are hard times. Either the Dragon got them or the Gharana did. That's the price of sending an Outsider on the salt run.'

Hafid nodded bitterly, hearing the note of reproach in Isham's words. He was the one who'd suggested Khyar take an untried Outsider on the salt-road and it had turned into a disaster. The Kahina herself had been so angry that she'd retired into Half-Death. Hafid was one of the Ten Bravest, and considered himself an honourable man, but now he wasn't sure if his motive in mooting the scheme had been entirely laudable. Had it been to test the Outsider's mettle, or simply to wash his hands of an embarrassing situation? He prided himself on seeking the honourable in every man, but hadn't he known deep down that the Outsider would never make it back? He was loath to give up the search, knowing he would have to face the Kahina, but as *gom* leader he also had the lives of his men to consider. And

Isham was right – even if Khyar and the Outsider were alive, there was no chance of finding them in the Dragon.

He wheeled his camel round sharply. 'Come on, we must go back.'

'Stop!' a voice cut into his thoughts like a sabre and he looked back to see Darash, the youngest of the troop, pointing his camel-stick back over the undulating cells of sand.

'Hafid!' the young man shouted. 'There's something down there!'

Hafid turned his camel and moved it back to the dune crest. He scanned the surface again in the direction the boy was pointing and at first he saw nothing but a string of boulders straggling along the edge of a great dune. His gaze skated over them, then switched back for a second view. As his eyes adjusted he became increasingly certain they weren't boulders, but moving things – no less than an entire camel caravan, perhaps fifteen or twenty animals long.

'By the heavens!' he cried, wrestling with his nervous camel. 'Your eyes are sharp as a hawk's Darash. Is it Khyar?'

'It's too far to tell, Hafid.'

'Then we must get nearer.'

'But Hafid,' Isham cut in, 'the Dragon is coming. We can't make it to the caravan and back to Ra'ul's Rock before it strikes.'

Hafid pulled his camel's head back. 'Spirits of the Sacred Imenan go with us,' he said grimly.

$$\boxed{32}$$

THERE HAD BEEN MANY VOICES IN his head in those days –
Johnny's voice, his father's voice, and most of all, Khyar's
voice. The Saghrani, half-comatose, in a carrying frame on the
camel behind him, had become his alter-ego – a spectral presence
that cut through the others like a razor, advising, cajoling, guid-
ing, explaining – keeping him on the narrow path that led them
back. For so long now he and Khyar had created their own small
universe in the nothingness, relying only on each other, that the
Saghrani seemed part of him.

He had experienced many other illusions, too – the glitter of
water in dune troughs, the flitting of spectral caravans across his
path, the blink of cats' eyes out of the night. Khyar had told him
he was in the grip of *khof al-barr*, the 'desert horrors', and when
he looked up and saw the six dark ghosts wafting towards him
on camels, trailed by scarves of dust, he dismissed them as more
creations of his disturbed mind.

Hafid and his men pressed their camels around Truman, but
he looked through them as if they were insubstantial, urging the
caravan onwards. 'Outsider,' Hafid yelled, pulling off his veil.
'It's me.'

Truman didn't halt or even look at them until Hafid reached
across and jerked the camel's headrope, bringing the animal to
a standstill. Then the Outsider's feverish eyes turned towards him

resentfully, and Hafid saw that his face under the blood-stained headcloth, was a mass of sunburn and scars. His features looked dull and introspective, as if he'd been interrupted while communing with the spirits.

'Go away,' Truman muttered, his voice thick with mucus, 'the Dragon is coming.'

'Light Mother's wrath!' Isham said. 'These are Gharana camels. Look, hyena brands. Khyar must have taken them from the enemy.'

In the basket behind, Khyar stirred and raised his disfigured head with some effort.

'Khyar', Isham bawled, noticing him for the first time. 'Khyar's alive.'

'What kept you?' Khyar asked feebly.

'What kept *you?*' Hafid demanded, peering at Khyar's bloodless countenance. 'Where are you hurt?'

'Gharana devils,' Khyar swore. 'Came on us on the tail of the Dragon. Took the camels. We had no water. They left me for dead with wounds in the head and thigh.'

'The Light Mother be praised!' Hafid grunted. 'You mean you tracked them down and took the camels with wounds like that?'

'No,' Khyar said. 'It wasn't me – it was *him*. He went after them alone and got them back. He killed three Gharana and brought all the beasts – theirs and ours. I never believed it was possible.'

Hafid stared at him incredulously. 'The Outsider?' he said. '*He* did that?'

'That and more,' Khyar said. 'He brought us here. He roped up the whole caravan himself – did everything while I lay here helpless. He saved my life.' The riders pulled their veils down, staring at each other in disbelief.

'I have never heard such a story,' Isham said. 'An *Outsider?*'

'I don't call him Outsider any longer,' Khyar gasped. 'I call him Antara. You remember the hero Antara – who was despised as a slave, but who brought back all his family's camels from raiders alone?'

195

At that moment there was a long moan from Truman. As Hafid reached to intercept him, he slumped and tumbled out of his saddle into the sand.

33

TRUMAN DIDN'T RECALL THE REST OF the journey back to the plateau. He remembered only Hafid treating his wounds with herbal linament, the roar of the Dragon as the troop and their camels sheltered safely in the cave at Ra'ul's Rock, and then the crowds of Saghrana waiting for him inside the plateau – more than he'd ever dreamed lived there. After the loneliness of the desert the world seemed full of people, and his nostrils were assailed with the warm smells of human beings – of goats, cook-fires, damp tent-cloth, cured leather and grease. The smells were both welcoming and repellent after days in the almost scentless air. Ranks of hooded men on camels cavorted backwards and forwards, executing mock charges, waving their swords, firing shots over his head. Women and children trilled ululations, clapped hands rhythmically and danced, chanting '*Antara! Antara!*'

Truman rode through the onlookers half dazed. He knew Hafid had sent young Darash on ahead with the news, but he could scarcely believe this reception was for him. He scanned the tattooed female faces hoping for a glimpse of Jamila, but found her nowhere.

As they couched their camels by the Nazir's tent amid a cheer-ing crowd, the old man strode out in his brown and tan burnoose, with only his cordwood face uncovered. He threw his arms round

Truman and shook his hand. 'Welcome back!' he shouted. 'You have done the tribe great honour. The Light Mother be praised for your safe return.'

Truman looked on as a troop of warriors hustled away Khyar's mutilated body. He felt a sudden pang of loneliness. In the desert there had been only the two of them and now it was almost as if a limb was being amputated. 'Stop', he said, hustling over to the makeshift stretcher. 'Where are you taking him?'

Khyar heard and raised his ashen, mutilated face an inch or two. 'Don't be afraid, my friend,' he whispered. 'They are carrying me to the Kahina to be cured. It takes more than a scratch or two to silence a Saghrani, you'll see.'

He put out a shaking hand and grasped Truman's weakly. 'You didn't fall short, my friend,' he said. 'You kept the water-pact. That is all a companion may ask. The Light Mother will repay you for your loyalty and courage.'

Heads bent over the fallen warrior, and the crowd in earshot hung on his words. It hit Truman suddenly that this was the stuff of legend, that the Saghrana would be telling – and exaggerating – around campfires for generations.

'We were a team,' he told Khyar. 'I couldn't have made it alone.'

Khyar smiled again as the men bore him away. Truman watched until the Nazir took his elbow and led him into the tent – the same tent he had sat in when he'd first come to the tribe as an unwanted guest. He collapsed on the same woven fibre mat, clutching his side where the Gharana sabre had sliced through his flesh. The warriors crowded round him, asking questions, while Hafid and his patrol took up their places next to him, and were slapped on the back and embraced. Mobs of women and children gathered round the tent, still ululating and bawling.

Seated near the hearth Truman noticed an owlish man with a face like wind-withered timber, who gazed at him intently through chrysophrase eyes.

'This is Sij Yasid,' the Nazir said, 'the Holy Man of the Kel.'

Truman murmured a greeting and examined the man curiously.

There was a stillness about him that set him apart from the jabbering crowd. The fire was stoked by unseen hands, and somebody began to mash coffee beans in a mortar with clear musical notes.

'This a real victory!' the Nazir rasped. 'This year it has all gone the demons' way. You have changed that. You have brought blessings and good fortune to the Kel.'

Truman looked up. 'They weren't demons. Just men with veiled faces. They were. . . . they died easily enough.'

The memory of his crazed, berserk onslaught on the Gharana raiders rushed into his head suddenly. Sitting here, amongst the Kel, it seemed impossible that he had murdered three men in cold blood. It couldn't have been him, he thought, not Dan Truman. Something had possessed him.

'I was the demon,' he said, 'not them.'

Sij Yasid's eyes sparkled. 'Many are the lessons of the *Mufarida*,' he said, his voice dry, empty of emotion. 'One of them is that there are demons in all of us.'

'Who are these Gharana?' Truman asked. 'Who are they really?'

'They are our shadow-selves,' the holy man said. 'The dark side of the Kel.'

'But they recognized Khyar – they knew him. I heard them talking.'

'Let us say no more of the Gharana here, Antara. Did you know that the area where a Saghrani pitches his tent is sacred? It is consecrated to the Light Mother, and the evil spirits are banished by incantations before the first pole is raised. We should not talk of evil things within its confines. Here, the Light Mother protects us all.'

'Who . . . what . . . is the Light Mother?' Truman asked. 'The Gharana talked about the Dark Mother.'

'The Light Mother is one aspect of the Great Mother,' the holy man said. 'The Gharana worship the dark aspect. The Light Mother is the sun rising in the east and setting in the west. She is the Light between the horns of the Sacred Ram – the mark of the Saghrana.'

199

'That mark,' Truman said. 'I've seen it before – on a column at the oasis of Siwa.'

'The Ten Bravest are here,' the Nazir cut in suddenly.

Truman looked up to see a group of warriors filtering into the tent. The others shifted and made room for them. They wore burnooses with the hoods flung back to reveal bearded faces under braided tresses of greased hair that hung about their shoulders. Some were badly scarred, but all held themselves loosely, as if poised for action, and there was a silence to them almost as forbidding as the holy man's, a sense of great power tightly coiled.

Each one carried a sabre across his chest, and Truman noticed that the lobes of both their ears had been slit, just as Hafid's were.

Hafid rose and each of the warriors greeted him silently. Then they faced Truman. One of them, a small, broad-shouldered man whose face was quartered by a sabre-cut running from his forehead, through a corner of his nose to his chin, stepped forward.

'I am Makhlud,' he said hoarsely, 'the senior of the Ten. We of the Ten Bravest salute you, Antara. All praise to the Light Mother for your safe return.'

The onlookers cheered, and as the warriors sat down the Nazir himself offered Truman coffee from a crow-beaked pot. Truman held his hand up.

'No,' he said. 'I don't want coffee. Give me water.'

The old man chuckled, put the pot down and filled a gourd of water from a bladder hanging from the roof. Truman took it reverently in both hands and looked at it – clean water, as clear as crystal – this was what he had dreamed of in the sands.

'This is the water of the Kel,' he said. 'The Light Mother be blest for our safe deliverance.'

The crowd halooed and clapped hands as Truman drank, savouring the coolness of the clean liquid. He understood now why water was sacred to these people. He knew he would never take its presence lightly again. When he'd drunk, four warriors entered carrying a young camel roasted and served in buttered rice on a massive brass tray.

'Ah,' the Nazir said. 'Feast your eyes before your belly. It is not every day we kill a camel.'

'It is a great honour,' Sij Yasid said. 'It is said, "he who lives long will see the camel slaughtered."'

The Saghrana crouched around the tray hungrily, and the Nazir broke off some succulent pieces of meat with his hands and placed them near Truman. Truman bent forward to eat, while the rest watched in hushed silence.

'Come!' Truman said. 'Eat!'

The Saghrana tucked in with gusto, but Truman's appetite had been diminished by near starvation, and he only went through the motions until the warriors sat back and licked their fingers, replete.

'Now,' the Nazir said to him, wiping a greasy palm on the tent flap. 'You have honoured the Kel, and yet we do not know your name. The Kel are already calling you *Antara*, but you may choose to be known by any name you like.'

Truman considered it for a moment. He shrugged. 'It's a good name. Let it stand.'

'So be it,' the Nazir said. 'From this day on you are Antara, and you have the countenance of the Kel. You may ask for anything, Antara – and if the Light Mother wills, it shall be given to you.'

Truman smiled raggedly. 'Friendship is enough reward, and a drink of cool, clean water. But there are two more things I'd like. The first is to see Jamila. The second is to meet Ossama Hadab.'

The babble of talk stopped abruptly and for a moment there was a chilling silence. The warriors froze in their places and stared from Truman to the Nazir. The old man fixed Truman with a predator's gaze.

'I told you when you first came here, you cannot meet Ossama,' he said. 'Unless Ossama wants to meet you.'

'I'm sorry . . .' Truman began, but the Nazir waved a hand at him. Suddenly the old man's grizzled features were lit up by a warm smile.

'But as for Jamila,' he said, 'perhaps that can be arranged.'

201

34

IT WAS LATE AFTERNOON WHEN THE Nazir led Truman to Termit rock. The sun was already dipping below the rimwall, turning the pillow-sand deep ochre, picking out the fissures and abrasions in the sandstone. Truman examined the ancient carvings on the buttress with interest, running his fingers over the rough, warm surface.

'The story of the Saghrana is written on this rock,' the Nazir said. 'Some of these scratchings go back to the time of the Imenan, our ancestors, who came here in the beginning. The first families pitched their tents right here, in the shadow of Termit. That is why this rock is the most hallowed of sites in the Sacred Land.'

Truman was fascinated. 'Where did your ancestors come from?'

The Nazir shrugged. 'It is said they came from the north. From the land of the Farun.'

'You mean the Pharaohs?' Truman asked. 'The ancient Egyptians?'

Tissi turned away. 'I'm a fighter,' he said. 'I know little of the oral history. Only the Kahina knows such things.'

He led Truman to a narrow opening in the rock, a slit just large enough for one man to pass through. 'The whole of the rimwall is honeycombed with caves and passages,' the

202

old man explained. 'Our ancestors found them in the Time of the First Reckoning and explored them all. It is said that those early years were a time of great struggle. Some evil things went on.' He shivered involuntarily and hesitated before the doorway.

'You will meet Jamila inside,' the Nazir said gravely. 'Pass through the small chamber and down the stone steps, and you will find a larger chamber. We call it the Cave of Wonders – the *Makrab al-Ajayib*. Jamila is there, waiting for you.'

He stopped and touched Truman lightly on the shoulder. 'My friend,' he said. 'I give you the same warning I gave Khyar before you went together on the salt-run. Be mindful that things don't always turn out as you expect.'

It was almost dark inside the chamber, but there was light beyond a sunken ovoid archway that led to the shallow stone steps. Truman ducked to pass through, and saw that the stairs were lit by smoky tallow-lamps hung amid twisted crystal columns that made up the walls. The columns were stalactites and stalagmites fused together over millions of years of slow accretion. Their existence bespoke the presence of water – vast quantities of fossil water – permeating the soft rock from above. He touched one of the columns and found it damp, and when he breathed in sharply, he could almost taste the water-vapour in the air.

He made his way down the steps carefully, marvelling at the patterns of exquisite delicacy the solidifying rock had made. The ceiling bulged in places with swelling cave draperies moulded by the trickle of fluid along the dipping surface, and set in the crystal pilasters were compact bands of onyx, webs of cave-coral and acicular stars like white sea-urchins with needles fine enough to draw blood.

Truman went ponderingly down the steps and paused at another deformed archway where the sound of dripping water was strong. Feeling a sense of foreboding, he stepped through the doorway and gaped. The low ceiling of the steps was sheared away to a domed roof high above him, hung with millions of crystal points like speartips, and in places with sweeping peri-styles that joined roof and floor. The cave was as vast as a cathedral – a gallery of wonders divided into grottoes and alcoves by scores of cable-like pillars formed by billions of fine calcite fibres. Gilded light flowed into the cave from a high natural window in the walls, reflecting on polished rock in the uneven floor, pitching back from concentric rings of pisolite and aggre-gates of turquoise and lapis lazuli.

Truman stared, overwhelmed by the place. On a natural dais behind a swell of smooth bluish rock a figure sat cross-legged by a flickering fire. The figure was clad entirely in black robes, its head shadowed by a dark hood. There was a beaten path weaving through the depressions and calcite spikes and Truman padded along it, feeling the cold rock against his bare feet, excite-ment and fear growing in his body. On the flatter surfaces around him he began to see etchings superimposed by human hands – disquieting images of headless men with limbs like wires, pipe-cleaner bodies swaying mesmerically, men with ram-heads who seemed to be leading giraffes on cords as fine as spider-webs, men with outstretched limbs racing after antelopes with bows and arrows, men with grotesque torsos and heads like space helmets, set amidst the imprints of hands, sun-disks, crescent moons and staring eyes.

Truman halted, half-hypnotized by the fire, his eyes riveted on the swathed figure. 'Jamila?' he said softly.

The seated figure stirred. A delicate hand materialized from beneath the robes and flung back the dark hood. There was an exotic swirl of wild black hair, and Truman found himself looking into eyes the colour of the sea – eyes neither green nor blue, but the colour of jade. It was Jamila, and Truman stared back fascinated by the face, more beautiful and alluring than he'd ever dreamed of. It was his goat-girl all right, and yet there was something subtly different about the face, some fine quality of knowledge and wisdom that hadn't been there before.

'Jamila,' Truman whispered.

 204

The girl shook her head sadly. 'I'm sorry, Antara,' she said. 'There's no Jamila. My name is Ossama Hadab, and I am Kahina of the Kel.'

35

'I'M SORRY,' THE KAHINA SAID AGAIN. 'The deception was unfair. But you were an Outsider who came looking for Ossama. That has never happened before. I had to be careful.'

'So you were spying on me,' Truman said slowly. 'But I thought you might feel something for me. Was I mistaken?'

Ossama looked away and tried to marshall the conflicting feelings that were battling for mastery within her. Ever since she'd set eyes on this man at the well she'd been fascinated by him. He was not the sturdy, predictable type like Khyar or Hafid, neither was he strikingly handsome. Yet there was something about his face that obsessed her – some combination in the set of mouth and eye that displayed both innocence and wisdom at the same time. Ossama had never met a stranger before, and there was an aura of magic around this being who had stepped out of another world. As a girl, she had been tortured by dreams and visions, an uncontrollable flood of them that had sometimes made her terrified to sleep at night. Often she had predicted the attacks of the Gharana, prophesied natural disasters, foreseen the deaths of people she knew. Through those dreams a stranger had walked, a being who had raised disquieting feelings in her body, unlike those she felt in the presence of any other man.

As she had reached maturity, her aunt, Tamghart – the Old Kahina – had helped her control this riptide of visions, to use them and harness them, but still the stranger had appeared to her, a stranger whose face she had never seen until now. Antara had shown courage, loyalty and endurance – three of the qualities most valued by the Saghrana, but he was not one of them, and a woman of the Kel could not love an Outsider. Yet she desired him as she'd never desired any other man.

'I have the Gift,' she said. 'I am supposed to *see* things, but I didn't see they had sent you on the salt-road. If I had known I would have spoken against it. Hafid knew, and when he told me I was angry with him – I retired into the Half-Death for three days, and then I *did* have a vision. You and Khyar stranded in the desert with no camels. That's why I asked Hafid and his *gom* to look for you.' She looked directly at him again with eyes so bright they were almost translucent. 'Do you believe in destiny, Antara?'

'I don't know what destiny is,' Truman replied. 'Only that I've been searching for something all my life, and suddenly I've found it. Life here is hard, yet somehow since I've been here I've felt more alive than ever before. It's as if I'd spent the whole of my life just going through the motions, and this is the real thing. I never want to go back.'

He tried to articulate his feelings, to form the maelstrom of images into words. He thought of the greed that had brought him here, of Maynard, Stein, Rybakov and the others, scheming and murdering for money. Yet here was a world where money didn't count, where people mattered more than things. It seemed suddenly more precious than all the palladium on earth.

He looked into Ossama's deep eyes, understanding more fully than ever before the savage possessiveness that men were capable of. This was very different from his youthful affairs, even from the love he'd shared with Natalie, which had been a sort of casual partnership. It was something that cut right down into the black abyss at the centre of his being, a pure animal longing so powerful that he knew he would easily have killed for her.

'When I was out in the Funeral Plains with Khyar,' he said, 'it wasn't my home I thought of, it was you. I *recognized* you the moment I saw you at Tarout. I knew I'd seen you before, in dreams I've been having since I was a child. I've seen this cave too, and somehow I have this feeling I was . . .'

'. . . meant to be here?' Ossama said. She smiled, enveloping him in a parcel of warmth. 'That's destiny, Antara, the sense that our lives are not empty of meaning, that they are leading up to something. I was expecting some intruder from the Outlands, but when I first saw you at the well you looked confused, bewildered. Yet there was something that shone in your eyes – an honesty, a certain humility – that told me you were no danger to the tribe. I knew you were meant to be here, and that we were destined to meet.'

Her aquamarine eyes shone like liquid in the last shreds of light through the high rock window. Truman took her hand, small and warm, in his own, and she did not resist. To his surprise, she was trembling slightly.

'How is it possible to see through time?' he asked.

The Kahina turned her face towards a shallow rock pool at her side. The water in it looked like transparent gold, licked with phantoms of flame from the fire. She dipped her hand into the water and lifted it out, so that the liquid ran off in trickles like strings of tiny gilded pearls. 'What colour is the water, Antara?' she asked.

'Gold,' he said.

'But it's not,' she said. 'Its colour is simply an illusion – the chance effect of light. Time is an illusion too. It changes shape depending on where you're standing. Meaning grows directly from the human soul. Your mind provides a structure of past, present and future, but those things are only aspects of our perception, not reality itself. In the real universe there is no absolute pattern, only the Divine. It has no past and no future: it is infinite – it simply *is*. What we call the Gift is the ability to dip into that ocean of infinity where the past, present and future become one.'

She stood up as gracefully as a dancer and moved across the rock floor. She stopped by a flat blue stone and pointed to a

 208

tableau engraved there. It was one Truman had seen often in his dreams – the strange headless men dancing, their limbs extended to the very edge of the picture. 'This was made by our ancestors, the Imenan,' she said. 'Long ago, in the time we call the First Reckoning. Many of them had the Gift.'

'What happened to their heads?' Truman inquired reluctantly, unwilling to break the spell.

'That signifies that they have moved beyond the world of al-Ada – the world of everyday things – and shifted into the dimension of Half-Death – the world of the spirits. In Half-Death there are no 'heads' – no individual minds – all individuals become one. All warriors enter Half-Death at least once in their lives, but for many the way is long, difficult and hard. I was blest with the Gift and can pass into Half-Death at any time.'

'And does your Gift tell you I love you?' he said suddenly.

The Kahina's calm features registered no surprise. She looked into his eyes and it was Jamila's fresh, guileless gaze that met his. 'My visions are imperfect but I don't need the Gift to know that.'

There was such tenderness in her face that Truman could feel the energy flowing from her in almost palpable waves. Just being in her presence gave him a sense of peace he had never experienced before. 'I told myself I was mad – that it wasn't possible. I was an Outsider who couldn't even match your women or your boys.'

Ossama smiled. 'With the eyes of al-Ada, I saw you as an effete outlander, ignorant of everything, but that was only the clothing – the flesh on the bones. Beneath it there was something rare and precious.'

Truman gasped. 'I wanted to talk to you,' he whispered, 'but it was as if there was this chasm between us that I couldn't cross over.'

Ossama moved back to the fireplace, knelt down and adjusted the fire with a twig, so that the flames leapt up. Truman followed her and sat down, taking in the miracle of the great crystal dome above them, the grandeur of the living sculpture that had been in the making for a million years.

Ossama knelt and took his head gently in her hands. 'I waited for you all my life, Antara, and at last you came.'

Truman looked into her eyes, overwhelmed by the power he saw there, and brushed her lips lightly. A spark of sheer energy ripped through him like fire, and he closed his eyes in ecstasy. Ossama pulled away suddenly and sat down.

'What is it?' he asked. 'Why did you turn away?'

'I told you my visions are imperfect,' she said, 'but I have had dreams about your people – Outsiders – who threatened to destroy us all. That's why I had to be so careful with you, Antara. There is great danger lurking behind you.'

'Yes,' Truman said. 'Yes there is.'

She drew herself up and Truman saw a new hardness in the jade eyes. He sensed instinctively that it was the Kahina talking now.

'Why did you wish to see Ossama?' she asked. 'What message did you bring?'

Truman suddenly felt overpoweringly ashamed. The idea that he could have agreed to sell out these people and their unique traditions for riches appalled him.

'The one-eyed man,' he stuttered. 'The one who came here some time ago? He died, and I found his body in the desert. He was carrying some bags of dust, and I took them back to my country. I didn't know what the dust was, but it contained traces of a substance my people treasure, something so precious they will lie and kill for it.'

'An evil thing?'

'No, it's only dust. The evil is in the people who want it.'

'They would tear the Sacred Land to pieces in the search for it?' she asked.

'Yes, and they would kill every man, woman and child who tried to stop them.'

A shadow passed over the Kahina's face. 'Then my visions were true,' she said, 'and it's too late.'

 210

'I don't know,' Truman said, starting up. 'You see they sent me here to bargain with Ossama – with you.'

'To bargain for what?'

'For the land.'

Ossama laughed, a laugh brimming with simple, childish amazement. 'The land!' she exclaimed. 'The Sacred Land cannot be bought and sold like a goat in the market. It doesn't belong to us. We may make use of it, but we don't own it any more than the plants and the creatures own it. We share it with them. It is the Sacred place of our ancestors from the Time of the First Reckoning, and their voices are here among the caves and the rocks. What would become of their voices if it was destroyed?'

Truman fell silent.

'Is that why you wanted to see me?' Ossama asked. 'To buy the Sacred Land?'

For a moment Truman hesitated, wondering how to explain. Out there on the Funeral Plains with Khyar he'd realized that he would rather die than let scavengers like Maynard, Stein and Rybakov tear this harsh but beautiful land up between them and crush this people who lived in such a delicate balance with their environment. The only things he wanted now were to be with Ossama, and to be one of them.

'They offered me riches,' he said. 'I admit I was tempted. But so much has happened since then. It was foolish of me, but I wanted to see you to warn you of the danger.'

Ossama took a deep breath and brushed back her hair again. It was getting dark in the cave and her face was lit from below by the wavering flames in the hearth, giving it a frame of unfamiliar new lines. 'I see the Light Mother's hand in this,' she said. 'You were called here, Antara.'

Truman bit his lip. 'You don't understand,' he said miserably. 'Those people are coming because I took the stuff back to my country. It's my fault.'

The Kahina shook her head calmly. 'No,' she said softly. 'If this thing is so valuable, others would have come for it. The

211

Light Mother called you for a purpose. You were meant to be here.'

'What purpose?' Truman asked.

'We know nothing of Outsiders,' she said. 'You must teach us, Antara.'

The daylight had almost gone, and the Kahina's eyes were pale pools reflecting the wan flames of the fire.

'I'll do anything you ask,' Truman said.

The Kahina contemplated him sadly for a moment. She perceived that Antara had a power that even he did not know about, a spirit that shone in his eyes and cast a spell over his listeners. He would have made a superb Nazir for the Kel. But she had been carried away by his presence, had almost forgotten that he was a stranger from the Outlands. She could only marry a warrior of the Kel, and only those who passed the *tafriq* could become warriors. Her heart failed her at the thought of Antara suffering the terrible trial of the *tafriq* – many who had lived all their lives here in the desert did not survive it. True, Antara had brought Khyar out of the Funeral Plains against all odds, but the pain of the rite was something infinitely worse than the thirst he had suffered out there. She was caught in a cleft stick. If she lost him to the *tafriq* she would never forgive herself, but if he did not attempt it then he would remain a stranger forever. She sighed, knowing that only the Light Mother could decide.

'You've brought honour to the Kel,' she said. 'You saved a tribesman. We don't forget easily, and you will always have a place here.'

Sensing the new formality in her voice, Truman looked at her sharply.

'I don't want just any place,' he gasped. 'There is no place for me without you.'

Ossama lowered her head so that the tangle of dark hair covered her face like a hood. 'There is still Khyar,' she said. 'He is my first cousin by adoption and by our tradition I am his by right.'

Truman felt his world slipping away, wandering out of focus.

 212

'By the law of the Kel,' Ossama went on, 'a Saghrana woman can only take a Saghrana warrior as a husband. You will always be welcome here, but you can't be a full warrior – not unless you undergo the *tafriq*.'

'But what is this *tafriq*?'

'It is hard for a Saghrani,' she said. 'For anyone else almost impossible. I beg you not to attempt it, Antara.'

'Is there a chance for us if I succeed?'

'I promise nothing,' she said, and now there was an unexpectedly sharp edge to her words. 'Many die in the *tafriq*, and many who live fail. Those who fail must . . . may not marry our women. And if you succeed . . .

'Yes?' Truman said.

A reflection from the crystals above caught the Kahina's eyes in the shadows and for an instant they sparkled yellow like the eyes of a cat. 'If you succeed you must swear to be ours forever. You may never leave the Kel for the rest of your life.'

36

THE WHOLE TRIBE, IT SEEMED, HAD turned out to watch the *tafriq* ceremony in the Makrab al-Ajayib, and the great cave was lit with dozens of tallow lamps and burning torches whose pinpoints of light were multiplied and thrown back a million-fold from the complex natural chandelier in the roof. As Sij Yasid, the holy man, led him to his place, Truman sensed the ranks of warriors closing silently behind him, heard the rustle of robes and cloaks, the shrill whispers of the women. Outside it was nearing sunset, the day's blue intensity fading into soft apricot colours, and the sun was visible through the natural window high in the caveside – half a gold piece hung on the rimwall in a smarter of zig-zag clouds and a halo of fine dust.

The Saghrana had flocked to Termit rock from every part of the plateau and the desert beyond, pitching their black tents in a vast semi-circle around it, and all day there had been feasting and ritual dancing to the sound of drums. Heads of families who had not met for months sat in small councils around campfires, passing among them ceremonial tobacco-pipes, and the roar of camels and the peal of coffee mortars was everywhere. Only Truman had remained aloof from the festivities as he sat fasting in a special tent separated from the camp, with the holy man as his companion.

The owl-faced man had become familiar to him now. For a

 214

fortnight he had been fasting with Sij on the bleak stony slopes of Tahert – the double volcanic plug that dominated the plateau – sleeping on great boulders that were roasting hot by day and freezing cold at night. Slowly he'd felt his senses and perceptions sharpen like a blade being honed. It was as if the landscape around him had suddenly come into focus after weeks of being blurred images. Every smell, every image had become almost unbearably acute, so that he felt he could hear the patter of a spider's feet on the sand, the stridulation of a scorpion-mother carrying her young, the sussuration of a puff-adder sawing through the sand, the wings of a kite snapping as it dived, the hiss of the wind in a tamarisk tree.

He had spent hours watching desert creatures – a kangaroo-rat playing by its burrow at sunset, a skink making an arabesque on a low duneskirt, a darkling beetle working its way over the hot face of a rock, a fennec fox peering timidly from its lair. To these creatures, he thought, the world looked quite different – different colours, different smells, different texture, different shape. That meant that the things humans took for granted – a world of green trees and blue skies – had no objective qualities at all. At last he'd begun to grasp what the Kahina had meant when she'd said that time and space were only aspects of human perception. These and other things men took for granted were part of the map of reality, not part of the territory itself.

One day on a lone walk he came across a single thread of desert sedge growing in the lee of a dune, far from any other life, and he sank down on his knees in the sand and stared at it for hours with the word 'miracle' bubbling through his head. Then, suddenly, he'd realized that this plant was not an island in the midst of desolation as he'd first thought, but a small part of a single vast organism called life, so powerful that it transcended even death itself. He'd trotted back to Sij Yasid's shelter on Tahert almost drunk with the revelation, and told the holy man about his vision.

'Why should it be so surprising?' Sij Yasid had asked him. 'The life force is the most powerful energy in the cosmos. It *is*

215

the cosmos. There is no real difference between you, me, the sedge, the sand, the rock and the stars. They are the same things arranged in a different order. All things must be respected – the plants, the animals, water, clouds, even the stones. They are all part of our bodies, for our true body is the cosmos itself.'

Slowly, Truman's perceptions of himself and his place in the landscape had begun to alter subtly. Before, he had loomed large in his mental image. It had been himself against the environment. Now, though, his image of himself grew progressively smaller until it was absorbed by the landscape. He was not in competition with it, he realized, but part of it. Steadily, the desert around him had begun to take on another shape – no longer a wild country, but a familiar place, a home. When he told Sij Yasid this, the sage laughed. 'The *tafriq* begins.'

Among the rows of dark faces, Truman saw Khyar. The Saghrani's features were still disfigured from his wounds, but the look of directionless aggression Truman had first seen in his eyes was gone.

'The Light Mother give you courage,' he rasped as Truman passed by, but the voice seemed to come from far off, clear but disconnected, like a voice from a distant world.

Truman moved through the glittering lights of the cave like a sleep-walker, hypnotized, his steps languidly slow. As he passed the wall-pictures of headless men and strange totem animals they suddenly seemed alive, and for a fleeting second he could hear the voices of the chanting men, the cries of the animals, and smell the odours of firesmoke and dust. The squelch and drip of water around him seemed almost deafening. He could actually hear the cave growing and changing. The holy man had prepared him for the ceremony with cryptic hints.

'There is pain,' he had said. 'Great pain. This is a test of courage, and whatever happens you must not cry out. Some of the initiates fail simply because they cannot stand the pain – others die. But the pain is only the beginning – it liberates the spirit from the bodily senses that keep it in thrall.'

'And if the initiate survives the pain?' Truman asked.

'Then he is given the Sharing Water – the *Maya al-Mushtarika*. It helps to free the spirit further, so that he may walk without hesitation through the plains of the Half-Death. There he meets with guides – spirits who may show him his true path. Some encounter dark spirits and return possessed by them.'

'And what happens to those?' Truman enquired.

'The answer can only be known by those who succeed.'

Now the holy man was silent as he led Truman to a smooth, oval boulder set on a sort of plinth in a shallow basin of rock. On the plinth Ossama waited, clothed in black from head to foot, and next to her stood the Nazir in ceremonial robes. Their figures looked tiny under the great vault of the cave. In hidden recesses drums began to beat, amplified by the crystal walls. He halted in front of the Kahina, who raised both her hands.

'In the name of the Light Mother!' she shouted, so that her words bounced off the walls and re-echoed eerily around the cave. 'In the name of Sacred Imenan, our Holy Ancestors back to the Time of the First Reckoning and beyond, we submit this man, Antara, to the trials of the Division, the Holy *tafriq*, that divides good and evil. May the Great and Holy Mother guide him to the *sabil al-mustaqim* – the undiverging path, and protect him from the demons of illusion.'

She paused and looked Truman in the eyes. 'Are you ready, Antara?'

'I'm ready,' he said.

'Do you swear that if you pass the Holy trial you will devote yourself to the Kel, to uphold its codes, laws and customs, and never forsake it for the rest of your life?'

'I swear.'

'Remember, you can stop the trial at any time by calling out "enough". Only you can decide when the pain is bearable no longer.'

There was a hush among the spectators as Truman was made to sprawl out face-down on the rock. Suddenly he could see nothing but the rock floor and the shifting shadows around him. He heard footsteps approaching him.

'Who wields the Holy *Farouq!*' the Kahina's voice asked.

'I do,' Khyar's voice came back. 'I am Khyar bin Kalash, a warrior of the Kel. Six men have I slain in battle with my blade for the honour of the tribe.'

'And what is your connection with the Seeker?'

'The Seeker is my friend,' Khyar said. 'The Seeker once saved my life.'

'Then strike hard and true,' the Kahina said, 'and the Light Mother protect him.'

The first lash took Truman by surprise. It was as if a bolt of high-voltage electricity had shot through his entire body, punching the breath out of him. For an instant all his muscles jerked tense, revolting against the terrible, searing pain that assailed them, and Truman stifled a scream. Sij Yasid had told him that to cry out was to invite disgrace. He let the air out slowly, but the muscles had only just relaxed when the second lash came, even more vicious and penetrating than the first. Truman's body went rigid and his heartbeat rocketed until his whole frame seemed to be shuddering. His breath came in deep, retching gasps and he felt something wet trickling over his back. Almost at once there was a third lash that sent Truman reeling to the frontiers of darkness. How could anyone withstand such pain? He fought to stay conscious, retching in agony, aware that he could call a halt to the ordeal at any time. Something – some stubbornness in his nature – prevented him.

There was a strange familiarity about this agony. His body told him he had been in this dimension before, but it would not tell him where or how. He had been here, and his mind had created some kind of cocoon around it, blotting it out of his consciousness. The fourth and fifth strokes came in quick succession as if in punishment for his obduracy, so savage that Truman heard a voice in his ear begging him to give up. It was his own voice, he realized.

Curiously, the sixth blow seemed less torturing, as if he were losing contact with his body, and from somewhere, far away, he heard the sound of drums and chanting. '*Six! Six! Six!*' the voices called, and he realized with a shock that the audience were counting the blows. The seventh lash felt like a scalpel slicing open the skin of his back, stabbing right into the core of his inner self, screaming, screeching with agony. '*Seven! Seven! Seven!*' the crowd chanted.

Truman closed his eyes, and had the impression he was running frantically down a backstreet in a city – a street where the buildings had been bombed and shellshocked out of true, where every window was a baleful, staring eye, where the substance of the construction lay in dead piles along the street. Was this a real memory or something he had dreamed? Suddenly he heard Paretsky's voice, as crisp and sharp as if the little Russian had been standing next to him. *When those assholes were going to stiff me in Beirut you downed them with karate moves. Best fighting I've ever seen. I'll never forget how you looked when you came racing down that street. Not scared in the least, but surprised. You looked like you just discovered Godzilla.*

He knew suddenly and with absolute conviction, that he had not dreamed it. He had not lied to Paretsky. That had been him, Truman, in Beirut, and he hadn't been charging towards the Russian, he'd been running away. Running away from something he had seen. *I saw something*, he whispered to himself, *something they didn't want me to see.*

He opened his eyes and in that moment the eighth lash connected. Truman writhed, stunned, his senses reeling. '*Eight! Eight! Eight!*' the crowd chanted. Light sherds were peeling away in his mind, revealing glimpses of a dark room with chains on the walls, men with olive uniforms and dark moustaches leering at him, electric connections being attached to his genitals. Truman tried to find his voice, but as he struggled to speak a ninth lash struck him like a scythe, and his body went rigid with agony. The vision of the dark room was gone. '*Nine! Nine! Nine!*' the crowd gasped.

Time seemed to slow down as he felt the pain penetrating its

219

caustic fire into every cell in his body. For a moment he wondered if he was going to die, and then the tenth stroke hit him like a tidal wave sweeping along the shore, bowling him along like a skittle. '*Ten! Ten! Ten!*' the ghostly voices wheedled, far off on another planet. Truman picked himself up out of the waves and groaned, waving his hand with all his strength.

'*Enough!* he mumbled.

The lashes stopped and Truman felt himself drifting gently downstream on a roll of emotion so intense it was almost ecstatic. There was a cheer from the multitude. Arms pulled Truman up and someone threw cold water over his back. He shivered. The starry dome of the cavern towered above him higher than the heavens. Truman blinked tipsily and sought out Ossama's face. She was still smiling palely.

'By the Light Mother!' Khyar's voice bawled in his ear. 'Ten lashes! I wouldn't ever have believed it if I hadn't seen it. I never knew anyone – not even the most hardened warrior – take more than eight.'

Truman's eyelids fluttered and he felt himself keeling over.

'Quickly!' the Kahina's voice came urgently. 'Give him the *Maya al-Mushtarika*. Let him enter the Half-Death.'

Truman heard the slosh of liquid in a bladder and something was forced into his mouth. He fought for breath, but a wash of nauseating liquid filled his mouth and he collapsed, feeling arms supporting him. He saw the sparkling galaxies of light in the roof fading into the distance, heard the voices becoming faint and distant, until he was lofted on a wave of energy, a pounding tide pulsing through stars and galaxies, drumming on and on for eternity.

37

HE WAS RACING ACROSS DESERT SANDS on feet like seven-league boots, bouncing from dune to dune, skating on air. It had been a long journey, but he was almost there. Far in the distance there was a rock aiguille with a cave half way up its side, and in the cave, he knew a woman was waiting for him. He closed his eyes for a moment and when he opened them again he was sitting in the cave, on a rocky shelf overlooking the desert, and the woman was watching him. Her features were indistinguishable – Truman couldn't even have said if she was young or old.

'Ah, it's you,' she said in a husky voice, that could have been masculine or feminine. 'I thought you'd be here sooner or later.'

Truman paused, 'Do I know you?'

The old woman cackled. 'You ought to,' she said. 'After all the time we spent together in that place in Switzerland.'

She leaned forward slightly into the light and a rush of recognition hit him like a headlight beam full in the face.

'You're the Oracle!' he exclaimed. 'The Hidden One! I've been trying to find you again ever since I got out of that place, but I couldn't remember why.'

'Now you know,' the old woman said. 'It's because I'm the one meditating you.'

Truman felt a sudden, unexpected surge of comprehension. 'I see,' he said. 'So you're the one responsible for all this.'

221

'Yes, of course. Who did you think it was? Now, do you have a question?'

Truman considered it for a moment. 'Yes. What I want to know is, who I am. I mean, who am I really?'

The old woman exploded with cracked laughter. 'Where does reality begin?' she asked mockingly. 'Where does the universe end? You're a character in my story, of course, a little bit of the universe or all the universe depending on where you stand. It's all relative, you see.'

'I don't get it,' Truman said.

She paused and shook her head. 'You want to have it spelled out, don't you? Very well then. Look at me. Look closer.'

Truman peered at her face, and saw that her features were moulding and changing into something familiar to him. The face he saw was the same face he'd seen in the mirror for countless years. His own.

He opened his eyes and found Ossama watching him anxiously. He was lying face down on the palette in the corner of her small living cave. When he tried to rise, starbursts of pain played a tattoo across his back.

'No,' the Kahina said, easing him back gently. 'Don't try to get up, Antara. It's time to rest now. The trial is over and you were successful. You took more lashes than any warrior in living memory.'

'I feel so weak,' he mumbled. 'I don't feel as if I could have succeeded in anything.'

'The signs are clear. The eyes are windows of the Half-Death.'

She smiled, inscrutably. 'What did you see in Half-Death, Antara?'

'I saw . . . it's so difficult to put into words.'

He closed his eyes for a moment and tried to grope for the fleeting images of his vision. It seemed to him that he had been on a long journey – all the way around the universe and back – that he had touched the Divine itself. All he could recall now, though, was a sense of utter euphoria – flying like a hawk on a spiral of air across rugged mountains. Running like an antelope across the desert. Fragments of memories came back to him. Harris's mummified body lying in the sand. A helicopter erupting in flames. A derelict street in Beirut. A black room with pain inside it. A woman with his own face. Rushing down a dune roaring like an animal. The Gharana warriors he had killed. *The Gharana are our shadow-selves*, the holy man had said, *the dark side of the Kel.*

'I understood one thing,' he said suddenly. 'The Gharana are the failures aren't they, the rejects? That's what the *tafriq* was meant for – to divide the sheep from the goats.'

Ossama looked troubled. 'It is said in the Oral History that in the Time of the First Reckoning, terrible things happened in the Sacred Land. Some of our people became possessed with *Afarit* – evil spirits. They began to . . . to hunt their own kind, their own families. They gained a taste for human blood. It would have destroyed the Kel. The *tafriq* was a way of distinguishing between the pure and the tainted ones.'

Truman's eyes opened wider. 'It was some kind of genetic defect?' he said, faltering, groping for a paraphrase in Arabic. 'Some trait that came to the fore because of inbreeding?'

The Kahina heard him out, mystified. 'I don't know those words. It was only found in men – it divided sons from fathers and brothers from brothers. The tainted ones had to leave because no one would cooperate with them. They created their own tribe, the Gharana.'

'But if it was only men, why didn't they die out?'

'For ages they have raided the oases of the Outside. They stole virgins and made them their brides. They used camels stolen from the Kel – with our brands – so that the Outsiders would blame us. The legend grew up that we were vampires.'

'But if what happened here was long ago,' Truman said, 'the gene – the thing that created the evil – it must have been bred out by now.'

'Certainly the young men who fail the *tafriq* cannot be distin-guished from their fellows before the trial. Many show great bravery and generosity as children. But the trial is absolute. No one who fails it can remain with us.' Truman watched her, appalled. 'You mean if I'd failed I'd have had to leave you, even though I brought back Khyar?'

She looked down. 'Yes. I tried to warn you Antara, but it's forbidden to reveal the secret to the uninitiated. Since the First Reckoning the Gharana have been our blood enemies. They pitch their tents outside the plateau and prowl the desert for Saghrana herds, probing for any weakness, seeking any opportunity to slaughter and steal. Since Goloi has been their leader they have grown bolder than ever. Only a few months ago they lifted some camels grazing outside the rimwall. They sneaked up under the cover of darkness and cut the throats of two young boys who were guarding them. Once they feared to enter the Sacred Land, knowing that within the plateau they would be killed on sight. But this year they have twice managed to get in by night to steal goats. No one knows how they did it.'

Truman squinted at her, perplexed. 'But you created your own enemy. Why?'

'That's the way it has always been. The Great Mother has both her light and dark aspects – one cannot exist without the other. Some of the elders say that without the Gharana we would destroy ourselves. Watch the hyena, Antara. It takes only the weak and sick animals. Those that are left are the stronger ones, who breed and produce stronger offspring. Many of the wise believe that it is so with the Gharana. They say our enemy has kept us strong, but I say that the desert itself has kept us strong, not the Gharana.'

Truman grimaced. 'You are the Kahina. Why don't you order them to stop it?'

She crouched down and touched him on the cheek. 'I can't. I can't order the Kel to do anything. The Kahina guides the tribe by dreams and visions. During the time of the migration to the south, the *nashoq*, the Kel's survival depends on my ability to predict the whereabouts of the new pastures. But it's not within my power to change our customs. They are decided only by tradition.'

'But how did you come to be Kahina?'

'I was chosen by my aunt, Tamghart, the previous Kahina. Ever since I was tiny I have been renowned for vivid dreams that foretell the future. Tamghart chose me from among nine other girls as her successor. But let's not talk of these things, Antara. You are here, and that's all that matters.'

Truman felt the whisper of her wild hair against his lips, and he gasped inwardly at the power flowing between them. He pulled himself up, groaning in pain, ignoring her protests, and for a long while he sat staring into her eyes. The whole of life was within them, as exquisitely beautiful and terrible as anything he'd seen in the Half-Death. His arms were trembling as he held her. 'Never leave me,' he whispered.

'You are my Antara,' she said. 'The one I waited for all my life. There is no power in the cosmos greater than this. Nothing can ever separate us now.'

38

RICHARD WHITEHAVEN MADE HIS WAY DOWN the basement corridor of MI6 headquarters with the jaunty step of youthfulness regained. Since his meeting with Morgan four months ago he'd trained harder than he'd done since his days in the Regiment, jogging three miles a day, shifting weights, swimming, blasting off rounds at the Small Arms School battle ranges, stripping and assembling weapons till he could do it blindfold. Even when his old knee-wound had played up on his parachute refresher course at Brize Norton it hadn't dulled his enthusiasm. He'd nursed it for a week and joined the next course.

Word had already come that the Russian column was on the move through Libya, and Whitehaven was expecting Morgan to give the go ahead any minute. The only hare in the gate was the nagging suspicion that his boss hadn't levelled with him about Truman. There was something afoot that didn't smell kosher, and before he took the irreversible plunge into the blue, he desperately wanted to find out what it was that Morgan was holding back. He halted at the door of the computer room and slipped his security-card into the socket. A green light clicked on and the door slid open silently.

Only the security camera watched him as he seated himself at a terminal, slotted his card into another socket and booted the computer. The big clock on the brick wall read 7.15 p.m. Past his normal working hours, but then Whitehaven had no reason to rush home to the empty flat above the pharmacy in Finsbury Park. It was a location that had nothing to recommend it except its anonymity. He thought of Margery and the cosy house in Shepherd's Bush where he was now persona non grata. Since Lance had left home, they'd found there was no longer any reason to stay together. Whatever it was they'd had to start with had been slowly eroded by his constant absences, his occasional infidelities. Margery had taken refuge with her boss, a kindly, home-loving man whose wife had conveniently died of cancer a year previously. Whitehaven had consoled himself with a mannish blonde from the secretarial staff until that too had ended as abruptly as it had started.

Whitehaven dismissed Margery from his mind and turned back to Truman. The archaeologist's trail had gone cold only a day after he'd arrived in Cairo, but since he hadn't reappeared, the chances were that he was either dead or still on the ground with the nomads. The fact that Morgan hadn't come clean about Truman was ominous. Only he and Morgan knew where these arms were going, and if Whitehaven didn't come back from the blue, the secret would be confined to Morgan alone. That worried him. MI6's forked tongue had already cost him one bollock, and he was fairly keen on retaining the other.

For weeks he'd been pulling in every favour he could muster from contacts inside and outside the Office, but still Q-ops had remained no more than a ghost. He'd even searched Archives for the Zinoviev tapes and transcripts, only to be told they didn't exist. Odd thing that, because Whitehaven remembered distinctly having taped the first two days of the Zinoviev debrief. And odder still, Whitehaven thought, that the Russian had dropped dead so soon afterwards. It was almost as if he'd never existed at all.

He'd thought over what Zinoviev had said about the Q-ops group doing a deal with the mafiya in Beirut in the eighties, and then about the rumour that Truman had been there at the same time. If there was any trace of Truman in the records he would be damned if he didn't find it.

227

His fingers worked like greased lightning over the keyboard. 'Beirut 1980 – 90' brought only a low-classified general digest on MI6 operations there. He keyed in 'Beirut-Q-ops' and as he'd expected the search came up blank. He tried Middle East 1980 – 90, and narrowed the search down to 'CXC' which signified deep-cover operations. A flashing block warned him that his pin number didn't clear him for this data, so he quit the file hastily.

'Logistics,' he thought suddenly. 'Medical Records.' 'Salary.' He keyed back into the *Beirut* file, and specified 'Incentives'. The tiny sand-timer icon flickered for a moment, then a menu appeared. He selected the 'Non-Permanent Personnel' file and a list of secure codenames came on screen. He worked down the list with the cursor and found three codenames against salary figures for 1981–3, the period within which Truman's dossier claimed he was 'travelling'. The names were *Haymaker, Sabretooth, Sawbuck.*

He memorized them and quit the file, then keyed into the 'Medical Records' menu and selected 'Casevac Payments'. To his dismay all three codenames appeared on the payments list. He scrutinized the figures against the names carefully. *Sawbuck* had received £920 for dental treatment in May 1981, and *Sabretooth* had been paid £2000 for minor burns in April 1982. Against *Haymaker* though, there was the massive figure of £40,000 for unspecified treatment, covering a period of six months between January and July 1983. Whitehaven consulted his pocket diary and noted that Truman had signed on for his Ph.D at Magdalen, Oxford, in August 1983. That didn't prove *Haymaker* was Truman, of course, but at least there was a theoretical possibility. He returned to Search and keyed in the name *Haymaker*. There were no further references, so he closed down.

It was not quite dark when he signed out of the office and made his way to the tube station, pondering the *Haymaker* file. Some serious aggro must have happened to *Haymaker* in Beirut to warrant six months of treatment at a cost of £40,000. That probably meant complete hospitalization for the entire period. There was a story behind that hospitalization all right, and somebody who'd been in Beirut in the early eighties had to know.

He slotted money into the ticket machine, collected his ticket and looked at the passengers pouring through the turnstiles. He gazed back through the arches at the blues and greys of coming night, reminding himself that an empty flat was all he had to go home to. *Beirut, 1980 to 83,* he repeated to himself. Then he stuffed the ticket into his pocket, and took out his mobile phone.

An hour later he was engulfed in the warm glow of the the Hare & Hounds pub in a backstreet in Rotherhithe, nursing pints of bitter through the drinkers to the corner table, where George Moore was painstakingly rolling a cigarette.

'Don't know why you bother, Sarn't Major,' Whitehaven told him as he laid the pints on the table. 'If you want to kill yourself why not use tailor-made?'

Moore grinned and stuck the perfect handmade roll into his mouth. 'It's not the same,' he said through his teeth, 'and by the way, they retired me as a major.'

Moore was an ex-Coldstream Guards warrant officer, who had served in the Guards' Parachute Company before finding a niche in MI6 – an incredibly lean, lanky man with brooding eyes and a groove either side of his face. He sported a prehistoric handlebar moustache and a silk cravat that together gave him the rakish look of a Battle of Britain fighter pilot in old fashioned boys' comics. Moore had taken early retirement, but in his days at the Office, he and Whitehaven had shared a cameraderie that included a pride in belonging to what they called 'the airborne brotherhood', and a disdain for 'Ruperts'.

Whitehaven sat and took out his pipe and his tin of Erinmore.

'Look who's talking,' Moore retorted. 'Still smoking that old rope after all these years.'

He lit his cigarette from a worn Zippo lighter with the Parachute Regiment logo engraved on it, and clicked the top back with a flick of the wrist. After the first puff he lifted his bitter and tasted it, wiping the froth off his moustache with his smoking hand.

229

'I know it's short notice, mate,' Whitehaven said, relapsing into ORs talk as if it was a secret mother-tongue, 'but I'm pushed.'

'No problem, Rich,' Moore said, smoking again. 'Always got time for a bevvy with my old mate. How's Morgan?'

Whitehaven closed his ears to the deafening banter of the early-evening crowd and lit his pipe, composing himself. He blew a smoke-ring at the ceiling. 'Same pain in the patella. Nearest he ever gets to the field is a Sunday afternoon drive with the Missis. The number of enemies he's got, I don't know how he survives.'

Moore cracked a laugh and coughed smoke. 'Morgan's not as bad as they say.' His eyes narrowed as he weighed Whitehaven up seriously. 'You mentioned Beirut on the phone,' he said. 'What's the score, Rich?'

'You were there with Int/Sec in 1981 to 83 weren't you?'

'Yeah, that was what I called a suit-job. Embassy attache. The real sharp-end stuff was done by Freds. I ran one of the teams myself.'

Whitehaven sipped warm beer. 'You ever hear of Q-ops?'

Moore put his pint down on the table heavily and pointed to the door with the two fingers holding his roll-up. 'See that? I'll be bugging out through there in thirty seconds sharp if you're going to ask me shit that's going to put my arse on the chopping block. I'm retired. I can do without it.'

'OK,' Whitehaven said apologetically. 'We don't use the Q-word. Let's try a codename. Ever hear of a *Haymaker?*'

Moore didn't pick up his beer. 'Yeah, I did. That's what you call the kind of punch that'll be connecting with your jaw just before I bug out.'

Whitehaven felt like laughing but didn't. 'George,' he said, 'it's my arse on the line, not yours. They're heaving me into the blue to play nurse to a bunch of nomads – in squeaky-clean fatigue, as deniable as shit. If I don't get a heart-attack at the door of the Herc it'll be a wonder. It sounds like a kamikaze deal, and I need to know what's what before I get clipped. Now for old time's sake, my old cobbler, talk to me about *Haymaker*. It goes no further than these walls, and I *need* to know.'

Moore stared at him and scanned the crowd. He looked longingly at the door, then back at Whitehaven. Finally he picked up his beer glass. 'Right. For old times sake, I say it once and I won't repeat. I'm giving no names because I don't know them myself, and if you ever drop me in the shit over this, I'll kill you.'

His roll had burned down almost to his fingers, but he took a toke on it anyway. Whitehaven remembered how roll-up smokers hated to waste even the smallest pinch of snout.

'Beirut, early eighties,' Moore began, as though dredging up images from the deepest channels of his memory. 'It was a training ground for all the intelligence services of the world.' He smiled fondly. 'The KGB were the best, even the Yanks had to admit it. Ruthless. I remember when the Soviet Ambassador's son was kidnapped by Hasabullah or one of those extremist sects. Know what the KGB did? The boss of Hasabullah had a son too. The KGB got hold of him, cut his balls off and sent them to the father saying the rest of the kid's body would follow in small packages unless the Russian boy came back unharmed. The kid turned up next day, clean as a whistle.'

He chuckled admiringly, and Whitehaven chuckled too, even though he'd heard the story before. Moore took a swig of beer. 'In '82 word was out there were Soviets working the streets of Downtown West Beirut. I don't mean Freds, I mean the real McCoy – KGB officers trained to talk Arabic like natives, and shit, they were good. Our Freds got mugshots from Int/Sec and were tasked to finger them so we could pick 'em up. Story went that one of our boys ran into a squad of thugs beating seven bales out of one of the Ivans, and clocked him from the mugshot. The thugs were about to put a nine-milly through Ivan's skull, so this Fred does a kind of charge of the Light Brigade to save the poor bugger. He wasn't even armed, apparently, but he was a big karate-man, and the story goes he downs four or five of the buggers, object being to collar the KGB guy and whisk him off to Tac-HQ before you could say 'shit'.

'Didn't work out like that, though. The Russian picks himself up, says 'Thank you very much, Comrade,' and bugs out. Our lad's going to go after him, but by this time the bully-boys are up and by Christ, they're hopping. 'If we can't have him,' they say, 'we'll take you instead.' And they did – put the bastard through intensive interrogation for a couple of weeks – cowprods, electrodes, you name it. But the Fred never says a dicky-bird, and just when they're about to clip him, their base is shredded by a bomb attack and the Fred's liberated by friendlies.

'By this time the guy's a veggie, of course – can't even recall his own name, so they casevac him back to Ukay. End of story. The Fred's codename was *Haymaker*.'

He paused and took a long drink of beer. 'I'm talking rumour, Rich,' he added. 'I didn't see it, and it didn't happen on my team, right? I'm repeating gossip, that's all.'

Whitehaven studied the bottom of his beer-glass assiduously as if great secrets might be written there. 'George,' he said, 'I've got two questions and after that I'll get you another pint. First, who was the KGB man *Haymaker* sprang?'

Moore laid out another superfine cigarette-paper and began sprinkling tobacco on it. He scowled. 'I told you I don't know names, but the Russkie's codename was *Cygnus*. I saw the mug-shot – a scrawny little bastard he looked, cropped hair and big glasses. That's all I can tell you.'

'OK,' Whitehaven said. 'Here's the big one. Most Freds are amateurs – some are the scum of the universe out to make a fast buck. They're expendable and if they get in the shit they're often just written off. Why should HMG spend £40,000 on hospitalizing *Haymaker* when they could have dumped him from a great height?'

Moore twisted his roll deftly between both thumbs and forefingers. 'This was no ordinary Fred,' he said. 'Think about it. First, the guy was good enough to pass himself off as an Arab and cool enough to walk round without even a piece on him. Second, he risked his life to collar a KGB officer, then took punishment for two weeks and never cracked. Freds like that aren't ten a penny, Rich. If the Office paid his hospital bills it wasn't out of the goodness of their hearts. You can bet your backside they wanted him on the phantom list.'

Whitehaven tried not to look surprised. He puffed his pipe. 'The what?'

Moore lit his roll-up and flicked the lid of the Zippo closed. 'I've already said too much,' he growled. 'You're a bastard, Rich.'

He thought for a moment, savouring smoke. 'OK,' he said. 'I might as well be hung for a sheep as a goat. The phantom list is a special roster of Freds who might go on for years until something comes up. The list isn't on record and it's only known to the DG. Maybe the phantom Freds never get tasked at all, but if something special comes up that HMG can't be seen to be involved in, and they happen to be qualified for, they're sent in cover so deep you'd need an excavator to dig them out. And there's a reason for that – phantom list Freds are mostly guys up to their armpits in shit – terrorists, gangsters, mafiosi, criminals, foreign agents who've been turned – guys who'd be snuffed by their own outfits if their real allegiance was known.'

Whitehaven grinned evenly. 'You talking about the letter that comes after ''P'', George?'

Moore blew smoke and rapped his empty beer-glass on the table. 'Never heard of it, and like I said, I don't repeat. But I tell you something, Rich. The phantom list is activated only for jobs that are arsehole deep in sewage, I mean, your genuine dancing with the devil. Stuff so dirty it might bring the government down if it was to come out.'

He took a long toke of his roll up. 'Now,' he said, 'didn't you say something about another pint?'

39

THE NIGHT WAS BALMY AND RIPE with stars, and Truman could never recall having felt so tranquil. He held Ossama to him, feeling the slight swell of her belly from the child she was carrying through her summer robes. Her wild hair caressed him, and the moon was a twin reflection in her brilliant eyes. Not far away, the entire strength of the Kel lay on the plain in a small city of black tents – among them the flames of cookfires twinkled like garnets. Even from here they could hear the lowing of the house-camels, hobbled close to the tents at night, the snap of saluqis, the eternal jingle-jangle of coffee mortars, the low murmur of storytellers round scores of hearths. Truman kissed his wife, closing his eyes and ears to everything, losing himself deliberately in the sweetness of the moment. In the four months since the *tafriq*, he had discovered a whole universe here within this woman, within the tribe – an entirely new dimension of life.

In his own culture people had become commodities, statistics classified according to how much they consumed or produced. The meaning of life had been reduced to economics, status defined by 'keeping up with the Joneses'. Truman had always known, deep inside, that there had to be a more profound meaning in the universe, a more fulfilling experience of life than simply amassing wealth. He knew he had found it among the Kel.

For them, possessions meant nothing. No one was accorded

 234

respect simply for what he or she owned, and no one had power over anyone else. Instead, the Saghrana lived by the cult of reputation, and reputation could only be acquired by showing courage, endurance, loyalty, hospitality and generosity – five qualities that together made up the concept of *miruwa* or humanness. If a person did not have humanness he was nobody, no matter how many camels he owned. The code the Kel lived by was absolute. Anyone who halted at a Saghrana tent had a right to hospitality and the protection of its owner, who for the sake of his reputation would defend his guest with his life even against his own family. To steal or harm a travelling companion was considered an unspeakable disgrace.

Money or power could never of themselves lead to happiness, Truman was sure of that now, only a deep-seated sense of belonging to the cosmos. That was the secret of the Saghrana. They had absolute faith in the Divine. They knew who they were and how they fitted in, even if they did not know that the stars were balls of gas spinning in space billions of miles away, or that the earth was round not flat. For Truman it was as if a veil he'd been wearing for the whole of his life had been whisked away. Often he felt he was not discovering a new world, so much as coming home.

The Kel couldn't amass possessions anyway. They were a moving people, and anything that wasn't portable was useless to them. They had to be able to load everything they owned on to the backs of camels and navigate the wastes between islands of vegetation, sometimes hundreds of kilometres apart. It was the Kahina's task to locate these pastures, and without her inner eye to guide them the tribe would have been lost. It was evident to Truman that the Kel held Ossama in profound respect – even awe. Yet she did not play the great lady. In everything she was modest and humble, never losing her patience, treating all her petitioners with the same forbearance and consideration. Though she was constantly busy giving advice to the scouts, conferring with the warriors, treating the sick, she always spared time for Truman, according him the courtesy due to a husband, making

235

him comfortable, cooking and looking after the tent, tirelessly explaining the customs and expectations of the Kel.

He kissed Ossama again, feeling the new fullness of her breasts under the gown, running his hand over the curve of her belly. 'I've found everything I ever wanted here,' he told her. 'I was lost till I found you and the Kel. My life before this was just a dream.'

'Don't talk of dreams, Antara,' she said softly. 'All of us are ghosts passing through each other's dreams. We must be content with the now.'

'It frightens me, though,' he said. 'I keep thinking that I'll wake up and find myself back in my old life, and you'll be a hallucination – a figment of my imagination.'

'We are all hallucinations,' she said, smiling. 'What are we but vapours of energy in the mind of the Great Mother?' Her eyes were tender. 'The Kel will soon be back in the Sacred Land for the summer, now the Lesser Sandtides are upon us. I'm no longer needed here, Antara, and there is news that one of the Burrowers we left there, Ayoub, is dying of sickness. I have to go back to the plateau and try to save his life.'

Truman placed a finger gently over her lips. 'Let me come with you,' he whispered.

She kissed the finger. 'For now, your place is here. The Nazir needs your strong arm and good counsel. I shall be riding Wald al-Asmar, the finest camel of the *bil*, and Khyar will ride with me. Ayoub is his uncle.'

'Khyar?' Truman repeated.

'What is it, Antara?' she whispered caressing his face. 'You have nothing to fear from him. He's your friend. He gave his consent freely to our *takhayim*.'

Truman smiled at her use of the old term *takhayim*, for 'marriage'. Its literal meaning was 'sharing a tent'. Among the Saghrana, tents were the property of the women-folk, the *haruum*, so no bachelor could be described as *takhayim*.

'I know,' he said uneasily, trying to ease the clutch of that savage male possessiveness that still affected him when he was with Ossama. The first thing he had been obliged to do after recovering from the *tafriq* was to seek Khyar's formal consent for his marriage to her. As her first cousin – if only by adoption – Khyar had the right to withhold his approval, but only if he intended to marry her himself. Truman had approached the young tribesman with trepidation, despite the fact that they had become so close during their desert ordeal. It was a formal occasion, with everyone dressed in their best robes, and Truman had taken Hafid along with him as support. Khyar had welcomed them into the brushwood shelter where he slept, and offered them water ceremonially. When everyone had drunk and murmured prayers to the Light Mother, Truman had asked Khyar to relinquish his claim on Ossama.

The youth had adopted an inscrutable expression, but Truman knew the depth of the passion he must be struggling with.

'There is no better *harma* among the Kel than my cousin Ossama,' Khyar said at last. 'She is beautiful, clever and accomplished. By the Ancient Imenan, any man who has Ossama as a wife is blessed indeed. You are an honoured warrior of the Kel, Antara, who has slain three enemies in face-to-face battle. The Light Mother knows, I owe my life to you. I give up my claim to my cousin. I give my consent to your marriage gladly, and I bless you both in the name of the Light Mother. May your days together be happy ones.'

Khyar had smiled merrily and slapped him on the back, but Truman could not forget how, out on the Funeral Plains, Khyar had repeated Ossama's name over and over in his sleep.

The Kahina sensed his misgivings now. 'Khyar's changed. He's one of the Ten Bravest, and he is no longer jealous of Hafid.'

'Yes,' Truman said, 'you're right. It's just that *I'll* be jealous of every moment you're in his company and not mine.'

'It's not long,' Ossama said. 'The Sacred Land is only ten days away for the Kel, moving slowly. We will be together soon.'

40

Ossama left at first light the following morning, and for the next few days Truman was busy with a thousand tasks as the tribe moved slowly back towards Bint Hammou with their herds. Every morning the camp of hundreds of tents was struck amidst a cacophony of jabbering and roaring, as the house camels were brought in and couched, tents were rolled, household items were packed in boxes or stowed in saddle-bags. Truman delighted in noticing that everything the Saghrana owned had a practical value – their possessions were like their bodies – knapped down to the bare minimum needed to survive. Despite the noise and the apparent confusion, it was always astonishing how quickly and efficiently the households were transferred to camels' back.

Before the sun was high the great procession would be on its way, a serpent of humans and animals winding its way across the Funeral Plains. The entire tribe on the move was the most magnificent sight Truman had ever seen – hundreds of families, with thousands of laden camels hauling all their worldly goods, processions of shaded litters that housed the pregnant women and small children, caravans of baggage animals from whose flanks dangled richly woven carpets and sheets of gazelle-skin decorated with cowries, and whose heads bore great ostrich plumes that fluttered in the wind as they marched.

Twice in those days, stragglers herding the milch camels were

 238

raided by Gharana bandits. Truman joined the warriors of the Kel as they tracked the raiders down and took their animals back. Truman had become an adequate tracker now, though he knew he would never be able to equal the best of the Saghrana, such as Hafid, whose abilities were legendary.

On the pursuit, they fought running battles with the enemy, and Truman was amazed to see that the Saghrana fought in the open, face to face with the foe. Each warrior would select an enemy and try to engage in hand to hand fighting with his sabre, yelling out his son's or his wife's name as he plunged into the fray. Killing with the rifle was considered a last resort. Truman's reputation was already legendary among the Saghrana – how he had killed three Gharana while dying of thirst, and brought Khyar back out of the jaws of death; how he'd taken ten lashes in the *tafriq*. He was already held in great esteem by the other warriors, even the Ten Bravest. For the first time in his life he began to feel that he was more than just an individual, that he was part of something greater than himself.

He had come to love the Kel: their bluff determination in the face of danger and hardship, their grace and dignity, their openness and generosity. He never pined for the teeming cities of his own country. Here, no one was just a face in a crowd – every individual counted. These people inhabited a different dimension from the one he had left behind – a place beyond the dominion of rationality, where security was replaced by a sense of harmony. The paradox was that this, one of the harshest of possible worlds, was actually a sort of paradise. He had long ago begun to see the landscape as they saw it, not as a hostile place, but as a place where the necessities of life were provided to those who had the skill to adapt. He knew that, whatever happened, he could never again return to his former life.

One morning as the tribe camped on pastures not five days from the plateau, Truman was awoken by the boy Yani. For a moment he was transported back to the days, long ago it seemed, when they had shivered all night under the rimwall cliffs. Yani's lopsided face was flushed with excitement.

239

'Antara', the boy hissed. 'Makhlud and Khyar have returned from the Sacred Land. They have news.'

'Ossama?' Truman gasped, rolling out of his covers. 'Is she all right?'

'Your Jamila is fine,' Yani said. 'They have other news to tell.'

He found Khyar and Makhlud seated by a campfire outside the Nazir's tent, drinking coffee, dusty and exhausted, their lips cracked and their eyes shot with sand. They rose to greet him formally, shaking his hand, giving him the triple nose-kiss of the Kel.

'The Light Mother be thanked your safe return,' he said. 'What is the news?'

'The news is good,' Makhlud said, his scarred face taut with fatigue. 'The Light Mother be praised. The Kahina is safe in the Sacred Land. She was in time to save old Ayoub's life. She greets you, Antara.'

'The Light Mother return her greeting,' Truman said, sitting down next to them. The Nazir put a tiny dish in front of him and poured a few drops of coffee from a hornbill-spouted pot. 'What else?' he inquired.

Makhlud's scar throbbed redly as his eyes surveyed Truman. 'On our second day after leaving the Kahina in the Sacred Land, we heard one of those flying machines go over.'

Truman opened his mouth to speak, but Makhlud held up his hand. 'Wait, Antara,' he said. 'There's more. The same evening we found sign from Outsider's boots – four men, heavily laden – and we followed them to a gully. We were almost upon them when they opened fire – thank the Sacred Mother we weren't hit. There were four of them and only two of us, but those are good odds for Saghrana. We boxed them in and every time they moved a muscle we put in a shot. They would fire back madly, wasting a lot of bullets, but by that time we had moved on. By sunset they weren't firing so much, so we knew they were either tired or low on bullets. We just lay there silently for a long time and they must have thought we'd gone. When one of them

240

showed his head, Khyar put a bullet right through it. Then we worked our way around behind the others and leapt on them with our sabres. We sent them all to the Light Mother's mercy.'

'They were wearing clothes mottled to resemble the colour of the desert,' Khyar said, 'and they had lots of weapons and machines, with big bags they must have carried on their backs.'

'Did any of them speak?' Truman asked.

'Yes,' Makhlud said. 'One was still breathing, and I asked him why they'd come to the *Mufarida*. He didn't understand my talk, but he said one word: "Truman".'

'I knew the word at once,' Khyar said eagerly. 'I told Makhlud, "that is the name of Antara. His Outsider name, before he became one of us."'

An icy finger ran down Truman's spine. He had tried to forget the chain of events that had led him here, subliminally willing them to vanish. But subconsciously he knew he'd been expecting something like this. He'd always known the Outside would catch up with him. He became aware that the others were staring at him, silently demanding an explanation.

There was uncertainty in their eyes.

'Did we do wrong, Antara?' Makhlud demanded. 'Were these friends of yours come to take you back to the Outside?'

Truman fixed him in the eye. 'I have no friends and no family save the Kel. You did right, Makhlud.'

The scarred warrior grunted. 'After we had killed them we searched their things.'

He delved in a leather saddle bag at his side and brought out something heavy wrapped carefully in a bundle of rags. 'We found this.'

He unwrapped a flat electronic device that looked like a lap-top computer, with a keyboard, a screen, and a telephone receiver attached. 'What is it, Antara?'

Truman scanned the device with interest. He took it on his lap and touched one of the keys. The screen lit up, making the warriors start.

It's called a satcom phone,' he said. 'It's used for talking to

241

others over long distances. You can speak to the Outside with this.' He pressed a key with a battery icon etched on it and a block appeared on the screen with four little boxes half shaded. 'It's still got power.'

The warriors watched the screen balefully. 'It's a thing of Jinns and evil-spirits,' the Nazir growled. 'Better destroy it, Antara.'

Truman considered it for a moment. He felt uncomfortable with this thing – it was a doorway to the outside world he'd left behind for good, and in these surroundings, with these people, it seemed alien. Suddenly he switched off the screen and closed the top.

'No,' he said gently, almost to himself. 'It's not evil, Nazir. It's just a machine. Machines aren't good or bad. It's the nature of those who use them that makes the difference. Light Mother's wrath – we may need this thing one day.'

The Nazir watched him distastefully. 'Who were these Outsiders, Antara? What does this mean?'

Truman surveyed the group gravely. 'It means the enemy is at the gate. The evil times the Kahina predicted are here.'

41

THE BURROWER AYOUB WAS A PURPLE speck against the pastel of the Funeral Plains, a drifting parcel of moisture evaporating in the glare of the early sun. He was barefoot, naked but for the remnants of his blood-stained burnoose, and the sand grains clung darkly to the lacerations on his limbs and body. Ayoub muttered to himself as he limped on, praying to all the spirits of the ancient Imenan to give him strength. He struggled for breath, gagging on the dryness of the air, turning over and over in his inner eye the horrific scenes of the past two days.

The Outsiders had arrived without warning. There had been only a handful of women, children and old men in the Sacred Land – the Burrowers and their families, the Kahina, and a few tribesmen who had been too sick to travel with the Kel on the *nashoq*. The first they had known was the terrific squeal of the big flying machines as they swooped over the rimwall, their shadows flitting across the valley like those of giant hunting kites. The machines had come down near Termit, and out of them had scurried men with guns in costumes stained to match the browns and tans of the desert's face. The flying machines had taken off again, but at almost the same time there had been a sound like thunder on the southern edge of the rimwall at Riyat Ash-Sha, where the ancient qanat had once stood.

The Saghrana had fought the Outsiders – the men, women

and children together, with sticks, stones, knives, anything they could find. They had even managed to send several of them to the Light Mother's mercy, but the punishment had been terrible. Ayoub had been weak from the sickness that had taken him to the brink of death, and only his frailty had saved him. All the warriors and the two other Burrowers had been shot, and most of the children with them. Some of the women had been taken alive and hustled into the recesses of the Makrab al-Ajayib, to the Light Mother knew what fate.

A group of Outsiders with faces like pigs had tried to manhandle the Kahina herself, and when Ayoub had tried to protect her, they had beaten him with their rifles and slashed him with big knives, leaving him for dead. Then a small man with a mask of a face, whose eyes were like bore-holes into hell, had arrived and spoken to the pig-men sharply in a croaking devils' whisper. They had let the Kahina go, but the small man's presence had been more terrifying than the beating – even Ayoub could see that there was an aura of darkness about him, as if he were the Angel of Death himself. The Kahina had whispered 'The Black Kahin' under her breath, and Ayoub had been startled to hear the fear in her voice. The Black Kahin had ordered her taken off somewhere, perhaps with the other women, and later that day the rest of the Outsiders had begun to arrive – so many he could not count them. They had come in wheeled machines – some small, some huge, heavy things like giant insects – and had started putting up tents in the lee of Termit cliff.

Ayoub himself had lain in the shade of a rock for a day and a night without food or water, as the tents sprang up around him like mushrooms, and the world had been full of the voices of the Outsiders and the noise of their machines. He had glimpsed some of the Saghrana women being hustled to the tents – the piercing screams that had followed told him how they were being used. Ayoub had tried to close his mind to those terrible screams. At least the Kahina had not been among the women he'd seen carried to the tents. He was a Burrower, not a fighter, but he knew the Kel lay only a few days away, moving slowly towards the Sacred Land with all their herds. He also knew that the Light Mother had spared him for one purpose – to warn them. The Outsiders had simply left him lying there to die, but he refused to die, and on the second night had summoned his strength and managed to slip away, hoping to find a camel. Most of the camels were out with the *nashoq* and though he had spotted Wald al-Asmar – the camel Ossama had ridden – grazing peacefully under Termit, he could not risk trying to catch it.

Instead, he had made use of the darkness and found his way to Riyat ash-Sha. What he saw there had astonished him. When the old qanat had caved in during his grandfather's time, it had left a canyon completely blocked with debris. Somehow, the Outsiders had forced their way through. Great boulders had been split into pieces or nudged aside like balls of camel-dung.

'By the Holy Imenan,' he whispered to himself as he recalled the sight, 'never since the Time of the First Reckoning has there been such a thing.' The pain in his body had grown almost unbearable now. He had been walking for a whole night and had eaten and drunk nothing for two days. At every step he had to will his feet to go forward and now he knew he no longer had the strength to carry on. 'I have to warn them,' he repeated to himself. 'Light Mother protect me, I have to tell them.' Suddenly there were fizzles of power like dry lightning inside his head, and he collapsed blindly into the sand.

It was Truman who spotted him first. He and Khyar had been riding with the main body of scouts, led by Makhlud, who were clearing the route to Bint Hammou for the mass of the tribe and the herds a few hours behind them. They raced their camels over to him and dropped from their saddles. Khyar turned the body over carefully.

'Light Mother's wrath!' he exclaimed. 'It's Ayoub bin Eser. He is my maternal uncle, one of the Burrowers.'

'Ayoub?' Truman repeated. 'But isn't he the man Ossama went to treat? What's he doing here?'

At the sound of his name the Burrower opened his eyes.

Truman cradled the old man's skull, feeling its egg-shell fragility. Ayoub's skin was hot to the touch. 'Water,' he told Khyar. 'Quickly.'

Khyar raced for his dripper and filled a bowl with water, while Truman tore off his headcloth and tied it loosely round Ayoub's head. A moment later Khyar was feeding him water from a soaked cloth.

'What is it, uncle?' Khyar demanded. 'What happened?'

The old man tried to speak and choked. 'Don't try,' Truman told him. 'Just drink.'

'No. No,' Ayoub coughed, grabbing at Truman's hand. 'You don't understand, Antara. There are strangers in the Sacred Land. Outsiders. They came two days ago with machines – flying things with blades that whirled round, and other contraptions I've never seen before. Machines that breathe fire and smoke. They smashed their way through the rimwall and now they are inside, by Termit rock. They are even in the Makrab al-'Ajayib. We were nothing but a few old men, women and boys, but we fought them. The Light Mother save us! It was monstrous. They killed almost everyone. Their leader was a man with a devil's face, who spoke in a whisper. The Kahina called him the 'Black Kahin'.'

A bolt of pure terror plunged down Truman's spine. 'Ossama?' he gasped, his voice quavering. 'What happened to Ossama?'

'The Light Mother alone knows.' Ayoub grunted. 'Some of the women they took for themselves, but I didn't see the Kahina among them. The last I saw she was being taken to the caverns.'

Truman felt his pulse racing. The 'Black Kahin' had to be Stein, he knew. He remembered how the Butcher of Berlin had murdered an eight year old boy in front of him. The thought of what Stein might do to his pregnant wife made him physically sick. He stood up and took a pace towards his camel. 'I've got to get her back,' he said. 'Khyar – I know this man. He is a monster. I can't leave her there.'

Khyar placed a restraining hand on his shoulder. 'No, Antara,' he said. 'You can't face so many alone. We have to wait for the Kel.'

Truman nodded, knowing Khyar was right. He cursed himself for a fool. He should have guessed that the enemy would come at the beginning of the hot season when the Kel were still away from the plateau. He should have prepared himself and the tribe for this moment, and above all, he should have stopped Ossama from returning to the Sacred Land.

'How many Outsiders are there?' Khyar asked, but before the old man could answer there were shouts and the groans of camels being barracked. Truman looked round to see Makhlud and Hafid with a group of other scouts running towards them.

'Holy Mother of Light,' Makhlud gasped. 'What's happened? A Gharana raid?'

'Worse,' Truman said grimly. 'Much worse than that.'

42

At sunset, the Kel pitched camp on an island of green beneath limestone cliffs, where there was enough to feed their animals for a night. The tents went up amid the roaring of camels, the shouts of men and women, the screech of children, the barking of the saluqis, the bleating of goats. The space outside the Nazir's tent was a haven of peace in the desert of confusion, and it was here – around a massive bonfire of brushwood – that Tissi bin Tamghar met with the Ten Bravest, the sheikhs of families, the holy men and the wise-ones of the Kel. Truman watched them talking in the half-light – small, lean, hawk-nosed men, with wind-ravaged faces, sitting very still and straight with their rifles in their laps. The last of the sun was gulped down by the desert, and the dry brushwood crackled, filling the air with the smell of resin.

Moonlight illuminated the circle of men in their light-hued burnooses, throwing their hooded faces into pools of shadow. The moon was bright above and the limestone cliffs behind them looked ghost-white in the darkness. All around them couched and hobbled camels moaned and rumbled softly, and coffee-mortars sounded bell-like notes out of the dark. There was an air of expectancy about the men that Truman could almost have cut with a knife. A greybeard named Khalis argued for negotiating with the Outsiders. 'We can't be sure what they want,' he said.

'Maybe they'll be happy to remain a few days and then leave us in peace.'

There were raucous jeers from the listening men. 'Light Mother's wrath,' old Ayoub cried, his face lost in the shadows. 'No, by the Sacred Ancestors! If you'd seen the way those devils dealt with the children, you wouldn't be talking like a camel's mouth bladder. Here's me a Burrower saying it!'

Khyar sprang up, his face pale, blue-shadowed in the jaw from his scar. He hurled his headcloth to the ground.

'It's a disgrace even to talk about it!' he bawled. 'Revenge is our sacred duty.' He faced old Khalis furiously. 'The Outsiders are without honour. The Great Mother's curse upon them! Saghrana blades are the answer they will get. Are our children and *haruum* to be slaughtered while we stand by and talk?'

'And what of the Kahina?' somebody cut in. 'Are we to leave her to the mercies of these strangers?'

Everyone began to shout at once, and Truman found it difficult to follow a word. Khyar was arguing heatedly with scarred Makhlud of the Ten Bravest, who was banging the ground with his camel-stick. One old sheikh in the front, with a wild shock of grey hair, was shouting for war and brandishing his rifle fiercely. Abruptly the Nazir leapt to his feet and drew his sabre, the blade scintillating in the moonlight.

'We are the Kel Saghrana!' he yelled above the noise, and for a moment the hubbub abated slightly. 'If fifty warriors will come with me, I will take the Sacred Land back from our enemies! By the spirits of the Sacred Imenan, we will take three lives for every man, woman and child they have killed!'

The tribesmen sprang to their feet, shouting, cheering and arguing at the same time, all claiming the right to take part in the raid. Only Truman held aloof. He watched the firelight drift over the faces grimly. For a moment he hesitated, knowing that what he had to say would not be welcome. He had undergone the pain of the *tafriq* in order to become accepted by these men, and he had no other wish now than to be one of them. Yet unlike them, he had lived in both worlds and knew just what they were dealing with.

The Saghrana were the toughest people he had ever met, but their way of fighting was dictated by generations of tradition and governed by the quest for honour. Here in the desert, honour meant everything, and the Kel had no concept of a culture whose object was greed, greed and more greed. Nor had they ever come up against the inhuman machines that culture had designed to deal with anything that interfered with its object. He knew that if the Saghrana tried to take on the enemy in their traditional way they would be massacred.

The paradox was that if he tried to warn them, tried to stop them attacking, they might regard him with suspicion. They might believe he wanted to spare the Outsiders, or even that his joining the Kel and his marriage to Ossama had been an elaborate charade. All the careful work he had done to gain acceptance would be lost. For a moment he weighed the balance. He could go along with them silently to almost certain death, or he could tell them the truth. He decided that it was his duty to try. He rose slowly. 'Wait,' he cried. 'Don't be hasty.'

For a moment the men stopped and turned to him with incredulity.

'Antara speaks for *negotiation?*' Makhlud said, his head cocked to one side as if he hadn't heard right. 'You want to *talk* to these sons of diseased hyenas?'

Eyes were burning at Truman now. Never since he'd passed the *tafriq* had he felt such an intruder.

'My wife is a prisoner of the strangers,' he said. 'No one has more right to join the raiding party than I. But I say we must be cautious. These Outsiders have flying machines. They have vehicles and powerful weapons such as have never been seen here before. This won't be like raiding the Gharana. They can destroy the whole Kel without even coming near us. They'll have devices which allow men to see in the night, machine-guns that fire so fast they could can cut down a hundred warriors in the wink of an eye. Khyar was right when he said the Outsiders have no honour. They fight with trickery and cunning. If we try to fight them in the way of the Kel, we'll be destroyed.'

There was a hushed silence for a moment. Then Mahklud jumped up and waved his camel-stick. 'Antara says Outsiders can see in the dark,' he yelled, laughing. 'Light Mother's wrath! Even if it is true, we have never run from an enemy. We are the Kel Saghrana!'

Everyone was yelling and gesticulating again, but Truman didn't move. He'd known all along that no one would listen. These men he'd come to love like his own family would march to certain death, and the greatest agony of all was that it was ultimately his fault. An idea occurred to him suddenly. 'I know these Outsiders,' he said. 'Let me go to the Sacred Land alone. If I have to, I'll exchange my life for Ossama's!'

There were shouts and murmurs from the crowd, as some of the tribesmen regarded him with renewed respect. Khyar was watching him silently, stroking his chin, and Truman wondered what he was thinking. Old Khalis stood up and pointed at Truman with a claw like finger.

'Antara says he knows the Outsiders,' he said. 'He reminds us that he himself was an Outsider before he came here. Perhaps he knows more than he is telling us. Perhaps he desires to return to his own tribe.'

Before Truman could speak, Khyar exploded with rage. 'Anyone who calls Antara an Outsider must answer to me,' he bawled, staring down Khalis. 'He saved my life in the Funeral Plains, by the Light Mother's Wrath!'

Tissi, the Nazir, stood again and waved a hand to calm Khyar down. 'Khalis is old,' he said. 'Even older than me. He forgets that no one who has passed the *tafriq* has ever betrayed the Kel.'

He turned to face Truman. 'No one can doubt that you are one of us, Antara,' he said, 'and no one has the power to stop you going alone. But will the strangers be satisfied when they have sent you to the Light Mother? Will they go away and leave us in peace after that? No. Never. They won't leave until we force them to leave, and we shall have lost a sound warrior for nothing. Even if you succeed in exchanging your life for

Ossama's, it won't change anything. We'll still be here and they'll be there where the water is.'

The clamour began again, the shouts and squabbling reaching a crescendo of noise. 'We will approach the plateau where the Outsiders have made the new entrance at Riyat ash-Sha,' Tissi cried. 'I shall lead the attack personally, and the Ten Bravest will be with me – all but Hafid.'

He sought out the hatchet-faced man in the firelight. 'Hafid,' he said. 'You will lead the rest of the Kel back to the Wadi Howa, where they will be safe from flying machines until we return.'

Hafid stood up to protest. 'Nazir,' he began, 'I am a warrior. My place is in battle . . .'

'The Light Mother alone knows what the night will bring,' Tissi said, cutting him off. 'Who will lead the tribe if all our best fighters fall?'

Hafid bit his lip and nodded in agreement.

'My proposal is that we move tonight, at once,' the Nazir went on. 'We shall be hidden by the darkness. There is a dune barrier near Riyat ash-Sha where we can leave the camels, and make our way to the new pass on foot.'

The men shouted and waved their sabres, but Truman swore angrily to himself and strode away from them. Khyar blocked his way.

'Come Antara,' he said. 'Do you refuse to face danger with your brothers? We need your courage and strength.'

He placed a hand on Truman's shoulder, but Truman shrugged it off.

'No,' he said bitterly. 'I can't refuse while Ossama is alive. I will ride with you, Khyar. But you should have let me go alone. You don't know what's waiting for you there. May the Holy Mother have mercy on us all!'

43

Two hours before dawn, Sergei Rybakov lay on top of a cliff near the new entrance his men had blasted through the rimwall. He lay full-length on a rubber mat, peering through a night-scope, watching the ant-like figures a kilometre away as they dodged from dune to dune, working steadily towards the plateau. The number was pathetically small – they would last about five minutes in the face of the heavy stuff he'd got dug in below, if that. He chuckled to himself. The rag-heads didn't dream what was about to hit them – they didn't even know they were being watched. He peered at them again – black commas in the greyness, moving with a purposefulness and a precision that impressed him. He suddenly thought of Afghanistan and reminded himself not to underestimate the enemy. The Afghans had been primitive rag-heads too, but they'd held an entire Soviet army at bay.

Up to now the operation had gone like clockwork, except for the obstinate resistance of the handful of old men, women and children they'd found in the plateau. They'd fought astonishingly hard with their antique rifles and swords – he'd seen kids of seven and eight face his men fearlessly, armed with nothing more than sticks, stones and pocket-knives. Casualties on the Russian side had been irritatingly high, considering what they'd been up against, but he put that down to the problems of a first contact

253

in unfamiliar terrain. He rested his eyes from the lens for a moment, and sniffed the air, scenting the odours of chalk and smoke. The met boys said the satellites were tracking a sandstorm working its way up from the equator, but they estimated it wouldn't be here until mid-morning, and he knew the party would be well over by then.

There were soft footfalls behind him and in the moonlight Rybakov made out a figure climbing up the rocky defile towards the OP. It was Stein. *Shit*, he thought, *here's Dracula. That guy gives me the creeps.* The feeling was succeeded by another emotion which Rybakov recognized as satisfaction. After all, he thought, Stein had scored a brilliant own goal. His ambition had got the better of him. The Colonel might think they had a deal, but by making his joint-operation gambit Stein had effectively wiped out Rand's chances of sharing in the palladium. He might believe that his company was going to bring in the plant and take half the dividends, but once Rybakov's troops set up in the plateau he'd have another think coming.

Rybakov congratulated himself on having succeeded in getting Stein to leave his army chafing in their barracks thousands of miles away, and scoffed inwardly at Rand's arrogance in believing that 'his cartel' needed the Corporation's name as a front. Maynard's company had indeed been too tied up legally to use any more, but what Stein didn't guess was that there were far bigger fish involved in this deal – bigger than Rand's, bigger than the Russian mafiya itself.

Stein was wearing desert camouflage like the rest of them, but even in the moon's paleness Rybakov could tell he wore it with elegant grace as if it were a dress-suit. He sat down on the rubber mat nearby. 'Any developments?' he croaked.

'They're gathering for the big push,' Rybakov said derisively. 'They'll move at first light. Is going to be easy as falling off a log.'

Stein's smile was hidden in the darkness. 'You said the same thing about those old men and women your boys encountered,' he said drily. 'How many casualties did you take? I saw two children no higher than my knee hamstring one of your boys and slit his throat.'

Rybakov rolled over and stared at him. He was dying for a Marlboro, but he'd seen too many men drilled by snipers in Afghanistan to risk his life for a smoke. 'You want to take over operational command?' he demanded. 'Be my guest.'

'No, Sergei,' Stein said. 'You are doing adequately I think. Battle command is not my forte. My job is intelligence.'

'You were supposed to locate Truman,' Rybakov said, 'and you got jack shit, so don't come here twisting my dick, Stein. If you can't do your own job, don't tell me how to do mine.'

Stein thought of making a sarcastic remark about the so-called search and destroy mission Rybakov had tasked to deal with Truman a couple of days previously. It had lost contact on the first day, and never made the RV. Instead, he frowned bleakly. 'I wouldn't dream of it,' he said, 'but letting the old man go seems to have done the trick.'

Rybakov nodded. He had to admit Stein's ploy of letting the old guy escape had brought home the bacon. Last night their thermal imaging devices had detected fires on the plains about twenty kilo-metres to the south. That was where the rest of tribe was holing up. Rybakov had nearly sent the Apache to hit them, but he'd decided to see what they'd got first. He'd got rocket-launchers, mortars, machine-guns on fixed traverse, a ring of claymore mines down there. No way the nomads were going to walk through that. They could clean the rest of them out easily afterwards.

'You can bet your ass if Truman's alive, he's back there with the women and children,' he said. 'Still, you shouldn't have stiffed them all, Stein. Ever heard of hostages?'

'There's one left,' Stein whispered. 'The woman with the blue-green eyes.'

Rybakov chortled. 'Why'd you let her off the hook? Fancy her do you, Colonel?'

'She's something special, if that's what you mean,' Stein croaked. 'You could tell that by the way the others treated her. That old man could hardly stand up, yet he leapt to defend her as if his life depended on it. He called her "Kahina", which the Dwarf tells me means some kind of Prophetess. She kept on babbling about somebody called "Antara" whom she reckoned would lead a holy war, and drive us out. From what I recall, Antara's some sort of mythical hero of the Arabs.'

Rybakov snorted. 'I get the idea,' he said. 'The dead king who's gonna come back and pull their nuts outta the fire. So where is she now?'

'I've got her tied up in that big cave with the pictures. I'm saving her for special attention. I didn't want to miss the fireworks.'

Rybakov looked at the luminous face of his watch. 'Stick around,' he said. 'The fireworks will start in about twenty minutes. You'll have grandstand view from up here. You can even take part.'

He pointed to a sniper's rifle with a laser-sight lying next to him on the mat. 'We can take turns to pot them, no?' he said. 'Will be like shooting fairground ducks.'

He rolled back onto his stomach and began focusing the night-scope again, watching the files of his men in desert camouflage taking up their positions behind rocks and boulders. He picked up the walkie-talkie that lay beside him on the mat.

'Major Antonoff, this is Rybakov,' he said softly in Russian. 'The rag-heads are still gathering on the dunes a klick south of you, but I think we'll be seeing movement forwards soon. You got your night-sights zeroed-in? Good – and remember, don't fire until the first claymore is tripped. Then I want every one of them sons-of-bitches whacked out.'

44

THE NAZIR LED THE FLOWER OF the Kel Saghrana towards the
rimwall in pale moonlight, fifty picked fighters in spearhead
formation, with the Ten Bravest scattered through them. Truman
marvelled at their silence – not a murmur, not a cough, not a
rustle of clothing nor even the slightest clink of a displaced
stone. It was like being among a legion of ghosts, he thought.
The night was crisply cold, but each man had stripped down to
his sirwal so that any wounds he received would be clean. The
warriors carried only their rifles with the slings tied up, and their
sabres and bandoliers of ammunition across their chests. Many
of them had oiled their bodies to prevent the enemy from grabbing them, and had braided back their shoulder-length, butter-
smeared hair.

They walked barefoot, feeling their way as surely as night
insects, as the dark edifice of the rimwall loomed over them. It
seemed the Saghrana advance had gone undetected, but Truman
knew that was too good to be true. The nearer they approached
the rimwall, the more certain he was that they were walking into
a trap. He could almost sense it closing in around him as they
advanced, yet he knew he couldn't just turn and walk away. He
had been accepted by these people and his acceptance had its
price. And anyway, he had to find Ossama whatever the cost.
At least the Nazir hadn't committed the entire strength of the

tribe to the attack, he thought. The raiding party had moved up to the dune barrier on camels in small groups during the night. The camels were now hidden behind the dunes, watched by Yani and a troop of herdsboys.

The moon rolled out from under a wing of cloud, and the Saghrana froze instantly. For a moment the entire company held its breath, knowing that they were perfect targets here in the open. From the corner of his eye, Truman could make out the Nazir at point, a lizard-lean shape, holding his old Mauser across his chest, his grey dreadlocks hanging around his shoulders. At least in this army, Truman thought, the chiefs led from the front. The pass lay no more than three hundred metres away, a gaping hole of shadow, and for a moment Truman wondered if the Nazir would order a charge to close the distance quickly. But the moon was swallowed by cloud again and the *gom* moved on. Truman felt his senses screaming – if they were in anyone's sights, then the shooting was going to start any second.

Suddenly there was an audible whizz like a firework going up, and a brilliant yellow light erupted above them, ten times brighter than the moon. 'Flare!' Truman cried. 'Get down!' Get down!' But it was too late to dive for cover. At a signal from the Nazir the warriors dashed screaming towards the rimwall, firing as they ran at the unseen enemy. There was an earsplitting crack as the first claymore exploded and Truman saw the Nazir come apart at the seams, vanishing in a puff of smoke. Then all hell was let loose.

A heavy machine gun drummed up from the shadows on the left, its tracer ripping through the night like a swarm of hellish fireflies, and almost at once another began on the right, a stuttering deadly drumbeat pumping out rounds at almost point-blank range. There were screams from warriors hit on both flanks, and then the deep-throated thunder of rocket-launchers, amplified by the rimwall, and the thump of missiles exploding among the attackers in great spears of orange flame.

Truman heard the whistle of mortar-bombs and ducked instinctively as two or three of them crumped into the sand nearby, sending shockwaves through the *gom*, knocking the men down like ninepins. Truman hit the ground next to Khyar who was firing back, working the bolt on his rifle like a madman, his face contorted with fear and confusion. More mortar bombs exploded far off to their left and a wave of dust and smoke lofted over them. The machine-guns kept up an unfaltering palpitation of fire from both sides, kicking up stones and spatters of sand, and another rocket boomed out and burst among them like a thunderclap. In its flash, Truman saw a scene of revolting carnage. The sand before the rimwall was a seething mass of broken bodies, of bloody, shrieking, mutilated tribesmen, many with arms and legs blown off. Those who were still on their feet were running round in circles like headless chickens, loosing off rounds so wildly that they were shooting their own comrades.

There was a momentary pause in the machine-gun fire, but it was replaced by a concentrated salvo of fire from men camouflaged in the shadows. More flares went up, and in their light Truman saw Isham, one of the Ten Bravest, leaping back towards him with his oiled hair flying, his torso already a bloodied pulp. Before he came within ten metres a high-velocity round from somewhere above sheared half of his head away, splattering Truman's beard with fragments of skin and brain. He heard the roar of engines, and saw a monstrous rhinoceros shape sliding easily out of a hidden berm – an armoured car, spluttering fire from its mounted gun. A search-light on its snout sprang on suddenly, transfixing them in its blinding beam.

'Kill that light!' Truman yelled at Khyar.

He saw the warrior tense as he caught his breath. There was a crack and a blade-shaped splurge from the muzzle of Khyar's rifle, followed by a crash as the searchlight shattered. Truman gripped Khyar's shoulder. 'Get out!' he shouted. 'Run!'

The warrior glared at him angrily over his rifle butt. 'A warrior of the Kel doesn't run away,' he bawled. A seam of tracer from the armoured car sizzled into the sand around them and Khyar jumped.

Truman gasped and jerked his arm back powerfully. 'If we don't run there'll *be* no Kel. Holy Mother's wrath, we have to warn the others. Come on!' Bullets spattered around their feet as they zig-zagged wildly towards the nearest nest of rocks, but the armoured car halted, its turret manoeuvring to come to bear on warriors trapped on the battlefield. Another armoured vehicle emerged from a berm on the left flank and rumbled across at an angle to cut off the retreat of any survivors. More flares popped open above them and the machine-guns stopped firing.

Once in the shelter of the rocks, Khyar turned to look, but Truman grabbed him and half dragged him through a narrow gulley between the dunes. As they emerged on to the sebkha beyond, and broke into a jog there was an ear-shattering howl of rotor-blades above them, and Truman looked up to see a dark ovoid shadow sailing across the dunes trailing a beam of light.

'That's an Apache gunship,' he screamed.

Khyar dropped on one knee and cocked his rifle, ready to take it on, but Truman jerked him away again.

'You can't fight it,' he grated in Khyar's ear. Rounds from the Huey's guns were ripping up the sebkha behind them, and the circle of light from its beam was sweeping the dunes, hunting them methodically.

'There's no escape!' Khyar cried. 'There's no way out!'

Truman spotted a dense focus of shadows at the base of a dune and made for it, zig-zagging across the salt-crusted ground, with Khyar trailing him. Close up he realized the shadows were the entrance to a disused hyena's sett, just large enough for him and Khyar to crawl into.

'Get in there,' he hissed. 'It's our only hope.'

They crept in and pressed close together in the darkness, just as the search-beam passed above them. The chopper stuttered over their hiding place and was gone, but moments later there were two crumping explosions from beyond the dunes.

'Light Mother's wrath!' Truman whispered. 'Yani. The camels.'

There was dead silence for a while, then Truman felt Khyar's body quaking with emotion. 'You should have let me die, Antara,' the warrior mumbled, his voice breaking. 'How can we face the *harruum* with all those warriors down?'

45

Truman's eyes watered bitterly in the smoke of the bonfire, but he was too weary to shift position, too numbed by what he'd seen even to remind the Kel that there were such things as thermal imaging devices that could pinpoint the fire from far off. Near him sat Khyar and the pathetic survivors of the raid on Bint Hammou – only seven men, almost all of them wounded. Yani was the only one left of the herdsboys who'd been guarding the camels behind the dunes. Truman and Khyar had found the youth, lying on a dune, screaming for the Light Mother, delirious with pain. He had been blinded in one eye by a piece of shrapnel from the Apache gunship's rockets. Truman shook his head despairingly as he remembered the sight – Yani was just a kid – he hadn't even passed the *tafriq*.

Of the fifty camels the Saghrana had left there, only ten were unscathed. The rest had been blown to smithereens or were so badly injured that Truman and Khyar had had to put them out of their misery. It had taken them and the rest of the survivors the whole day, dicing with the Lesser Sandtide that had blown up at mid-morning, to rendezvous with the main body of the Kel in Hawa gorge.

Now, the walls of the narrow chasm echoed with the ghostly sound of women keening and children crying, and Truman brushed the smoke-tears from his eyes to focus on the sea of shadows beyond the group of survivors – five hundred warriors who hadn't taken part in the raid. They were bareheaded, their hair frizzed out in unkempt mops, their faces smeared with ashes as a sign of mourning. There was a hush over the company and Truman looked up and saw the moon emerge from behind a cloud, casting a silken luminescence across the ash-covered faces. Almost at once, he was struck by the preternatural aura of calmness about the men. There was a fearsome energy here that was almost palpable – an energy kept in check by generations of austerity and desert discipline. It was the same calm he'd felt in the air while waiting for the Dragon.

The Sandtide had petered out at sunset, but Truman knew it had saved them all. It would have sent the enemy's communications equipment haywire and grounded the Apache, covering the tracks of the thousands of camels that had ferried the tribe here. Hawa itself was a deep limestone gash cut through a warren of fish-scale dunes – a natural hiding-place whose walls were riddled with caves and rocky overhangs. He knew Hafid had posted sentries on the dunes and sent pickets far into the desert on every side. He prayed to the Light Mother that tonight, at least, the enemy would leave them alone. *The enemy*, he thought bitterly, *my own people – Outsiders. No, no longer my people. I am Saghrana now.*

He tried to turn his mind away from from those terrible moments at Riyat ash-Sha, yet the images came back and back, making him quake. Behind those images were others, tantalizing shadows of a past he'd forgotten, memories liberated by the *tafriq*, that had returned to him again and again over the past weeks, each time more detailed and more vivid. His body remembered the pain of the black-room in Beirut, the terrible suffering it had been subjected to, the electrodes on his genitals, the burns on his neck, the slashing and lashing and beating, the removal of his nails with rusty pliers. The pain had almost destroyed him and he'd escaped from his body into a safe-haven beyond, for an eternity. When he'd finally opened his eyes and found himself in that place in Switzerland, it was as if he'd been born again.

The massacre at Riyat ash-Sha had opened the floodgates, and now images rushed back on him like a riptide. He recalled waking up in the Sanatorium Berghof, not knowing where he was. He recalled wandering down a bleak hospital corridor and into a room where an elderly, balding man in a white coat was sitting at a desk. Behind the desk was a window giving a breathtaking view of snow-capped mountain peaks. The man had red cheeks and wore silver rimmed glasses, his eyes watery blue and shifty beneath them. When he'd asked how he'd got there, the white-coated man had shown him a form committing him to the Sanatorium, signed by his mother, Lady Fiona Truman-Keynes.

'But she wasn't the one who brought you,' the man said. 'His name was Morgan. I assumed he was a friend of the family.'

Truman tried to push the memory aside, forcing himself back to the present, to the debacle at Riyat ash-Sha. He was still shocked by its suddenness, he realized. It had all been over in minutes. So devastatingly final. He had fought men face to face with a sword in his hand, but that had been nothing beside this blind massacre of human souls. He felt numb at the idea of facing the enemy once more, but he knew he had no choice. He would go back for Ossama, even if he had to take on all the enemies alone. He became aware suddenly that the holy man, Sij Yasid, was speaking, his eyes like sink-holes in the owlish, ash-white face.

'We commend the souls of the dead to the safe-keeping of the Light Mother,' the old man recited, holding his hands palm-up in supplication. 'They are gone but they will remain with us always. Their voices will always be here among us – in these rocks, in the Sacred Land, speaking in the winds that cross the Funeral Plains. Death is but the horizon, and the horizon is but the limit of our sight. The Light Mother have mercy on them.'

'*The Light Mother have mercy on them*,' came back the refrain from a thousand mouths.

As the voices died away, Hafid rose from the ranks, his hatchet face obscured by ash, his body naked but for a loincloth and his sabre slung on a baldric across his chest.

'Brothers and sisters of the Kel,' he began in a low voice. 'Our war-leader, Tissi bin Tamghar, is dead, among forty two of the finest warriors of the Kel. Of the Ten Bravest, only Khyar and myself are left. Worst of all, the Kahina – our eyes and ears – is held hostage by an enemy whose faces our warriors never even saw.'

There were growls and cries of disbelief from the audience, and Khyar rose heavily to his feet, his face wild, bug-eyed under a covering of ash. 'It's true, by the Sacred Ancestors! Ask any man here of the seven that lived. We were as quiet as snakes. We got near enough to smell the sweat of the enemy, and then the whole world exploded around us. It was as if those people could see in the dark. Antara warned us but we laughed at him. We didn't even see anyone to shoot at. It was over in a few winks of an eye, by the Light Mother. Never in my life have I seen anything like this.'

The buzz had become an outcry now, and suddenly an old man stood up and hurled his burnoose to the ground, shaking his wild hair across his shoulders. He unsheathed a dagger, and as the crowd watched he slit his naked chest from the base of his withered neck to his abdomen, until blood gushed from it. He raised the bloody dagger high and the curved blade scintillated in the light of the flames. '*Eeeeeyuh,*' he screamed. 'Revenge is the sacred duty of the Kel. For every warrior fallen, there will be a price!'

There were hysterical yells from the onlookers, and an eldritch ululating from the watching womenfolk. More warriors leapt up screeching, throwing off their cloaks, mutilating the flesh of their naked torsos with sabres and knives. Truman watched them with a feeling of disbelief. The transition from stoic acceptance to frenzied action had been so sudden it shocked him.

Khyar held up a trembling hand. 'Stop!' he croaked, almost pleadingly. 'Listen! We can never fight these machines. Don't you understand? They saw us in the dark and destroyed us before we even got in range with our rifles. They even had a flying machine that chased us, and destroyed the camels with its fire. Our weapons are nothing against these enemies.'

He halted, and Truman saw that he was fighting back his emotions. 'I am a warrior of the Kel. Six men have I killed in battle, and never, until today, have I run from the enemy. I wish I had died on the field with the Nazir and the others, but it was not the Light Mother's will. We can't fight these Outsiders.'

There was silence again. The men who had mutilated themselves halted and stared at him. Khyar was a notorious hot-head – one of the most aggressive hawks of the Kel. His statement astonished them.

'But the Sacred Land?' a warrior protested. 'There is grazing here for a few days and no water. Without the Sacred Land the *bil* will die. If the *bil* die, the Kel are finished.'

Khyar wiped dust away from his lips, and stared around him. 'The Outsiders fight in a way we have never seen, but there's one of us who understands them – Antara. Antara must teach us. Antara must be our war-leader, our new Nazir.'

Truman felt himself blushing. He gazed at the curling flames of the fire and wouldn't meet Khyar's eyes.

'*Antara!*' the crowd yelled. 'Antara must speak!'

Truman sat rigid, glued to the ground. He dug his fingers into the warm sand beneath him, praying that the crowd would turn their attention to someone else.

'*Antara!*' the warriors roared. '*Antara!*'

Finally he lifted his eyes to Khyar. 'I can't,' he whispered urgently. 'I'm a newcomer here. I can't be your leader. Don't do this, Khyar.'

Instead, it was Hafid who rose to his feet. The Kel cheered. Hafid was known as a sound and reasonable man as well as a brave one, and Truman understood why the Nazir had left him in charge of the tribe. If anyone could fill Tissi's footsteps, he thought, it would be Hafid. The warrior held up both hands. 'I agree with Khyar,' he said. 'Antara was once an Outsider, but he has proved himself a brave and resourceful warrior of the Kel. He was the only one here who knew what to expect, yet

266

still he went along with the *gom* to face death. If we are to regain the Sacred Land, only Antara can lead us. The Kahina is his wife and she carries his child . . .' he broke off and stared at Truman with eyes that were dark gaps in the ashen face. 'He can't refuse us now.'

The warriors began to shout his name again, and Truman felt a rush of fire pass through his body. He cast left and right for a way to escape, but knew there was no way out. Being part of something worked two ways – it had rewards, and it also had responsibilities. Sweat began to pour down his face. He had to get Ossama back, but how could he fight the Outsiders with swords and a few antique rifles? He closed his eyes, and suddenly another image flashed behind them. He had an idea. It was a last resort, but it was their only hope. He stood up unsteadily and there was a gasp from the audience.

'*Antara*!' they shouted.

He lifted his hand. 'I'm not fit to be your leader,' he said. 'There are many finer men here than me – Hafid and Khyar for a start. But Hafid's right. I would die before leaving the Kahina to the mercies of these men. We can't defeat them in open battle – Khyar spoke true about that. We must fight fire with fire. We need help, and if you will trust me, then by the grace of the Light Mother, there might just be a way.'

When the crowd had dispersed he called Hafid and Khyar to him. 'Khyar, where is the satcom phone? The thing you and Makhlud found among the possessions of the Outsiders who came to kill me?'

'It's in my baggage, Antara,' Khyar said. 'But why? You said that thing was a doorway to the Outside. If we use it we will be opening the way for more of our enemies.'

Truman weighed these words up, sensing the truth in them. Khyar was uncannily near the mark, he thought. Who knew what can of worms a simple phone call would open up?

'The Light Mother is our strength,' he said, 'but our only help comes from the Outside now.'

While Khyar was bringing the satcom, Truman scoured his own baggage to find his clothes – the ones he had worn when he'd first come to the Sacred Land. He found them screwed into a ball at the bottom of a saddle-bag, and he pulled out his old jacket. It was an artifact from another planet – a thing that seemed foreign and useless to him now. In its pockets, though, he found a bunch of receipts and, finally, Whitehaven's card, wrinkled and dog-eared, but still legible. He closed his eyes and pictured Whitehaven. The pipe, the old parka, the big man pushing the card across the table at Gatwick airport. He had seemed so sure they would meet again, and Truman felt reluctant to fulfil the Englishman's expectations. Then he thought of the Kel and the dead warriors at Riyat ash-Sha, Whitehaven was their only chance.

When Khyar returned with the satcom phone, Truman sat it on a rock and switched it on, setting the antenna and orienting it by the stars. Then he tapped in Whitehaven's number. There was a long pause, broken by a female automaton's voice 'Please state your name, and give the name of the person you require.'

46

Richard Whitehaven stuffed his folded canopy under a rock next to his helmet, and pulled the release-catches on his container. Inside was his bergen, his belt-equipment, an M16 rifle with 203 grenade-launcher underslung, and two 66 mm rocket-launchers. He picked up the rifle, slipped a magazine out of one of his pouches, and clicked it into place. He shot the breech-block back once, nudging a round into the chamber, and set the safety-catch, then, cradling the weapon in the crook of his arm, he pulled a water-bottle from its pouch and took a long, grateful swig.

He felt more confident now he had his feet on the DZ. The time for butterflies was always in the aircraft before the green light came on. He breathed in the clean desert air and thought once more of Oman in the seventies. Until that mortar bomb had come whistling overhead he'd had the time of his life there, and it was good to be back at the sharp end. Previous missions with MI6 had taken him to the streets in Berlin and Moscow, but it wasn't the same.

There was some special attraction about this landscape that he could never quite define. Perhaps it was the absence of anything standing between you and eternity. Maybe it came from being born in the industrial sprawl of Manchester – miles and miles of dripping red brick streets, infinity shut out by walls, roofs and windows. From the age of seventeen, when he'd run away from the tedious apprentice plumber's job in Salford, he'd wanted nothing more than to be a soldier. His father had been a milkman, and though he'd never suffered a day's illness in his life, it had always seemed to Whitehaven that he'd been more dead than alive. The only time he ever got animated was when he told his stories about being in the navy during the war. The Atlantic convoys – U-boats, torpedos, men drowned – it was only then that Whitehaven realized what courage and resolution could lie in the heart of even the most ordinary of men.

Most of all though, Whitehaven recalled the misery of those mean streets – cats' piss in the snow, porridge for breakfast, stealing pennies from the church collection-box. His father had always insisted that a sound apprenticeship would set his son up for life, but Whitehaven had no desire to be set up for life in that twilight world. He'd craved adventure, action, drama – all the things his father had once known. At the Parachute Regiment Depot in Aldershot he'd found that not only did he enjoy the imposed hardship and discipline, but he also thrived on it. He'd passed out top of his class and received the baton for best recruit. He'd done three tours in Northern Ireland in quick succession, shot a terrorist on the street in Belfast, and seen five of his mates blown to pieces by radio-controlled mines.

He had already decided, though, that he wanted to go further than the Paras. The Special Air Service Regiment was the best, and he'd applied for selection and passed first time. With the Regiment he'd been involved in secret operations all over the world, culminating in Operation Storm, Oman 1972, when a communist mortar had put paid to his active career with the army. After that, MI6 had been a poor second best, despite the fact that he was officially promoted major. He'd thought about jacking it in for good, of course, but by then he'd been married to Margery with Lance growing up, and what other employment could a trained killer-cum-intelligence agent find at the age of forty?

The truth was that Whitehaven had always felt a fish out of

270

water in MI6. He thought of himself as a straight arrow, and he just didn't have the Machiavellian frame of mind required to do well in 'the Office'. MI6 people were liars by profession, yet Whitehaven admitted to himself, almost guiltily, that he was a poor liar – his nose didn't actually grow longer, but his mother had always said there was something about his face. He supposed he still saw himself as a white knight fighting evil, and the wheeling and dealing got him down. Nothing was ever what you thought it was.

Take Truman, for example. When he'd first met him at Gatwick he'd formed an impression that the guy was a straight man like himself, let down by forces beyond his control and doing the best he could. Now it appeared that he might have been in on the affair from the beginning. Whitehaven didn't have certain proof that Truman was *Haymaker* other than a coincidence of dates, but the fact that the archeologist had suddenly contacted him out of nowhere, asked for his assistance, and told him exactly where the drop should be, seemed another unlikely coincidence. Whitehaven had pondered why Morgan had delayed sending him in, even though they'd got word long ago that Rybakov's mercenaries were on the move. Now the enemy were already established in the plateau and the task of driving them out was going to be that much more difficult. It was almost as if Morgan didn't want to win. They could have tracked the Saghrana migrations by spy satellite, dropped in close to them any time. Morgan had procrastinated for day after day, but as soon as Truman had phoned he'd given the green light, and they'd been airborne within 24 hours. It looked as if Morgan *knew* Truman was going to call, and had been delaying the mission deliberately, waiting for his contact.

And what if Truman was playing a double game? True, Maynard was dead, but what if 'Sir Daniel' was still working for Kortex, and the whole thing was a set-up? When he'd put this to Morgan, his boss had seemed totally confident. If Truman was still loyal to Kortex, he'd argued, there would have been no point in his drawing attention to himself by a phone call. Whitehaven hadn't been satisfied with this answer, and had thought more than twice about refusing to go in. In the end, though, he was a soldier and it wasn't his to reason why. He'd bitten the bullet and jumped as planned, but he still didn't like the sound of it at all.

He set the water bottle back in its sheath, took his binos from a pocket of his bergen and got down on his belly, sweeping the serir from horizon to horizon. It was still early morning and the sun was a pale ecliptic hanging over cream-icing dunes in the east. To the north he could just make out the broken-tooth outline of the plateau, and to the south the serir stretched on, a soft-padded plain of sand punctuated by nests of boulders and smaller patches of pea-gravel. It was a good DZ, but appalling cover. You couldn't even have hidden an ant on this serir.

Not far away – less than a kilometre he reckoned – he could see the drogues of the first of the heavy-drop containers billowing slightly in the breeze. Beyond that he could see four more containers distributed along a crooked north-south axis, each one a few hundred metres apart. God bless the Brylcream Boys. Only special forces dispatchers could have put the goods down so tight. Other than the fluttering parachutes, though, he saw no movement. He smelt chalky desert scents and felt the lambent heat in the air. He'd worked out the exact coordinates of the drop-zone from Truman's description, and before he'd hurled himself out of the C130, just before dawn, he'd seen the signal-fires he'd asked Truman to light. Truman and his boys had to be here somewhere, but it beat him where, because there was nowhere to hide in this place. There wasn't even a sniff of smoke from a fire.

Whitehaven put his binos away and rolled over on his back, pulling a Mars bar from the top pocket of his smock. He sighed as he shucked the wrapping. Old habits never died, he thought. You always kept your Mars bars in your top right hand pocket so as your oppo would known where to look when you went down. In the old days it had almost been an SOP. He wolfed down the chocolate and consulted his leather-capped G10 watch:

06.25, and the sun had been up half an hour. If they didn't get the weapons off the DZ pretty soon, he reckoned the enemy would be here.

He sensed a movement to his left and sat up abruptly, grabbing his M16. Then he gasped as four or five figures seemed to pop up out of the ground not fifty metres away – small, savage-looking men with thick beards and shaggy haircuts, naked except for loincloths or baggy pants dyed the same colour as the serir. They were carrying antique WW1 bolt-action rifles, and swords slung across their chests, and they looked like they meant business. There was another tremble of movement behind him, and he glanced back to see more of the elf-like men materializing from the ground. *Shit*, he thought to himself, *they were there all the time. Shit, these guys are good.*

He snapped into a kneeling position and slipped the rifle-butt into his shoulder, drawing a bead on the nearest man. This one was a head taller than most of the others, a beanpole of a fellow with a matted mass of whisker and a scrag of filthy hair. He wore baggy trousers held up by a thick belt with a dagger in it, and his ectomorphic torso was draped with a sword-belt and an ammunition-bandolier. In his left hand he carried a rifle, but the weapon wasn't pointed at Whitehaven, and the man's posture was relaxed.

'*Agif!*' Whitehaven snapped. '*Ma tiju gharib*. Don't come any closer!'

It wasn't until the rag-head stopped that Whitehaven realized there was something familiar about him. 'Jesus Christ! Truman? Is it you?'

The rag-head with the matted beard smiled truculently. 'Welcome to the *Mufarida*, Mr Whitehaven,' he said.

47

THERE WAS A SHARP DETONATION AND a whoff of orange flame from the rear of the 66mm rocket launcher and a hundred metres away a granite boulder ruptured into a thousand pieces. The nomads were cheering, but Whitehaven put down the empty rocket-tube and directed their attention grimly to the straw dummy he'd erected behind him, which was now burning fiercely.

'Backblast!' he said in Arabic. 'This baby'll knock out almost anything moving at a hundred and fifty paces, but remember – you stand behind it and you'll get fried.'

To give them an idea of the range he and Truman had paced out a kilometre along the valley floor and marked it with rocks at hundred metre intervals. It was amazing how quickly the Arabs had picked it up. 'OK,' he said. 'You now know how to use the 66mm. Each one of you now goes and instructs ten more, and when they've got it, each of them tells another ten. And no test-firing until . . . Antara says so.'

He watched as Truman dismissed the men, doling out a rocket-launcher to each, and marvelled once again at the respect they gave him. They seemed to think the sun shone out of his backside – he could almost hear the admiration in their voices. They listened to Whitehaven politely enough, but they would do nothing until Truman OK'd it. He felt like a crow in the Regiment again, with the old hands pretending he wasn't there. That didn't bother him. Even in Oman it had been the same. The SAS had trained the Firqan, but the nomads had always remained slightly aloof and wouldn't take orders from anyone except their own chiefs.

When things had got noisy, though, the Firgan had always known that they could count on the Regiment to back them to the hilt – and vice versa, as he knew to his great advantage. He respected their right to distance. After all, this was their own land, even though the country was ruled from far away Khartoum. As he saw it, British aims here were much what they'd been in the Gulf in the eighties. Train the locals, defeat the foreign enemy in a secret war, earn the gratitude of the government in the form of millions of dollars worth of contracts for British companies. It had worked a blinder in Oman and it could work here as well. Britain was the Sudan's former colonial power, and relations had remained cordial up to the coup in 1989. After that they'd been strained, but ever since the country had started exporting oil a year back, Britain had been looking for a way to restore the old ties.

Morgan had dropped hints that the FO had come to a secret agreement with Khartoum. The Sudanese government was fighting rebels in the south and couldn't afford a campaign in the desert as well. The British would be their proxies. The palladium and platinum here would provide a welcome boost to the Sudan's economy, and if Britain secured it for the Sudanese government, a British mining company – a legitimate one – would almost certainly get the job of extracting it. There would follow British contracts for arms, roads, construction, infrastructure, security advisors – all manner of spin-offs. What troubled Whitehaven most, though, was the fact that the plateau was a sacred site for the Saghrana. Sudanese-British mining interests would be protected by government troops, or another army of mercenaries. No one had told the Saghrana they were being trained to kick out one enemy only to find them replaced by another. Whitehaven owed it to himself, and to the nomads who'd saved him in

Oman, to make sure these Bedouin got a square deal before that happened.

He was suddenly dog-tired. He was getting too old for this, he thought. From the moment they'd got the weapons off the DZ yesterday, he'd been lecturing the boys on small-arms – the Heckler-Koch L85 rifle, the 66mm rocket, the L2 grenade, the 5.56mm light machine-gun – even night-scopes and sniper-rifles. You had to hand it to these guys, he thought, they might be illiterate, but they were damn fast learners. It was a crash course of a crash course that would normally take a couple of weeks, but they were naturals. Most of them got it right the first time, and anyway they were dead shots – right on the money. The weapons had cost a small fortune, he reflected, but whatever Morgan's real motives in sending them, it'd probably been a sound investment. They'd got themselves an army of natural fighters here at zero expense.

Whitehaven sat on a rock and lit his pipe, observing Truman's shrewd handling of the men. Life here in the desert brought back vivid memories of the old days – same tents, same faces, same smells. It was interesting to see that people still lived like this in the twenty-first century. There was something admirable about the Saghrana, that he had to admit, but you wouldn't have caught him togged up like one of them, or making oaths to this 'Light Mother' like Truman did. Truman had 'gone native' in a way that wouldn't have been possible for himself, no matter how long he stayed with them. It was odd how the east seemed to take Brits two ways, he reflected. Either they ended up aping the natives and their customs, like Truman, or they became more emphatically British than ever – like himself.

It had happened to him in Oman, he remembered. The longer he'd been there, the more ideal his image of Britain had become, so that actually going back there was a disappointment. He'd seen the same thing, but much more dramatically, among Brits who'd spent their whole lives abroad. In a way he envied Truman his ability to switch roles and cultures, but on the other hand he knew it was basically a con – a way of controlling them. What

276

would Truman himself have thought of an Arab who tried to pretend he was a Brit? These Bedouin might find Whitehaven a tad less chummy, but at least they couldn't accuse him of pretending to be something he wasn't.

He scanned the floor of the canyon, where rifles, machine-guns, grenades, ammunition-clips and other kit lay strewn on blankets and rugs like an arms-dealer's yard-sale. Truman picked up an L85 rifle and weighed it in his hand. 'So light,' he said. 'It's incredible the stuff they have now.'

Whitehaven puffed smoke and grinned cheesily. 'Better than that old Martini you've got, anyway,' he said. 'Weighs about 4.5 kilos with a full mag on. Fires 650 rounds a minute semi – up to 800 fully automatic. Effective range of 400 metres. With these little darlings, and the LSWs and sixty-sixes you can take on anything on the ground, even those APCs they've got.'

'And the Apache?'

Whitehaven shook his head. 'No way,' he said. 'Those kites have got Kevlon-bonded boron chloride shields. Carry laser-guided Hellfire missiles that can strike more than five kilometres away, and take out any known battle-tank. Only way to deal with the son-of-a-bitch is on the ground. Get in there and put a charge on the air intake or the rotors.'

Truman frowned and cradled the rifle in his arms. The day was meandering towards sunset, the gorge criss-crossed with alternating sequences of light and shade. Out on the skyline, beyond the walls of the canyon, the dunes were outlined in a pinkish gauze. 'Who exactly are we fighting?' Truman asked in Arabic. 'Is it Rand's or Kortex?'

'Rand's and Kortex are partners now,' Whitehaven said. 'But these are Russian mercenaries. Ex-Spetznatz vets hired by the mafiya. They're the guys I warned you were behind Kortex, remember? They're good as mercs go, but your ragheads will do fine, Truman. If we can ground the Huey, that is.'

Truman scratched his rough beard and scowled. 'I'd like to get two things straight, Mr Whitehaven. First, these men aren't ''rag-heads'' – they're Kel Saghrana – a very proud people.

Second, my name's not Truman any more. I'm Antara, acting Nazir of the Kel. And I'd prefer if we talk in Arabic, otherwise they'll think there's some sort of conspiracy going on. The Kel are very curious, and they don't have hidden agendas.'

Whitehaven guffawed. 'That's a bit rich coming from you.' Truman looked at him sharply. 'What do you mean?'

'Nah, nothing,' Whitehaven said. 'You've got to play the part, I suppose.'

Truman turned on him, his eyes flashing. 'Look, things have changed since you collared me at Gatwick, right? I'm not playing a part. I found something here that I spent my life looking for, and I'm never going back. I'm one of them now.'

'Yeah,' Whitehaven sneered, 'and I'm an eskimo. You can drop the high-and-mighty act with me. I know who you are. Five months ago you were an out of work trowel jockey, now you're bloody Genghis Khan. Either you're a complete screwball, or you're hiding something.'

For a moment Truman's brow furrowed under the wild mop of hair and Whitehaven thought he was going to take a swing at him. Then Truman relaxed and turned his back. He pulled off his burnoose in a single movement, exposing the deeply-etched tracklines of the lash, traversing his back from buttocks to shoulder.

Whitehaven almost dropped his pipe. 'Christ!' he gasped. 'What the hell did they do to you?'

Truman replaced the burnoose quickly. 'It's a kind of initiation. Like I told you, I'm one of them, and whether you happen to approve or not doesn't matter a damn, because *they* think I'm one of them, and it's their rules I'm playing by. I don't know what you think I am, but I used that satcom phone for one reason – to return these people, my people, to their land, and to get my wife back.'

This time Whitehaven did drop his pipe. 'Your what?'

'My wife,' Truman repeated. 'She's being held hostage by those bastards in Bint Hammou.'

Whitehaven waved his hand pacifyingly and retrieved the

 278

Falcon from the sand. He lifted it and blew dust away from the bowl, wondering whether Truman really was out of his box, or if this was just part of the deep cover. *A wife?* If it was cover, he was playing it right up to the maker's nameplate on this one. He stuck the pipe in his teeth and wheezed with false laughter. 'OK,' he said. 'Have it your own way, but I reckon you and Morgan cooked up something between you, and since my tender arse is on the line I want to know what it is.'

Truman eyes flickered wide at the mention of the name Morgan, and though it was only for a fraction of a second, Whitehaven noticed. That proved it, he thought. Truman knew who Morgan was all right.

'I don't know anybody called Morgan,' Truman said.

It was a lie, Whitehaven thought, and it sounded like a lie. 'Yeah?' he said contemptuously. 'Then where d'you think all this kit came from, Santa Claus?'

Truman watched him with a face made deliberately blank. 'OK, Mr Whitehaven. What do *you* think is happening here?'

'What I think is going down is that HMG has made a pact with the Sudanese government to kick out the interlopers, like we kicked out the commies from Oman in the seventies. That will leave the site open for legitimate British companies working under Sudanese patronage.'

Truman eyed him speculatively. 'And where do you stand on that?'

'I agreed to the deal because I owe my life to guys like these nomads, and I want to make sure they don't get scragged. There aren't many indigenous cultures like this left. You once called that my "holier-than-thou" attitude, remember? Well for your information, what you see is what you get.'

Truman laughed. 'Then we're on the same side. I can't see the problem.'

'The problem, Mr Antara, is that there's an alternative scenario. That you are working for someone very high up in the British government, who thinks they ought to have the rare earth for themselves, and these nomads are being played. By you,

Truman. You promised to liberate their sacred plateau from the enemy, but when the scrapping's over, maybe you're just going to hand it over to a new boss-man. If so, then I'm the dumb piggy in the middle whose going to wind up up shit creek.'

Truman looked at him incredulously. 'That's ridiculous.'

'Is it? I can't help remembering that you're the one who got us into this. If you hadn't brought those rare earth samples back and handed them over to the Office, there'd be no issue. None of us would have been here, and your nomads would still be living in ignorant bliss. You've worked for my bosses before, Truman, I'm sure of that. Now I've got the feeling that someone out here is working for Q-ops, and since I know it isn't me, I see only one possible candidate.'

Truman was suddenly confused and angry. Almost without thinking, he let the L85 slip into his hands. Whitehaven sensed menace in the movement.

'You're talking horse shit,' Truman said. 'There's no secret plot except in your paranoid mind. And I didn't give the samples to anybody. I sent them to Maynard, because they were his. As for this "Q-ops", I don't know what the hell you're talking about.'

Whitehaven's eyes were glued to the rifle now, and he saw that Truman's hands were slowly squeezing its stock. 'Yeah?' he said again, in English. 'And I don't suppose you know who *Haymaker* is, either?'

Truman blanched suddenly, and Whitehaven noticed beads of sweat trickling down the side of his face. That was two to nil, he thought. Truman knew Morgan and he knew *Haymaker* too. He watched Truman's knuckles tighten on the weapon.

'I could take you out right here,' Truman said through gritted teeth, 'and nobody would say a word. The only thing that's stopping me is that it would be against the Saghrana code of honour.'

They faced each other tensely for a moment and then a long shadow fell between them. Whitehaven looked up and saw the hatchet-faced guy Truman had introduced as Hafid standing with his back to the sinking sun. The tribesman looked very alert, poised on the balls of his feet, rocking forward in his sand-hued burnoose, with one of the new rifles clutched across his chest as if it was something precious. He looked from Truman to Whitehaven and back. 'Is anything wrong, Antara?'

'No,' Truman said. 'We were just discussing plans for the attack.'

'Good,' Hafid said. 'I've brought old Ayoub with me as you requested.'

He made a beckoning gesture and the old man appeared from behind a nest of boulders, a scrawny figure in a ragged, pepper and salt burnoose. As they squatted down together, Truman noticed that Ayoub's eyes were bloodshot, the lacerations on his face and limbs swollen, his cheeks hollow cavities, his skin sallow and pale. 'Are you still ill?' he inquired.

The old man peered at him. 'No,' he said. 'But I'm not happy with myself, Antara. The Light Mother forgive me. It's my fault the Nazir and all those warriors were slaughtered. I know now why the Outsiders didn't kill me. They tricked me – let me escape on purpose, knowing I'd tell the Kel and lead you all into the trap.'

Truman put a hand on the old man's emaciated arm. 'It's not your fault,' he murmured. 'If you hadn't warned us, we'd have ridden right into them with the women and children anyway. Maybe there'd have been no one left at all.'

Whitehaven noticed that he didn't say anything about the fact that it was his fault the bloody Russkies were there in the first place. 'All this is very touching,' he said, 'but it doesn't get us anywhere. What we're faced with is frontal assaults on two well-defended passes, manned by superior numbers with superior firepower. In text-book military terms we're talking a big no-no. Theoretically you'd need ten times your full strength to do it. OK, the *esprit* of your assault force counts for a lot, but you're looking at huge casualty lists.'

Truman shook his head. 'The Kel can't stand heavy losses. This isn't a professional army we're talking about. These men are individuals, not numbers, and every loss means a cut in the tribe's ability to survive. What we need is a third way – over the rimwall maybe. Is there any way it can be climbed, Hafid?'

The hatchet-faced man shook his head. 'It's too steep. The only weak point was the one the Outsiders found.'

'What we need is a Trojan horse,' Whitehaven said.

Ayoub's rheumy eyes suddenly filled with excitement. 'Wait, Antara. There is another way into the plateau – a secret way that only the Burrowers know.'

Truman stared at him expectantly and Whitehaven cocked his ears, trying to pick up the words of the unfamiliar dialect.

'Long ago,' the old man said, 'the Imenan built many qanats in the Sacred Land, to carry water to their fields and orchards. In those days – the Time of the First Reckoning – the Sacred Land was a paradise. Many of the tunnels are now lost, but when I was a boy, my father took me on expeditions with him exploring some of those he knew. It was his dream that they would one day be used again, and that the Sacred Land would become the garden it used to be.'

He paused and swallowed drily. 'One day, we found a qanat we'd never seen before on the northern side of the rimwall. It was very ancient – in places we had to dig through roof-falls, and in others we had to crawl on our hands and knees to get through. We followed it for a whole day, and just when we were beginning to think it went nowhere, we saw daylight ahead. We made our way out into the light and found that we were on the other side of the rimwall – the Imenan had somehow cut the tunnel through solid rock. We were above what looked like a plain of flat sand stretching as far as the horizon – a plain without a stone or a growth of sedge. I wanted to go down to it, but my father held me back. He picked up a stone and threw it at the sand. The stone sank right through the surface and vanished from sight. Then I knew where we were – it was the great quicksand Umm al-Baka, the Mother of Tears.'

Truman grasped the old man's hands. 'If we could get in that way we could creep up on the enemy from the rear – we could destroy their machines before they discovered us.'

Whitehaven nodded, impressed. 'A small, well-equipped party could do it.'

'We can coordinate surprise attacks on both entrances with the infiltration,' Truman said. 'Hit them from all three sides at once. It needs careful synchronization, but I think we can do it.'

He turned to Hafid, who had remained curiously quiet during the exchange. 'What is it?' Truman asked him. 'Is something wrong?'

Hafid sighed. 'It's a good plan, Antara, but it won't work. To get to the qanat you have to traverse the Umm al-Baka and no living Saghrani has ever crossed the Mother of Tears. The legends say there are ways across it, but they've long been lost to the Kel. And that place is treacherous. One wrong step and you're gone forever.'

'There *are* those who know the secret paths,' Ayoub cut in.

Hafid made a wry face at him. 'That's true, by the Holy Ancestors,' he said. 'But you're as likely to get help from them as from a camel-spider.'

'How come?' Truman said.

'Because Umm al-Baka lies in the heart of Gharana territory, Antara,' he sighed, 'and those devils would rather go to the Light Mother than take us across.'

48

It TOOK THE WHOLE NIGHT TO reach the northern edge of the rimwall, and as the sun came up, Truman called a halt. The men – Ayoub, Khyar, Whitehaven and half a dozen warriors – couched their camels and began collecting camel-dung to make fires for tea. Whitehaven groaned as he flung himself down on the sand next to Truman. 'Remind me to heavy-drop a pinkie next time,' he said. 'Jesus, there isn't a muscle in my body that's not aching from that damned animal.'

Truman grinned at him. 'You get used to it. But don't let any of the Kel hear you curse a camel. To them, the *bil* are next to God.'

Whitehaven had acquired a new respect for Truman in the past twenty four hours. He didn't believe anyone else could have persuaded the nomads to accept the idea of sending a raiding party through the territory of their traditional enemies. Truman had held a meeting with the entire strength of the tribe, and the debate had gone on for hours. The main stumbling block seemed to be that he was proposing some kind of truce with the Gharana. Warrior after warrior had stood up to denounce the idea, declaring that there was blood between the two tribes going back to the ark and that they'd killed uncle Fred or cousin Joe and on and on. Finally Truman had said something that astonished Whitehaven.

'We all know who the Gharana really are. They're brothers, sons and cousins of all of you. If they're devils, then they're the brothers, sons and cousins of devils. We need the help of Goloi and the Gharana, and if we don't get it, we're finished. Would you rather see the end of the Kel than negotiate with your own relatives?'

There had been a murderous silence after that, and Whitehaven thought Truman had well and truly lost it. He realized that the Englishman had turned their whole world on its head. It was a remarkable tribute to his directness and powers of persuasion that he'd brought them round – slowly, begrudgingly, perhaps – but in the end they'd agreed.

Whitehaven watched in fascination as Khyar struck a flint against his sabre-blade, dropping sparks on to a cotton-like pad taken from a desert plant. As the fluff began to smoulder Khyar blew on it gently, nursing up a tiny flame. Then he began to lay pellets of hard dung over the flame.

'I hate to say it,' Whitehaven said, 'but this is not tactical. The smoke can be seen for miles.'

Khyar swept back the hood of his burnoose and looked at him. 'You think the Gharana don't know we're here? They've been tracking us since midnight.'

Whitehaven shrugged and pulled out a box of Swan Vestas. 'In that case, why not do it the easy way?'

Truman chuckled. He checked the G10 watch Whitehaven had given him, one of scores he'd doled out to the tribe with instructions on how to tell the time. He scanned the desert. The light was encroaching slowly in long arcs across the sandy plain stretching as far as a vast eroded buttress that marked the northern end of the rimwall. Old Ayoub flung a pile of camel-turds down next to the fire, and followed Truman's gaze.

'There!' he said, pointing a crabbed finger. 'See! Where the desert changes colour from red to brown. That's where the quick-sands begin.'

Truman gasped. The transition of colours was hardly percep-tible – he doubted he would have spotted it at all without Ayoub's help – and it began less than a kilometre away. If they had continued for a few more minutes they would have blundered right into it.

Whitehaven surveyed the quicksand through his binoculars. 'Shit!' he said. 'You can't even tell it's there. Looks just like ordinary sand.'

Suddenly Ayoub crouched down and made a crossed index-finger sign. 'The enemy!' he growled. 'The Gharana are here.'

Khyar and Truman instantly grabbed their rifles and rolled into the sand. Whitehaven dropped the binos and crawled two paces to where the light machine gun he'd brought with him stood on its bipod legs at the base of a jagged stone. He eased the stock into his shoulder and peered through the sights. In front of them a host of shadows had sprung out of the desert – men in flowing black robes, swaying purposefully out of the haze towards them on camels, so silently and effortlessly they seemed to float. Truman crawled up next to him and Khyar and Ayoub took the flanks. Truman glanced behind him to see that the rest of the Saghrana had gone to ground, merging invisibly with the desert surface.

Whitehaven cocked the mechanism and the harsh mechanical sound grated against the morning silence. There was a spatter of metallic clacks from around them as the Saghrana fighters armed their rifles. Truman cocked his own weapon and watched the riders, remembering the fear he'd felt when they'd come upon him and Khyar out in the Funeral Plains. His mouth went dry. More Gharana were materializing now, twenty or thirty of them fanning out into line abreast on their mounts, riding unbent, eyes hidden behind their black veils, their old rifles clasped across their chests in their bridle-hands, leaving the other hand free for their camel-sticks. There was a curious aura of dignity about them, Truman thought, like horse-guards on parade. The sun popped up suddenly behind them giving the sinister riders distinct outlines, glistening in hazy circlets around the heads of their camels.

'I could take out the lot right now,' Whitehaven whispered.

 286

'No,' Truman snapped. 'Don't fire.'

'See the one on the big dun camel in front?' Khyar said. 'That's the leader. Goloi himself is here.'

Slowly, very slowly, Khyar slipped off his head cloth. He left his rifle on the ground and grabbed a handful of sand. He rose carefully, joint by joint, flapping the filthy headcloth from side to side, tossing the sand into the air. Truman lined up his sights on Goloi – the shrouded man on the big dun camel riding in front of the advancing horde. More and more riders appeared out of the sand-mist behind him, until it seemed as if an army of shadows was marching on them.

'Jesus wept,' Whitehaven muttered under his breath.

Khyar shuffled forward, waving the cloth, stooping to pick up more handfuls of dust. Truman waited for the shot that would bring him down, and wondered what he would do if it happened. One shot would ruin everything, and Ossama's life might depend on the Gharana. On impulse, Truman let go of his weapon and stood up behind Khyar, waving his own headcloth. Goloi's camel was within a hundred metres of them now, and the muzzle of his rifle was pointed lazily in Truman's direction. Khyar shuffled forward again with Truman two or three paces behind him, and Truman knew suddenly that if this gambit failed there would be no retreat – Whitehaven might mow the Gharana down with the light machine-gun, but not until he and Khyar had been riddled with enemy bullets.

Suddenly, Goloi reined in his camel, yanked the headrope and tapped the beast on the head lightly with his stick. The animal made a yawning sound, and did an elegant curtsey as its legs folded. Before it had settled, the Gharana chief had slipped out of the saddle and stood facing them thirty metres away. The advancing camel-men halted, and three or four swung out of their saddles and strode up behind their leader. Goloi held his rifle in his elbow with his camel-stick crossed in his other hand. He reminded Truman of an ancient Egyptian mummy with the hands crossed ritually in death with the crook and the flail. The Gharani stood like a statue, his face a featureless patch of dark, his voluminous ebony-coloured mantle fluttering, until Khyar and Truman halted ten paces from him.

'Peace be upon you,' Khyar said.

For a second there was silence. Then Goloi said, 'I never thought I'd live to hear you wish me peace again. How can you stand there and pretend I'm not your own brother?'

For a second Truman wondered if he'd heard right. Goloi must be speaking figuratively he supposed. The chief's voice was deep and rich, and there was an edge of mockery to it.

Khyar stood stock still. 'I have no brother. I had one, but he is dead.' A rumble of laughter came from behind the veil, and suddenly Goloi stripped off the cloth with a single violent movement. With a shock that sent his heart stuttering, Truman saw that Goloi and Khyar were almost mirror images, or rather Goloi was what Khyar might have looked like had his life been abandoned to bitterness and misery. The Gharana chief was thicker-set, and older, and his face seemed to have adopted an aspect of Khyar that Truman had glimpsed occasionally when they'd first met. In Khyar it was a passing expression in a vast gallery of nobler ones, but for Goloi it was as if his face had become trapped in it and had got no further.

He stared from one to the other, bemused. 'Is this true, Khyar?' he demanded. 'This man is your own brother?'

'Our father and mother are the same,' Khyar said. 'But he is no brother of mine. My brother is dead to me – he no longer exists.'

Goloi snorted. 'You call us demons and devils. Yet you cast your own kith and kin out into the wilderness. I ask you, which are the devils, you or us?'

Khyar looked at the sand. 'The *tafriq* is the way of the Imenan,' he said. 'The way it has always been.'

'And now,' Goloi said, 'I suppose you come to ask us for help against the strangers who are sitting with their machines inside the Sacred Land. Is that so?'

Khyar glanced helplessly at Truman, who moved cautiously up his shoulder.

288

'You think they'll stop with the Saghrana?' Truman asked. 'Once they've wiped us out, do you think they'll let the Gharana remain here? I know who those men are. They want nothing less than to destroy the Sacred Land.'

Goloi fixed Truman with a cold stare. He raised a hand, pointing a crooked finger from black drapes that fell almost to his midriff. 'You,' he said. 'I know who *you* are. You are the Outsider who killed three of my warriors on the Funeral Plains.'

He glanced over his shoulder, 'Mumtaz!' he shouted. 'Send Mumtaz!'

A dark-robed, veiled and hooded warrior came striding through the ranks, and halted at Goloi's shoulder. He peeled off his veil and Truman was confronted with the face of the Gharani who'd escaped him many weeks ago on the Funeral Plains. In a rush he recalled how he'd shivered the man's sabre to shards and cloven him across the face. There was a deep, livid scar running diagonally across his cheek, mouth and jaw. The Gharani spat into the sand in front of Truman. 'This is the man, Chief,' he said.

Truman felt an icy flush down his spine. 'I had no choice.' 'You took our camels. We would have died.'

'The camels you took were mine,' Khyar said. 'This man saved my life.'

'They recognized you,' Goloi said. 'That's why they didn't finish you off. But who stole whose camels is not relevent and you know it. The law of the tribes is an eye for an eye and a tooth for a tooth. Before you leave his life will be ours.'

'Antara is our Nazir,' Khyar said. 'We need him to fight the Outsiders. If you take him, we'll never defeat them.'

'What's that to me?' Goloi said. 'Why should I care about your precious Kel or your Sacred Land? What's to stop me from ordering my warriors to wipe you all out right now?'

'Nothing,' Truman said. 'But many of your people will die. There are few of us, but we have powerful weapons – Outsiders' weapons. We'll all die, maybe, but then the strangers will still be inside the plateau, and you'll have to face them sooner or later.'

Goloi scratched the tuft of beard on his chin. 'Perhaps I'd be better advised offering my services to them.'

'Perhaps,' Truman said. 'But you can trust them as far as you'd trust a scorpion. At least you can believe the word of a Saghrani. We ask for a truce, and a guide to take us across the quicksands.'

'The quicksands?' Goloi asked. 'Why?'

'We have to get to the ancient qanat in the rimwall,' Truman said. 'We'll filter into the plateau from there.'

'Ah,' the chief said slowly, 'the Umm al-Baka tunnel.'

Khyar stared at him in surprise. 'You knew about it?'

Goloi snorted. 'How do you think we took those goats from under your noses twice this year?' he said. 'Why there've been times, brother, when I could have slipped into your hut and slit your throat while you slept! But no, I thought – much as you deserved it, I couldn't do it. I remembered too well how close we were until the cursed *tafriq* separated us.'

He sighed. 'Anyway the qanat is old and treacherous. Three of our warriors were killed in a cave-in last time we went through – We don't use it any more.'

He watched them silently for a moment, while the Gharana camels shifted impatiently behind him. He cocked his head to one side. 'If I grant a truce, what do I get out of it?'

Khyar looked at Truman again.

'Name your conditions,' Truman said.

The Gharana chief's eyes turned hard. 'First,' he said, 'you end the *tafriq* forever.'

Khyar gasped audibly. 'The Kel will never accept . . .' he stammered.

Truman looked at him, then back at Goloi. 'That I can't promise,' he said. 'Only that you have my word I will present the idea to the Kel with my support.'

Goloi nodded. 'Second, that you divide these new weapons you have equally between us when the fighting's done.'

'Agreed,' Truman said. 'You have my word as a Saghrani on that.'

 290

'Third,' said Goloi, his gaze not leaving Truman's face. 'You – Antara – your life is forfeit for the death of my warriors, after your fight with the Outsiders is done.'

Truman met the man's stare unflinchingly. It was Khyar who spoke. 'There are blood feuds in plenty between us. Why choose Antara?'

Goloi's face darkened. 'Because,' he said bitterly, 'two of the three warriors he killed were my sons.'

For a moment the breath rushed out of Truman's body, and he staggered slightly. Here was the counterpoint of his frenzied killing – the sudden realization that the enemies he'd cut down like cattle were someone's children, who had been nurtured and loved.

Truman looked at Khyar, who shook his head. 'Don't accept, Antara.'

'It's that or nothing,' Goloi said. 'The blood of my sons is on this man's head. I'll have my revenge, or you won't go through Umm al-Baka. You'll need all your prayers to the Great Mother to get back alive.'

'But Antara is our leader,' Khyar said. 'We need him.'

'You think I didn't need my sons?' Goloi replied.

Truman stood up straight, knowing that he was being asked to make the supreme sacrifice. He realized instinctively that to assent to Goloi's demand would be no evening promise to be broken at sunrise. If he promised and broke his word there would be no future for him among the Kel, where a man's standing depended on his honour. He didn't want to die. Life had become precious to him now and in the past few months he had attained a peace with himself that he had never known before. Part of it was the love of a good woman, part the prospect of a new child, and part the sense of identity he'd acquired by being absorbed into the Saghrana. But in a way the price of his acceptance had been the lives of the three Gharana he had killed, and he knew that even though he had been saving his own life, he had to answer for them. Goloi was right. By desert law no extenuating circumstances justified a killing.

Whatever the case, a life demanded a life in payment, and if he refused to sacrifice himself then in fifteen years' time vengeance might fall on the head of his yet unborn child. Before that happened, though, Ossama and the whole of the Kel might be a memory, no more than a few incomprehensible scratchings on the rocks. He couldn't bear the thought of this unique culture being destroyed because he had fallen short. He feared death – perhaps more than most people. That was why he'd always challenged it. His extreme fear had forced him to run towards it instead of fleeing, and out in the Funeral Plains that instinct had paid off. Yet submitting himself to formal execution would be very different from dying in a mad clash with the enemy. He shivered involuntarily at the thought, and wondered longingly if there was any means of squirming out of this fate. He knew there was not. The only way to save the Kel was to cross the Umm al-Baka, and the only way through the quicksands was to accept Goloi's terms.

He stared the Gharana chief out and raised his chin. 'I agree to give myself over to you . . .' he began.

'No Antara!' Khyar said urgently. 'You have no idea what demonic rites these. . . .'

'Rites!' Goloi spat. 'You talk about rites? What rite is worse than one that splits brother from brother and takes children from parents? What custom is it that turns blood relatives into devils and demons? Can any custom be more inhumane than that?'

From where he lay, Whitehaven watched the conference uncertainly, aware of how exposed they were. If there was a firefight now they'd take out dozens of Gharana, but they'd still have little chance of getting out alive, even with the weapons he'd brought. He realized that Truman had been put in an impossible situation and knew he had no choice but to appear to agree. He'd heard the story of how 'Antara' had killed three of these Gharana to save his own life and Khyar's, when the bandits had stolen his camels, and he'd been impressed. He had to admit that a guy like Truman was worth his weight in gold as a 'Fred'.

He had no doubt, though, that in offering his life, Truman was

 292

lying through his teeth. The archaeologist had guts all right, but Whitehaven would have bet his shirt that putting his head on a chopping block wasn't part of Morgan's masterplan. What amazed him was the fact that Goloi hadn't clipped Truman the minute he'd set eyes on him. Hard men didn't waste time talking about revenge, they took it, and Whitehaven was nagged by the notion that there was something here he'd missed.

'I agree to the condition,' Truman said solemnly. 'My life is yours – as soon as we have chased the Outsiders from the Sacred Land. I swear it in front of all these warriors, as acting Nazir of the Kel.'

The Gharana chief regarded him gravely. 'Very well then. I will guide you across the quicksand myself. For now, you may go in peace.'

49

ALL DAY GOLOI LED THE SMALL party across the quicksands, walking with their camels, as the sun tightened above them into a pale fireball, pounding them with hammer-blows of heat. They marched carefully with all their senses alert, for the secret path was narrow in places – a neck of solid sand winding through vast bottomless pits. 'I once saw a whole herd of camels blunder into the quicksands,' Goloi told Truman as they walked abreast. 'One moment they were there and the next – whoosh – they were gone. We Gharana say Umm al-Baka is a dragon with an open mouth, waiting to devour the careless.'

'How were they formed?' Truman asked.

'They're the work of the Dark Mother,' Goloi said. 'According to our legends there was once abundant rain on the plateau. The rainwater flowing down from the rocks filled huge depressions under the sand. The ancient Imenan must have built the Umm al-Baka tunnel to harvest the same rains. They were clever beings the Imenan – this place could have been the garden of Eden. But then the ancient skills were lost and the *tafriq* began.'

'Is it true that some of the Kel began to thirst for human blood?'

Goloi grunted. 'Who knows? Perhaps. But that was long ago. I know they say we're vampires who keep virgins shut up in caves and feed on their blood. I know they say we hold bloody ceremonies to the Dark Mother. It's all camel-droppings, Antara. Look at me – do I seem any different from my brother?'

'No,' Truman said. 'A little bitter, maybe, but even Khyar has his bitter moments. I don't believe there's any real difference – Saghrana, Gharana, Outsiders, Insiders – we are all just leaves of the same tree. I truly believe the *tafriq* should end.'

'By the Dark Mother,' Goloi said. 'You're a straight man, Antara. It will almost be a shame that I have to kill you.'

There was a sudden scream from the back of the column and Goloi turned abruptly.

'Brahim!' someone bawled. 'Brahim has stepped into the quicksands!'

Truman dropped his camel's headrope and made to run back, but Goloi grabbed his arm with a grip like steel. 'Take care!' he hissed. 'One step and you're under. It's too late to save him, anyway.'

Truman and Goloi dodged back through the line of camels to where a small group of Saghrana had gathered, tottering perilously on the invisible path. When they arrived Brahim's camel had already disappeared under the sand, and the tribesman was immersed up to his chest, struggling to catch a headcloth somebody had thrown to him.

'Help me!' he screamed. 'I'm standing on my camel's head. For the love of the Light Mother help me!'

Goloi whipped a loose rope from one of the camels and flung it to the struggling man. Brahim's flailing hands grabbed for it but missed, and a second later he was up to his chin in the sand. 'Help!' he wailed, his eyes almost popping from his skull. His hands flapped impotently on the quicksand's rippling surface. Goloi threw the rope again, but already the tribesman was suffocating, his mouth full of wet sand. He spat, snuffled and blubbered, his eyes fixed on the other tribesmen as he fought frantically to get his hands free. The Saghrana warriors yelled and scrabbled for him.

Don't move!' Goloi warned them. 'Not even one step. Otherwise you'll all be dead.'

Brahim had stopped struggling now, and Truman saw the light of hope had gone from his eyes. Those eyes – almost bursting with terror – were the last thing he saw of Brahim, as the warrior's head sank slowly under the surface. For a moment the company stood shocked as the liquid sand closed over Brahim's head.

'Jesus wept!' Whitehaven said over Truman's shoulder. 'I never saw anything like that.' Truman could hear the shudder in his voice.

'How did this happen?' Truman demanded.

'It was his camel,' one of the warriors said. 'It lost its footing somehow and tumbled into the quicksands. Brahim tried to stop it and was pulled in.'

'The Light Mother have mercy on him,' Khyar said.

Goloi looked up grimly. 'I warned you the path was treacherous,' he growled. 'From here on we rope the camels together. Walk exactly in my tracks and do not deviate, otherwise not a single one of you will make the journey's end.'

They walked sombrely and silent after that, each man brooding over what they had seen. Truman worried that Brahim's camel had taken down two waterskins and Whitehaven that two of the sixty-sixes had gone under with it. By early afternoon the rimwall loomed over them, breathtakingly sheer, a recumbent monster with flaked and fluted skin, ruptured and rumpled by the ancient cascade of water. There was a bight of rock where the wall was indented into a bay, and soon Goloi was leading them between the high walls. Truman didn't breathe easily until they were couching the camels by the screes of shattered boulders along the base of the cliffs.

Old Ayoub gestured excitedly up the rubble-strewn slope to where the mouth of what looked like a cave was visible, perhaps three hundred feet above them. 'That's it!' he cried. 'That's where my father and I came out all those years ago.'

Truman sent two men up to reconnoitre the tunnel, while the rest of them unloaded the camels, laying out the rocket-launchers, the two light support machine-guns, optics, grenade-launchers, cyalume sticks, the boxes containing plastic explosive charges, L2 grenades and ammunition. Whitehaven divided the gear into man-sized loads, while Khyar and Truman filled plastic military waterbottles from the drippers.

'I'm sending two men back with the camels,' Truman told Goloi. 'I know I can trust you to escort them back to the Salaba.'

The Gharani grinned ruefully. 'I'll be there. To collect my price.'

'You realize that both of us, and everyone here, might be dead by that time,' Khyar said.

Goloi stood up straight and faced him. 'Then the Dark Mother will be appeased. If we meet again, Antara, I will be coming for your life. The Dark Mother is all-knowing, but I would have wished otherwise. In our brief time together, I've learned you are a man to respect. But the blood-feud divides us, and it must be so.'

'*Why*?' Truman said. 'If the *tafriq* can end, so can the blood feuds.'

'Nothing lasts forever,' Goloi said.

Khyar was staring at him, and for a moment Truman thought he was going to embrace his lost brother. 'Remember when we were small?' he said. suddenly to Goloi, as if speaking with great effort. 'You used to carry me on your back. The children of the warriors used to call us "moles" because we were Burrowers, but there wasn't a single one of them you couldn't best.' He gulped. 'I called you a demon and a devil, brother but you were right. *We* are the devils to perpetuate this custom. You haven't changed. You carried all of us on your back today. You could have led us into the sands and drowned us all, but you didn't. It is a brave and generous thing you've done.' He inclined his head slightly in salute. 'I shall not forget.'

50

THERE WAS SOME FINE STONEWORK AROUND the tunnel entrance, emblazoned everywhere with the ram's head and sun-disk symbols of the Saghrana. Old Ayoub pointed out the remains of stone feeder-channels which had once directed water from the cliffs into a hewn-rock cistern, long since eroded away. 'See!' he said, smiling toothlessly in admiration, 'the work of the Imenan. Imagine! It has been here since the Time of the First Reckoning.'

Truman examined the markings with professional interest. 'This symbol,' he said. 'The ram's head with the sun disk? Where did it originate?'

'It is said that the brand represents an ancient relic the Kel brought with them from the land of the Firun,' Ayoub said. 'It is from this relic that the Kahina derives her power, and no one is allowed to see it but the prophetess herself. Maybe there is no relic. Maybe it's just a story, anyway.'

Whitehaven was busy kitting up the warriors, slinging bandoliers of ammunition and 66mm rocket-tubes over shoulders, clipping on grenades, helping them fit the unfamiliar webbing-pouches that held their water and food.

Ayoub watched him grimly. 'This is not going to be easy. I remember there were places where we could only just scrape through.'

 298

'And Goloi said there'd been a cave-in,' Truman added. 'We may find ourselves having to dig our way out.'

'I came well jacked-up for that,' Whitehaven said, holding up two folded entrenching-tools. 'But I hope nobody here suffers from claustrophobia.'

'Let me go first,' Ayoub said. 'Give me light and one of those tools. I'm used to these places. I've worked in them all my life.'

Whitehaven picked up a cyalume stick and squeezed it so that the end flared with chemical fire. He handed it to the old man. 'After you, Pop,' he said.

The first stretch dropped steeply through the belly of the cliff, and Truman, in second place after Ayoub, found himself running his hands along the sheer stone walls in admiration. 'How on earth did they do this?' he wondered out loud.

'The Imenan knew many secrets we have forgotten,' Ayoub said. 'The Sacred Land was different in those days. My father told me there were orchards and open pools – animals like ostriches, giraffes and crocodiles.'

Soon the shaft levelled off and curved away into pitch darkness, becoming lower and narrower so that in places Truman had to duck down. There were piles of debris scattered across the floor, and occasionally huge cubes of shaped stone which had separated themselves from the roof. Ayoub worked his way forward doggedly, moving the cyalume stick from side to side, pointing out obstacles, giving an expert running commentary on the state of the shaft. Truman could do nothing but scrabble after the spurt of chemical fire, occasionally glancing behind him to check that Whitehaven and Khyar and the four other warriors were there. 'Keep closed up,' he told Whitehaven. 'If anyone stops, pass the word along. We mustn't get separated here.'

The qanat twisted and turned through the rock, first narrowing then opening out suddenly into long galleries. It was as hot as an oven, and airless, in some places they had to walk crouching, and once they were forced to crawl on their hands and knees. After two hours they came to a gallery that was blocked by a roof-fall of rubble, and had to work in shifts of two, shovelling

299

the dirt and stones backwards and spreading it out along the sides. It was harrowing work, labouring elbow to elbow in the spluttering light of the cyalume torches, catching their breath in the heat and the foul air. Old Ayoub worked tirelessly, his illness forgotten, proud to show the skills he'd acquired from his ancestors, and he had almost cleared a path through when he froze. 'Light Mother's wrath!' he whispered. 'Look at this!'

Truman and Whitehaven craned their necks, to see a human skull grinning at them vacantly out of the debris. 'This must be the cave-in Goloi talked about,' Truman said.

Whitehaven shivered, 'I hope there's no more where that came from.'

They left the Gharana skull where it was, and forced their way through the remaining rubble into the clear part of the tunnel, where they sat close together and passed water-bottles around. Whitehaven glanced at his watch and fretted. 'It's sunset outside,' he said. 'I hope we're going to be out of here well before first light.'

'We are almost half way now,' Ayoub said.

They continued, crouching, ducking, gasping for air. Whitehaven suggested killing the cyalume sticks on the easy stretches so as not to waste what little oxygen there was. They were making their way through a particularly low stretch when there came an angry rumbling from above them.

Ayoub stopped abruptly and listened. 'What the hell's that?' Whitehaven gasped. 'Please tell me it's not rain! The last thing we need is a shower right now.'

The noise came again, louder this time.

'Not rain,' Ayoub said. 'We call it the Giant's Footsteps. It's a sound you often hear in these tunnels. My father told me it happens when rocks that were hot from the day's sun suddenly get cold at night and crack open. See, the rocks grow and change just like Adam's sons.'

The rumble came again, even louder and a shower of small stones and dust began to rain down on them from the roof.

'Jesus!' Whitehaven said. 'She's going to cave!'

'Move!' Truman screamed, and they began to monkey-run along the qanat as bigger stones began to plunge down to the tunnel floor.

'Holy Mother protect . . .' Khyar began to shout, but his words were drowned out by a terrifying crack as the tunnel-roof behind him split apart and tons of stone and dirt cascaded into the gallery. There were muffled screams and shouts from behind them, but they could do nothing but lie flat with their hands over their heads waiting to be crushed. A second later the rumbling ceased, and old Ayoub wormed his way out from the pile of sand that had half buried him and squeezed the cyalume stick. In its flickering light they saw that the tunnel behind them was completely sealed. Truman crawled back painfully to the roof-fall and set his ear against it, listening for any sound from the warriors who had disappeared behind the cave-in. He heard nothing. Khyar crawled up to him and began pulling away some of the larger stones frantically.

'No!' Ayoub shouted hoarsely. 'Don't Khyar. You'll bring the whole lot down on us!'

Khyar paused. 'What are we meant to do then? There's four of our brothers behind there.'

'Or maybe under it,' Truman said. 'Perhaps they're all dead.'

'The Light Mother have mercy on them,' Ayoub whispered. 'If we try to dig them out we'll be dead too.'

'OK,' Whitehaven said, panting in the thin air. 'We're all right, so maybe they are. They've got an entrenching tool with them, so they'll have a chance of digging through, depending on how broad the cave-in is. Or they can go back to the entrance. You can't get lost in here, that's one thing.'

No one spoke for a moment and there was silence but for their heavy breathing. Truman realized that he had to make a decision. 'We dug our way through the Gharana cave-in,' he said. 'Why can't we do the same here?'

'The other roof-fall was in one of the big galleries,' Ayoub said. 'And it was old. The roof had had time to settle. Here, without props to shore it up, we won't stand a chance.'

301

Truman inspected his G10 watch hastily. 'We'll have to leave them,' he said heavily. 'We have no choice. The Light Mother grant that they get out alive.'

Whitehaven nodded, knowing Truman had had to make a leader's choice – the men or the mission. If they delayed to dig out the lost men, then the whole operation would fall through, and they would probably end up getting buried themselves in the process. He thought of something and groaned softly.

'What is it?' Truman said.

'The sixty-sixes,' Whitehaven said. 'We've got none with us. Those four guys were carrying them all.'

51

OSSAMA FEARED THE BLACK KAHIN. HIS face was a ritual mask concealing a terrifying demon within. Each time he moved in the half-light of the tent, she caught a glimpse of something standing behind him – a grotesque, featureless ghoul-figure three times his height. The man himself was small, neat in his desert-camouflage dress, and at first glance the features were smooth and even. But in his eyes, Ossama saw something she'd never seen before, even in the Gharana. She knew the telltale signals of men – the way their facial muscles rippled and ordered them-selves – the sex signals, the greed signals, the signals of lies and betrayals. The first thing that had drawn her to Antara was the openness of his face, a face that shone with honesty like a lamp. But this man's face was cloaked in darkness and his eyes vultur-ine – the shell of a being who took no ordinary interest in her sex, except to inflict pain. It was the Black Kahin she'd seen in her visions, and she shuddered as he stood over her now, the pale features betraying no emotion at all.

Ossama did not struggle at the ropes that bound her to the chair. Everything around her – the table, the battery-fed strip lamps, the steel boxes, the flickering machines with symbols on their faces, even the chair itself, belonged to a different world. She had never sat on a chair before in her entire life, and the strange upright posture it enforced made her back ache. There were two big men behind her – the pigs of men who'd dragged her from the cave to this tent. Them she did not fear. They were dirty and smelt of sweat and grease, but she had no trouble in reading their faces. They were simple, brutal men to whom she was merely a female body to be used for gratification. Only their fear of the Black Kahin had held them off until now.

The Black Kahin turned from her and started talking to a fat little bald dwarf with a beard, the man whom she called The Tongue. The Tongue was the pot-bellied shape of Termit cliff and had a face as large and white as a new-born baby's. He had no interest in her as a woman either, but she had seen how his eyes devoured the younger soldiers who had passed through the tent. She watched as the Black Kahin leaned over a pile of jute sacks in the corner – sacks that gave off the smell of putrefaction, as if they contained dead animals. He picked up one and rummaged in it for a moment, bringing out a wizened object the size of a cooking pot. He held it up triumphantly before her face, his eyes now rimmed with excitement. Ossama gagged. It was a severed head – the head of an old man with curled rats-tails of grey hair. She tried to look away, but one of the pig-men behind her grabbed her head and wrenched it back.

The severed skull was tarry with congealed blood and partly charred by fire, but Ossama recognized it at once. It was the head of Tissi bin Tamghar, her father. For a moment the tent began to spin, and she fought desperately to prevent her inner core from imploding, knowing that she was teetering on the edge of a deep abyss. This was the vision she'd had months ago in Half-Death – the blackened face of her father staring at her with reproachful eyes. She groped out of an ocean of horror. *'Father!'* she whispered through trembling lips. *'Father! Father!'*

The Black Kahin watched her with new interest in the pale ritual mask of a face, then looked at the Tongue, who was translating her words. He spoke curtly to the dwarf.

'The Honoured One says this belongs to a man who was leading the force of warriors that dared attack us,' the Tongue said.

Ossama closed her eyes and tried to control her breathing in the way she'd been trained long ago. When she opened them, the Black Kahin was talking again.

'The Honoured One says he's pleased to tell you they were all killed,' the Tongue said. 'Almost all of them anyway.'

This time Ossama didn't betray her emotions. The breathing exercises had rallied her and she stared at the ground, forcing her body to go limp. She divined instinctively that with men like this the best strategy was to appear submissive, to pretend frailty while secretly gathering strength. She had no doubt about what awaited her here. She'd heard the dying screams of Fatiha and Huda even while she'd been tied up in the cave behind Termit, and she realized that she had been saved until last. Like most Saghrani women, she was capable of resisting pain, but she had to think of the baby she was carrying. She was three months pregnant and just beginning to swell, yet she knew she was still as fast and determined as any warrior of the Kel.

One small chance was all she needed, and she focused her attention on watching for it. She would mourn her father and the rest of the warriors in due course. She prayed to the Light Mother, though, that Antara was not among the dead. She could not bear the thought of losing him now – their time together had only just begun. Then the Tongue said something that made her heart flutter.

'The Honoured One wants to know about a foreigner who came down in a helicopter,' he said. The little man puffed out his cheeks and made a chittering sound that was meant to suggest the noise of a flying machine. 'His Presence says he knows you are a prophetess among these vermin. He knows your father was leading the attack and must have been the chief. He noticed how the others deferred to you.'

Ossama's delight in the knowledge that Antara had not been among the fallen was stifled suddenly by the terror that the Black Kahin would discover that she was Ossama Hadab. Antara had known her name when he had come from the Outside, so this creature might know it too. True, Antara had thought Ossama was a man, but one slip might give away the secret, and the Black Kahin would know what a prize he had. That the knowledge might save her life didn't alter her conviction – better her life be forfeit than the tribe betrayed. She suddenly understood why Antara had seemed so determined not to return to the Outside. It was this monster who'd been waiting for him there.

'If anyone would know about this foreigner,' The Tongue translated, 'it would be your father. And if your father knew, you must know. Where is the foreigner now?'

She stared at the table opposite, noting the belts that were fixed to it and the telltale bloodstains in the wood. This was where Fatiha and Huda had met their end, the place she herself was intended to die.

'I know no foreigner,' she said. 'I know only the Kel.'

The Tongue stumbled over his translation, and the Black Kahin waited with impatience. He said something that sounded harsh to her ears. 'His Presence says that is a lie,' the dwarf translated. 'He found the wreck himself and there were tracks leading away from it towards the plateau.'

Ossama shook her head. 'I know nothing of any foreigner,' she repeated.

The Black Kahin nodded as if he'd understood, and his eyes blazed. He spoke again in his harsh-sounding language. 'The Honoured One says that if you refuse to tell him about the foreigner he will kill you,' the dwarf said. 'And not only you but all your people. They can't resist our weapons. He knows where they are and he will rid the earth of you vermin forever, men, women and children.'

Ossama stared at her bare feet again and said nothing, taking strength from the knowledge that Antara was alive. In a few short months she'd grown to know his soul completely. He'd brought Khyar out of the Funeral Plains when death had seemed certain, and she knew that while there was power in his body he would not leave her or the Kel to die. She looked up to see a hideous smile on the Black Kahin's face, and realized that he would kill her, and all the Kel, whether she spoke or not. She tested the strength of the ropes that bound her wrists tentatively. They were tight, but they were ropes, not steel. The Black Kahin was talking in a croak to the Tongue again.

'The Honoured One will give you a short time to consider it,' the little man said. 'and when he returns he expects an answer. If not, then your precious Light Mother will not save you.'

Ossama lifted her head defiantly, knowing it was the wrong move, but needing some gesture to reassert herself, if only for the sake of her own pride. 'We shall all die when it is time,' she said. 'The Great Mother gives and she takes away.'

The Black Kahin snarled something and swept out of the tent, followed by the dwarf. The pig-men hovered around her for a few moments, their eyes ogling her with lust. One of them – a man with a shaved head and a filthy moustache that almost covered his mouth – slipped the rifle off his shoulder. The rifle had a big knife attached to its end, she saw, and he began to manoeuvre it towards her, muttering something she guessed was obscene, as saliva drooled from his mouth. He touched her ankle with the cold blade, and brought it up slowly against her calf so that it lifted her tattered robe. She stifled a sharp intake of breath as the blade scraped against her knee and began its journey up her inner thigh, pushing the hem of her garment up and exposing her slim brown legs. The man's eyes bulged at her, and a trickle of sweat ran down from his brow. She could smell the stale breath and the male heat on him. Then a voice called sharply from outside the tent and the soldier froze. His companion said something, and he pulled the rifle away, staring at her for a moment, licking his lips. Then he shouldered the rifle and stomped out of the tent.

As soon as the two pig-men had gone, Ossama closed her eyes and fell into meditation. She drew deeper and deeper breaths, letting the air wash her body from the crown of her head to the tip of her toes, feeling powerful new energy sweep through her like fire. She channelled the energy to her wrists, where the rope bound her, her breaths growing longer as wave after wave of power swirled through her arms. Suddenly she felt her being

307

split into two separate entities, and knew she was entering the Half-Death. One of her selves hovered somewhere above her and she was looking down on her physical body – a woman with dirt-spattered hair and ragged garments tied to a chair. Her physical body was motionless, but inside it had already become a raging inferno of heat. She felt something stirring in her spine, and knew the serpent Anak was uncoiling there, releasing new energy with every shake of its tail. Sweat began to pour down her face in ribbles and her heart thumped like a hammer. Her body was white-hot, her blood liquid fire, and she knew that she had driven herself dangerously near the edge of survival.

'Light Mother!' she whispered. 'I am the Light!'

She mumbled a mantra, her mind focusing every mote of power on her bindings, feeling the muscles in her wrists expand, feeling the blood burning through her arteries there. Then suddenly the ropes gave way and her hands were free. Almost at once she sensed danger and the part of her floating above saw the tent flap thrown back and the pig-man who had caressed her leg with his blade stalked into the room. The big knife was in his hand now, and she saw him halt before her and sniff the air like an animal. At once the fear brought her back to her physical body, and she was staring at the guard as he slit the hem of her robe up to her waist with his knife and jerked her legs apart. He grunted in surprise as he felt the heat in her flesh. His eyes flickered furtively and the perspiration raced down his fat face as he stuck the knife in the sandy floor, humping over her and scrabbling with his flies. As he exposed his rampant sex to her, she let her body go rigid and kicked out with her right foot, straight into his windpipe. It was not a particularly powerful blow, but the aim was as true as an arrow and the pig-man lurched back, clutching his throat and gasping for air.

In that moment she snatched her hands out of what was left of her bindings, grabbed the heavy bayonet and brought it up with all her might into the guard's testicles. She felt the flesh give. The man screamed, paralysed for an instant, and collapsed whimpering. Ossama's robe was heavy with blood, so she tore the remains of it off, standing naked but for a loincloth. She picked up the soldier's discarded rifle. There was a movement behind her, and she vaulted across the tent with the speed of a gymnast towards the second guard who was staring with popping eyes and going for his weapon. She swung the rifle like a club with all the force of her leap behind it. It cracked against the guard's temple so hard that the butt snapped off. He fell like a dead weight, and a second later she was out of the tent and into the galleries of shadow under Termit, running as fast as a gazelle.

She was dimly aware of cries behind her and bullets wazzing and humphing past her ears. Then suddenly the gunshots stopped, and she looked up to see the Black Kahin and the dwarf with three or four guards behind them, standing at the entrance to her living-cave, barring the way. The Black Kahin's eyes were burning.

52

F ROM WHERE THEY LAY, ON THE soft peak of a dune that hugged the rocks near Termit cliff, the four men heard the gunshots. Truman rolled to the edge of the dune-slope in time to see the nearly naked figure of Ossama being hustled back to the tent. His blood froze and he almost leapt out of his position.

'Ossama!' he gasped. 'Ossama's down there!'

Whitehaven grabbed his arm. 'You bloody fool!' he hissed. 'She's going to have no chance if you get yourself shot. Your boys are in position by now. We've got to kill the Apache or it's all over.'

Truman closed his eyes. His breath was coming in gasps and he had to slow it deliberately. Whitehaven had his binoculars in his hand, and Truman grabbed them and peered at the figures hundreds of feet below him.

'Careful!' Whitehaven warned. 'If there's anyone switched on down there they'll clock the sunflash.'

Truman ignored him, focusing the binos on the tent. He saw the bodies of two guards being carried out, and a small, lean man stalking angrily alongside them. 'Stein!' he growled.

As he watched, the Colonel caught one of the big guards by the hair and delivered two smashing punches to the man's face. Truman's gaze followed Stein as he turned on his heel, and he wondered if the Colonel would return to the tent where Ossama

310

had been taken. He was uncertain whether he would be able to restrain himself in that case, but mercifully Stein walked along the line of marquees and entered another. Truman memorized the position of both tents carefully.

The sun was a gold penny lodged on the rimwall, and the great tower-block knappes that rose out of the valley floor cast giant pillars of shadow across the pink and amber pillow sand. Truman took more deep breaths, willing himself to patience, and tweaked the focus-wheel on the binoculars, scanning the scores of bell tents that had been pitched around the pot-belly of Termit cliff.

There was a lot of activity going on – mercenaries refuelling vehicles from jerrycans, tinkering with motors, cleaning up weapon-systems, while others patrolled the perimeter in twos and threes. It was hard to believe so much destructive power was concentrated down there, he reflected, when the whole mercenary camp was dwarfed into insignificance by the vast scale of the valley. He shifted the lenses to where the Apache stood on a marked out LZ, a silent wasp-queen disdainfully ignoring the scurrying drones around her. Light flashed brilliantly on the helicopter's bristling Hellfire missile-tubes as a ground crew serviced them with what looked like practised efficiency.

Whitehaven looked at him, then adjusted the light machine-gun on its bipod, checking the sights. He glanced at his watch. 'Look, I know you're itching to get her out. I'd feel the same if it was my old lady. But remember this is a very big deal – the whole future of this tribe depends on what you do now. Mission first, personal objectives second. We got another half hour of daylight, then we get this show on the road.'

He drew Truman gently back to their little nest under the cliff, where old Ayoub sat cleaning a weapon. Khyar followed. Whitehaven opened the bergen he'd been carrying and took out the shaped plastic charges, laying them on a strip of rug. 'Now get this straight,' he said. 'You can jump up and down on this stuff and it won't go up. It's the dets you've got to watch – they're volatile. Can you do it?'

'Trust me,' Truman said.

'Antara,' Khyar cut in, 'let me do this.'

Truman shook his head. 'Khyar, I'm already dead. Have you forgotten the promise I made to Goloi?'

Whitehaven frowned. 'Come on,' he said. 'You can stop the play acting now, Truman. You know damn well you didn't mean what you said. If it's any consolation, I think you did the right thing.'

Truman and Khyar exchanged glances.

'You're a good man, Richard,' Khyar said, 'but you know nothing of the ways of the Kel. Among us a man is no more than his word – without that he is nothing.'

Whitehaven shook his head and turned away, but inside he was troubled. The nagging feeling that he was missing something had returned. Despite his conviction that Truman was double-dealing the Saghrana, there was, he had to admit, an air of conviction about the man that was deeply impressive. The way he'd handled himself, the way he'd really seemed to care about these people, especially the woman down there, had warmed Whitehaven's heart. Then he remembered what Moore had said about *Haymaker*. *This was no ordinary Fred . . . the guy was good enough to pass himself off as an Arab . . . he risked his life to collar a KGB officer . . . Freds like that aren't ten a penny*. Maybe it was Truman's ability to play the part so perfectly that had made him such an asset to the Phantom List.

'Anyway,' Truman said, cutting into his thoughts. 'I've got to get Ossama out. I'm not coming back without her.'

Whitehaven looked at him and for the first time he wondered if he could be wrong about Truman. He didn't want to contemplate it. If Truman really was what he said he was, then Whitehaven would have followed him into hell and back. But nobody could be that straight.

'I'll say it again,' he said. 'Your boys start their assault exactly one hour after sunset. The first thing the Russians are going to do is send the Huey up. If it's still in one piece by then, the tribe is mincemeat and we are too. So make your choice, Antara.'

'Let me do it,' Khyar said eagerly.

Whitehaven touched him sympathetically on the arm. 'Your heart's in the right place, my friend,' he said, 'but you haven't been trained. Anyway, you're a crack shot, and I need your dead eye up here with me in case any of those *adoos* gets trigger-happy. We call that "covering fire".'

He pulled out a case holding a night-scope and showed the instrument to Khyar. 'You'll be amazed what a difference this thing makes.'

While Khyar examined the night-scope, Truman picked up the initiator – a small plastic box with an antenna, like the remote of a radio-controlled toy. There were two lights and a single red button in the middle.

'The dets are instantaneous,' Whitehaven told him. 'So if you're not out by the time you press the red button, you can kiss your arse goodbye.'

53

W HEN HE WAS CERTAIN STEIN WAS engaged in his interrogation
of the girl, Sergei Rybakov entered his tent. He pulled a
satcom phone out of its case, oriented it by compass, and tapped
in a number on the keyboard. Things were going as planned,
and he wanted to make sure those he had to answer to back in
London knew about it. He listened to a burst of static, then
suddenly there were shots and raised voices outside. Rybakov
heard a woman scream, and then the unmistakable croaking tones
of the Colonel abusing the guards. He resisted the temptation to
investigate, but a moment later there was a flurry of movement
directly beyond the doorgap. Hastily, he cancelled the call and
wiped the number from the phone's memory. He was just replacing the receiver when Stein entered.

'I told the guard no disturbance,' Rybakov muttered with irri-
tation. 'What's going on out there?'

'That little bitch,' Stein said. 'The Prophetess. She just
knocked down two of your so-called ''special forces'' and almost
escaped.'

Rybakov chuckled. 'You want to be more careful, Colonel.'

Stein advanced into the tent, eyeing Rybakov curiously. He
took a mincing step over to the satcom on the trestle table and
examined it.

'What were you doing, Sergei?' he demanded.

 314

'Wass it look like?' Rybakov snapped. 'Communications.'

'I thought we agreed all comms should go through the rear-link operator for security reasons,' Stein said. 'Didn't you tell me yourself that satcom was wide open to direction-finding equipment?'

Rybakov sighed impatiently. 'I said if it was transmission of more than ten seconds.'

Stein nodded slowly as if a mystery had just been revealed. 'Who are you communicating with?' he asked.

'Who do you think? The boys who pay for all this, that's who. I was sending sitrep to my cartel.'

Stein glanced at the device again then watched Rybakov carefully. 'Must have been a pretty concise sitrep to go through in ten seconds.'

Rybakov slammed his fist down hard on the table suddenly. 'Stein, I said no disturbance. I don't want nobody disturbing me, see? You think you so clever doing sneaky-pete around spying on people. You got your own job to do and you ought to get on with it. You make that bimbo talk?'

Stein tore his eyes away from the phone reluctantly. 'Not yet,' he said. 'But I will. She knows something about Truman, I'd swear it. Right now she's strapped to the table in my tent, and I shall be working on her very soon. I'm surprised you haven't sent the Apache to bomb the nomads' camp, if you're so sure Truman's there. Didn't you say your men would crush all opposition in a day?'

'We crushed opposition,' Rybakov snapped. 'You know how much it costs to keep that kite airborne? You know how much one of them missiles runs? When your Mr. Rand is forking out you can afford to criticize, but until then keep your trap shut and do the job.' He never finished his sentence, because his walkie-talkie buzzed. He picked it up, listened attentively, and spoke quickly in Russian.

'What's going on?' Stein said.

It was Rybakov's turn to examine Stein's face curiously. 'Major Antonoff, at the pass, just picked up a couple of Land

Rovers carrying a patrol of your Afrikaner boys. You order them to tail us Stein?'

For a second, Stein looked surprised. 'This is nothing to do with me,' he said quickly. 'Maybe it's the advance guard of the plant column.'

'No,' Rybakov said. 'That's not due for another week, and you know it. And as it happens Antonoff got one of them to talk before he snuffed it. The guy said they were doing recce for a fighting column that arrives here tomorrow. The column was dispatched on personal orders of Marcus Rand.'

54

Truman and Khyar slithered down the warm face of the dune. The darkness had come quickly, first gathering in ever deeper purple under the eaves of the rocks, then filling the whole of the valley with a darker matrix of blacks and greys. The remnant of the day was a glow-line along the western edge of the rimwall, and above them the stars began to break cover into the colossal landscape of the night. There were fires around the bell-tents – chemical fires whose discordant odours tainted the air – and all around them there were foreign voices and the glow of cigarettes.

For a few moments they lay full-length at the base of the dune, letting their senses adjust to the new environment. Truman felt the sand sticking to the camouflage-cream on his body, and tightened the straps of the pack so that it wouldn't flap as he walked.

Khyar touched him on the arm. 'This is as far as I go, my friend,' he said. 'From now on the Light Mother will be your companion.'

Truman slipped the initiator out of the webbing pouches that contained his spare magazines. He handed it to Khyar. 'If I'm not back in one hour,' he said, 'press the button.'

'But Antara,' Khyar whispered, 'I can't do it.'

'You can,' Truman growled urgently. 'My life is already

promised, Khyar. If you fail then the whole tribe will die, and I can't trust myself to choose between the Kel and Ossama. I know you'll do the right thing. You have the watch Richard gave you?'

Khyar nodded. 'One hour,' Truman repeated, and then he was off into the night.

Everything he'd learned from the Saghrana came to his aid now. He moved like a ghost under a cloud of invisibility, feeling his way pace by pace, all his senses sparking acutely. He skirted the bell-tents, past bubbles of light in which men sat in huddles, smoking, cooking on hexamine stoves, playing cards, drinking beer. They were like portholes into a different dimension, Truman thought, these men were sharing the same space as him, but living in an alternative world, their senses closed to the landscape.

When he halted he could hear the wind scouring softly across the rimwall, feel the invisible small eddies in the sand beneath his feet, and sense the myriad creatures stirring within the earth and upon it. He felt invulnerable – almost transparent – and sometimes he came so close to the guards that he could have touched them. He experienced a strange sense of lightness, even one of exultation, in the freedom of this moment. Destiny, Ossama had said, all the roads of his life had led him here. This was his moment. Tomorrow, if he survived, Goloi would turn up to claim him, and he could not deny his promise. His supreme concern was Ossama. He would get her out, even if it meant only one moment in her arms before he died. Here in the desert he had found everything he'd always dreamed of – a place, a family, a world where a man could still feel the wonder of belonging to the earth.

He skirted the guards at the vehicle park, and worked his way around the electric arc-lights. Somewhere a generator was thumping like a heart-beat. He wove a path through the jeeps and trucks, dodging from shadow to shadow until he came to the armoured cars. They were parked close together, brooding steel maggots in the night, and he ducked down between them in the soft sand. There was the scuff of desert boots nearby, as loud as an engine, and Truman slipped off his pack and rolled under the wheels of the first APC.

He lay there, trying to control his breathing as two men stamped past the row of vehicles, chuntering gutterally in Russian. He smelt the coarse tobacco of their cigarettes as they went by. He opened the sack and slid out the shaped charge, fixing it beneath the gearbox as Whitehaven had instructed him. He set the guncotton primer in the material, then nursed the detonator out of its box and set it gingerly in place. He waited a few seconds, listening, then crawled under the second vehicle, laying a charge in the same place. When it was done, he crept out and dodged back in the shadows of the soft-skinned vehicles. There wasn't time for them, and with their new weapons, the Kel warriors would easily take them out. As long as he grounded the Apache, that was.

The heli stood less than two hundred metres away, and Truman covered the darkness as rapidly as he could. His watch told him only fifteen minutes had passed since he'd parted with Khyar, but already it seemed he'd been in the arena a whole lifetime. Every scent, every sound, every movement seemed acute, every second an era. Occasionally he halted to prick his ears, and made out the scurrying of mice and the trick-tricking of darkling beetles in the sand. Once, an owl flitted across his path, making him freeze.

The Apache stood in shadow, among a retinue of steel boxes and oildrums. He took in the scent of aviation fuel and oil nearby, and then the smell of human sweat. There were guards here, hugging the shadows, and as he watched, one of them betrayed himself by a small movement. The man coughed and moved out of the darkness, now a pale shape in his light desert camouflage gear. Truman slipped the sling of his L85 over his naked shoulder and brought the bayonet Whitehaven had given him from its clip on his pouch. He stood still, listening, watching for other movements. The man had his back to him now, and Truman crossed the fifty feet between them, his bare feet dead silent in the sand. At the last moment, he let his pack fall to the ground.

The guard sensed movement and had half turned when Truman caught him around the neck with a hand clamped over his mouth. He whipped the big knife across the man's throat and began sawing powerfully, feeling the blood spilling over his arm. The guard struggled, making sucking noises with his mouth, trying to bite his hand, but Truman held on, sawing desperately through his windpipe until the neck was almost severed. When the guard finally went limp Truman kept his hand in place, fearing that even in his death throes the man could scream a warning. For a full minute he propped up the heavy body, letting the blood course into the sand, feeling the last twitches of the muscles. Then he let him drop like a wet sack to the ground.

He stood poised, ready to fight again, but there was no movement from the shadows. He had just slotted the bayonet away when another guard walked around from the other side of the Huey, not more than ten feet away. The man went rigid with surprise and jogged the AK47 from his shoulder. By the time it was in his hands though, Truman had taken a world-class skip across the distance that separated them and delivered the most powerful karate kick of his life directly into the sentry's throat. There was a sound like ripping cloth, and the man spluttered as he went down. Truman landed on him, ready to wrench his head forward and break his neck, but the limpness of the head told him instantly that it wasn't necessary. He withdrew panting and quivering, taking breaths in great gulps.

Neither guard had got off a warning shout, but Truman knew he had to proceed cautiously. He could not afford to be seen. He picked up the pack and stole around to the other side of the Apache, crouching in the lee of some oil-drums to take out the last two charges. He set one up on the undercarriage, and climbed up on fuselage footholds to place the last charge inside the air intake. This one was tricky as he was working blind, and his hand shook slightly as he reached for the detonator. He stopped, steadied himself, and fixed it with a firm hand on the guncotton primer. Then he slipped down, ditched the pack behind a pile of rocks not far off, and began to move stealthily back to the living quarters, threading a circuitous route across the three hundred metres. By the time he reached the bell-tents his watch told him he had only fifteen minutes left.

55

SOME OF THE TENTS WERE LIT from the inside, and Truman could see naked and half-naked male torsos projected on the walls like a cinema screen. This was good, he thought. No one was alert, no one was ready for an attack. These guys obviously thought they were on vacation. He worked his way along the line until he found himself by the big marquee into which he'd seen the guards hustle Ossama. He glanced at his watch. Twelve and a half minutes to go. He paused close to the marquee walls. From inside there came voices – a man speaking Arabic, a female voice answering in monosyllables, and another male voice grating like a fingernail on a blackboard. Truman shivered. He would have known Stein's voice anywhere. He pressed himself into the darkness by the tent, and searched along it till he found an air vent at eye-level. He peered in.

The interior of the tent was smoky from an oil lamp standing on a box, and in one corner a laptop computer and a VHF radio were set up on a table. A woman, naked but for a loincloth, was strapped to another table in the middle of the tent-space, her long dark hair flowing over one end and almost touching the ground. A grotesque little man with a beer-belly and pop-out eyes was standing close to her on one side, while on the other stood the elegant figure of Colonel Julius Stein. As Truman watched, the colonel swept back his sleek hair. He stepped forward and caressed the naked belly of the woman lightly, insinuatingly, with both hands.

'Tell the bitch,' the Colonel croaked, 'that the unborn child in here will be the first to die. Tell her I will perform a breech operation myself, with this.' His hand darted to his pocket and Truman saw the familiar shark-toothed knife spring into his hand. He laid the flat of the small blade on the woman's rounded stomach.

'Tell her I want to know where the foreigner Truman is,' he snapped, 'or I shall root out the foetus and show it to her before she dies.'

The little man repeated the words in Arabic, with lisping, stumbling diction. Stein leaned over the woman's face to sneer, and suddenly she lifted her head and spat right into his smouldering eye.

'The Great Mother curse you!' Ossama's voice shrieked. 'You want to know where Antara is? You fool! Antara is here now!'

The bayonet was already in Truman's hand as Stein jerked back, wiping saliva from his eye. He ripped open the wall of the tent in a single movement and was inside even before the colonel's knife came up. His first burst from the L85 winged Stein's elbow and sent him reeling, the second took the dwarf in the bulging midriff and stove his belly in. By the time the Colonel was on his feet again, Truman had slit the straps that held Ossama and was peeling her off the table. Instead of falling into his arms, though, she grabbed the bayonet out of his hand, facing Stein.

'I told you he was here!' she hissed.

For the first time in Truman's experience, Stein's impassive face cracked with astonishment. He backed away towards the door, still grasping his little slicer and clutching at his damaged elbow. There were shouts from outside and a sentry in desert camouflage appeared at the door-gap. Truman shot him, and the head disappeared.

'You,' Stein whispered. 'You're Antara.'

As Truman levelled the rifle at him the radio suddenly crackled to life.

'Charlie Sierra this is OP Alpha,' a mechanical voice stuttered. 'Sir, there are Bedouin advancing on both passes. Estimated numbers five, six hundred, men and women . . .'

The voice faltered momentarily, and Truman caught the distinct sound of an explosion. 'Jesus Christ!' the voice grated. 'They've got anti-tank rockets down there . . .'

'Roger,' another voice cut in, 'we are sending up Hellfire. Repeat, sending up Hellfire.'

Truman glanced at his watch. Two and a half minutes to go. They were going to get caught by the charges.

'Get out!' he screamed at Ossama. 'Get out now!'

Ossama heard the urgency in his voice and leapt across the tent and out through the hole Truman had carved. Truman levelled his weapon at Stein, but as his finger tightened on the trigger a shiny grey object rolled in through the doorgap. Truman leapt back instinctively and the thing went off with a shattering clap that knocked Stein clean off his feet. Truman's eardrums felt as if they were caving in, yet otherwise he was unhurt.

'A stun grenade!' he thought, and at that moment the tent wall opposite was ripped down and a squad of soldiers stood there with AK47's ready to fire. Truman rallied himself for a heart-beat and emptied his magazine into them. Then he ducked out of the tent after Ossama.

56

OUTSIDE THE TENT THERE WAS PANDEMONIUM. Mercenaries were running about – some of them half-dressed, diving for non-existent cover, and trying to shoot back at the light machine-gun that had opened up from high on the rimwall. As Truman raced past them, he found himself hoping desperately that Whitehaven and Khyar would recognize him through the night-scopes. The rat-tat-tat of the light machine-gun came in short, economical bursts, but it was deadly accurate. Truman saw two or three of the Russians go down as he lurched by. In between bursts there came the phizz-pop of one – no, two – L85s. Khyar and even old Ayoub were doing their bit, Truman thought. Ossama had vanished into the darkness.

Over at the MT park, jeep and truck engines were being gunned frantically, men were bawling orders and squads of mercenaries were assembling, then breaking up in confusion as bullets zapped around their ears. From the direction of the Salaba and the Riyat Ash-Sha passes to the south and north came the sound of gunfire and the staccato eruptions of high-explosive. Suddenly a heavy machine-gun mounted on one of the APCs started up, its bass *boom-boom-boom* adding to the confusion. A tent near Truman burst into flames and its former occupants rushed straight at him as he sped along through the wreaths of fire.

'Stop him!' Stein's voice croaked from behind.

He saw understanding on their flame-lit faces, and squeezed the trigger of his L85. There was a dead-man's click as the pin sprang forward on an empty chamber, and Truman reversed the rifle and used it as a club. Five or six men were on him now, and he laid about them with the stock of his weapon, following through with karate kicks. Two or three went down, but more filled their places instantly.

'I want him alive!' Stein growled, almost in his ear. The wooden butt of an AK47 lammed into the side of his head, stunning him, and in a moment the rifle was wrenched out of his hands and his world became a blitzkrieg of kicks and punches.

He dropped on to his knees, trying to protect his head with his hands, but a size twelve commando-boot stabbed through his defense and connected with his forehead, severing his contact with the world outside. For an instant he was power-gliding across a ripe meadow of stars, and the cosmos was silent and free of all pain. He was in the dimension of the Half-Death, he realized, where time stopped and became a singularity. The memory of his capture in Beirut and the black room rushed back on him like a rolling wave.

He remembered how he'd arrived in Beirut, a law graduate just down from Oxford, full of himself, confident that he didn't need the title he'd been born with to succeed in the world. He'd picked up Arabic as easily and perfectly as he'd picked up karate – the world was his oyster and nothing could stop him. He'd been the best freelancer they'd ever had, so assured of his ability that he didn't even carry a gun. He'd been riding the crest of a wave until the day he'd seen something he wasn't supposed to see. Then he'd run away in terror and blundered into Paretsky by chance. After that there had been the black room, and he'd known nothing more until he'd woken up in the sanatorium Berghof in Switzerland, with two years of his life lost in terra incognita. Truman knew he didn't want to go back to that room again, and he fought to stay where he was, but when the inner eye opened he was tied to the bumper of a jeep, with Stein looming over him, and next to him a tall, slim man with oriental eyes and a gold ring in his ear, holding a walkie-talkie.

The first sound he recognized was the slashing of the Apache's rotors as the Huey prepared for take-off. Truman ignored Stein and struggled to get a glimpse of his watch. There was still a minute to go before Khyar pressed the button. The APCs were both within a few metres of him, and he knew his body would be ripped to shreds. But Ossama was safe. Stein had wrapped a piece of his shirt around the injured elbow. His clothes were torn and bloody, his hair wild, his eyes showing confusion from the stun-grenade.

'I'm glad you're awake to see the end of your adopted people,' Stein said. 'Mr Rybakov here was going to let them off the hook. They could have vanished silently into the desert and that would have been the end of it, but no – they had to come back for more. This time the lice will be squashed. Every last one of the vermin will be expunged from the face of the earth.'

Truman stared at him. 'You're insane,' he stammered.

Stein's hollow eyes flared. 'We are all insane, Truman,' he whispered. 'You, me, Maynard, Rybakov here – the whole lot of us are stark-staring bonkers. And so what? The norm is merely an artificial construct of modern society. Ask your precious nomads if there are any madmen among them, and they won't even know what you're talking about! Morality is another con-struct – a system we are indoctrinated with, but whose real purpose is to make sure those in power stay in power. The reality, Dr Truman, is that nothing is good or bad unless we make it so ourselves.'

The tall man with the earring was listening to his walkie-talkie. 'Stein!' he shouted impatiently. 'The Bedouin are forcing a way through the passes. They've got rockets and mortars – even high-velocity rifles. We have to get the APCs and the helicopter into action right now.'

All around them men were piling into trucks and jeeps and roaring off in splashes of sand. The APCs were rumbling to life. Truman was dimly aware that the rattle of Whitehaven's machine-gun up on the rimwall had stopped. Only a lone L85 was cracking out from up there. Khyar. The sound of the Apache's rotor's had reached a crescendo.

'Leave him here!' Stein shouted at the men. 'I'll be back for him!'

'*In your dreams you asshole!*' Truman told himself.

Truman watched Stein and Rybakov jump into a jeep with a beatific smile on his face. He twisted his watch-arm up to count off the last ten seconds. The APCs were already off, the Apache hovering, about to get airborne. Images from his life rushed through his head. Ossama was kissing him under the desert stars. He closed his eyes and reached out to eternity.

Nothing happened. There was no explosion. Truman opened his eyes and saw a camel charging straight towards him – a huge, white camel pounding along at the gallop with its great legs working like pistons and its neck stretched out like a giant swan. For a moment he thought he was dreaming. He recognized the camel instantly as Wald al-Asmar – the one he'd ridden when he'd first come to the Sacred Land – the same camel Ossama had brought back to the plateau. Hanging on to its headrope with one hand, Khyar was braced against its flank, using the beast as a living shield against pot-shots. The animal thundered to within a metre of Truman and dropped to its knees. Khyar slipped off and shot two mercenaries who were dashing towards him with his L85, firing one handed. He slashed through Truman's ropes with his sabre.

'The charges!' Truman screamed, 'Why didn't you do it?'

'I couldn't!' Khyar shouted back. 'You saved my life. The blood burden is upon me!'

Before Truman could protest, Khyar smashed a hard fist into his jaw, almost knocking him down. His senses dimmed for a moment, and an instant later he was bent across the camel's back, and Khyar was lashing a rope across his body.

'What the hell are you doing?' Truman grunted.

'Repaying a debt!' Khyar bawled over the noise and confusion.

 328

'And by the way, I lied to you, Antara. I've always loved Ossama. Tell her that and salute her from me!'

Then the camel was up and with a final slap on the rump from Khyar it burst into a bombing gallop along the line of blazing tents. Truman fought desperately to free himself from the rope, but by the time it was off, the beast was out of control. He gripped its hair desperately, and looked back just in time to see Khyar poised with the initiator in his hands, standing up straight, and screaming, *'I am Khyar bin Kalash, a warrior of the Kel Saghrana!'*

There was a massive detonation like thunder, as all four charges went off simultaneously. The Apache, hovering a hundred metres up, went up like a supernova, a radiant fireball raining streams of burning fuel and molten kevlon in all directions, before hitting the desert surface with the force of a meteor and exploding again in a brilliant aurora that lit the night. Nearer to him, the two APCs disintegrated in blinding flashes, sending fragments of white-hot armour-plating searing across the camp. Khyar and everyone around him disappeared and at once the shock wave from the explosions struck, clapping the tents as flat as pancakes, bowling the camel off its feet and sending Truman crashing into the sand.

57

HE ROLLED CLEAR AND THE FIRST thing he saw was Whitehaven sashaying down the nearby dune with the light machine-gun in his hands and an M16 with grenade launcher slung over his shoulder. He looked like a refugee from Che Guevara's army, with two Browning pistols stuck in his belt, his torso criss-crossed with ammo bandoliers, and L2 grenades clipped on his pouches.

'I thought they'd got you!' Truman said. He had a splitting headache and his jaw throbbed where Khyar had punched him.

'Sorry old cobbler,' Whitehaven grinned. 'Copped a stoppage. Bloody sand.'

A jeep was tearing towards them, laden with foot-soldiers, its gears grating and headlights flashing. Whitehaven thrust the LMG at Truman and pulled the pin on an L2. He ran forward, hurled the grenade and hit the deck rolling. There was an ear-splitting crack as the jeep burst into a fireball and tipped over. An entire wheel steamed past Truman's head leaving a vapour-trail of smouldering rubber fumes, and flaming bodies flew, screaming like hellish angels. Instinctively Truman squeezed the trigger of the LMG, spraying the burning wreck. Vehicles were buzzing everywhere and flak was incoming from at least two directions. Truman could see orange and green tracer slicing across the valley. Whitehaven made an ecstatic closed fist 'up yours' gesture at the downed vehicle and threw himself down by Truman.

'They're on the run,' he gasped. 'Your Kel are through the passes. The Russkies are bugging out! We got 'em! *Yes!*'

'Where's Ossama?' Truman asked.

'Up there on the dune with Ayoub,' Whitehaven yelled back. 'Nice lady. Lucky bugger.'

Mercenaries were rushing past on foot in disorder, firing behind them, and Whitehaven gave them a few bursts of 5.56mm from the L85 on automatic. Truman followed up with a series of double-taps from the LMG and bodies hit the sand. It was a scene out of Dante, he thought, utter madness. The mercs had gone out of control and were driving around wildly looking for a way out. The APCs, the Apache and the soft-skinned vehicles caught in the blasts were still burning, and as he watched more jeeps and trucks erupted into flame from rocket-launchers wielded by unseen Saghrana warriors advancing across the plain. He saw soldiers fighting each other desperately to get on the trucks. Whitehaven took the LMG from Truman and put in a deadly burst here and there among them just to keep things livened up. He was hooting like a schoolboy.

'Khyar's down,' Truman said during a momentary lull.

'I know,' Whitehaven replied. 'I saw it all. That boy was crazy as a coot. He spotted that camel mooching through the ranks, and as soon as Ossama broke, he yelled some sort of Indian warpath cry, scooted down the dune and grabbed it. Of course, if I knew you'd given him the damned initiator, I'd have set it off myself.'

'I owe him my life.'

Whitehaven wasn't listening. Another brace of jeeps was haring towards them out of the night, weaving drunkenly, and he sent a 203 grenade from the underbelly of his rifle skimming their way. The round missed and the jeeps roared past oblivious, lit up by the flames off the battlefield. In the light of the flames Truman saw a small figure crouched in the front of one of them – Colonel Julius Stein. Whitehaven knelt, ready to give them another dose of 203, but suddenly swivelled as he came under

331

fire from the left. A group of mercenaries were pepper-potting determinedly towards him. He threw the M16 down and reloaded the machine-gun with a new mag.

'OK, you buggers,' he growled. 'Chew on this!'

Truman rolled away from the incoming fire and stole a glance at the jeeps behind him. They had pulled to a stop not a hundred metres away, and in the firelight he saw Stein and a handful of soldiers jumping out, making for the Cave of Wonders behind the buttress of Termit. He grabbed the M16.

'It's Stein,' he shouted at Whitehaven. 'I'm going for him.'

Whitehaven fired a short burst and reloaded again. He unclipped bandoliers of 203 grenades and M16 rounds and thrust them at Truman. 'I'll hold the fort here. Run for the buttress. I'll give you cover.'

Truman sprinted across the open ground, stitching a zig-zag pattern to avoid the rounds that whizzed around him. He collapsed by the buttress-wall, pressing his head against the rough stone, listening to the crescendo of noise from the battlefield. Dark figures had begun to appear out of the night on the periphery of the Outsider camp – elvish men in loincloths with their hair splayed out wildly, running forward, falling, rolling and firing at the retreating mercenaries. From the darkness came the occasional whumph and thump of 66mm rockets detonating as they found their targets among the jeeps and trucks. A shroud of acrid smoke and dust lifted over the valley. He ducked behind the rock and made for the entrance to Ossama's living cave. Two shadows, their light desert smocks ghostly in the moonlight, closed on him from the entrance and he fired a 203 at them, followed by a burst of 5.56 mm rounds. The grenade hit the rock and ruptured with a starburst crack, twisting the two bodies round and hurling them against the wall. Truman didn't halt to find out if they were dead.

He plunged into the darkness of the small cave, then down the shallow stairs beyond. The tallow lamps were burning and he made his way into the big cave cautiously, with his M16 ready. At the base of the stairs he slipped into the shadows. The place seemed deserted at first, but as Truman paused, listening, he caught the hiss of breathing. Gripping the rifle he stepped forward, following the beaten path, past the murals dating from the Time of the First Reckoning. Above him that vast, billion-faceted chandelier of stalagtites scintillated, casting back the dim light of the lamps lit in nooks and crannies. At the back of the cave was another natural doorway, opening on a wide gallery hung with pilasters of limestone as white as salt, where more lamps flickered. He stepped through. In the centre of the cave, Stein was standing motionless. He was no more than ten paces away, but he was not alone. His left hand gripped the hair of a Saghrana boy with a lop-sided face, whose one good eye bulged from its socket. Even in the half-darkness, Truman recognized Yani.

The Colonel's face was an alabaster plaquette in which only the burn-hole eyes seemed alive and his right hand held his fang-shaped blade to the artery under the boy's ear.

'You know I'll do it,' he whispered. 'You've seen me in action before.'

Yani tried to say something but only a croaking sound emerged. 'Shut up!' the Colonel spat. He looked at Truman. 'Of course, you could try to shoot me before I slit his throat, but I wouldn't rate your chances highly. The question is, can you afford to take the risk?'

Truman hesitated, remembering the Desert Fox's boy at Kharga, and how Stein had murdered him gratuitously. He was caught in a cleft stick. Even acquiescence now might only accelerate Yani's death.

'Let him go, Stein,' he said.

Stein smirked. 'Oh no, Dr Truman. This child is my safe passage out of here. You're going to escort me back up those steps and make sure I pass through your lines, otherwise the boy dies. Rand's mobile column is already within a day's drive. You are going to make sure I rendezvous with it in one piece.'

Truman nodded. 'So you cheated on the Russians after all.'

Stein spat again. 'Not me,' he said. 'It was Marcus Rand. He had to go and mess up everything I set up, simply because he couldn't stand the idea of working with the mafiya. But no matter. Now your nomads have routed them. Rand's men will come in handy. I shall take command of the column, move in and take over where the Russians left off.'

'You'll never take over this place, Stein,' Truman said.

The Colonel chuckled. 'Then who will?' he said. 'You and your Brit backers? Did you tell your pregnant bitch woman that you were working for British intelligence, Antara? Did you explain that the price of throwing in her lot with you was the dismantling of her precious Sacred Land for the rare earth it contains? You masquerade as one of these savages, but in reality you're just cheating them out of the thing they value most. At least I have never lied to myself. Now, drop the weapon or the boy dies.'

Truman watched the shark-tooth blade as it rose and fell. He lowered the MI6 gently to the rock floor.

'Kick it over here,' Stein ordered.

Warily, Truman pushed the stock of the rifle hard with his bare foot, so that it skittered over to Stein's feet. Stein pinned it under a booted foot.

'You really are a fool, Truman,' he scoffed, 'to fall for the same thing twice. You really think I need you or this half-blind shrimp to get out of here?'

He thrust Yani away from him and stooped to pick up the weapon in a single fluid movement. At that moment, though, there was a flicker in the shadows and Sergei Rybakov charged out with a knife gripped blade down, between thumb and forefinger. Truman ducked instinctively as Rybakov let the blade fly straight as an arrow to thump into Stein's chest. The Colonel took a step backwards, his features rippling into an expression of sheer surprise. He stretched out a lean hand to grasp Yani, but the boy was already squirming away from him across the rock. For a second his hand flailed in the lamplight, then he collapsed in slow motion on to the cavern floor. Rybakov bounded over to him, his Makarov in his hand.

'You fucking double-crossing bastard!' he spat.

Stein's eyes opened narrowly. 'You're the traitor, Rybakov. You lied to us. Do your bosses know what you really . . .'

Rybakov shot him at hard-contact range, and Stein's skull exploded into fragments of flesh and bone.

58

OUTSIDE DAWN WAS COMING AND THERE was a hush over the valley, as if all its creatures, animals, plants, humans – friend and foe alike – had suspended hostilities to wait for the entrance of the sun. There was a flush of firegold up on the rimwall, the first beams of light piercing through a haze of smoke from smouldering vehicles and tents. Everywhere the dead lay strewn in the sand, and groups of captured mercenaries were being hustled by tribesmen, dressed again in their hooded burnooses against the early morning cool. Camel-men were trotting about in squads, but the atmosphere was subdued and without exultation. Truman realized he was witnessing a historic moment – when a traditional nomadic tribe came face to face with the 21st century.

A voice called his name and he saw Ossama rushing towards him. They ran into each other's arms and for a moment his world was only Ossama – energy poured into him and out of him, and tears washed through the blood-steaks on his face. He could not bear to let her go, so precious were the few moments that remained to them. He crushed her to him. 'I love you,' he said. 'I'll always love you.'

'Thank the Light Mother!' she breathed in his ear. 'You're safe. You're safe.' Their lips met and time hauled up and slowed. Reluctantly he tore himself away. 'Ossama,' he said, 'I promised to give myself up to Goloi. That was the price of our victory.'

Her face fell. 'But that's impossible. In my visions . . .'

Others crowded round them now, and Ossama broke off. Hafid held his rifle up solemnly, his dark brow ridges glistening. 'Now we need never fear anything again,' he said eagerly. 'These weapons were a gift from the Light Mother, Antara.'

Truman laughed emptily. 'The weapons don't change a thing my friend,' he said. Even as he said it, he knew it was a lie. The weapons changed everything. Nothing would ever be the same again.

Rybakov was there, being guarded by two of the Kel. Hafid drew his sabre and held it to the Russian's throat. 'Now I take revenge for Tissi, Makhlud and all the fallen warriors. In the name of the Light Mother.'

'Cock-sucker!' Rybakov grunted.

Hafid raised the sabre, but Truman grabbed his hand. 'No. This man saved Yani.'

Hafid let the hood of his burnoose fall back and eyed Truman with a piercing stare. 'He was one of the leaders. Revenge is the Sacred Duty of the Kel.'

'Look around you,' Truman said, gesturing to the dead, burned and mutilated bodies scattered across the valley. 'Don't you think there's been revenge enough?'

'Antara's right,' Ossama said. 'We've had enough bloodshed to last eternity.' Hafid let his blade fall doubtfully.

Truman faced Rybakov. 'What happened?' he inquired. 'Did you get cold feet when you found out about Rand's column coming across the desert?' Rybakov glared at him. 'Rand is double-crossing bastard,' Rybakov said. 'But he and Stein was never in the picture. I got my own plans. I'd have stiffed Stein sooner or later anyway.'

Whitehaven cast a glance at Rybakov and sat down on a stone and lit his pipe. 'What are we going to do about him?' he asked Truman. 'And about the bloody South Africans. We've jumped out of the frying pan into the fire, and if they don't end up snaffling the palladium, then our own people will hand it to the

Khartoum government on a plate. Whatever happens, the Kel are going to end up on a casualty list.'

Truman turned on him. 'No one's going to be snaffling anything here, Richard,' he said. 'This place will remain the Sacred Land – that's what we were fighting for.'

'Nice speech,' Whitehaven said, savouring smoke. 'Very nice. But why don't you come clean with us all? OK, you've done a great job in leading the Saghrana, but why don't you admit that Morgan sent you out here? That you're selling out their Sacred Land for the sake of British interests. Tell them what they were *really* fighting for.'

Ossama stared at Whitehaven belligerently. 'What are you saying?'

Whitehaven cocked an eyebrow at her. 'Your loverboy here's been working for the British government all the time,' he said. 'In fact he's been with them on and off for years. Used to be called *Haymaker*. They sent him here under deep cover to get you poor sods to fight for them. How do you think these weapons turned up so quickly? It wasn't the Light Mother and it wasn't Santa Claus – it was signed, sealed and delivered by Her Majesty's Government.'

'But isn't that who you work for?' Ossama demanded.

'OK, it is,' Whitehaven said. 'But I only agreed to come out here because I thought I could help you. Some nomads like you once saved my life, and I wanted to repay the favour. You people are something special. I'd like to see the way of life preserved as it is, but I suspect Antara here is under orders to sell your land out for money to another master.'

Ossama's jade eyes searched Whitehaven's face. 'I don't believe it.' Truman lifted his eyes and locked on hers for a long silent moment. 'It's not all lies. I did work for British intelligence once. I was called *Haymaker*. I worked in a place called Beirut doing secret things. I was captured and tortured and hurt so badly that my mind tried to blot out the memory. I woke up in a sanctuary in a place called Switzerland, and two years of my life had gone up in smoke.'

Ossama's eyes were wide now, and the tribesmen were riveted, only half understanding his words, but knowing some deep revelation was happening here.

'But that's all,' he said. 'I swear it upon my unborn child, and in the name of the Light Mother. I have never worked for the British government since then and I'm not working for them now.'

'Yeah?' Whitehaven said. 'Pull the other one. You used these guys. You rigged this whole job up with Morgan.'

'I told you,' Truman said. 'I don't know any Morgan. Except. . .'

'Except what?'

'Except Morgan was the name of the man who committed me to the sanatorium in Switzerland. I don't even know who he is.'

There was a spluttering expletive from somewhere close, and everyone looked at Rybakov who was still being held by two tribesmen. The Russian grinned back at them nonchalantly.

'You say something, Ivan? Whitehaven said.

'Yeah,' Rybakov said. 'And it's *Mister* Ivan to you. I say you're a bloody dickhead and Morgan is too. Truman here had nothing to do with the mission. Is me that's Phantom List.'

Whitehaven dropped his pipe. 'You what?' he stammered. 'That's just not bloody possible. You're on the wanted list, Rybakov. You're mafiya. You murdered Amersadiqi, Maynard, and God knows how many others.'

Rybakov croaked with mirth. 'So what? You think things are black and white, *comrade*? Black hats and white hats? Good guys and bad guys? Cowboys and Indians? I bin working with Q-ops ever since I came to UK.'

Whitehaven's fingers twiddled with the safety catch on the LMG, still slung on his shoulders. 'That's shit,' he said. 'Why would Morgan fly in a planeload of kit to fight you, if you were already working for him?'

Rybakov snorted arrogantly. 'Who said I work for Morgan? Listen, the boys that run me – the Q-ops group – are the real power inside your Office, Whitehaven. Guys who realized long time ago that is better to get rich yourself than to waste your life fighting for property of others. We don't have no agreement with Khartoum. Never did have – that was eyewash for sake of Morgan. My bosses planned to take over the mining op here themselves under cover of so-called mafiya. Fill their bellies. Keep the civil war boiling in the Sudan so as government never has chance to get interested, then move out. Morgan's bin sniffing around my handlers for years. He suspected what was going on but he had no proof. He worked a flanker on me and my handlers sending you in with the weapons, though, the bastard.'

'Zinoviev,' Whitehaven muttered.

Rybakov snickered bitterly. 'Yeah. The fat bastard nearly let cat out of bag. My bosses fixed him up all right though. They give him poison-tipped umbrella on the King's Road, and bury his files. Of course, it didn't hurt to let people think it was Truman who was on Phantom List. I found out he'd bin a Fred in Beirut in eighties. Turns out that in '83 *Haymaker* stumbled onto a meeting between Q-ops group and mafiya. The one Zinoviev told you about. The boys tried to pick him up, but he escaped and they couldn't get him back, because he'd been taken by Hasabullah and was getting cowprod treatment.

'They might have got him eventually, only he was liberated by cell working for Morgan, and Morgan was clean. He was hopin' *Haymaker* would spill on Q-ops group and kept him in a sanatorium. Only problem was that when he came round he couldn't remember a fucking thing. Morgan was pissed, but was lucky for Truman. Q-ops took him off hit-list, and that's how come he's still walking round today.'

'But what about the samples?' Whitehaven said. 'They had to have come from Truman.'

Rybakov chortled. 'Truman had nothing to do with it. We got samples by breaking into his place in Oxford. My bosses passed them to Morgan with story that they'd come from customs. They asked him to have them analysed, so they wouldn't be implicated. He gave them to you. Nobody knew Amersadiqi was mole for Rand's – that was just coincidence.'

'And Maynard?' Truman asked. 'Was that a coincidence too?'

Rybakov looked serious. 'I never whacked Maynard. My handlers told me to have you clipped because they were afraid you were in it with Morgan. I used idea to put pressure on Maynard, but I didn't know he had a dicky heart. Was an accident.'

He shook his head and smoothed off his camouflaged jacket. 'Now, I've told you what I know. If there is jeep still in one piece after all this shit, steer me to it, and I'll say bye-bye. I don't want to be here when the Rand column arrives.'

Whitehaven swung the machine-gun towards the lanky figure and cocked the working-parts. 'Hold your horses, comrade,' he said. 'You're going nowhere till you start naming names. I want to know who's behind this can of worms.'

Rybakov paused, glancing at the machine-gun. 'I don't know names,' he said, shrugging. 'Is a crazy mixed up world, no? You never know who you're working for.'

He grinned at them and his gold teeth glinted in the first strands of sunlight blinking over the rimwall.

Whitehaven tipped his head to one side suspiciously. 'You know what strikes me as fishy?' he said slowly. 'The fact that you're singing like a harpsichord, Rybakov. Nobody put pressure on you, so why'd you come out with this all of a sudden? I think you're protecting somebody. This is all a smokescreen, isn't it?'

Truman watched Whitehaven, his senses becoming more and more acute. For a moment he saw another face where Whitehaven's should have been. The face of Paretsky, saying *I'll never forget how you looked when you came racing down that street. Not scared in the least, but surprised. You looked like you just discovered Godzilla.* He had seen something they didn't want him to see all right, and thanks to Rybakov he now knew what it was.

He'd stumbled on a meeting between British and American intelligence agents and the Russian mafiya in a derelict quarter of Beirut. He'd managed to sneak in and listen, and to his utter astonishment he'd realized that they were making a deal about drugs – a massive operation to ship heroin and cocaine to Europe, and to divide up the profits. He had been so shocked that he'd

341

betrayed himself to the guards and they'd started shooting. That was what he was running away from when he'd bumped into Paretsky. Now, for the first time in all these years, the memory came flooding back, details, names, faces.

'Whitehaven's right,' he said, speaking with such certainty that Rybakov gawked at him, and Whitehaven bit his tongue in surprise.

'You see, Mr Rybakov,' he went on slowly, 'I've remembered who I saw at the meeting in Beirut, hobnobbing with known terrorists. One of them was then the head of the Middle East desk of MI6.'

Whitehaven's face looked like a slot machine into which Truman had just inserted a coin. 'The Middle East desk 1983!' he gasped. 'That guy is now the Director General. That's it, Truman. That's who he's protecting!'

He turned angrily on Rybakov. 'That crap about your so-called 'bosses' was just hogswill. There only ever was one boss. Only the DG himself had access to the Phantom List file, and he was your boss, *Mister* Ivan. He's the shit behind all this.'

Rybakov had suddenly turned a sickly shade of pale. 'It won't do you any good. You got no proof, Whitehaven – only say so of a screwball who likes playing Lawrence of Arabia. I'll make sure you get whacked the moment you step back on your own soil.'

'I'll take my chances,' Whitehaven said. 'After all, your boss never managed to get rid of Morgan, even though he must have been behind all those stories about the guy's incompetence. I think I owe Hugh an apology. And if I was you I'd keep my gob shut, because right now I'm the one holding the gun.'

Rybakov wheeled on Truman. 'I know you won't let him do nothing to me.' 'Not after you promise me protection. Against your shitty desert law.'

'You're right Mr Ryabakov,' Truman said, his voice ice. He turned to Hafid. 'Escort him to Riyat ash-Sha with any of his men who are still standing. Give them each a litre bottle of water and throw them out into the Funeral Plains.'

He stared at the Russian. 'Nobody here's going to kill you, Rybakov.' he said. 'But your only way out is north. You should be running into Rand's column in a couple of hours. Maybe you can persuade them to take you back to Libya, I don't know. Or maybe they'll just shoot you down like dogs. Before they do, perhaps you could pass them a little message from me. We have your weapons now as well as our own, and if they or anyone else comes within five kilometres of the plateau we'll blast them to pieces, and that's a promise.'

Hafid nodded and two strong warriors seized Rybakov. 'You fucking cock-suckers!' he shrieked. 'Fuck you Truman! Fuck you to hell!'

Truman turned his back on the struggling Russian as the tribes-men dragged him out of earshot. Ossama wrapped her arms around him. 'I knew you couldn't have betrayed us, Antara. Some things can't be hidden. You'll always be one of us.'

Dozens of tribesmen and women had collected around them now, and were chanting 'Antara! Antara!' It reminded him of the day he had arrived back at the plateau after bringing Khyar's caravan out of the Funeral Plains. A group of warriors, their bodies smeared with blood, joined hands and did a twisting, triumphal dance in his honour.

Only Whitehaven looked on dismally. 'I owe you an apology too. I suppose I knew deep down you couldn't have been playing a part. I envy you, Antara.'

Truman was eyeing him steadily. 'What will you do now?' he asked.

Whitehaven shrugged. 'You're going to need friends on the Outside,' he said. 'The way the world is today no group can make it on their own. I'll try to persuade them that there's no palladium here, or that the plateau's the source of some devastat-ing disease like Aids that could wipe out the whole world. Sure, they'll be back sooner or later, but this time the Kel will be prepared.'

A cry suddenly went up from the audience and the dance halted abruptly. Truman looked back to see Goloi and a group

343

of Gharana warriors approaching, walking their camels, their black robes fluttering in the light breeze. With them came an escort of Saghrana led by young Darash, who walked gravely, carrying his L85 tight across his chest. It looked like a funeral procession, Truman thought. Then he remembered – it *was* a funeral. His own. The Gharana stopped some way off, and Darash approached Truman.

'Antara,' he said. 'These . . . demons claim you made a pact with them. They claim that you promised them half our new weapons.'

Hafid's eyes filled with disbelief as he recognised the Gharana chief. 'Goloi!' he said. 'Here in the Sacred Land! You defile the place. The Light Mother strike me if I don't kill you myself!'

Goloi loosed his veil and watched Hafid calmly, with a touch of amusement.

'You'd kill guests travelling under the Sacred Word of Truce?' he inquired.

'Who gave you the Sacred Word?' Hafid demanded.

'I did,' Truman said. 'As is my right as war leader. Without Goloi, we would never have won, Hafid. I promised half our weapons. I also pledged my life to him in return for the truce, and now I give it freely.'

Hafid bowed his head. 'I'm humbled, Antara. No one can doubt that you are one of us. I offer myself in your place.'

'Thank you old friend,' Truman said. 'But your task is to help the Kahina lead the Kel in the most difficult time of their history. It won't be easy. She'll need a man like you.'

Goloi threw back his black cloak, revealing the sabre hanging from his bull-like chest. He drew the blade gravely. 'I take my revenge here, now, in front of all. Let me see you face death like a man.'

Whitehaven swung his gun round on the Gharana party. 'Truman,' he whispered. 'I can take them out.'

Truman scoffed at him. 'Don't you get it yet?' he said. 'This is honour. If you don't have it you don't have anything. A promise is a promise.'

 344

Ossama clung on to him. He kissed her and gently unpeeled her arms.

'Ossama,' he said, fighting the sob from his voice. 'These few weeks we've had together have been a whole lifetime for me. They are precious beyond all the treasures imaginable. If I had to live them again knowing I was going to die so soon, I'd still have done everything I did – had everything as it was.'

Ossama stood up straight and brushed the tears from her eyes. 'You'll never be forgotten,' she said. 'Your voice will always be here in the Sacred Land, in the winds that scour the Funeral Plains. Death is but the horizon, Antara, and the horizon is but the limit of our sight.'

Truman tore his gaze away from her. Death was waiting in the Gharana chief's face – a face that was so like that of the brother who'd denied him, the brother who'd given his life for Truman. He felt eyes riveted to him, measuring, assessing, as he walked steadily towards the gleaming blade. There were many things left undone, he thought, many wishes unfulfilled – but in the past few months he'd at last come to some kind of peace with himself. He halted in front of the chief.

'I have something to say,' he said.

'Speak,' said Goloi.

Truman turned and faced the crowd, who were now shoulder to shoulder. He surveyed the wind-bitten, bloody faces.

'I have only one thing to say,' he began, 'and it's this. A people divided is weakened, a people united is strong. The Sacred Imenan had a good reason to start the *tafriq*, but that reason is long ended. The *tafriq* must be abandoned. Out there, the universe is always changing. Change with it and you will survive.'

There was silence for a moment, then someone yelled '*Antara! Antara will never die!*' There was a roar of accord from the audience as Truman turned to Goloi.

'I'm ready,' he said.

Goloi grunted and raised the blade high. 'This is for my sons, Hadasha and Yassim!' he cried.

Suddenly the sun rolled over the rimwall, a searing injection

345

of light, a bubble of energy pulsating beams in rainbow colours across the spectrum. Truman's heart leapt at its beauty. He could hear voices in his head, thrumming music out of the earth's bowels, the song of the planet, changing, growing. The new light caught the sabre-blade as it fell, and flashed once in its mirror. Then the blade struck the sand at Truman's feet.

Goloi scowled grimly at Truman's shocked face. 'There's been too much killing. Too much pain and heartbreak. You looked death in the eye, Antara. That's enough.'

He held out his knobbled hand and Truman took it. It felt hard and dry as a metallic stone. A keening sound of utter wonder and amazement rose from the onlookers, and Truman knew that this act of clemency from the leader of the Gharana would never be forgotten.

'One day,' Goloi shouted. 'When the accursed *tafriq* is ended, perhaps Gharana and Saghrana will be one again, as they were meant to be. Until that day, there is blood between us, and if I meet any of you out on the Funeral Plains, I shall try my best to kill you. Until then, go in peace.'

He slotted the sabre back into its sheath, turned on his heel, and was gone.

59

TRUMAN FOLLOWED OSSAMA ACROSS THE CATHEDRAL of the Cave of Wonders, where crystals in millions watched them from the great domed roof like glittering eyes. She led him by the hand past the cavern where he had faced Stein, to where the tunnel roof sloped lower and lower, until they had to walk crouching. Finally, the space became so confined that they had to crawl on hands and knees to get through. Memories of the desperate journey through the qanat came back to haunt Truman.

'Hey,' he called. 'Where are you taking me?'

'Trust me,' Ossama whispered from the darkness.

Presently the womb-like space opened out and they were able to stand upright again. Truman heard the strike of flint on steel as Ossama lit a cotton pad, then transferred the flickering flame to a tallow lamp. Shadows fled away from them against the solid wall of a gallery cut in the rock. They were standing on a narrow platform on the edge of a sheer precipice whose depths were lost in the darkness. A narrow ledge wound along the curving wall and disappeared around it.

'Be careful here, Antara,' Ossama said. 'One slip and you're in the abyss.'

The ledge was no more than half a metre wide and Truman dared not look down in case he lost his balance. The trek seemed to go on and on till soon they were moving in complete darkness again. Suddenly Ossama halted, and Truman almost ran into her. He heard the flint on steel sound once again, then blinked in the eruption of light from another tallow lamp. They were standing on a second platform above the abyss, in front of what looked like a massive stone door, locked with a chain and a huge, rusted padlock. Ossama brought out a heavy key and unlocked it with a sound that echoed off the gallery walls. She pulled away the chain.

'Few men have been permitted to see what you are about to see, Antara,' she said. 'This is the treasure the Imenan brought with them from the land of the Firun.'

The door was a solid slab of granite that must have weighed tons, but it had been pivoted so ingeniously by a ball and socket system that Ossama was able to swing it open without effort. She picked up the oil-lamp and ushered him into the cave. It was not large, nor did it contain any wonderful crystals like the Makrab al-Ajayib. Instead, the walls were honed smooth and covered from floor to ceiling in rune-like symbols, cursive script and pictographs that reminded Truman of ancient Egyptian hiero-glyphs. He examined a section of the wall in the light of the lamp and gasped.

'This is ancient Greek,' he said. 'I know this language.'

'It is the writing of the Imenan,' the Kahina said. 'Its meaning has been lost to us. We have only the oral history now. But this is not what I brought you to see, Antara.'

She pointed to a large object standing in the centre of the cave, that looked like a carved stone sarcophagus. Truman moved over to it and saw that a large ram-and-sun-disk symbol was etched at the base of the stone side. He glanced at Ossama – a shadow of gentle curves, her features lost in a swirl of dark hair.

'This is the secret of the Imenan,' she whispered.

Trembling, Truman peered over the lip of the sarcophagus and held up the lamp. Inside was a mummified figure swathed in funeral cloth with arms crossed over its chest in the ancient Egyptian manner. The face of the mummy was invisible under a hood of cloth. Truman sucked in his breath.

'What is it?' he asked, his voice quavering.

'It is the body of the Great Mother,' Ossama said. 'The Oracle of Ammon, the Hidden One. She is my ancestor, the ancestor of us all – Saghrana and Gharana alike.'

Truman stared at her, and caught the gleam of her jade-coloured eyes in the lamplight. 'Where did she come from?' he asked.

'She was brought here by the Imenan,' Ossama said, 'from the land of the Firun. Where she came from originally, I don't know – from a lost civilization, perhaps, or even another world. For countless ages she lay in the Temple of the Hidden One at Ammon, an oasis in the far north.'

'Siwa!' Truman gasped. 'She is what I was looking for. I thought she was buried there.'

Ossama didn't seem surprised. 'Why were you searching for the Oracle, Antara?'

'I don't know exactly. Perhaps I thought if I could find her, I'd find the bit of myself that was missing. But I have already found it.'

'It is said,' Ossama recited, 'that it is not the goal but the quest itself that matters. Truth lies not in the material world, but in ourselves. For many ages the great and powerful of the world came to the shrine of the Oracle to discover the truth. But the Oracle was only a mummified body. They carried the answers to their questions with them and the body of the Oracle only provided the connection they needed – the connection to the Hidden One in themselves.'

'Why did the Imenan bring her here?'

'The world changed. Outsiders with new ways came to Ammon, and the power of the Oracle was ended. The Imenan fled into the desert, carrying the Oracle with them, and journeyed for weeks until they found the Sacred Land. They made a home here, but they had to change their ways too, to live in the desert. At first they tried to tame the land, building their qanats, planting crops, but slowly the old skills were lost and new ones were acquired. Only the Gift was passed on.'

She placed a hand on his and he looked deeply into the ocean-coloured eyes. 'Long ago the Kahina of the Imenan foretold that an Outsider would come to the Sacred Land – a man whose innocence shone in his face. He would bring with him new ways, new knowledge, show us a different path. The first time I saw you, I knew you were that man, Antara.'

'I don't want to change anything,' Truman said. 'But like Richard said, others will come for the precious thing buried in these hills. If we are to stay here we have to be as strong as they are. Already we have new weapons, but that's only the beginning.'

Ossama smiled. 'Nothing remains as it is. There are no fixed things. The ancient law-givers taught us that all the suffering in the world stems from our attempts to cling on to fixed thoughts, people, ideas – when all these things are impermanent. The enlightened being is the one who moves with the flow.'

She moved to the back of the cave, and opened another door. Beyond it lay a flight of stone steps leading up out of sight. Truman followed her silently up to a natural archway that opened on to a promontory on the rimwall. They stood close to each other, savouring the chalk-and-flint breeze from the Funeral Plains that stretched on and on to the horizon, a mystical sea of dunes bathed amber by the light of a dying sun.

'I know nothing lasts forever,' Truman said. 'But to be with you, to be part of the Kel, here, now, at this moment – that is enough.'

He looked into eyes that were neither blue nor green, but both colours at once, and thought he could see eternity there. Far below him new flows of sand-waves formed and broke across the dune crests, and the sun was a fire opal melting into the netherworld, beyond the limits of his sight.